Praise for *Sunshield*

"Clever, thrilling, and full of heart, this is epic fantasy done right."

—*Publishers Weekly* (starred review)

"Filled with unforgettable characters that you'll truly care about, *Sunshield* is fantastic! Emily B. Martin expertly weaves together multiple narratives with precision, passion, and excellence to create a riveting tale that will stick with you long after you finish reading. I loved it!"

—Sarah Beth Durst, award-winning author of *Race the Sands*

"An exciting take on the fantasy genre with its mix of Wild West and a tempered glass court. The three main characters seamlessly weave together a diverse tale of deceit, highway robbery, and political machinations. I hope you enjoy it as much as I did."

—Jeff Wheeler, *Wall Street Journal* bestselling author of the Harbinger, Kingfountain, and Muirwood series

"*Sunshield* is an adventure story with credible and heroic characters you want to cheer for. An excellent read."

—Luanne G. Smith, author of *The Vine Witch*

"*Sunshield* by Emily B. Martin is a richly imagined, beautifully textured fantasy that will leave you clamoring for the sequel. I couldn't put it down!"

—Elle Katharine White, author of *Heartstone*

FLOODPATH

ALSO BY EMILY B. MARTIN

Outlaw Road duology

Sunshield

Creatures of Light trilogy

Creatures of Light

Ashes to Fire

Woodwalker

FLOODPATH

A NOVEL

EMILY B. MARTIN

HARPER Voyager
An Imprint of HarperCollins*Publishers*

FLOODPATH. Copyright © 2021 by Emily B. Martin. All rights reserved. Printed in the United States of America. No part of this book may be used or reproduced in any manner whatsoever without written permission except in the case of brief quotations embodied in critical articles and reviews. For information, address HarperCollins Publishers, 195 Broadway, New York, NY 10007.

HarperCollins books may be purchased for educational, business, or sales promotional use. For information, please email the Special Markets Department at SPsales@harpercollins.com.

Harper Voyager and design are trademarks of HarperCollins Publishers LLC.

FIRST EDITION

Designed by Paula Russell Szafranski

Maps by Emily B. Martin

Library of Congress Cataloging-in-Publication Data has been applied for.

ISBN 978-0-06-288859-4

21 22 23 24 25   LSC   10 9 8 7 6 5 4 3 2 1

To my family

THE
OCEAN
WEST

the Outer Islands

Cape Coraxia

N

W   E

S

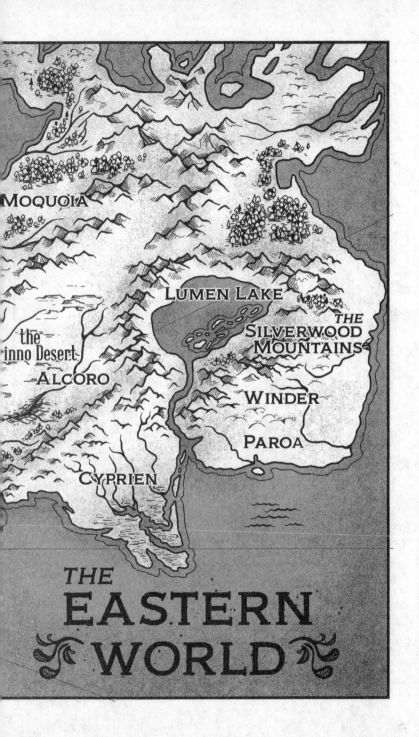

MOQUOIA

the
inno Desert

ALCORO

LUMEN LAKE

THE
SILVERWOOD
MOUNTAINS

WINDER

PAROA

CYPRIEN

THE
EASTERN
WORLD

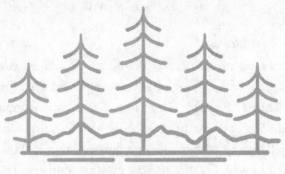

VERAN

I'm being followed.

I noticed them a few hours ago, as the sun rose across the rugged Ferinno Desert, turning the distant wash of the South Burr to eye-searing gold. To give my watering eyes a break, I had twisted in my saddle to look back into the lingering purple dawn, and that's when I saw them—the helms and tack of soldiers, glinting in the dust, following my line across the sagebrush flats.

I chew my lip and scan the ground again. Thanks to the still-damp soil from last night's hellacious thunderstorm, my horse Kuree is leaving deep hoofprints as clearly as if I was stamping a trail for the Moquoian soldiers to follow. I'm well off Lark's course, so I've yet to see any prints left from her horse, or an errant paw mark from a loping coydog, but maybe that's just part of her power—leaving no mark on the landscape.

I try to shake that notion. Lark's not a magical desert sun goddess. And she's not a bandit, either.

She's a princess.

Drowning my anxiety at the pursuing soldiers is a now-familiar wave of . . . of, Light, I don't even know what this emotion *is*. Shame? Regret? Astonishment at my own stupidity? I traveled with Lark for six days across the desert, saw her eyes from inches away as she hauled me down a ridge, saw the freckles mixed in with the dirt and the eyeblack on her cheeks, and not once did I make any connection to her twin sister, Eloise.

She was wearing a bandanna, I insisted to Rou just hours ago as we both stood aghast in the rain. The eyeblack, the dreadlocks, the hat, the be-damned sun always blazing behind her . . .

But no. In the long, lonely ride through the night, I've finally realized what I wasn't seeing. Lark's difference from Eloise goes further than hairstyle and sunburn. Eloise is like her father, Rou—amiable, generous, easy, with a quick smile and a ready laugh.

Lark—Moira—Moira Alastaire, she isn't like Rou.

Lark is like her mother.

The way she stands with her shoulders thrown back, the way she uses silence to intimidate and establish power, the way she turns a rock or a bucket or her horse's saddle into a throne, the judicious way she hands out approval.

The way she uses all that hardness as a front for how much she actually cares about the people around her.

Eloise is like Ambassador Rou.

Lark is like Queen Mona.

I twist in the saddle again. The dust cloud seems closer, or maybe the growing light is just making it more obvious against the long shadows thrown by the dusky sage. I'm leading them right to her, right to the hidden camp in Three Lines Canyon.

But I don't dare veer off to try to lose them in a creek or rocky rise—once Lark reaches her canyon, she's not going to stick around. And I can't risk losing her trail.

If I don't find her in Three Lines, if she disappears into the Ferinno, there's no way I'll see her again unless she wants me to.

Which, given current circumstances, is beyond impossible.

I shake myself, slapping my cheeks. I've pushed Kuree through the night, only stopping to rest once the Owl star rose, and then for less than an hour. I didn't sleep. I paced back and forth under the wheeling star as it eased above the horizon.

The Owl star. I grimace. I am such a faker, pretending to be one of Mama's scouts, pretending I've sat through the night watches in the canopy platforms, sharing the culture of the Wood Guard around the campfires. Bat star, Wolf star, Owl star, Whippoorwill star. I know all the good-natured grumbles about each one, all the jibes and jokes about who takes which watch, how the Wolf star is the worst, because no matter how you slice it you never get a decent sleep, how the Owl star is the loneliest, how the Whippoorwill star will make you crazy with the predawn birdsong.

I know it all, but it's not mine. Not truly. I'm no Wood-walker. I'm no scout. My chances at entering the Wood Guard were foiled long ago, when it became clear my childhood seizures weren't just freak occurrences. At ten years old, when my friends were all being fitted for their trainee uniforms, I was being tailed by a physician, ready with ointment and nausea pills and clean clothes for when I puked or pissed myself as my body relaxed after seizing. They moved me from Vynce's room back into the old nursery, so my physician could sleep in the adjoining nurse's room. They made me sit instead of stand, walk instead of run, take long rests after dancing. They made me stay at my father's side in the council room, instead of hurrying along with my mother as she ran ridges and checked caches and trained scouts in the language of the Silverwood.

Thinking of Mama and Papa does nothing to ease my anxiety. They would die if they knew where I was and what I was doing. Not the racing after a notorious outlaw—they've both done worse—but rushing into the merciless desert, alone, after a string of near-sleepless nights, without enough supplies, and after I've already had two seizures within a week of each other. That's the shortest lapse between episodes I've had since I was fifteen.

What choice do I have, though? I twitch my head, trying to banish the cobwebby exhaustion fuzzing the edges of my brain.

Three Lines. Have to get to Three Lines.

I look over my shoulder again at the pursuing Moquoians. I've spent so much energy worrying about Lark and Rou and Eloise and myself that I've spared almost no thought for Tamsin and Iano. Tamsin is, after all, the reason I first rode out into the desert to find Lark. Despite being weak and starved, she made it through the ride from her prison cell over the past two days, but the chance I thought she'd have to recuperate in Pasul was whisked away by the soldiers combing the town for her and the Moquoian prince. Instead of resting, she and Iano had to bolt into the mountains, angling for a hamlet in the giant redwood forests of the western coast.

By the Light, I hope she's all right. I suppose I should be glad the soldiers are following me and not her. If she and Iano can stay hidden long enough to find out who kidnapped her and blackmailed Iano, then something might be salvaged of this smoking wreck. But if they're caught before they can pinpoint who their enemy is . . . my mind wheels. It could mean a coup in Moquoia.

And as the Eastern ambassadors—me, Rou, Eloise—are purportedly involved, it could mean full-out war.

I almost laugh, giddy with lack of sleep and gripping anxiety. I set out on this journey to Moquoia two months ago with dreams of political victories to call my own, and instead I may have started international war.

Kuree noses toward some tough grasses, and I squeeze her flanks with my knees.

"Come on," I murmur. The South Burr is nearer—soon I'll ford the water, and then it's just a matter of finding that grassy trace leading up into the caprocks. Hopefully I'll find the little track left by the comings and goings of Lark's camp. If I'm lucky, I may even spot her making for the mouth of the canyon.

And if I'm really, *really* lucky, she might decide *not* to kill me on sight.

TAMSIN

I open sticky eyes to a yellow morning. Impulsively I shift to look for the light from the tiny window in my cell wall, only to realize the light is everywhere. Morning is everywhere, not trapped beyond dingy adobe walls but rising, nudging, laying wet over the cloak wrapped around my shoulders. I shiver and then regret it—the movement replaces the hazy sleep with a spiky headache.

"Tamsin?"

I roll over, clumsily, because half my body doesn't feel like it belongs to me and the other half feels full of rocks. A face swims just a few inches from mine, golden-pale against the loose fall of black hair.

"Ia'o," I say, and wince.

"Tamsin," he says again, and I wonder if this is just what life is now, repeating each other's names in lieu of conversation. He shifts upright a little more, and I realize the warmth along my back wasn't from the cloak, but from him pressed up against me.

"How are you? Did you sleep? Don't . . . you don't have to try to speak." A hopeless kind of look crosses his face, as if he can't come up with a suitable alternative. "Just . . . do you want to sit up?"

I wrap my grimy hand around his and let him help me struggle upright. I hang my head for a moment, waiting for the throbbing in my temples and tongue to lessen. It doesn't. Iano rubs my back.

Memories of the last twenty-four hours are coming back to me—the flight from Pasul into the hills with nothing more than a half-lame horse and the clothes on our backs, hours of silent travel uphill, probably a few more hours where I fell asleep on the horse's back, and then the short foray off the trail to find a decent place to lie on the ground and continue sleeping. I lift my head. The place we chose is little more than a marginally flat place on the upper slopes of the Moquovik Mountains, populated by talus, wind-bent juniper, and a dastardly breeze. The horse stands a few paces away, cropping the pitiful strands of grass clinging to the rocks. I realize that we aren't quite as unequipped as I thought—leaning against the horse's tack on the ground is Iano's bone-white longbow and quiver of blue-fletched arrows.

"I think we're getting close to the rainshadow," Iano says. "We got higher than I thought we would last night. Tonight's camping . . . may be harder."

I'll say it will be. The eastern slopes of the Moquoviks are cold and sparse but dry, at least. If we cross the rainshadow today, though, chances are high we'll be soaking wet as well as cold, and we have only Iano's traveling cloak to share between us. Realizing said cloak is wrapped only around my shoulders, and not his, I start to slip it off, but he puts his hand on mine to stop me.

"Keep it on a little longer, Tamsin. You look . . . you just keep it."

I look atrocious, most likely, spider pale and sheep shorn, cheeks swollen with the unhealed wounds in my mouth. As if following my thoughts, his gaze drifts down to my lips.

"Would you let me see again?" he asks quietly. "In the daylight. I didn't get a good look yesterday."

Gingerly I part my lips. He places his thumb gently on my chin and tilts my face toward his. I'm facing into the morning sky, so it must be no trouble to see the swollen split in my tongue. His chest rises with a short breath, and he draws me against him.

"I'm sorry." His voice is anguished against the murdered fuzz of my hair. "Tamsin, I—I'm sorry. I never thought . . ." His grip tightens. "I'm going to find them. They'll pay for what they've done, I swear it. And then I'm going to marry you and crown you queen of this country."

Now *that's* an amusing image—me floating silently around Tolukum court in Queen Isme's scarlet silks, with her twin jeweled combs perched on my shaved head. I shake my head against his chest and lean back, in part because hearing him talk this way turns my stomach, and because his shirt button is pressing into my lip and it all hurts too much.

I swipe a patch of dirt beside us and scratch a few letters with a twig.

HIRES, I write.

He frowns at my word. "The Hires?"

I nod.

"What about them?"

I circle my hand, wanting him to think about the group of fanatics who planned the attack on my coach. One of my captors, Poia, was a Hire—a group with the firm political belief in the hierarchy that places slaves and bond laborers at the very bottom of society, while wage earners like herself occupy a higher rung.

When Iano doesn't comment, I write in the dirt again.

STILL OUT THERE.

"Well, of course they're still out there," he says. "I didn't know they might be involved until last night."

Surely he must realize that we can't accomplish anything until we can pinpoint who in our court is affiliated with the Hires. It's not a desirable or admirable label to be branded with, despite the fact that some of them have literally branded themselves with tattoos stating exactly that. Those can be kept hidden, though, and whoever the traitor is has clearly kept their association a secret to avoid losing allies. But those extremist views must have colored all of their politics, and that, ultimately, is what makes them dangerous—a vocal supporter could be pinpointed and their influence diluted.

A quiet one, a secret one, who can influence without being exposed . . . that's the real threat.

I try to put some of this into words, scratching them carefully in the dirt, but there are too many, and the soil is too pebbly. Iano puzzles at my work, and my frustration spikes at the piling up of words I can't speak. My head still aches, my body buzzes with fatigue, and my stomach rumbles, ravenous again after breaking my hunger strike. But before I can muster the energy to clear the ground for writing again, we both freeze.

From the direction of the path comes the unmistakable sound of horses' hooves on rocky ground. We're about a bow shot off the track, but there's little cover between here and there, only a few boulders shielding us from view. All anyone would have to do is . . .

"Hang on, look," says a muffled voice. "Doesn't that look like prints? Somebody veered off the path."

"Probably a shepherd."

Yes, it is absolutely a shepherd, listen to your idiot friend, please listen. My mind wheels and I lock gazes with Iano. His fingers creep toward his bow and quiver, but hesitantly, as if he's not sure what he'll do with them once he gets them in his grip.

"Tending what, rocks? There's no grazing up here, not even for goats. Come on, let's just take a look and then we'll head on down. The captain won't notice a five-minute delay."

Hooves crunch on stone; rocks go slithering down the slope. Behind us, our horse lifts his head from the grass.

Iano's fingers close on his bow, but by now we both know who's coming around the bend—two soldiers, in the black-and-white livery of Tolukum Palace, with the redwood cone crest on their chests.

They're in single file, so the first one rounds the nearest boulder and practically falls off his horse in surprise.

"Oh!" he says. His gaze flicks between the two of us. "Oh . . ."

"What?" says his companion, still behind the boulder. "What is it?"

He's young, and wearing the orange belt of a new recruit; he's probably never seen a portrait of Iano, let alone been in close enough proximity to see his face. And neither of us is looking particularly royal at the moment—Iano's hair is loose and rumpled, with no pin or jewels, and his shirt and trousers, though finely made, are filmed with dirt and mud. I, of course, look worse. Maybe we can pass for innocent travelers.

But the soldier's gaze doesn't linger on Iano—it jumps to me.

"Oh!" he says again, and his hands begin to fumble around his saddle.

"Dammit, Olito, *what is it?*" demands his companion, attempting to edge his horse around the boulder.

"That's—it's the accomplice!" Olito says frantically. "It's . . . look, look—she's just as the orders said . . ."

Accomplice?

I realize now what he's fumbling for. A crossbow. He wrenches a quarrel from under his saddle flap and jams it in place, awkwardly winding the crank.

"Let me see, Olito, move your damned horse—"

Iano jumps to his feet and draws his bow. It's a beautiful movement, graceful and fluid, wonderful for a relaxed afternoon of targets at the royal hunting lodge, but not at all comforting when facing the prospect of two loaded crossbows. All the thrilling appreciation I've ever had for his clever handling of his artisanal bow vanishes as I wonder why on earth he didn't choose a more modern weapon to train with.

Olito draws his crossbow up to sight, but his companion is finally maneuvering his horse around his, making the animal sidestep and bob and Olito's aim waver.

"Hold your quarrel, Olito, hang on, let's just make sure—*by the colors.*" His companion finally gets a clear look at me, twisted halfway in the saddle as his horse negotiates the rocky slope. "You're right!"

I do the only thing I can think of given the circumstances. I flee.

I scramble on leaden fingers and toes for the cover of another boulder. I hear the whir of a crank, and a quarrel skips off the rocks where I'd been sitting.

"Hold your quarrel!" Iano roars behind me. "How dare you—by order of the crown, hold your quarrel!"

But several things then happen at once. There's another wind of a crank, and then a twang of a string as Iano releases, and all those afternoons of targets and darts and fox-in-the-hole funnel right into his arrow as it punctures the young soldier's throat. Olito slumps in the saddle, his reloaded crossbow clattering to the rocks. The horses spook, their frantic movements dislodging rocks and adding to the disarray. The second soldier panics, first grabbing for his crossbow, and then abandoning it for his saddle horn as his horse bolts instinctively down the mountainside. But the terrain is too loose, and too steep, and the animal makes it only a few strides before it stumbles. The soldier is half-thrown from its back, but he barely makes it to the ground before the horse rolls right over him. There's a horrible sight of four flailing hooves in the air, of flying rocks, and then the horse disappears over the sharp lip of the mountain, the sound of grinding stone following it down.

The soldier doesn't move. He stays facedown in the rocks, one of which bears a wet, straggled line of red.

Iano drops his bow and stumbles backward.

"Oh, Light," he gasps.

Slowly, I rise from my half-crouch by the boulder. I wish I felt ashamed for running, but I don't—staying put would have only earned me a quarrel. I wobble back toward Iano, who's staring at Olito still slouched half out of his saddle. As we watch, the horse takes a few nervous steps down the path, and the soldier's head bumps the boulder. With a slow, terrible slide, he falls to the ground.

Iano's palms fly to his head, his lips white. "*Oh, Light . . .*"

I grip his shoulder to steady both of us. His frantic gaze jumps to me.

"He was . . . he would have shot you! But I didn't . . . I didn't mean . . . oh, Light . . ."

I squeeze him, fighting down my own panic. His gaze moves down the slope, where the second soldier is still unmoving on the rocks. There's no sound from beyond the lip of the cliff.

Iano suddenly bends at the waist, his hands on his knees, gasping as if he's going to be sick. I sink with him—my legs are reedy and trembling from my burst of movement. I peer up into Iano's stricken face.

"I killed him," he whispers to the ground. "I killed them both. Our own soldiers . . ."

Perhaps it's because I know I can't offer any condolences, but suddenly there's something else I want him to focus on. I swipe at the ground below his face and drag my fingernail through the dirt.

ACCOMPLICE? I write.

"Who's an accomplice?" he asks.

"Me," I say. I point to the soldiers. "Called me . . ." I point to the word in the dirt again.

"They called you an accomplice," he says, and then his brow furrows. "They must have had you confused with someone else."

They'd seemed pretty certain, though, and there was no

hesitation in how they should act upon it. They were ready to shoot on sight.

I rise and slowly approach the riderless horse, stepping carefully around Olito's body. The horse tosses its head, still uneasy, but I grasp its dangling reins and reach for the saddlebag.

"What are you doing?" Iano asks.

I gesture to the bag, unhooking it from the saddle. Bringing it back to Iano, I open it and rifle through the contents. The topmost items are camping goods—packets of food, a tinderbox, a canteen. But below these things is an oilskin pouch, crinkling with parchment inside. I pull it out and open it.

It's a stack of documents, all marked for the captain of the garrison in Pasul. I unroll the first and come face-to-face with Lark, the woodblock-printed image staring out in crisp black ink from under her broad-brimmed hat and raised bandanna.

Wanted: Dead or Alive
The Sunshield Bandit

for the Murder of Ashoki Tamsin Moropai,
Abduction of Prince Iano Okinot in-Azure,
and Attacks on Moquoian Industry.
Subject Should Be Considered Armed and
Dangerous.
Reward: Two Hundred Crescents
Fifty Crescents for Accomplices, Dead or Alive

"Oh no . . . ," Iano breathes, reading over my shoulder.

My own chest is locked tight with dread. Lark is being blamed not just for my faked murder, but for Iano's disappearance, too? My gaze travels down the page, where there's a splash of red wax at the bottom. Iano's fingers jump to grasp the parchment, lifting it closer to be sure. He draws in a sharp breath.

It's his mother's seal—the stamp of Queen Isme Okinot in-Scarlet.

We lock gazes—his eyes are creased with shock.

"Not . . . ," he begins. "I mean . . . just because . . . she authorized the bounty, it doesn't mean that she . . ." His anguished gaze drops to my lips. "Does it?"

I shake my head, but it's a worrying thought, that Queen Isme might have been the one behind my attack.

"She's *not* a Hire," he says firmly, almost angrily.

I don't say anything. I can't. Instead, I tap the phrase at the bottom, with the reward for accomplices.

"Vee," I say.

"V?" he repeats, and a full five agonizing seconds pass before his expression clears. "Oh—Veran?"

I nod.

"I suppose this puts him at risk too—assuming he finds her."

I nod again, release the bounty sheet, and rifle through the other documents in the pouch. They're all copies, meant to be posted throughout Pasul. They're hastily made—the woodblock was clearly carved in a hurry, with uneven spaces between the letters and smeared ink where they hadn't been left to dry long enough. I close the oilskin pouch and lift out the one beneath it, also full of parchment. I have a sinking feeling in my stomach, a growing dread at why, exactly, the two soldiers recognized me as an accomplice.

I open the pouch and pull out the first sheet.

"Great Colors of the Light," Iano blurts out in shock.

Sure enough, there's my face, or as near enough as the wood-carver could come. It's rounder than it appears now, more like it used to be when I was a healthy weight, but the most damning thing is my hair. It's gone, just as mine is now, suggested only by a few sparse black lines on my head. At the bottom, just like Lark's, is the queen's seal.

Wanted: Dead
Accomplice of the Sunshield Bandit

Name Unknown
Moquoian National. Amber Si-Oque, Possibly
Forged. Shorn Head. Mute.
Subject Should Be Considered Armed and
Dangerous.
Reward: Two Hundred Crescents

We stare in silence. I fix on that one word at the top, the finality of it lending some sense to our soldiers' panicked reactions. *Dead.* I'm not supposed to be brought in alive.

"What . . . *how*?" Iano finally asks, his voice weak. "How could someone know what you look like? How could they know that I gave you back your *si-oque*? How could they know that you're . . . about your tongue?"

I turn the heavy parchment over and sweep the ground for a pebble. I roll it in the dirt and use it to form an inelegant scrawl.

OUR BLACKMAILER DID THIS.

It's the only answer I can think of. The court had already been twitchy about the Sunshield Bandit, but the only person I can think of who would know these details about me, besides my now-dead captors, is the person who orchestrated the attack itself.

Which means they must know that I've escaped. And this is their way of getting rid of me before anyone finds out that I'm the *ashoki* who didn't die.

Iano's right—just because his mother's seal is on the bounties doesn't mean she's the mastermind. But it does mean she's been drawn into the lies.

It means we're even less safe than we thought.

Iano scrubs his face. "We need to get to Giantess Township. We have to get to Soe's, find somewhere we'll be safe. This is getting out of control—someone in Tolukum is somehow one step ahead of us. I just hope they haven't figured out where we're going."

I don't know how they could, but we can't afford to linger anyway. Together we pile the bounty sheets back in the saddlebag. For one terrible moment, we both pause, and then simultaneously look to the riderless horse.

Iano inhales.

"You get on," he says, his voice tight. "I'll get the rapier."

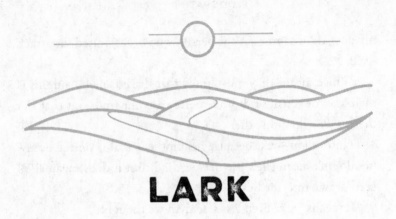

LARK

The South Burr is running high.

I stand on the far bank, my boots inch-deep in muck, staring at the rushing, rust-colored water between me and the trace leading up to Three Lines. Last night's thunderstorm was no typical desert shower—the grass along the banks is slicked flat and strewn with debris, and the water is still well above its usual course. As I watch, a cottonwood tree bobs hurriedly downstream, shedding green leaves along the way.

We never needed to worry much about flash flooding in Three Lines. The worst that ever happened was that the freshwater seep would overflow and send a creek down the side of camp, but since all our gear and stores were on the higher slopes, we were never in any danger. I see that telltale creek now, trickling down the grassy trace, but now I'm on the wrong side of the Burr, and what was usually a line of defense is a barrier.

It doesn't matter, though. Flooding or not, I have to ford it. I have to get my campmates out of the canyon, out of the Ferinno.

I have the barest head start. If we leave everything, we can get away before anyone comes looking.

And Sedge's crossbow is in camp. So I can deter anyone trying to follow.

I shouldn't have thought of the crossbow. Thinking of the crossbow makes me think of Saiph, and then of Rose, and then of the disaster all our lives have become. Saiph is missing, either lost along the road or injured, or killed, or captured by slavers, or in prison in Pasul—and I don't know how I'm going to find out which. Short of following the track he was supposed to take south of the water scrape and then knocking on the sheriff's door, I can't figure out how I'm going to find him.

And Rose . . .

It's been two weeks since the catastrophe with the slave wagon, the one that killed Pickle and wrenched the last good bit of Rose's amputated leg below her knee apart. And it's been five days since I left her with the others, feverish and unconscious.

I've grown sicker and sicker with dread this whole ride, afraid of what's waiting for me in camp.

And I *loathe* the self-absorbed, manipulative prince Veran Greenbrier.

Jema stands with her head drooping over the rushing river, nose almost to the water. Poor Jema. I finally stopped to let her rest once we reached the shiprock, but it wasn't enough, and I need her to keep going.

We have to get across the Burr.

"Rat," I call. "Here!"

Rat lopes up the bank, leaving paw prints in the deep mud. I grab hold of his ruff and wrap my arm under his chest.

"You're not going to like this," I warn him. "Bear with me, okay?"

I hoist him off the ground, and immediately he whines and wriggles, smearing my trousers with mud. But they're about to get soaked anyway, so I move forward and take up Jema's reins. I maneuver upstream of her—if she slips, I don't want to be in her path. With a cluck, I slosh forward into the thick, muddy rapids.

We're okay, at first. The slope is gentle and the ground is pebbly. Rat gives a stringy coyote whine at my hip, and I clutch him tighter. Jema snorts, tossing her head.

"It's okay," I soothe them both, leading us farther out into the river. On a typical day, a ford here would barely get my knees wet, but just a few feet in, the surface is already over the tops of my boots. They flood, dragging my steps.

By the time we're ten feet in, the water is sloshing against my thighs. Something—a branch or root washed free by the current—slaps my knee, and I lean into Jema's shoulder. She tosses her mane, her nose high.

"It's okay," I say again. "It's okay, Jema. Jema, come on . . ."

The water's at her chest, and she doesn't like it—she keeps trying to turn away from me, to move downstream.

"Jema," I say breathlessly. "*Jema . . .*"

And Colm.

The name slams into me and I slip on the rocky bottom, clutching the reins to keep from falling. Rat's claws catch my trousers.

A familiar voice enters my head.

You named your horse after Gemma Maczatl? The Last Queen of Alcoro?

I'd scoffed at Veran a few days ago, glad to use his affront against him, but I hadn't given his comment much thought. The night I stole Jema was two years ago, in Teso's Ford. There was a group of university officials in town for a lecture, and as I lurked around the back of the amphitheater, pinching coins from pockets, I heard that name dropped more than once. When I stole one of their horses, a big, burly black mare, I gave her that name.

I liked it. It felt fancy, felt right.

Felt familiar.

"No, no, no," I murmur, gritting my teeth. I wrap Jema's reins around my fist, trying to pull her along, but now I can't get that other name out of my head—the one that often accompanied the first.

Gemma and Colm. Colm and Gemma.

Your uncle's coming to visit . . .

Look, we got a letter from . . .

"NO."

I drag Jema forward, trying to outrun these ghosting half-memories, trying to drown them in the raging water. The ground dips under my boots, and suddenly I'm up to my stomach. I hoist Rat up under my arm, his paddling legs clawing my shirt.

Those memories aren't mine. They don't belong to me. I've got no past in that lofty, untouchable world, a world of queens and kings and castles all built on the backs of innocent people. A world that trades in flesh and blood.

This was a bad decision, choosing to ford here. I should have continued downstream to the place where the current eases, but that would have taken me two miles out of the way. Two miles from Three Lines, two miles from my campmates. *Two miles safer.* I shake away that thought and take another step.

The water's at my chest; I lift my chin above the dirty droplets leaping from the surface. Rat clambers over my shoulder, his wet fur sticking to my face. I can feel him shaking.

"S'okay," I spit around the hair and spray. "Come on, halfway there . . . no, *Jema*—"

Jema's had enough. She turns downstream, her ears flat against her skull. I haul on her lead, but with both her and the current tugging me in the same direction, my feet slide, and I pitch forward. My head slips under the surface. Rat's claws scrabble at my shoulder, tearing my skin . . .

And then he's gone.

I suck in a dirty mouthful of water, my body free in the rapids. I bounce off a rock, jarring my injured shoulder. By chance my toes catch the riverbed, and I fight to dig my heels in. They pop free almost immediately, but it gives me the chance to thrust my head above the surface, spewing out water.

"Rat!" I fling my soaking dreadlocks out of my face—my hat is gone—and desperately scan the water downstream. It's a raging mess, foaming and plunging, branches appearing and disappearing as they tumble. I'm rushing along with them—rushing past the trace to Three Lines. In a moment I'll be swept past and have to double back, losing those precious minutes . . . I give a wordless shout and start to stroke—I'm no swimmer, never had to be a swimmer in the desert, *not since the lake, stroke from your shoulder, not the elbow, fingers into spoons, not forks, sweetheart—*

My next shout is more of a gasp, and then I see Rat—he's twenty feet ahead, paddling for the shore we started on, where Jema is cantering out of the river, shedding streams of water. But the coyote is already being carried past the horse, floundering in the middle of the current.

"Rat!" I take one long shoulder stroke downstream before something slams into my stomach, knocking the breath from my lungs. Something wild and waving punches my ribs—a branch. I've hit a tree lodged in the bottom, stopping my progress. Rat shoots farther and farther away from me.

"Rat!" I scream. The current is so strong it's moving me sideways, along the angle of the tree. It's shifting me toward the far bank, toward Three Lines, but now Rat is out of sight. I fight to free one leg from the net of branches. I nearly have it thrown over the blockage when from the corner of my vision, a figure comes barreling down the riverbank, near where Rat just disappeared. It dives into the torrent.

The tree I'm flattened against judders, and I go under again. The current pushes me down its length, every twig and knob finding a way to pinch or scrape or slap. I emerge, choking, and realize that I'm nearly in the first reeds on the far bank. My boots grind on the bottom, and I lift my shoulders free. Gasping, I wind my fingers in the reeds—bless you, cattail—and haul myself into the pebbly muck. The water tugs at my boots, but now I can crawl, coughing, through the weeds and up onto the bank.

I'm a uniform dirty brown, from my hair to my once-white shirt to my boots. I slouch for a moment, drawing rattly gasps of air, my ears still full of the rushing water.

Stupid, stupid, stupid.

Stupid.

My dread now cresting like a swell, I lift my head and stagger to my feet. I barely get my boots under me before I hear the last voice I want—or expect—to hear.

"Lark! Lark, I got him!"

From the willows staggers an equally-brown Veran, his sopping clothes hanging off him, hair plastered to his forehead. He's clutching a bedraggled Rat in his arms. An anxious coyote whine rises over the sound of the current, and my dread flushes into something like relief.

Something, but not quite.

I glance across the river—Jema is safe, nosing along with the pretty palomino Kuree, both their reins dangling. My buckler winks on her saddle, along with my sword hilt. I look back to Veran as he stumbles forward eagerly, eyes bright.

"I got him," he gasps again. "I wasn't sure I could, but I learned to swim with Eloise as kids—your ma made sure I could . . ."

A searing, irrational bolt of anger flares through me, and I slap my thigh. "Here, Rat."

Rat struggles out of Veran's grip and hops toward me, panting. Veran doesn't stop, picking up his pace to close the distance between us.

"Lark," he says. "You have to let me talk to you. Please—"

I don't wait for him to slow down; I take one step toward him, the heel of my hand out for his sternum, aiming to tip him off-balance and maybe kick him once he's down. But before I can make contact, his hand flies through the air to clamp over my wrist.

He smothers his own look of surprise at his reflexes. "I thought you might try that," he says. "I'm not *entirely* stupid, you kn-*oow, blue blessed Light*—"

His remark is cut short as I finish twisting his arm. His fingers release, and in the brief few seconds he takes to clutch his wrist, I break into a run for Three Lines.

"You follow me and I'll shoot," I shout over my shoulder.

"Lark!" he cries. "Wait—stop! There's something I need to tell you!"

But I'm fueled by anger now, and my shaky exhaustion is replaced by a burst of energy. I race up the grassy slope, Rat tearing along behind me.

I don't stop to wonder why there's nobody out in the trace— Andras should be here with the ox and the horses, watching the road and letting the animals graze. Lila should be gathering greens, maybe with little Whit at her side. But the slope is silent and empty. Perhaps it's too early in the day, or they're waiting until the river recedes so they can bring the animals to water.

Perhaps some horrible thing has happened, perhaps the canyon flooded in the night, perhaps it caved and they're stuck inside, perhaps lightning struck and set the place burning, perhaps, perhaps, perhaps.

I run faster.

"Lark!" Veran is following me, stumbling over the rocky tussocks. I hope Sedge has the crossbow oiled and loaded— maybe if I shout he'll do the aiming and shooting for me. My lungs burning, I reach the lopsided boulder at the entrance of the canyon. The three wavy lines carved into the rock, the ancient glyph proclaiming a water source inside, blur as I rush past them.

"Sedge!" I call. "Lila!" My voice bounces off the rocks. "Rose! Andras, Whit, Moll!" *Pickle. Saiph.* The litany of my campmates cycles through my head, my throat hitching at the two I've already lost.

"Sedge!" I shout again. "Get your crossbow! Get the horses!"

I hop over the stream coursing over the path from the over-flowing seep. On any other day it would be a blessing, fresh water running right by our toes, but now it's only another un-nerving anomaly—where *is* everyone? Are they hiding? Does Sedge have them sheltered above the seep? And where—I crest the little rise to the flat place where we keep the horses—*where are the horses?*

"Lark!" Veran calls again. "Stop!"

I break through the scrub oak fringing the camp and skid to a halt.

There's nothing, nobody. The fire ring is black and cold. The mud-and-stick lean-tos are in stacks on the ground. One of our rock walls has been disassembled and lies in a pile. There are no blankets, no pots, no bits of survival scattered around. No, that's not quite true. There's the ax handle I broke a few weeks ago, still missing its head, and the dinged-up metal staff Pickle used to throw to jam stagecoach wheels.

But everything else, every*one* else, is gone.

Veran crashes through the scrub behind me, gasping. "Lark—"

I don't let him finish. I take off in the direction of the seep. They must be there, up the little slope—maybe the water rose too high, maybe Sedge decided it would be easier to defend . . .

"Damnation, Lark!" Veran shouts. "They're not up there! They're not here! They've left—I sent a wagon!"

I slide to a stop again, rocks scattering under my boots. My blood rages in my ears, and I stare up the slope without seeing it, my vision spotting white.

"I mean, not a wagon, like—that kind of wagon," he continues behind me. "A cart. In the letter I wrote to Iano—that Saiph carried to Pasul—I told him to send Saiph back with an eight-seater cart. We paid the driver—they're probably nearly to Callais by now. No, wait—"

I pivot toward him, and he throws up his hands. "I was going to tell you in Pasul. I thought the sooner they could get help—"

I advance on him, ready to break his nose, his fingers, his knee. He stumbles backward on the rocks. "Lark—"

"You have taken every single thing away from me!" I snarl.

"You wanted me to get them out, you wanted me to help them, I thought—"

"You've *ruined. Everything!*" I shout. "You and your stupid hero complex, you've ruined everything I ever had!" I stoop down and scoop up a stone, cocking it back over my shoulder. He flings his arms over his face, crouching by the scrub.

I stop. From this angle, on the other side of the stacked lean-tos, I again catch sight of the pile of rocks from one of our walls. But it's not just a pile. Something's wrong about it—it's arranged too neatly, too purposefully, and in too recognizable a shape, longer than it is wide, with a large, flat stone propped up at the far end . . .

I drop the rock. Veran looks up half a breath later, but I've already veered toward the pile. He rises slowly from his crouch.

"Lark . . . is that . . . ?"

I stop at the foot of the mound, first staring directly between my toes, where a frayed corner of a blanket peeks out from under the rocks. I catch more glimpses of the fabric through gaps, wrapped neatly, tightly, around something inside . . . my gaze travels to the big, flat stone at the head of the pile, leaning against the canyon wall. I recognize the stone—it was one of our general work surfaces, something we'd use to stitch leather or hammer metal or beat corn into meal. The face has been cleaned, and the remnants of black smudges, drawn on with charcoal, fleck the surface. The thunderstorm has rendered them unreadable, but it's clear they were initially letters.

A few letters, spelling out a short name.

The name of someone I left here, near death, at the reckless whim of a royal stranger.

Rose.

My heart shudders to a stop. My knees buckle, and I land at the foot of the cairn, staring again at the frayed corner of the blanket that's serving as a shroud. The blood has ceased roaring in my ears, leaving only a vast, noiseless void.

"Rose." My voice is hoarse, abraded by muddy water and too much emotion. My fingers clench on the rocks, and I fight the sudden, wild urge to tear away the cairn, to rip open the shroud beneath.

"Is it . . . how do you know?" Veran whispers behind me. "It's just . . . there's no name . . ."

I clench my jaw so hard it pops. How do I know? Which one of my campmates did I leave unconscious while I rode off to Utzibor? Which of my campmates had already lost a calf because of me, and now, thanks to my mistakes at the wagon, lost her life? My oldest friend, the closest thing I've ever had to family . . . my chest tightens, crushing my breath. I wind my arms around my head and squeeze.

"Lark," he says again, seemingly ignoring my silence. "Listen, I know . . . I know this is bad, but we need to get to the horses. We need to get on the road, head toward Callais. I sent your campmates to my friends there, to Gemma and Colm, and if we start now, we can be far enough away before the soldiers—"

I snap.

I jump to my feet and whirl around in one sharp movement. He leaps back a second too late—I've already lunged and caught him by the collar. He staggers and we both go down, his breath whooshing from his lips as he lands with me straddling his chest. The packed ground sends spikes of pain up my knees, but I barely feel it. I cock my wrist back.

"Lark," he croaks. "I'm sorry, listen, I'm sorry—"

I pause to aim. I'd like to break his teeth, or his jaw, but that would hurt my knuckles. I decide to settle for his nose, his pretty aquiline nose—that's going to hurt, too, but at least I shouldn't get anything embedded in my skin. I hinge back a little farther.

He blinks up at me, his chest rising and falling under my legs. Some of the dirt from the river has sloughed off, and underneath I can see the pink scar over his eyebrow, and the purple-green bruise on his forehead, the lingering mark from where he hit his head after collapsing in a seizure a few days ago. Down above his right ear is the blistered patch from rescuing Tamsin from the burning building. On his neck is a fresh wound, a long, thin scrape, as if from a flailing dog's claw.

My fist trembles in the air. My own burns sting; my shoulder twinges from the blow from Dirtwater Dob's mattock. My scrapes and bruises from the flooded Burr throb.

He continues to gaze at me with those sagebrush eyes, his palms shaking on the ground.

"I shouldn't have sent them away without telling you," he says slowly, softly. "I'm sorry, Lark. I made that decision before we ever left Three Lines—I thought I was doing you a favor, getting a head start on things, that you'd appreciate it later. It was only after we'd been traveling for a while that I realized I messed up. And I never imagined someone might die while you were away. Lark." His voice cracks. "Hit me if you want, if it'll help, but then let me fix some of this. I know I can't fix all of it, but the rest of your campmates are all right—Saiph is okay. If he weren't, the others would still be here."

My shoulder aches with holding my fist back. I rearrange my knuckles. He winces in anticipation but doesn't toss up his hands.

From down the canyon comes the echo of a voice.

Veran's eyes widen a little. "Uh, that's the other thing. We're being followed."

My arm spasms, and my gaze drifts to the rocky earth just over his right shoulder.

"Don't—!" he warns, but my fist is already flying down. I ram my knuckles into the dirt by his ear. We both suck in a breath at the same time—he in shock and me in pain. But I don't waste any more breath. I roll backward, my left hand still closed on his collar, and drag him upright.

I hold his face inches from mine.

"What do you mean, *we're being followed*?" I snarl.

"The soldiers from Pasul," he gasps. "From the Moquoian palace—they followed my trail after I set out after you. I didn't think they'd move this fast, but they're on fresh horses."

The horses. "And you just left Jema and Kuree by the river?"

His eyebrows knit. "Well, you did, too!"

I shake him. "Because I was planning to *shoot you* and be done with it." I look over his shoulder. "How many?"

"I never got a good count. Five or six, maybe?"

"Armed?"

"Yeah, definitely."

I grind my teeth again and glance around, but Sedge and Lila were thorough—all our caches are cleaned out, empty. Not so much as a blunt knife. I let go of his collar—maybe with an extra shake—and stalk to the old ax handle and metal staff. I toss him the handle. He drops it, and then stoops to pick it back up.

"We'll have to go over," I say.

"Over what?"

"The canyon," I say. "We can climb up the track to the water pocket and then over the ridge. We can come down the draw on the other side and try to get to Jema and Kuree."

"And then Callais?"

"One thing at a time, okay?"

The dirt on his face cracks as he smothers a smile.

"What?" I demand.

"You got that from my ma."

I point at him with the metal staff, my collar hot. "Look, rule one is you absolutely shut up about—*any* of that, you understand? I am still *so close* to punching you."

He twists the corner of his mouth, trying ineffectively to smother his smile. "Got it."

I nearly swing the staff at his head, but now the canyon walls echo with clattering rocks. I turn away from him, my stomach dropping as my gaze passes over Rose's cairn again, and then I start for the overflowing seep.

"Keep up," I say without looking back.

VERAN

The climb up the canyon headwall is steep and loose, with several slips saved only by a grip on clumps of stringy grasses. A few scorpions and a tarantula skitter from our approach, and at one tight twist, the air fills with the gut-wrenching whisper of a snake rattle. But Lark only growls impatiently at the creature, giving it just enough berth, as if she's angry at it as well as me.

I shouldn't have grinned at her down there, not after seeing the grave, but by the Light, so much about her makes sense now. I want to point them all out to her, connect all her mannerisms and turns of phrase, but climbing takes all my breath, and chances are high she'd use that metal staff to send me over the edge.

There's a shout from down the canyon, and I glance over my shoulder.

"They've spotted us," I call. Lark twists, frowning at the knot of soldiers pointing up at us. She pulls her bandanna up over her nose and mouth—it looks odd without her eyeblack and broad-brimmed hat. She turns back and keeps climbing, using the metal staff as a hiking pole.

"Is this just about my bounty?" she asks gruffly.

"No, I don't think it has anything to do with your bounty," I say. "I think they're after me."

"Oh, is that all? Why the gall am *I* running, then? Is there a reward?"

"Ha," I reply flatly. "I'm sure they'd be just as happy to get their hands on you, too, so I wouldn't risk it."

"What've you done to make a bunch of Moquoian soldiers chase you from Pasul?"

"Rescued Tamsin, obviously."

"Obviously," she mimics, a snarl in her voice. "I thought we rescued her for the prince. I wouldn't have thought that would result in jail time."

"Tamsin isn't just a court noble," I say. "She was the *ashoki,* the—"

"The folk who sing at everybody to tell them what to think?"

"It's a little more complicated than that," I say, annoyed. "They don't just tell people what to think, they bring things to their attention, frame things in ways people haven't thought of. Tamsin got caught up in the slave trade several years ago. She made it her goal to play for the court to make lawmakers see the system doesn't work like they think it does, that it's not a just institution."

"Funny that somebody had to explain that to them," she says shortly.

I sigh. "I won't argue that point. Politics can be an insular world, I don't deny it. And I won't defend it. Folk are resistant to change, at their best, and greedy and corrupt at their worst.

But that only makes Tamsin's work all the more remarkable—she completely changed Iano's frame of mind. The next king of Moquoia, Lark. He has no compelling reason to disrupt the status quo, except she helped him see that he should, and he could. Don't you think that's remarkable?"

She doesn't answer my question. "So what you're saying is, some of the politicians in court got angry that she was rocking the boat?"

"That's a Lumeni phrase," I point out.

"What?"

"*Rock the boat.* You learned that in Lumen Lake."

She stops dead and turns to me, her bronze eyes blazing over her bandanna. The end of the metal pole hovers an inch from my nose.

I wave it away. "Sorry, couldn't help it."

"You'd better start helping it."

"Come on, the soldiers are starting up."

She looks down, to where the first Moquoians are starting the ascent up the headwall, hindered by their crossbows. She makes a frustrated sound and continues.

I press on, wanting her to have the full story, still fighting the guilt of not telling her about the wagon. "You're right, though—Tamsin made enemies in court. The problem is, we don't know who. There are plenty of people who would be against upsetting the slave trade, and in favor of Iano appointing an *ashoki* with more traditional politics. The minister of infrastructure is at the top of my list." I recall my handful of unpleasant interactions with Minister Hetor Kobok, coupled with his long absence around the time Tamsin was abducted. "But it could be anybody, really. It could be the new *ashoki*, or an ally of hers determined to keep a proslavery voice in power. Or any of the ministers who depend on exploited labor. Or someone with some other motive; I'm not familiar enough with the nuances of Moquoian politics to—"

"Veran," she says.

"What?"

"Shut up. Focus on breathing, or you're going to pass out. If you do, I'm leaving you."

I fall silent, following the crunching of her bootheels. Rat's panting is the only other sound.

"I mean," she says suddenly, as if realizing what she'd said. "I'm not going to leave you if you . . . that's not what I—"

I allow a dismissive sigh, letting her hear my irritation. "Oh, so it's one thing if you shoot me yourself or knock my brains out, but blessed Light, you couldn't bring yourself to leave me if I have a seizure? I don't want your pity, Lark."

She doesn't turn around, but her steps slow just a bit. A few rocks scatter under her boots.

"Sorry," she says.

"You can shut up, too," I snap.

We toil upward. My thighs burn from the climb, my breath hitching in my chest. Every now and then I glance down at the Moquoians—we're keeping pace ahead of them, thanks to Lark's familiarity with the nigh-invisible path. I work to keep my footprints as light as possible, to avoid making the way any clearer for them.

"Here's the pocket," she says after a while. I follow her over a lip of stone to see a shallow depression. Lying in the center is what looks like an oblong puddle, but I know from our last foray up the sandstone bluff a few days ago that it must be deep to provide such a reliable water source.

We drink from the pocket in silence, the cool, sweet water washing some of the mud out of my throat. I splash my face and hair and let the droplets fall through my fingers. I wish we could carry some with us—I wish we had a canteen or a bottle, a pot, a skin, anything. Lark seems to be thinking the same thing. She crouches at the edge of the pocket, gripping the lip with her knuckles in the water, staring down into its depths.

"It never ran dry," she says. And I realize then that she's not just climbing out of Three Lines Canyon—she's saying good-bye to it. With the soldiers behind us and her campmates in Callais, she might never be back in this place again.

My thoughts flicker briefly to the Silverwood, to the dark slopes and ancient trees, and my heart squeezes a little tighter. I've said good-bye to my home plenty of times, but I've never expected I'd never return.

I glance down the canyon—the helmets of the soldiers bob as they scramble up the slope, still over a quarrel shot below us. My gaze drifts out to the canyon floor, and I frown. Instead of continuing up, two of the soldiers have turned around and are running back through Lark's camp.

I bite my lip, not wanting to rush Lark through her good-bye, but she tears herself away from the water before I say anything. Without looking at me, she turns for the slope.

"We're close to the top, but the last bit's a scramble," she says stiffly. "We never had much need to go over the rim. Come on, Rat."

"Where does the adjacent canyon let out?" I ask as we start up the crumbly incline.

"About half a mile downriver."

I glance back at the two soldiers running back down the canyon. "And if we can't get out that way?"

"Why couldn't we?"

"Two of the soldiers are going back. What if they blockade the canyon entrance?"

"How many are following us?"

"Four."

"Then we have nothing to worry about. You said there's only six."

"I said I didn't get a good count."

She grunts cryptically. "Well, we can't go back. We have a head start. We should reach the end of the canyon before them."

"They probably have horses."

She spins on me, her arms spread wide. "What do you want me to say, Veran?"

"I just want you to know all the angles," I say hotly.

She makes a disgusted sound and goes back to climbing. "If you hadn't followed me, we wouldn't have this problem."

"If you hadn't *run*—" I blurt out before I can help it, but even if I hadn't stopped myself, I wouldn't have been able to finish. With a shout of anger, Lark whirls around, the metal staff wheeling wide. It's only thanks to the steep slope that I'm able to duck under its path.

"We have to go, Lark!" I gasp, my feet sliding backward down the incline. I crouch again as the staff makes the return arc, ruffling my hair. "We don't have time—"

Lark pulls back for another swing, her eyes burning and her feet wide. She'll make contact this time. I scramble to get out of the reach of the staff, but before I make it far, Rat barks. Lark's gaze jumps past me just as I hear the familiar wind of a crank. And then the staff isn't slicing toward my head—she lunges and hooks the end in my tunic like a sailor's gaff and shoves me into the canyon wall. I swear breathlessly—the end pins me to the rock, bruising my shoulder. A quarrel shatters off the path where my torso had been.

I glance down between my toes—the first of the soldiers has her arms hooked over the lip of the water pocket, her crossbow sights trained up at us. She swipes another quarrel from one of her companions below her and jams it in place.

"Get up!" Lark snarls, as if I'd been rolling around on the path for no reason. She withdraws the staff and snatches a handful of my tunic, and then we're running—bent nearly double as we race to get back out of range. The sound of the crank is lost to the shower of rocks washed loose from our scramble, and the next quarrel hits near Lark's grip on a juniper root. Without pause she scoops up the quarrel and wedges it down in her ponytail for safekeeping.

In another few breaths, we're out of range again, but now the soldiers have summited the bowl of the water pocket. I race after Lark's boots, choking on the dust she kicks up and trying not to panic when my toes slide on loose gravel. There's no space for panic, though. No space for thought.

Only flight.

We reach what amounts to the rim of the canyon—merely a broadening of the incline, so that we can run upright instead of scramble. Lark takes off through the thick sage and juniper, occasionally shouting things over her shoulder like, "Snake!" or "Burrow!" I labor after her, my lungs seizing on my breath. I haven't put my body through these kinds of paces in . . . forever. Not ever. Even during the few times I've managed to slip into the forest on my own, I've been careful to take things slowly, to rest and drink and eat, to scan my body for the occasional telltale signs that meant I'm pushing myself too hard. Fatigue, nausea, headache—sometimes these things warn me that my body's about to give way. But not always. And not now. Now my body's just a mess of screaming muscles and blurry vision and adrenaline. Two days without sleep, two nights of frantic riding, a swim across a swollen river with a flailing dog, a run up a canyon wall . . .

I don't think I can make it.

"Lark," I gasp aloud, stumbling numbly over a rock. "Wait . . ."

My voice isn't loud enough for her to hear, but to my surprise, she stops anyway, her boots skidding in the gravel. I practically crash into her a second later, unable to change the mindless pace of my legs. She swears and widens her stance, gripping my shoulders to steady me. I lean unapologetically on her, dragging air into my burning lungs.

"Hot damn," she says grimly, and I look up. We've reached a knoll on the canyon rim, high enough to be able to see down to the canyon on the far side, as well as the grassy trace leading to the river. I suck in an agonized breath.

The bank and both canyons are swarming with soldiers. Most are mounted, cantering this way and that, but some are weaving up the canyon floor, wedging themselves behind rocks. The climbing sun flashes off swords, off helmets, off quarrels.

Across the foaming brown river, I can just make out Jema and Kuree hitched to two Moquoian mounts, their saddlebags torn open.

"Six," Lark says.

"I said I didn't get a good look!"

"Six is a lot different from twenty!" she snaps.

I can't even be bothered to argue. I bend at the waist, still clutching her arms, trying to slow my breathing.

She twists to look over her shoulder, scanning for the four pursuing soldiers. I can't find the strength to turn my head, but I don't hear the crunch of approaching footsteps yet.

She lets out a breath and turns back to the canyon. "Blazes." She hitches me up a little higher. "Okay. Okay. There's a bit of a climb, and then the rim here turns into a mesa. There's no descent on the southern slopes, but we can probably find a way down the northwestern side . . . except . . ."

She trails off.

"Except what?" I ask.

"Except it leads out into the water scrape," she says. "About fifty miles, give or take, with no water."

I've heard of the water scrape. It's been the bane of planning the final western reaches of the proposed Ferinno Road, and it's what made Lark's camp on the South Burr so strategic. Every traveler, every stage and caravan and slave wagon, had to come to the Burr to water their animals. The official track to Pasul, as it exists now, makes a dramatic bend southward to minimize the distance between the South and North Burr. If a driver could cut across the water scrape, they'd reach Pasul two days earlier, but their animals would die of thirst halfway across.

The idea of *walking* across it is nothing short of laughable.

"Can we descend the mesa on the northwest side and then circle back around for the eastern side?" I ask.

"Are the Moquoians expecting you to go east?" she asks.

After Rou and Eloise took off east, after I fled east from Pasul, after I brought the wrath of the Moquoian court down on the Eastern Alliance?

"Yeah," I say, straightening as much as I can.

She looks again at the soldiers in the canyon, and then down at the trace, and then to Jema and Kuree across the river, and finally over her shoulder. She sighs again, lifts my arm, and settles it over her shoulders.

"Let's just focus on getting across the mesa first," she says.

"One crisis at a time," I say, because I'm lightheaded and it feels like a lifeline to repeat my mother's mantra.

Lark snorts. "Oh, we're *way* past the luxury of only worrying about one thing at a time. Come on. If we get out of sight, the soldiers behind us may think we've gone down the next canyon."

She starts me forward, veering away from the drop into the canyon and instead up the incline spreading to our right. It's studded with boulders, and within a few feet, we're screened from the immediate view of anyone following. I set my feet carefully, wobbly—but at least I'm not as completely spent as a few days ago, when she had to all but carry me down the ridge after I collapsed. After getting my breath back, I take some of my weight off her shoulder.

"I think I can walk now," I say, sliding my arm from around her neck.

She frowns at me over her bandanna and then hands me the metal staff. "Here. Use that to balance with. I'll need it back if there's fighting to be done."

I take it, trying not to show how relieved I am to have something to lean on that's not her.

"I see you've lost the ax handle," she remarks.

"Yeah, I dropped it when I thought I was going to get my head bashed in," I say tersely. "Too bad you missed—you could have been rid of me."

Something flickers on her face, but she smooths it out—by the Light, she's *exactly* like her mother—and turns up the slope again.

"If I had really wanted to hit you, I would have," she says.

I take one step and then stop. "What?"

"Come on. Keep quiet. We're hardly safe here."

She continues on, hopping nimbly among the rocks. After a moment, I shake my head and follow, more silent but less steady than she, and now emotionally exhausted as well as physically from trying to figure out if we're allies or enemies.

TAMSIN

Rain patters through the canopy, punctuating the birdsong ringing in the branches. I've been listening to the birds almost in a trance for the past hour—in recent years Tolukum Palace has been sealed up to keep out the fever-bearing mosquitoes, making it muffled and hushed inside, and over the past few weeks, the bats were more prevalent than birds outside my tiny cell window in the Ferinno. Now, engulfed in the dense maple forests east of the redwoods, the air resounds with their whistles, buzzes, chirps, and cadences. A whole choir of master songwriters, all yelling at each other about sex and territory, while I sit beneath them, silent.

We stopped a little while ago about a mile outside Perquo Branch, a foresters' hamlet on the western slopes of the Moquoviks. After seeing the bounty sheets in the soldier's saddlebag, there could be no question of me going into town, so Iano left me in as comfortable a nest of brush as we could manage and went in to purchase supplies with our last few coins. I've spent the hour wrapped in the dead soldier's cloak while the horse we took from him browses nearby.

The sound of rustling branches rises over the sounds of the rain and birds, and I open my eyes to see Iano leading the other horse through the ferns, soaked from struggling through the dripping fronds. He sets down a sack and settles beside me.

"Are you okay?" he asks.

I nod. "You?"

He still seems caught off-guard when I manage to speak, even the few words I can say without mangling their consonants. "Yes, I'm fine. I got some supplies at the general store."

He pulls out a few tins of biscuits, the hard, flavorless kind that keep for decades, and then produces something else—a small slate, about eight inches square.

"This is the best I could find," he says. "It wasn't even for sale—I saw it behind the coin box and asked to buy it." He hands it to me, along with a bag powdery with chalk pieces.

I take it, my stomach turning. He waits, perhaps thinking I might write something, but I don't. I don't want to. Selfishly, I hate it. I direct all my anger at it in a single, burning ray. Eight inches and some chalk—this is what my voice is now.

I set the slate and chalk down. I pat his knee by way of thanks and reach for one of the boxes of biscuits.

"I've been thinking," he says. "About the bounty sheets, and who our most likely suspects are. The most obvious person I can think of is Kimela Novarni."

The same thought had occurred to me. That at face value, the person who would have the most to gain, politically and professionally, from ousting me is the woman who replaced me as *ashoki*. Kimela Novarni comes from the money of the rice plantations on Ketori Island, and aside from wanting my position, preserving slavery would be a given for her. She was a contender for *ashoki* back when I was first being considered. That I—a loud, unknown newcomer who'd practically walked in from the street—had been appointed over such an old and storied family had ruffled plenty of feathers two years ago.

Clearly, some had stayed ruffled.

"In my mind, she's the most likely culprit behind all this," Iano continues. "All the blackmail was focused on her appointment. And only someone with a nuanced understanding of court politics, like her, could have orchestrated it all."

I purse my lips, uneasy with the obviousness of Kimela's motivation, and unsure why I should feel that way. I realize I'm going to have to use the slate after all. Dispirited, I pull out one of the chalk pieces and start to write. I hold it up to Iano to read.

HOW DID KIMELA LEAVE THE LETTERS?

"In my room, you mean? I don't know. She must have been paying someone. Though," he admits reluctantly, "the servants swore they'd never seen any of the letters. I questioned them all, from my hearth maid to the head of staff, Fala. Still, one of them could be in Kimela's pay." He sees my look. "No?"

I tap the chalk pensively a few times, organizing my thoughts, reflecting on the bounty sheets with Queen Isme's seal. Kimela could perhaps have swayed the queen to authorize them—*ashokis* are master wordsmiths, after all, and are expected to know a great deal about the court. But bribery isn't supposed to be involved. It's not just an ethical concern—it affects how the *ashoki*'s message is received. If word gets around that the court teller gets her information by buying it, or makes her mark by lining people's pockets, her reputation goes from social strategist to clumsy gossip, and it's difficult to come back from such a fall. Several *ashokis* throughout history have been relegated to this status, whatever clever lyrics or subtle messages they may have achieved swallowed by their reputation for purchasing secrets and popularity.

It could be argued that when my attack occurred, Kimela wasn't *ashoki* yet, and could easily have stooped to unsavory methods to win the position. But, if that's true, she's playing a dangerous game. If she's found out—if word leaks that she bought and blackmailed to get her position, rather than being selected on her merits—it could undermine her whole career.

Somehow I suspect writing *It's not what* ashokis *do* won't get my point across. Seeing Iano still waiting for my response, I finally shrug and write, I DON'T THINK IT'S KIMELA. BUT—CAN'T RULE ANYONE OUT.

"No," he agrees. "We can't. Who do *you* think it is?"

I shake my head. There are so many people it could have been, a dizzying number, even more frightening when considering all the lives impacted beyond just mine. The two soldiers from yesterday, merely following orders, lost their lives because of this. And people died in the attack on my coach, too—several guards were killed, and the driver. My maid, Simea, was killed when she threw herself over me to shield me from crossbow fire.

I close my eyes, fighting despair, when a high-pitched whine rises over the rain and birds. I look up to see a mosquito land on Iano's forehead. Without thinking, I lash out and smash my palm against his head. He reels backward with a yelp.

"What was that for?" he demands.

I show him the crushed insect on my hand as proof. I gesture pointedly, and then pick up the chalk again.

RAINSHED FEVER, I write. HAVE TO BE CAREFUL. Actually, I'm surprised he didn't bring back any salve or ointment from the general store to keep insects away. Out here in the forest, there are no glass windows to keep the mosquitoes out.

He sits up, rubbing the red spot on his forehead from my palm. "Oh," he says. "We might not have to worry about that as much out here. Turns out . . . well, Veran has a theory about it."

I tilt my head. ABOUT RAINSHED?

"Yes. Sort of. About the mosquitoes. He thinks they're worse in the city because so many birds die from hitting the glass domes on the palace. That if the birds were alive, they'd eat the mosquitoes." He waves nonchalantly. "I'm not sure I believe him, but—there's no denying the fever is less rampant out here than in Tolukum, and that it started rising once the atriums were built on the palace."

I raise my eyebrows in surprise, and then look up to the canopy, still thick with birdsong. It seems such a fanciful observation, far-fetched in its simplicity, but then . . . a lot of birds do die on the windows. And Veran comes from a country famous even on this coast for a steadfast devotion to their natural landscape. If anyone could make that connection, it would be him.

"He thinks we should cover the glass," he says reluctantly. "Or string up mirrors. But . . . I don't know how we could justify the expense."

IF IT BRINGS DOWN THE FEVER . . . I write.

"That's what he said," he says. "It just seems like such a big leap of faith, and rationale."

I frown, bothered by his reticence. CAN'T HURT TO TRY.

"It could if the ministers think the idea came from the Eastern delegation," he says. "They were already on edge with them sitting in on council sessions."

YOU COULDN'T GET THEM TO SEE REASON?

Iano spreads his hands. "I was focused on finding answers about you, and keeping you safe. I didn't have the time to set things straight in court."

My fingers tighten on the chalk. His comment should make me grateful, that all his energy went into searching for me. But all I feel is numb. All that work he and I did to bring the Eastern delegation to Moquoia, all the letters we wrote, the plans we devised. All wiped away like the dust on my slate by our elusive enemy.

Iano watches as I hover the chalk over the slate, but I can't think of what to write. A scolding feels ungrateful, and anything else is too exhausting to contemplate given my means. Finally, I draw a long breath, pat his knee, and write one word.

SOE'S.

He nods. "Yes. Let's get to Soe's. Maybe some of this will make more sense there."

I doubt it, but at least we may have a place to sit where prying eyes aren't hunting for us. We bundle up his purchases, shake the rain off our hoods, and mount the horses—Iano helping me struggle into the saddle. Again I'm struck, not with gratitude, but with gloom. As he takes his own seat and nudges his horse through the brush, I shake myself, guilty. Maybe it's just the fatigue of the journey. Maybe it's the weeks of poor food. Maybe it's leftover insanity from the cell in Utzibor.

Whatever it is, I hope I can push past it—sooner rather than later.

Because we have work to do.

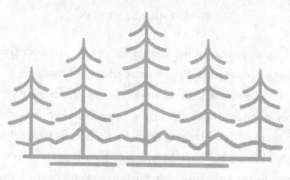

VERAN

We reach the northward slope of the mesa in the late afternoon.

We've been lucky, I guess. The four soldiers pursuing us from Three Lines split up, with two disappearing into the second canyon and the other two picking their way over the rim. But they stuck to the southern side, probably assuming we were trying to find another way down to the river. Instead, Lark led us slowly northward, climbing the rise of the mesa and then following its slope downhill, until we lost sight of the river and canyons completely.

There's been plenty of water so far. Last night's thunderstorm left a patchwork of puddles in the dips and divots in the rocks, so many that we don't stop to drink from them all. And while clouds gather on the north horizon later in the afternoon, they don't blow our way. I mention this once to Lark, suggesting the shade might be nice, but she shakes her head and gives a one-word reply.

"Lightning."

I'll concede that point. Mama never cuts any corners where lightning is concerned. And there's plenty of evidence that this ridge sees its share of ground strikes—several times we've passed through stands of trees that have been scorched by brushfires over the years, the blackened husks thrust up wearily against the sky. This would have been a terrible place to be last night, but now there's only heat and sun, snakes and beetles, rock and scrub.

We barely speak again until we reach the dramatic mesa drop-off.

"The water scrape," Lark says without emotion.

I lean on the metal staff, staring out at the land spreading away in front of us. Where the land to the south and east of Three Lines is rocky and gray-green with sage, the flats before us are an almost uniform sepia, the short grasses punctured by spiky yucca and the occasional dark smudge of juniper. They roll away to the horizon, broken by nothing but the final line of sky. It's a barren, inhospitable sight, so utterly different from the rich forests I grew up in. At home, the land is life—it's food, and medicine, and shelter. It provides everything.

Here, it's nothing.

Lark sighs. I sneak a glance out of the corner of my eye—she's looking at the water scrape with something close to misery, the expression plainer without her hat and eyeblack. She's tied her bandanna over her forehead to keep some of the sun off, so I can see her lips purse in unhappiness. Her fingers trail absently through Rat's fur as he sits on her foot, panting.

I try not to acknowledge the twinge of guilt in my gut. Not everything was my fault, I reason to myself. It wasn't my fault she ran from Pasul. Not my fault she had to leave Jema on the bank. Not my fault one of her campmates died while we were away.

But it *is* my fault the soldiers followed us, which is precisely what's put us right here at the edge of this wasteland.

She surveys the slope in front of us. "Fifty miles to the North Burr," she says, taking a few steps. "We can probably make another seven or eight before midnight."

My mind wheels to a halt. Seven or eight miles? Midnight? I'm lucky to still be upright and sucking in air, and she wants to keep going?

"Lark," I say. "I'm . . . I'm going to need to rest."

"Rest, then," she says shortly. "I'm going to keep walking."

I straighten off the staff. "We can't split up."

"Then keep up. Come, Rat."

I stare at her, and then back out at the endless sea of brown grass, and at the sun hanging low in the sky. A flood of memories stolen from the Woodwalker handbooks and Mama's lectures to her scouts comes pouring back to me.

Prioritize, Mama would say, repeating the words of a string of Woodwalkers before her. *Know the difference between what's important, and what's urgent. Prioritize. Start with what you have.*

"Lark," I say, more firmly. "Listen. We need to be smart about this. I know you're upset and angry at me, but those aren't good reasons to just tear off across the water scrape."

She doesn't stop or turn around. "I'm tearing off across the scrape because we have no other choices, and because I want to get somewhere that I can steal a horse and a sword and a canteen and go back to being left alone."

"That's not going to happen, Lark," I say. "You know that,

right? Not now that Rou and Eloise know who you are. They'll comb the Ferinno to find you—they'll send out the Alcoran and Cypri armies, they'll send out the Silvern scouts and Winderan hunting dogs. And if you don't want them to find a damned *skeleton* and break their hearts all over again, let's just wait a hot second and think about this."

She whirls on me. I impulsively brandish the staff even though she's too far away to strike.

"Don't you *dare* try to make me feel guilty," she snarls. "I don't owe anyone *anything.*"

I take a breath. Somehow I have to find our common ground.

"No," I agree. "But you owe it to yourself not to die in a heap in the water scrape, and I owe you payment, like I promised."

She gives me a consternated look. "How stupid do you think I am? You're not going to pay me. You're being chased by Moquoian soldiers—we can't just walk into the bank in Pasul and take out a load of keys."

"No, we can't. And we're not going to make it to Callais without transport, either. But I *will* pay you, Lark—you said that's what you wanted." I gesture out at the water scrape, to the northwestern horizon. "But I think our only chance right now is to meet back up with Tamsin and Iano. They're the only ones we know we can trust between here and the coast."

Lark huffs. "They could be anywhere."

"They're at Giantess Township," I say, remembering Tamsin's hasty note just before we parted in Pasul. "At the house of Soe Urkett. It's not that far from the Moquoian border. And if we can make it there, we can get help—maybe hide for a little while, maybe help figure out some things." I eye her. "Make travel plans. *Then* I can pay you."

"I'm not going to Callais with you," she snaps.

"Not to meet back up with your campmates?"

"I'm not going *with you*," she repeats with emphasis.

I shrug, trying to feign indifference. "I won't make you, then. You do whatever you want. But you can't deny we're going to need a place to hide while the Moquoian soldiers are searching for us. We can figure out our next steps later. But look, I'm not going to lie to you—if we try to go farther tonight, I'm going to collapse."

She frowns, and I'm not sure if it's in concern or irritation. But I've got a hook now—I need to follow it up. The handbook chapters on crisis survival are trickling back to me—I used to devour those pages, imagining myself stranded on Thunder Ridge or carrying a wounded comrade up from the Echoes. A little flare of that rookie excitement flutters in my chest. "Why don't we take stock of what we've got, maybe gather a few things to bring with us, and get as much rest as we can? Both you and I have been running for almost three days now."

Without her bandanna, I can see her grinding her teeth. She looks out at the dull brown of the water scrape again. My heart jumps in my chest, and I wonder if she really would leave me here, if I'm about to watch her and Rat disappear.

"Fine," she says shortly. "We'll spend the night."

"Oh good." There's no masking the relief in my voice. The excitement kicks back up. "That's good. This is what all the handbooks recommend."

"What—the what?"

"The Woodwalker handbooks, for the scouts." I unbuckle my belt. "They have all kinds of scenarios, all kinds of emergencies, and they all start with being slow, being smart—

prioritizing, knowing the use of what you've got. *Start with what you have.*"

She goggles at me. "Do you think this is some kind of game? Like you'll earn a badge at the end?"

"No!"

"This is real life, Veran—this is survival."

"*Active* survival," I say. "Not just reacting. Not just hoping. That's worlds different. It's something we can prepare for. Look."

While she watches, I crouch down and lay my belt on the ground. I pull Iano's *bintu* knife out of my boot. I reach into my pocket and produce the dirty polishing rag she gave me to use as a bandanna. I lay them all out on the ground in front of me, Mama's voice prickling in my head. It's just like one of the crisis exercises she puts her trainees through.

You're on the Kit Ravine Shelf, she says. *You have a fire hatchet and three strips of jerky. The north slope's burning and the sun is down. What do you do?*

I consider my gear silently.

More, Mama demands. *You have more.*

I reach up and untie the laces on my tunic collar, pulling them out of the eyelets. I finger the fringe and the silver laurel medallions on my boots—I can't think of what use they'd be, but at least they're there. I look up at Lark, who's simply staring.

"What do you have?" I ask.

"A half-blunt pocketknife and the staff," she says.

More! Mama says.

I study her up and down. "And your bandanna, and the tie in your hair, and the quarrel you picked up from the soldier, and your belt and bootlaces, and . . . and your buttons. Your earrings."

"My earrings," she repeats flatly.

I press on. *Start with what you have.* "And . . . we both have our boots, and your vest and my tunic." I look around. "And Rat's fur. And sage, and juniper. Yucca. There's a cottonwood. What's that fleshy plant—is that purslane?"

"Yeah."

"Edible, right?"

"In a pinch, I guess."

"So yes. And grass," I say, gazing out again at the scrape.

We're both silent. My mind flicks over our list of objects. The metal blades mean we can clean game, if we can catch it. The string and fringe mean we can lash things together, maybe create a bow drill to start a fire—if I can remember how it's done. The double layers of clothing mean we can stanch bleeding. The purslane means we won't starve right away.

But the main thing . . .

"Priority one has to be fixing something we can carry water in," I say, squinting at my line of gear, racking my brain for some use I've missed. What could serve to transport water? A boot? Surely boot water would be better than no water. But my boots won't hold water for long. Lark's might, but then she'd be barefoot. Could we waterproof an article of clothing? What makes a thing waterproof? "If only there were pitch pines around . . ."

Lark huffs. "Even if we had pitch, we don't have a way to boil it."

Think, think, think. Half-remembered diagrams of esoteric

survival techniques flicker in and out. "I think there's a way to melt it on a rock, maybe with coals . . ."

"But it doesn't matter, because we don't have pitch," she says impatiently. She picks up the metal staff. "Listen, I'm going to set a few deadfall traps and look for some flint."

Flint! Of course—with the right kind of rock, our knives can produce sparks. I chide myself for forgetting.

She whistles to Rat and then gestures back to me. "Why don't you shred some of that yucca there to make a tinder nest?"

"Hm," I say in vague agreement, turning my gaze on the yucca.

As Lark disappears through the rocks, I reach for the nearest frond on the spiky plant. It's tough and waxy, with a razored edge. I pick up Iano's *bintu* knife and hack away at the base of one withered spike. It comes away in a bundle of stiff fibers.

Something to weave.

When Lark comes back a half hour later, her bandanna bulging with purslane and clusters of some red berry, she stops short.

"What are you doing?" she asks, staring at the piles of disemboweled yucca leaves piled around me, and then at the tangled mess in my lap. "That's not how you make a tinder nest."

"I made one," I say, gesturing with my elbow to a ring of rocks I set aside for a fire pit, along with a small stack of brittle wood.

She sets her bandanna down and pokes the nest, apparently unable to find anything wrong with it. She looks again at the fibers in my hands. "What's that?"

"A coil," I say, holding it up. "At least—I'm working on it. I've never done it before, but I've read you can weave baskets to be watertight."

"Lila did that once," she says, settling down by the fire ring and taking a handful of rocks out of her pocket. "It leaked."

"I still want to try—if we can't carry water . . ."

"We're going to have to rely on seeps and puddles," she says, examining one of her rocks. "With luck there will still be some left from last night. Come on, put that down. Eat some of this stuff while I get a fire going."

"I can't—I'll lose the coil." She rolls her eyes, and I point out, "You'll thank me later if it holds water."

"*If*," she says, selecting one of her rocks and holding it over the yucca nest. "If there's one thing I've learned, it's to stay away from *ifs*. A waterproof basket is an *if*. Purslane and buffalo berries are here and now."

"To think you once scolded me for having no foresight," I say.

"I have lots of foresight. I foresee you fighting with yucca when you could be fueling and resting."

"I'll eat," I say. "And rest. Just give me a few minutes."

She makes a disgruntled sound and pulls out her pocket-knife. She turns the blade to the blunt edge, and with a short, sharp flick, strikes the metal against the flint. A small burst of sparks rains into the tinder.

I watch her surreptitiously over my work. Mama still makes her scouts learn all the main firelighting techniques—Cypri-made matches are a new convenience, after all—but I've never had the opportunity to try it myself. Lark does three more hits before she gets a spark to catch, holding the tinder up to her lips and puffing gently. A tendril of smoke curls into the air. When the spark blooms into little petals of flame, she lays the nest in the fire ring and feeds it a few twigs.

I tug on the ragged bundle of yucca fibers in my lap, trying not to feel jealous of how effortlessly she did something I've secretly practiced on my balcony, with only variable results. She begins to stack a few larger sticks in a cabin formation around the nest—Mama teaches the tent formation at home, but then, there's no lack of available fuel in the Silverwood. Here, in Three Lines especially, it must be important to conserve wood. Another detail I hadn't thought of.

"My ma would love you," I say before I can stop myself.

She looks up at me and then back down at her healthy fire. "Why?"

"You know everything. You've done everything."

"But not to earn a badge or anything," she says. "To survive. I've made plenty of mistakes that almost cost me my life. That almost cost my campmates their lives. That *did* . . ."

She breaks off, her gaze on the fire, her hands still.

"But how many more times did you save their lives?" I ask. "How many more times did you protect them, provide for them?"

"It went on too long," she says distantly. "I should have made more of an effort to get them out before things got so bad."

"You did all you could with what you had."

She looks up at me, and I'm surprised to see anger in her eyes. "You don't know that—you *can't say that*. You still have this . . . this delusion of who I am, this image of some wild, tragic hero. But all you know are the tall tales—you weren't there for the scrapping from day to day, the splitting firewood and hauling water and spoonfeeding little Whit when she was too sleepy to eat."

"By the Light, Lark, that's *why* you're a hero. I don't know about wild or tragic, but all that other stuff—folk depended on you to survive, and you did what it took. And I'm telling you, everyone at home is going to love you."

"Shut up, Veran."

"You don't care at all?" I press. "You're not curious at all? You'd just turn away—knowing who you are now—and just come back out here?"

"After I figure out what you've done to the rest of my campmates—yes."

"You don't want to know—"

"No. I knew everything before I met you."

Her voice is so firm and her gaze is so steady that I almost believe her—*almost*, except . . .

"What about Port Iskon?" I ask. "What about the man's name on your sale papers? Sold by someone with an Alcoran name in a Moquoian port—someone we know now wasn't your father. How did you get around the cape only to wind up back out in the Ferinno? You're not still curious about that?"

"What does it matter now?" she asks.

"It could fit some of the pieces back together," I say. "How you were abducted, where you were brought—"

"I don't care!" she says forcefully. "Will it help me live through tomorrow? Will it help me keep my campmates safe? My past is the same as that stupid basket—it's an *if*, it's a *maybe*, it's a question, not an answer. It's not going to help, and I don't care."

She holds my gaze, her eyes sharp and her silence profound. Queen Mona. I was never good like Eloise at using or enduring silence and stares. I look down to the fire ring.

"Oh," I blurt out. "Watch it!"

Without thinking, I fling the twisted pile of dry yucca fibers. Lark cuts her gaze away to watch the shapeless bundle land on her nearly-dead pile of ashy tinder. The cabin of sticks collapses. A tiny tongue of flames shoots up and licks the yucca, and then my doomed coil bursts into flames. The surrounding sticks flare with light.

We watch the growing fire for a moment.

"It was about to die," I say, feeling absurdly as if I have to offer an excuse.

Lark grunts, and feeds a few sticks into the fire. "At least it was good for something."

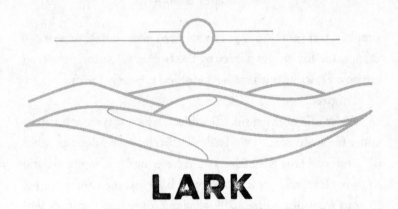

LARK

Early in the morning, the water scrape is not particularly dry. The drooping yellow grasses are thick with dew, soaking us up to our knees. We use our handkerchiefs to sop up water from the stems as we walk before wringing them into our mouths. Mine consistently tastes like dirt and sweat, but I expect Veran's tastes like blade polish. He doesn't seem to care, though—he was absolutely delighted by this innovative water-harvesting technique, one that Rose and I used to do every morning when the cows had mucked up the river.

Rose . . .

I'm empty inside—the billowing anger that fueled me yesterday is all dried up, and I can't summon the energy to feel much of anything. I just want to get across the water scrape, though I don't know what I plan to do on the far side. I could easily leave Veran to find Tamsin and Iano himself, and I do want to meet back up with my campmates as soon as possible. But a trip clear across the Ferinno is going to take planning, supplies, transport—things I'm going to have to steal or work to earn, made fifty times harder by the fact that Pasul and the road are now crawling with soldiers looking precisely for us.

I'm tired.

We've said nothing since breakfast, which was more purslane and a few wild rosehips. My deadfall traps were all empty, but it's a mixed blessing—game would have meant hanging around to skin, clean, and cook it, and we'd have lost the cool morning. Instead we walk, occasionally scaring grouse into flight. Pronghorn lift their heads, watching our progress from under their stubby black horns. A ferret summits a rock to scream angrily at our invasion of its intense privacy. A dry breeze wicks the sweat off my skin, already stealing my water.

I'm not sure what we'll do come the afternoon. Anyone used to traveling the Ferinno knows the desert is at its most dangerous past noon, and doubly so if you happen to be without water, food, and shade. Heat, dehydration, sun blindness, thunderstorms, rattlesnakes . . . normally it's not worth the risk. But I hate the thought of all that time slipping by with no progress to show for it, lengthening the days we'll be stuck out here. Traveling at night has its own problems. Even with moonlight, the ground becomes a treacherous maze—a bad step and a sprained ankle could doom us out here.

Death by sun? Death by moon? I can't decide which one to risk.

I'm conflicted, too, about how quickly to move. So far, I've been walking in front of Veran, with Rat loping along between us. I'd like to take off, space out, put the sun over my left shoulder and just fall into a stride. But I worry too much about leaving Veran behind. What if he collapses, and I don't realize it?

What if he calls out, and I'm too far away to hear? For the hundredth time, I muse bitterly on the fact that he's somehow made me hate him and care about his well-being at the same time. I strike an unsatisfactory balance—walking just far ahead and fast enough to discourage casual conversation, but close enough that I'll hear if he falls into the crackling grass.

Because I don't trust that he's going to keep his silence, if given the chance. I don't trust that he won't start spouting stories and snippets that keep nudging my hazy brain. I don't trust that he's not going to hide that knowing smirk when I drop some thoughtless phrase, as if my words are an insight into who he thinks I am.

The morning crawls on.

I focus on water. The thunderstorm that roared through Pasul and the southern route toward Three Lines two nights ago must not have stretched this far. The grasses are shriveled and bent—these are the dog days of summer. As August wears on into September, the rains will come back, but for now, the sky is bright and bold with lack of moisture. I alter our course now and then to weave toward low dips where brushy thickets of catclaw and greasewood stand out dark against the grass, but they're hardly productive. We find one rock shaded by yucca that has a little collection of dew in a crack—I point it out to Veran.

"If you lie down, you can sip some of that up."

He crouches down. "What about you?"

"There's a little more over here." It's mostly just a damp patch in the rock, nothing I can drink. I pull Rat down toward it, and he licks the rock. I use my bandanna instead to sop up the last bits of dew held in the spines of the yucca. It amounts to only a few drips.

Veran sits back on his heels, wiping his mouth. "Better than nothing, I guess. Did you get enough?"

"No," I say.

"No," he agrees. He looks up at the sky. "How far do you suppose we've come?"

"I don't know, a few miles."

"And this whole place—it's just more of the same?"

"Not as glamorous as you thought?"

He frowns. "I never expected it to be glamorous. I'm just wondering how we know what kind of progress we're making."

I look northwest across the flats. "The land will rise for a while, and then this afternoon we'll get into some of the boulder fields. We can climb some to try to find pockets, but they don't hold onto water like the ridges farther south. Eventually we'll be able to see the River Tell to the north."

He looks back down at me. "There's a river?"

"Two dozen miles north, out of the way. It forms a wash you can see from a distance."

"But we're heading north—I mean, eventually. Why go west and then north fifty miles if there's water twenty miles away?"

"Most folk are trying to get to Pasul."

"Well yeah, if you're in a carriage. But we're not, Lark. Why are we staying south of the river? Wouldn't it be smarter to cut toward it and follow it into Moqouia? That cuts the distance without water in half."

"Because we can't. Come on, let's keep going."

But he doesn't get up. He squints at me. "No, you've piqued my curiosity now. Why would Lark the Sunshield Bandit, expert desert survivalist, not want to head toward ready water?"

I flick my right arm—the hem of my sleeve twitches up my wrist, over the circular brand.

"Take a wild guess," I snap.

His face changes, his eyebrows sliding upward. "Oh, the River Tell. Which, obviously, is the location of Tellman's Ditch. Where you spent—how many years as a slave?"

"Before you get all soppy and sympathetic," I say, "let me explain this isn't about bad memories. It's a dangerous route to take if you're not a slaver. The quarry spans almost a mile along the river, and the rest of the way upstream to Moquoia is lined with mule tracks for the barge tows. It's not a river we could just walk along. If we were to cut north now, we'd hit the Tell downstream of the quarry, where it's just slurry and sludge. Upstream we'll run into the biggest slaving operation outside Tolukum Palace. Make sense?"

"Perfect sense," he says.

"Good," I say, turning away.

"Mules, though," he says.

I roll my eyes and turn back to the west. "Come on."

I don't miss his sigh, but I ignore it and continue out into the scratchy grass.

The sun climbs. The air hazes with the buzzing of grasshoppers and drumming of grouse. Rat catches a ground squirrel. We eat some of the purslane in Veran's belt, sucking the green liquid out of the leaves. We find a small barrel cactus—with some difficulty I cut through the tough rind and show Veran how to put the pulp in his bandanna and wring the juice out of it. Our short knives aren't suited for the task, though, and I can get only so much out without earning a hand full of spines. I wring out a final trickle into my mouth and pass it to Veran.

"Finish it," I say.

"Did you get enough?"

"No. Stop asking that question, it's a stupid question."

"I just want to be sure you're taking enough."

"I am. More, though, I don't want you to keel over. I don't feel like carrying you." I glance out at the western sky—the sun is just starting to edge beyond its peak overhead. Soon it will be hanging in front of us. "On that note, here."

While he drinks the rest of the liquid in the cactus pulp, I shake out my grubby bandanna. I fold it in half and lift it toward his head.

"What are you doing?" he asks.

"Hold still. The sun's going to be in front of us soon. If you cover your forehead and pull it down over your eyebrows, it'll give you a little bit of shade."

He waits while I tie it behind his head. "If I didn't know any better, it would feel like you're watching out for me."

"I told you, I don't want to carry you."

"How far to the River Tell? Fifteen miles?"

"What does it matter?" I ask.

He shrugs. "Just curious."

I'm not in the mood for his jokes, and I don't feel like thinking about Tellman's Ditch getting nearer. I hitch up my sleeve again. "Listen. You know about the slavers' brand?"

His face becomes guarded, and his gaze flicks from my wrist back up to my face. "The concentric circle?"

"That's the incomplete brand. When your bond is up, they set a vertical line through the circles to show you're done and not, say, a runaway. Guess what I don't have?"

He looks again at my wrist, where the tattoo of my long-sword punctures the scarred circles, a make-believe release line.

"It's not a curiosity, Veran," I say. "If we went poking around the river and were caught, and they saw my incomplete brand, guess where I get to go? And if you think any of your notions about who I really am would matter at all . . ."

He tosses up his hands. "I didn't say anything."

"No, but you were thinking it."

"Not until you brought it up."

"Like being related to the right people is all it takes to be above the system." My fists clench. "Like having an imaginary title before your name gets you out of anything and *everything*."

"Don't get mad, Lark," he says, spreading his arms. "You're getting mad at me for something I didn't say—something I didn't even think. You're just . . . mad."

"I'm just mad," I repeat, enjoying the kick of emotional energy I had yesterday. My head blurs with the beginnings of a headache. "I'm mad at you."

"But I didn't do anything. I mean—I know!" He waves emphatically. "I know I made mistakes, all right? Believe me, I know. But you're acting like I schemed this whole thing, like I purposefully fooled you into trusting me so I could toss you into the arms of your emotional long-lost father and deathly ill twin sister. I *didn't* know, okay, Lark? I wish you'd stop treating me like I'm out to intentionally ruin your life. I didn't know you're Moira."

I hate—I *hate*—hearing that name. It stings more and more each time I hear it, a scar reopened and then prodded over and over. I turn on my heel, digging up a clump of sod, and storm away from him. He calls after me, but I don't stop. Screw staying close together—he can keep pace for all I care. Rat springs after me, his tongue lolling from his mouth. Around us, the grasslands shimmer.

I know Veran's following me because he calls out every so often, his voice indignant and distant. I don't slow down. The land slopes gently uphill, forcing me to swing my arms to keep my fast pace. The sun edges downward, burning with full force on my unshaded forehead and cheeks. I consider stripping off my vest and fixing it around my head, but I'm in a stride now. I don't want to stop, driven by anger that started out feeling justified but now just feels mean.

I'm mean, I'm heartless. I'm stupid.

My head hurts.

When did I last have a drink?

The trickles from this morning don't count.

The water pocket yesterday, back home in Three Lines. But it wasn't a long drink, tailed by those Moquoian soldiers. And before that, there was the race from Pasul, and the race *to* Pasul, and the swordfight that killed Dirtwater Dob, and the fight before that wrenched my shoulder, and the burning building in Utzibor—*Rose*—and carrying Veran down the sandstone ridge before summiting again to fetch more water—there. The water pocket on top of the sandstone ridge, just before he collapsed in a seizure. That was a good drink—cold water, clean water, no cows, no dirt.

The sky's too bright—the grass is too bright. The sun is straight ahead, white and wide.

I lift my hands, aiming to clamp them over my eyes and stumble on blind, just for some relief, but I'm surprised by how heavy they are. Lifting them from my waist takes a huge amount of effort, and once I get them up, I can't hold them there—they drop like cast iron back toward the ground.

I've felt this before, just before that juniper tree not so very far from here, when I crawled through the sawgrass away from the slave wagon, when I walked, and walked, and walked with an unfinished circle burned on my arm . . .

The sun bleeds into the sky.

The grass turns white.

I tilt and disappear.

TAMSIN

I love my friend Soe Urkett for a lot of reasons—not the least of which was how we kept each other sane when we realized what we'd gotten ourselves into working for the black-market slavers—but I don't think I ever fully appreciated her unflappability before. When she opens the door and sees the prince of Moquoia and me—swaying and nearly unrecognizable—on her doorstep, she doesn't gawk or exclaim. After quickly securing our horses' reins to her front porch, she clamps a hand on both of our shoulders, steers us inside her cabin, and practically pushes us into seats at her kitchen table.

The deep, nutty aroma of toasted walnuts envelops us. When Soe and I worked for the slavers, she was the cook, but now she makes her money pressing oils and wines. She has the only three presses in Giantess Township, and her days are filled with crushing salal berries for *tul* and walnuts for oil. A basket of half-hulled nuts sits on the kitchen table; she sweeps it aside as I sit down.

"I *knew* it wasn't true," she says, slamming her hands on

the tabletop. Her long black braid swings over her shoulder, the curly ends brushing the wood. "I *knew* the rumors were wrong. I had my doubts when I heard all the fuss about the bandit attack out by Vittenta, but when people started throwing around news that the prince had defected, I knew you'd never died, Tamsin."

"They're saying I've defected?" Iano asks, taken aback. "To whom? The East?"

"That's just one of the stories in town," she says. "I heard it last week. I'm Soe."

"Iano," he says.

She nods and pushes back from the table. "How do you take your tea?"

"Uh, strong, please."

As she turns to a cupboard, Iano looks at me. I gesture pointedly at Soe's back.

He clears his throat. "Soe, before we start on anything, you should know—Tamsin *was* attacked outside Vittenta. They cut her tongue. She's having some difficulty speaking."

Soe stops rummaging in the cupboard. The clatter of crockery goes silent. Slowly, she turns, a glazed mug in each hand, and fixes her gaze on me. Her eyes are two different colors—one dark brown, like mine, the other a pale, crystalline blue, her iris startling in comparison. I rest my cheek resignedly against my fist, returning her look.

Without warning, she slams the two mugs down on the table. Iano and I both jump, my fist dropping in surprise. Flinging a dish towel over her shoulder, she rounds the table and puts her thumb on my chin. I tilt it at her touch and open my mouth.

When Iano first saw, there was only anguish in his face. But Soe's tightens with anger, her lips pursing in a close-lipped snarl.

Her thumb remains gentle on my chin, however, her fingers soft. When she speaks, her voice is quiet.

"Tamsin with the words," she says, tilting my face a little more toward the lantern light. "Tamsin with the lyrics, Tamsin with the voice. Tamsin with all the answers to all the world's problems. Oh, my friend."

Maybe I was too tired to cry when I first reunited with Iano, or maybe I just let his own tears stand in for mine, but under her gaze, faced with this burst of genuine anger on my behalf, my eyes begin to burn. A string of memories I thought I'd forgotten trickles back—us together in the little room over the warehouse where the illegal slave ring had operated, the click of the lock every night. Soe's stoic tenacity when we realized we had essentially signed ourselves up for three months of voluntary prison. Her cajoling me into reciting poetry or passages from the texts I used to copy to pass the brief time we spent not working. Her showing me the fingerings on her dulcimer with the thought that it might stretch my arthritic scribe's wrist. Her feigning interest when I went on one of my political tirades, me storming around the tiny room, she musing over a deck of cards, encouraging me with an occasional "mm-hm."

I blink, and a tear rolls down my cheek. She brushes it away and cups my chin, easing my mouth closed. She kisses the top of my fuzzy head. With a sigh, she releases me and goes back to making tea.

"Fill me in on the story later, if you want," she says. "For now I'm more interested in the present." She opens the window and draws a jar of milk out of the water bucket on the sill. "What *is* going on up at the palace, why have you arrived on my particular doorstep, and what exactly are we doing about it?"

Iano looks sideways at me. I wipe away my tears and wave at him to go ahead. I'm hardly going to sit and write out responses all night.

"Unfortunately, we don't have many answers," he says. "Tamsin was attacked outside Vittenta back in July and held captive by two unfamiliar guards out in the Ferinno Desert. One of them was a Hire—she had the tattoo."

Soe makes a sound of disgust. "Figures. What did they want?"

"They made Tamsin sign her name on blackmail letters, which then came to me, telling me to appoint another person as our *ashoki* at the end of the month, when my mother abdicates and I'm crowned."

Soe glances at me as she pours milk into a saucepan. "I don't suppose this new *ashoki* has the same interests as you?"

I press my lips and shake my head.

"I think she's the one behind it," Iano says. "She has the most obvious motive."

Soe catches my look. "You don't think so, Tamsin?"

I shrug. I still don't have a good reason for not suspecting Kimela beyond professional intuition, so I don't bother trying to put my thoughts into words.

"Hm," Soe says. She leaves the milk simmering on the hearth and pulls down a bottle of *urch* syrup. In the palace our tea is made from either larch or birch sap, but in the countryside it's more common for the two to be mixed, sometimes with pine resin, to make it last longer. Some courtiers call our tea *urch* to be quaint, but out here that's simply what it is—not larch, not birch, but both. *Urch*.

As she stirs it into the hot milk, I pull out my slate and scribble on it.

"Hey," I say, tapping to get Soe and Iano to look up.

TELL US ABOUT DEFECTION

"Oh, yes," Iano says, straightening. "What's this about me defecting?"

"It's just one of several stories," Soe says. "First came the news that the *ashoki* had been tragically murdered by the Sunshield Bandit, and then just a week or so later, we heard that there was to be a new *ashoki*. It seemed awfully quick—I remember there was a gap of nearly six months back when Tamsin was appointed. I expect that was in response to the first bit of blackmail?"

"Yes," Iano says, accepting the hot mug from her. "My mother was set to transition the throne to me next month. I got the first blackmail letter on July thirteenth instructing me to announce Kimela's appointment to the court."

"What did your mother say when you told her you wanted to appoint such a drastically different *ashoki*?" Soe asks. I'm glad she asked. I cut my gaze sideways to watch his reaction. His expression doesn't change.

"She seemed perfectly agreeable," he says.

I snatch my slate and chalk. NOT SURPRISED? I write. NOT UPSET?

He shakes his head. "No, she . . . she seemed fine. I assumed she was glad the decision was made before the transition of the throne."

Soe and I exchange a glance as she hands me my tea. I take it, and then, against my better judgment, I rummage in Iano's bag and pull out one of the bounty sheets from the soldier's saddlebag. I unroll and show it to Soe, pointing to the red wax at the bottom.

Her eyebrows lift. "Is that the queen's seal? On your bounty sheet?"

Iano's face tenses. "That *doesn't mean* it was her. It only means she authorized the bounty. Please—don't make me think about my mother. Don't make me think about her hurting you, and tricking me. She and I were never as close as I was to my father, but we weren't enemies."

SHE WAS AGAINST MY APPOINTMENT, I point out.

"She was . . . not *thrilled* about your appointment," he says. "Mainly because she knew the status quo of the court, and she wasn't comfortable with the idea of angering our allies. But she was never *against* you. You wouldn't have been appointed if she had been. I know . . . I know we can't rule her out, either, but please. Not right now. And anyway, like I told you, she's *not* a Hire."

I frown, wanting him to clarify if he *knows* she isn't, or if he just *hopes* she isn't.

Soe rolls the parchment back up and settles down at the table. "Well, it's a question we can't answer right now, anyway. Where was I? Oh, so after the news of the new *ashoki,* things started getting strange. Word was you had disappeared, Your Highness, in the middle of the night. I think at first the palace tried to play it off as you retreating to the hunting lodge for a week before your coronation, but then other, unofficial reports started leaking out. There were tales that you had run away with one of the Eastern ambassadors, then tales that you'd been kidnapped instead. That turned into rumors that it was all part of an elaborate coup the East had orchestrated right in our very court, and things really broke loose. Some heard that Queen Isme had the ambassadors hanged—which made the pacifists angry—and others heard that they'd escaped in the night—which made the nationalists angry. Then word went out that they'd been deported, and folk flocked to the main road to holler at every noble-looking coach that went by. I expect they got their targets wrong nine times out of ten, but it made travel a nightmare for pretty much everyone."

I glance again at Iano. No wonder the Cypri ambassador had been so angry when we arrived in Pasul. Not only had diplomacy been sabotaged by some unknown malcontent, and the princess taken ill, but they were run out of the country by a mob. For that disgrace alone, we'll be lucky to avoid war.

Soe takes a sip of her tea and nods at Iano. "Some said you had been seduced by Eastern propaganda and were selling out the country, while some heard that you had negotiated some kind of back-door peace treaty. And *everyone* was talking about the bounties for the Sunshield Bandit, with stories that she was behind everything—that the East had been using banditry for their muscle all along. There have been reports of folk seeing her everywhere. The latest runners came through yesterday, saying you still hadn't been found."

Iano and I both let out a breath at the same time.

LEAKING PIPE, I write.

He nods at my words. "I can't believe how much misinformation has spread. Rumors are inevitable, of course, but so many of those events should never have reached the public. We were so careful about how we announced the visit from the ambassadors back in *Sernsi* for that very reason—we wanted to be sure people knew it was a diplomatic visit, with peaceful intent."

I tap my slate. SOUNDS LIKE SOMEONE INSIDE

"Someone leaking information?" Iano asks wearily. "Someone abducted you, maimed you, and kept you hostage in the desert, blackmailed me into appointing Kimela, framed the Eastern ambassadors, and now they're leaking rumors out to our citizens? What are they trying to do—tear the country apart?"

We share a moment of silence around the table.

"Well, it does no good to worry about it right now," Soe says. "You're here, and you're safe for a little while, at least. That's the main thing. It's also good to know the prince hasn't abandoned Moquoia, and we're not *quite* at war with the East."

"For the moment," Iano says, echoing my thoughts. "Though our enemy seems to be closer than we think—on our way over the Moquoviks, we encountered two Tolukum soldiers, and . . ."

He can't finish—I can see the two deaths at his hand still flickering behind his eyes. His throat works. "And . . . well, people are hunting for us. With luck they'll think we're heading back to Tolukum, but if this much information is getting out, someone might know you and Tamsin are friends. They may expect us to look for shelter here."

"We'll just have to take what precautions we can," Soe says. "Tomorrow we can head to the salal thickets and the walnut grove—it will let us keep an eye on the road, and give me stock to press so we can buy supplies in town." She nods to me. "You need a fresh outfit, anyway, and my medicine kit is low. For now you can hole up in the workshop—it's warm enough, and dry. We might have to move the big press, but that's fine." She sets down her tea and gets up.

I unfold my palm on the table and nudge Iano's elbow.

"Tamsin says thank you," he says, rising with her. "And so do I. I promise you'll be repaid for your trouble—once I have access to the treasury again."

"I'm just glad to find you both alive. I didn't know what to do with myself when I thought you'd died. Sit down, Tamsin." She waves at me—I'd started to stand with Iano. "Stay there. I have something for you."

I sink back down, closing my hands around my mug. They disappear into the workroom, and my eyes drift shut. I've slept in Soe's workroom before—it's cramped, and the floor is sometimes oily, but after the emptiness of my cell and the harshness of sleeping on the ground, I have never been so grateful to be offered a safe space in the house of someone not holding me hostage.

Still, I can't fully relax. My mind won't stop racing with our conversation, the growing details, the muddled facts. Now that I'm out of the hands of our enemies and back within our borders, things seem so much closer, so much more severe. A week ago, I couldn't be sure I would have the luxury of finding out who orchestrated my capture, or what they were hoping to accomplish with it.

Now, I can't get it out of my mind.

I reflect on the two names we've come up with so far— Queen Isme and Kimela.

Did Queen Isme secretly orchestrate Kimela's appointment? The seal on the bounty sheets seems to suggest so. But I've known the queen for several years now. I know her history and her politics; I've studied her habits and preferences. I've sung about her to the court—not always in the most flattering terms—in front of her very eyes. She never looked at me with the same malice as some of the more easily offended courtiers. Was she just that skilled at hiding her feelings? More important— would she seriously have tortured her son with gruesome tales and mind games? She hasn't abdicated her throne yet—it would have been easy to appoint Kimela herself. Why manipulate Iano into doing it for her?

It doesn't add up.

Which leads me to Kimela.

The *ashoki*-elect has the right politics—she's nothing if not patriotic. Tradition is her lifeblood. She might even be a Hire. Are her morals that skewed, to stoop to blackmail and extortion in a position known for operating above such things?

Is the queen gullible enough to believe her?

Or just that desperate?

I rub my grimy face, thinking back to that night I sang "Storm Gathering," the damning composition I'd performed just days before I was attacked. It was the most to-the-point piece I'd sung in my entire tenure, and it created waves of palpable reactions in the hall. I sift through the distant memories of the crowd, scanning the faces. A dozen-odd ministers and courtiers with competing interests, their faces reddening with outrage. Minister Kobok, glaring so hard I thought the curtains might catch fire. Allies of industry, opponents of Iano, stewards, servants. So many people, so many possibilities for private sabotage.

I nudge the back of my teeth with my spliced tongue.

That's the thing—it wasn't *just* politics.

It was personal.

I hear scraping in the workroom of the big press being pushed across the floor. I open my eyes. A moment later, Soe bustles back in, clutching something—one of the small pots from her shop, like the kind in which she keeps walnut oil. She drops onto the bench next to me.

"Here," she says. "Let me see your hands."

Puzzled, I give her one, my skin chapped and cracked. She pops the cork off the little pot, revealing a thick salve. A waft of lavender and beeswax curls toward my nose. She dips her fingers in and takes my mangled hand, massaging the cream into it. It's all I can do to not gasp at how good it feels.

"I expect the Ferinno is murder on a person's skin," she says matter-of-factly.

I watch, silent—obviously silent, but I mean mentally silent, as well. My brain has completely blanked at the enormous comfort in this small offering. She kneads the cream along my cracked nail beds and scuffed knuckles, and then up my wrist, where she knows it goes stiff and hot with scribe's arthritis.

She looks up when I can't hold my sniffle back anymore. My nose has clogged up, which is annoying because I want to keep smelling the lavender. I wipe my cheeks with my other hand.

Soe leans forward and wraps her arms around my shoulders. I rest my head on her. I open my palm between us to try to convey my thanks, but she doesn't see it.

"Oh, Tamsin," she sighs. "What an absolute mess. I'm sorry."

I feel the same rush of gratitude I did just a moment ago, but this time it's not just about a safe space in her workshop. It's born instead from the long weeks surrounded only by people hoping to keep me right on the threshold of death. By the empty insanity of my cell's four walls. By the quick rush of unfamiliar faces in Pasul. By the soldiers aiming their quarrels at my head. By the secrets and lies and unknowns, and the death sentence now attached to my picture.

A friend.

How nice it is just to have a friend.

LARK

Something forces its way between my lips. It's hard and metallic, but it brings a trickle of liquid after it. It coats my tongue, a tiny amount, running down my throat and leaving a silty taste behind.

Water.

The hard metal object disappears from my mouth, and then comes back, followed by another minuscule dribble. My throat works, dry and aching.

I don't open my eyes because it doesn't strike me as something that seems achievable. My whole body is heavy, dark. The metal object comes back again, and again, bringing another tiny mouthful of water each time. Grit crunches between my teeth. The world smells like dirt, like hot grass. Grasshoppers click and rasp. Air puffs against my cheek.

At the next trickle between my lips, something wakes up deep in my belly. It cramps at first, then twists, then *writhes*. I suck in a breath, scattering droplets of the next offering of water.

I roll to one side, land with my face in the grass, and puke up the miserable contents of my stomach. Dry grass stabs me in the eyes and cheeks, but I don't lift my head—I simply lie bent over, elbows shaking.

"Earth and sky . . . Lark?"

A hand grips my shoulder and tries to haul me away from the damp patch of my vomit. The best I can manage is to collapse onto my back. My stomach clenches again, and I clutch it, groaning.

"Here, open your mouth."

I wrench my head away, gritting my teeth against a fresh wave of cramping, spreading out from my stomach down my legs, my toes, the arches of my feet.

"Lark, I've got water—open your mouth."

Something slides behind my neck, and my head and shoulders are hauled off the ground. The grinding pain in my stomach spikes. The metallic object bumps against my lips again, and I fling my head in the other direction. I don't want more water!

There's swearing.

"Look, there's not so much of it that you can just . . . hold still, dammit! If you're in pain that means you're rehydrating, that's what all the books say. Come on, keep it together."

Hands drag me back into place—new pain flares unexpectedly in both shoulders, but at the next moment, there's rock against my back again. An arm flattens across my chest, holding me still, and the metal object—it feels like a disc, almost like a coin—pushes once more into my mouth. Water splashes against the back of my throat. I cough, and a hand clamps over my lips. I can hear my heart pulse in my ears, I can feel my fingers buzz and burn. I swallow. The hand leaves my mouth, but the arm stays flat across my chest. The water disc comes back again. And again. And again.

"Stop," I croak, still unable to open my eyes. "Stop it."

"It's okay. It'll be okay, if you'll just—stop moving your head away. Think about something else. *Raindrop one, raindrop two*—you remember that one? All the Lumeni kids sing it, with those little hand motions. Uh, let's see, it's been a while . . .

> '*Raindrop one, raindrop two*
> *Cloud of gray, sky of blue.*
> *Raindrop three, raindrop four*
> *Rocky ridge and sandy shore.*
> *Raindrop five, raindrop six*
> *Fall and flow, swirl and mix.*
> *Raindrop seven, raindrop eight,*
> *Lightning first and thunder late.*
> *Raindrop nine, raindrop ten*
> *Storm is coming once again.*
> *All the drops together make . . .*'"

Whirly, pearly Lumen Lake.
I know that line.

"Oh, damn, hang on, the mud's getting thicker." The metal disc disappears, and I hear the shlucky sound of digging. The nursery rhyme rings in my ears, jangling with my too-loud heartbeat and pounding headache. There was always a childish anticipation of the end, when the final line was squealed while spinning round and round.

"There was one Rou used to sing, too." Veran sounds out of breath. "I can't remember how it starts, though. Something something, came to the creek, *hop over, hop over . . .*"

And the little one knocked her head.

I slit open an eye. The world is intensely bright, all the colors washed out. Veran's head bobs near the ground—with a huge amount of effort I tilt my chin down to see him better. He's flat on his stomach with his arm swallowed up to his shoulder in a sandy hole. Rat lies beyond him, panting in the shade of a catclaw shrub. I shift—my back is against rock. My feet are in the sun, but the rest of me is in the shade.

"Okay, here." Veran struggles to his knees and carefully removes something from the hole. It's round and silver, with a slight curvature to it, turning it into a tiny bowl. It's only as he adjusts his legs and I see the hacked fringe on his boot do I realize what it is—one of the silver laurel flower medallions.

He holds it to my mouth again. A teaspoon of water shivers in the little bowl. Still squinting through one eye, I sip it.

"You made a seep," I rasp.

He turns back for the hole. "It was all I knew to do."

"It worked," I say.

"Barely." He leans down to refill the medallion. "I had to get down twelve inches before it started to collect. I thought for sure it was going to take too long." He rises again and holds out the medallion. "Blessed Light, Lark, why didn't you tell me you were getting dehydrated? You were so focused on keeping me and Rat going you forgot about yourself."

He sounds rattled. I peep open the other eye to get a better look at him—his face is screwed up as he concentrates on keeping the precious water in the little bowl on its way to my mouth.

I sip again. "Where are we?"

"Not far from where you fell. There was a boulder field down the slope a little way."

I hadn't even seen it. Tunnel vision, I guess.

"You carried me?"

"Dragged you. Your arm's probably going to hurt later. I did try to use the one you weren't favoring before."

"Two hurt shoulders, then."

"Dammit, Lark, what was I supposed to do?" He sits back, the empty medallion clutched in his fist. "You were tearing away across the flats, and then you just went down . . . I didn't know what to do. *I'm* usually the one that other people have to revive—I've never done it my damned self! People make it sound like it's no big deal, the books lay it out as so straightforward, but that was scary, Lark, not exciting or easy at all—are you *laughing*?"

I'm surprised he can tell, because it sounds more like choking. Nothing seems to be working right—certainly not my brain. Everything feels giddy and funny. Funny to think of him dragging me like a sack of corn. I flutter a hand at the indignant look on his face. "Not at you."

"At *what* then?"

"Okay, at you. Only you would think dealing with an unconscious person was supposed to be fun and exciting."

"People always seem so calm!" he exclaims, decidedly not calm. His curls are stiffened with sweat and dirt and flung back from his face, and his eyebrows are thrown sky high.

"People are probably trying not to freak you out, you know that, right? Poor Veran." I laugh again, but it's sticky, gritty, like it doesn't belong in my mouth.

He stares at me for a second, then pivots around on his knees. Silently he reaches down and collects another bead of water. As my vision clears a little more, I see the mud caking his arms and flecking his face—he had to dig the hole by hand. Bits of fringe from his boot are scattered over the ground.

My giddiness muddles into shaky exhaustion. A line of fire races up my back, collecting in my right shoulder. That same image of him hauling me down the slope, step by step, returns, only now it's not funny.

It wasn't ever funny.

My neck twinges; my lower back stings from scraping over a rock, a stick, a thorny shrub. Veran turns slowly with the medallion, his gaze on the water. His fingernails are cracked, and several of his knuckles are bloody. His knees are coated with dirt from his awkward shuffle back and forth between me and the seep. How many times has he made the two-step trip?

He leans forward with the medallion, and from this close I see the scrunch in his nose, his lips, his one-scar eyebrows.

The last traces of nonsensical humor slip away.

Fire and dust, have I always been this mean?

"Veran," I say.

"Here." He hands me the medallion. I'm not ready for it—my hands shake, and half the water jumps out to fleck my trousers.

He gives a frustrated growl. "Be *careful*."

I sip the few droplets, and he takes the medallion back without looking at me. He turns for the seep, dashing his muddy hand under his nose.

"Veran," I say again. "I'm sorry. I . . . I shouldn't have laughed. I didn't mean to laugh. And earlier, I shouldn't have . . .

I was being stupid, and selfish. I shouldn't have taken off like that. I didn't mean to scare you."

"Like *that* matters." He shakes his head and swipes at his eyes. "What if you had *died*?"

"I'm not going to lie, that would have made things a lot simpler for me."

"Don't joke, Lark, don't do it."

It wasn't a joke, but I fall silent as he dips his arm into the hole again. My head is still throbbing, but the cramping is getting less sharp, leaving me trembly and weak. I try to shift, to shake some feeling into my legs, but moving leaves me lightheaded.

He turns on his knees again and holds the silver flower out.

"Why don't you drink some?" I say.

"I did, in between a few of yours," he says shortly. "Besides, it tastes nasty."

"Then just sit for a minute. I'm okay for a little bit. Come here into some of this shade."

He sighs, lifts the medallion to his own lips, and tosses it back like a shot of whiskey. Pulling a face, he edges as far away as he can get from me and still be out of the sun. He rubs his face, leaving grime over his bruised forehead.

We sink into a bleary silence. The hot breeze slinks through the grass, rattling the dry stalks.

"Sorry about your boots," I say.

He grunts. "I can get more."

Now *he's* trying to be mean, but it only feels like a reflection. A mirror turned on myself.

"You can get more," I say. "Back home, in the Silverwood Mountains. Where your pa's the king and your ma is the queen and a . . . forest walker."

He makes a disgusted sound at my bad guess, sets his chin in his hand, and stares away across the flats.

"Why's it a flower?" I ask.

He turns the medallion carelessly in his free hand without looking at me. "Mountain laurel is the traditional symbol of the Silverwood monarchy."

"But you've got a bug on your seal ring."

"Fireflies are the symbol of the country, not the monarchy."

"I see."

Silence passes.

A long silence.

"What's the symbol for Lumen Lake?" I ask.

It seems to take a moment for my question to sink in. The idle, angry fidgeting with the medallion stops, and he goes unnaturally still.

"The bulrush," he says. "Two crossed bulrushes surrounded by twelve pearls."

"Bulrush."

"Cattail," he says.

A flood of memory comes back to me—Cook sending Rose and me to the river time after time to gather cattail pollen or cobs or stalks or fluff or new shoots. Biscuits, tinder, soups, reeds for roofing, filling for bandages. Cattail has seen me through every season. One of the few things I could count on.

My gaze blurs on the horizon. My stomach cramps. Sweat prickles my upper lip—another sign my body is slowly rehydrating. I should drink more.

"How old am I?" I ask.

I half-expect him to snark or jibe. It's nothing less than I'd deserve. But he sighs and runs his fingers through his ruffled curls.

"Nineteen," he says.

"That's *it*?" Rose and I had thought I was well into my twenties, like her.

"Not for long."

"Why?"

"Because your birthday is next month. September twenty-sixth."

The breeze rustles the grass. From somewhere close by comes that jumble of fluty notes that Veran told me was a meadowlark.

"And . . . ," I begin. I close my eyes against the glare of the sky—maybe I can ask these things in a void, hear their answers, and then wake up and leave them behind.

"I have a sister," I say.

"Eloise. Your twin."

"We don't look anything alike."

"Actually, you kind of do." He sounds tired. "Her skin is paler than yours—it's not as sunny at the lake as it is out here, and she spends a lot more time inside. You're skinnier than she is. And her hair is probably what yours would look like if it wasn't locked. But your eyes are the same. Your noses are the same. You both have freckles. I expect your smiles are the same."

"You expect?"

"I don't think I've seen you smile. At least, not without your bandanna."

I open my eyes. That doesn't seem right, but in the next moment, I can't help but concede it. There was precious little to smile about in my life before, and almost nothing after the wagon disaster that killed Pickle and ultimately Rose. But it seems strange, because there were moments when Veran and I were traveling to Utzibor that seemed . . . less terrible than others.

I resist the urge to reach up and prod my face, afraid I'm going to hit stone.

Still woozy. Still borderline delusional.

"I'm going to pull up some more water," Veran says, rolling forward onto his knees. "Do you want some?"

"I guess. Yes. Please."

He crawls forward and reaches down into the hole. He takes a few sips from the medallion and then props onto his side to hand it over to me. I take it and drink. Given a little time to collect in the seep, the water is less cloudy than before. Veran holds out his palm, but I pause, clutching the flower.

"And that man," I say. "In the posthouse."

"Rou?"

I nod. I remember the way he came at me, the way I first thought he was ready for a brawl, arms out, face wild. How instead his palms clamped flat on either side of my face, his eyes inches from mine.

Veran props his head on his fist. "That was Rou Alastaire, Lumeni ambassador."

"He's not Lumeni."

"No. He's from southern Cyprien. He married Queen Mona the same year my oldest sister was born."

"So why isn't he the king?"

"He didn't want to be," he says. "He was more comfortable being an ambassador. You know Cyprien has no monarchy?"

I rack my painful brain for this knowledge. I've never had to think much about the makeup of governments beyond whatever local sheriff is in charge of the town I'm robbing.

Veran jumps at my hesitation. "Sorry, I shouldn't have assumed. Cyprien has never had a monarchy. They have an Assembly. A group of senators who are elected to office. Rou was a representative for them before he and Queen Mona met."

Slowly I hand him the medallion. "The Assembly—that's like Alcoro, right?"

"Right." He dips the flower into the seep and hands it back. "Queen Gemma dissolved Alcoro's monarchy and transitioned them into an elected government, after Cyprien's model, before I was born."

I take another sip. I turn my head and spit out the sand that's crunching between my teeth. I stay looking that way, into the wisps of sedge growing under the rock. This was a smart place to dig a seep—he knew to look for a low, shaded spot where plants were growing. Guess those books of his weren't totally useless.

"But Lumen Lake is a monarchy," I say, my stomach wobbling.

"Yes. And your mother is the queen."

"And . . . they all live there. At the lake."

"Yeah. Your pa travels some, mostly to and from Cyprien, but yes—they all live at the lake."

"I—we, me and . . . the other girl—we were born there?"

"Yeah."

I draw a breath. "I have been dreaming of water since I can remember what dreaming is."

Water that never seemed big enough, deep enough, clear enough. Water that rushed and foamed, that sprayed and misted.

Cold water, silver with fish and sky. The kind of torrent I had tattooed on my arm in stages, cascade after cascade, until it was a flood from shoulder to wrist.

Veran lets out a long, deep sigh. Out of the corner of my eye, I see him droop a little, as if the last of his justifiable anger is puddling on the ground. "Lark . . ."

But I'm not ready for his sympathy yet—I was doing better under his frustration. I hand the medallion back without looking at him.

"The name," I say.

"Which name?"

"The name. *My* name."

He takes the medallion. "Moira Alastaire. You're the oldest—you got the matrilineal name. Morigen, Myrgen, Myrna, Mona, Moira. Eloise is named after one of Rou's brothers who died when they were kids."

"Him—that man, the ambassador," I say, stumbling for words. I can't say the word *father* yet. "What's he like?"

"He's really friendly, Lark. The kind of person everybody likes. He tells bad jokes. He can play the mandolin, and he spins poi, those chains with fire on the end. He taught me how to play spoons."

"He seemed unhinged." I don't know why I say it—I guess it's not so easy to just quit being mean on the spot.

"Well, he sort of was, at that moment. You have to understand what they went through. I was kept from the worst of it, as a kid, but I've learned more since then. He had some kind of breakdown when they called off the search for you. And then he got really protective of Eloise."

"You said something about her being deathly ill."

"Rainshed fever—that sickness that's on the rise in Moquoia, carried by mosquitoes." He sighs and runs a hand through his grimy hair, and I realize that while I've been mourning Rose at every turn, he's probably been thinking of his friend making the grueling trek across the Ferinno. "She's friendly like Rou, and smart like him, too," he says. "Good with people, big-hearted, that kind of thing."

My meanness twists inside me again. The opposite of me, then. That's something that can't be chalked up to too much sun and bad food.

I reach for the only thread left, the only possibility that there might be something tangible to link me to this pretty, pleasant family.

This *royal* family.

"And—the queen?"

He doesn't answer at first. He dips the medallion and hands it to me. I drink and hand it back, and he dips it again, all without speaking.

"Well?" I ask.

"I . . . I don't know. I don't know how to describe Queen Mona as a mother. She's . . . powerful. She's a legend. She took the throne in Lumen Lake as a child and staved off civil war just a few years later. She was ousted from power by Alcoro and then fought her way back out of exile, alongside my ma. She won back the lake, and helped make peace with Alcoro and unite the East."

Nothing, then. No realistic connection. A soft-hearted princess, a friendly ambassador, and a legendary queen. If all this is to be believed, I slipped through the cracks and have now emerged a run-down, mean-spirited outlaw, with a price on my head, an unsealed slave brand, and a bad reputation that's bled past the borders of the Ferinno.

Veran shakes his head. "I don't know what else to tell you. To be honest, Queen Mona has always scared me a little. But she and my ma are about as close as you can get as friends, so don't feel like you have to trust my judgment. Obviously Eloise could tell you more. Or Colm or Arlen."

Oh, blazing Light—*Colm.*

"Colm's my—?"

"Uncle, yeah, congratulations. You crashed and robbed your uncle's stagecoach."

I groan and drag my legs up to my chest. I bury my aching head on my knees. Crashed and robbed was the least of it. I hit him and stole the shoes off his feet.

"Who was the other name?"

"Arlen? Your other uncle. Queen Mona's youngest brother. His wife is your aunt Sorcha, and their daughter Brigid is your cousin. Shall I get into your lineage, as well? I can probably recall a few generations on both the Alastaire and Roubideaux sides, though I always get my Lumeni kings mixed up."

"No, stop." Having an immediate family—a blood family— is overwhelming enough; I don't know that I can take hearing about a string of foreign nobility all related to me. I let out a breath. "Fire and dust."

"Since we're on the subject, maybe you should know you swear like a Cypri."

I pick up my head an inch. "What?"

"*Hot damn, blazes, fire and* whatever—those are all typical Cypri expressions. Alcorans use sky terms, not fire terms, and Moquoians swear by the *ophoko* colors. But you swear like Rou."

I set my head back down. I grind my forehead into my knee-caps, trying to counteract the pulsing in my temples.

"More water?"

I flick my fingers without looking up. "You drink some. I'll have more in a minute. Has Rat had any?"

"He dug around under some of those catclaws and came up with his nose wet, so I think he got a little."

"Okay."

Yes. Okay.

I latch on to the lie.

Okay.

Okay, I nearly blew it. I let myself fall apart. I let the past few days do the worst thing possible—distract. We're in one of the worst places to be unprepared, and I let myself get completely sidetracked from simply surviving.

Okay, I've made mistakes.

Mistakes I've made before, that should have killed me but didn't, because I was dragged away from death, first by Rose and now by Veran.

Okay.

"Thanks."

"What?" he asks.

I turn my head away, toward the flats, my temple on my knee. "You heard me."

"I don't know, I might be hallucinating."

"I said thank you."

"You're not angry at me anymore?"

I let out my breath.

"Because if you are—" he begins.

"I don't know what I'm feeling, Veran." I look back at him.

He's on his back now, his head by the seep, gaze on me. "None of it seems real. None of it seems right. I don't want to believe it, because what if you're wrong? Nothing good has ever come from me getting my hopes up. But then, all these little things—things you keep saying . . . I remember those nursery rhymes. I remember some of the names. Arlen . . . does he have only one eye?"

"Well, he has two," Veran says. "One's just blind. He wears an eye patch."

"And was there a waterfall?"

"At Lumen Lake? Lots."

My eyes drift closed, still burned by the bright, hazy sky. "I can't recall ever seeing a waterfall. But I remember them."

"It's you, Lark, I'm telling you. It's all real. You're Moira Alastaire. And if you don't believe me, believe Rou and Eloise. Believe Tamsin. They all recognized you before I did."

They did. Without my bandanna and hat and eyeblack, they recognized me right away.

I rub my eyes. My head muddles with a stream of names and places. Colm Rou Eloise Arlen Mona Lumen Lake Cyprien bulrush hot damn Moira.

"Can I . . . set some rules?" I ask.

"Be my guest."

"Don't call me Moira," I say.

He closes his eyes, his face turned up toward the sky. "Okay."

"Okay."

I go quiet. He waits. I'd thought I'd have a million specifications, conditions, boundaries to wrap tight around me to keep all this at bay. But now I can't think of a single thing besides the name.

"Is that the only one?" he prompts. "Or am I still just sup-posed to cut the sass?"

Condition one is you cut the sass, I'd told him one week ago, when I stood over him in Three Lines, hesitantly agreeing to accompany him to Utzibor. Back when my life was mine, and he was simply a means to an end.

"I guess . . . for now."

"Got it."

He stays on his back, eyes closed and fingers laced over his chest.

"Are you all right?" I ask.

His fingers flicker skyward before settling down again. "Oh, sure. It was only the most terrifying moment of my life, that's all."

"The *most* terrifying?" I repeat. "Veran, you've been shot at by multiple crossbows. You rode out into the desert alone to be robbed. You smashed a bandit with a pickle jar and ran into a burning building. And that's just in the last few days. What about the time you fell off the walkwire at home?"

His eyes fly open, his gaze still up at the sky. "Yeah, but all those times, I was only responsible for my stupid self! I got my-self into those messes, and the only life they impacted was mine! But it wasn't my life on the line this time." He rubs his arm over his face. "I just . . . earth and sky, Lark, you have to understand, I've spent my life wishing I could do the things I read about, and then when I'm finally faced with the opportunity—"

"You did just fine," I finish, bewildered. "You succeeded. You dug a seep in one of the meanest places on earth and dragged me back from the edge of dehydration."

"While panicking out of my mind."

"Who says everybody else doesn't panic in the same kind of situation?" I ask. "When you collapsed up on the ridge the other day, I was shouting a blue streak—at you, at Rat, at the sky, at myself. Taking charge of someone else is scary. Maybe the stuff you read leaves those parts out."

He heaves a shaky sigh and flops his arm over his eyes. "Well, at any rate, don't do it again. I don't think I can take it."

"I won't. I said we're getting across the water scrape, and we're getting across. How much time did we lose, do you think?"

"Two hours, maybe. The sun's getting low."

"We'll rest until it goes down, keep drinking what's in the seep. Then we'll keep going. That is, if you think you can."

"Yeah, give me a little while."

"All right. Hey." I shift my leg until I can nudge him with my foot. He picks up his arm to look at me. "Thanks. I mean it. You saved my life."

His green eyes flicker. "Well, you saved mine. A couple times, now."

"Let's not keep score, okay?" I reply. "I'm trying to say thank you."

He turns his head to face the sky again and closes his eyes. "You're welcome, then. Please don't make me do it again."

"Don't worry," I say firmly. "I won't."

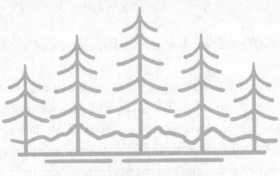

VERAN

It's the cold that wakes me. In the Silverwood, the humid air holds on to all the day's heat, leaving an August dawn just barely cooler than noontime. But out here in the dry water scrape, the morning cold is as persistent as the midday heat. I shiver. Without a cloak or bedroll, the only warmth comes from Lark's back pressed against mine, and Rat burrowed between our legs.

I ache all over, but it's the muscly, twinging ache from hard walking, not the deep-set, weary ache that sometimes signals a seizure. My forearms burn and my hands sting from digging an arm's length into the dirt the previous afternoon.

Walking last night was barely easier than it was during the day. The cool darkness was a blessing, but the land that seemed so flat and featureless in daylight became a maze of surprise holes, rocks, brush, and hummocks. The moon was nearly full, but it rose late, and while the stars washed the sky into pockets of purple and indigo, there was barely enough light to avoid obstacles. We moved slowly, dazedly, each of us falling more than once.

Carefully, I shift, leaving the warmth of Lark's back. I sit up and peer down at her. Yesterday, while she was slumped unconscious next to the seep, I'd been startled by the paleness in her cheeks and lips. And while I'd dripped sweat, digging at the earth first with our scavenged crossbow quarrel and then with a rock and then with my bare hands, her skin remained dry and cool. It had come on so suddenly. And while I was hacking the laurel medallion off my boot, something else struck me—there's nothing in the scout manuals to prepare someone for the utter *uncertainty* of an emergency. There are step-by-step breakdowns, tips, tricks, testimonials—all designed to lead, ultimately, to success. None of it prepared me for the sheer terror of not knowing if Lark was going to wake up or die.

I hadn't been joking when I told her that shook me up, bad.

My stomach squeezes again with the same panic that flared then, and I attempt to push it away. It's too dim to see the color of her skin now, but she seems to be breathing easily enough. Her hair is filmed with tiny beads of water—dew. I look across the water scrape, lavender-gray in the dawn, where the bobbing grasses are heavy with moisture. I pull my handkerchief out of my pocket and carefully, quietly, reach for Lark's under her belt. I lift it out. Rat rolls his head to look at me, but Lark doesn't stir.

I consider taking off my tunic to gather up the moisture on the grass, but it's filthy and would probably only produce mud and diluted sweat. Armed with the two handkerchiefs, I get stiffly to my feet and wade out into the wet grass.

I slowly sop up the water like Lark showed me yesterday morning, wringing it into my mouth. After I cool the scratchy burn in my throat, I start to collect some for her. Several stalks of grass hang particularly low, burdened with some kind of seed head. I bend closer, wondering if it's something we can eat, when I realize they're not seeds at all—they're grasshoppers. Dozens and dozens of grasshoppers cling to the tops of the grasses, frozen into a nighttime torpor. They must latch themselves up on top when night falls to make most use of the early sunlight. I prod one; it doesn't move at all. I pluck it straight off the stem like a fruit and hold it in my palm.

My folk eat a fair amount of grasshoppers, cicadas, and crickets. On market days, it only costs a few coppers for a bag of hickory-roasted grasshoppers, and my sister Ida's favorite meal is the juniper-cricket stew we eat on the autumn equinox. But I've never had one raw. I turn it in my hand—its big thorny leg twitches with the warmth from my skin.

I look across the landscape, picking out the stalks of grass drooping with insects, easier to see as the light grows. I could fill the skirt of my tunic as easily as picking berries, and I might even be able to get a fire going with the handful of yucca scattered around, but I can't think how I'd cook them without something to put them in. I squint at the distant horizon as if it might help me think, honing in on a bright smudge that I first take for mist. Then my brain catches up with my eyes, and my breath hitches in my throat.

Not mist.

The river.

I stare harder, trying to make absolutely sure I'm not hallucinating, that it's not a mirage or rocks or nothing. But no—I can see the glint of moving water, and the line of dark foliage along it.

We've neared the River Tell.

We must have strayed too far north during our march last night. We tried to be careful in keeping the polar star on our right shoulders, but there were certainly times I spaced out, too focused on my feet to pay attention to the sky, and I expect Lark, still weary from dehydration, was little better. At any rate, we've closed the distance to just a handful of miles.

It will be easy enough to simply aim a little farther south once we get going today. But I can't help but scan the horizon again, wondering, calculating. I turn back to Lark. The grasshopper, warmed from its torpor by my palm, springs into the air and disappears into the grass.

I crouch down. "Lark," I whisper. "Wake up."

I touch her shoulder. She picks her head off her arm, bleary-eyed. A rasp comes from her throat. She swallows and tries again. "Veran?"

"Here. I gathered some water. I can get more once you've squeezed it out. But listen, I think we turned too far north last night. We're in sight of the Tell."

She blinks several times and pushes herself into a sitting position, letting her head hang for a moment. Her dreadlocks curtain her face, loose. She rubs the back of her neck and then straightens.

"How close?" she asks, accepting the soaking handkerchiefs.

"It's hard to say with the slope—maybe five or six miles."

She wrings the bandannas into her mouth and swallows.

"We'll have to turn south," she says. "Head for the North Burr where it comes out of the highlands, and then turn upstream . . ."

"But, Lark," I say. "That's going to add miles we don't need, swinging south and then doubling back. Can't we keep heading straight across?"

"I've told you before, we don't want to be spotted anywhere near Tellman's Ditch and mistaken for escaped slaves."

I gnaw my lip, thinking. "How is the compound set up?"

She eyes me warily. "There's a tent city, where the workers live. It's split up into quadrants, all surrounded by pike walls and guard towers. The quarry itself is downstream—there's a fenced route between it and the tent city."

"Where does everyone else stay?" I ask. "The overseers, the drivers, the off-duty guards?"

"The headquarters compound," she says. "Upstream."

"And I expect, if the focus is on guarding the slaves where they're kept, there's less security around the compound?"

"I wouldn't know—I was only there a few times for health screenings." She frowns at me. I fidget with the mangled fringe on my boot. "I don't like that look," she says.

"What if—" I say.

"No."

"No, but listen—"

"How about some more water?" she says.

"If we could get into the compound—if we could get even *around* the compound, we could make off with something that could help. Even just a canteen . . ."

"We'll be seen," she says, staring at me like I'm suggesting we casually throw ourselves off a cliff. "And when they take a look at my arm—"

"Why would they assume we're runaway slaves on sight? Why not folk traveling to Vittenta? If we'd broken out of the tent city, we'd be dressed differently, and not looking like we've been half-dragged across the water scrape. And neither of us look Alcoran *or* Moquoian—you look Cypri, and they're not going to know what on earth I am. I almost think we could just walk in and say we're lost . . ."

"No." She shakes her head. "We've taken a lot of risks together in the past week, Veran, but this one's too big. I'm not walking into Tellman's Ditch."

"Then we don't walk in," I say. "We'll just poke around the edges. Grab a canteen—or even a mule."

"A *mule*?"

"After nightfall," I press. "It'll be dark—we'll sneak in and out." She's shaking her head again, and I rush to continue. "I know it sounds crazy, but, Lark—I'm starting to think walking across the water scrape is even crazier. Correct me if I'm wrong, but we're not going to survive another day like yesterday, walking through the afternoon on only morning dew and wet rocks. And if we *don't* travel in the afternoons, and only stick to morning and after the sun sets—well, you saw how well that went last night. We're nowhere near where we wanted to be. At this rate, it will be days before we reach the Moquoian border, and longer still until we reach somewhere we can pass into the mountains, and by that time the soldiers will have fanned out through Pasul, Vittenta, Tolukum—you name it, they'll be there. Word will be out that we're being hunted. The only advantage we have is staying just ahead of the bad news, and connecting with Tamsin and Iano before they're found, too. How else are you going to get to Callais?"

"I'll figure it out."

"Yeah?" I press. "Think you can do it before one of us dies out here?"

She glares at me but doesn't reply. She looks out across the scrape, her brow furrowed and lips pursed—she looks startlingly like Eloise when she does that.

She lets out a breath. "It's a really, really bad idea."

I jump at the omitted concession. "Let's just skim around the edges. Stay a few miles out, rest in the afternoon somewhere we can see down to the compound. Make some plans. Then when it gets dark we'll slip down and cause a little mayhem."

"We will *not*," she says, turning back to me. "Listen, I'll admit that we can't go on like we did yesterday, but you have to promise me you're not thinking of tiptoeing in and turning the place over. No fires, no riots, no prison breaks. Because after you run off all giddy with a couple of mules, you know who it'll come down on? Who'll take the blame and have to clean up the damage? Who'll be whipped or hanged for causing an uprising?"

"Oh. The slaves."

"*Oh*," she says mockingly.

"Sorry," I say, flushing. "I hadn't thought about that."

She shakes her head. "You and your hero complex, I swear. If I get any *inkling* you're thinking of doing something that's going to bring misery to the couple hundred workers down in the tent city, we're forgetting the whole thing and striking off south, got it?"

"Got it."

"Good." She plants her hands on the ground and stiffly rises to her feet. She hands me one of the bandannas. "Here. We'll drink while we move. Come on, Rat."

I follow her back out into the grass, her boots carving a dark line through the dew. She swipes her bandanna over a few stalks and then stops.

"Hoppers," she says, pinching a blade bent under a grasshopper.

"Yeah," I say. "There are so many . . . I wish I could figure out how to eat them."

"You have to pinch their heads off," she says, plucking the one off the grass. With a flick, she twists off the head and then plucks off its wings. "And then squeeze the guts out, otherwise they'll make you puke." She gives it a little shake, and a blob of innards flies into the grass. With no other fanfare, she pops the rest into her mouth, legs and all.

I stare, openmouthed. She catches sight of the look on my face and pauses halfway through chewing. A moment of silence hangs around us as I grapple with the fact that I just watched the daughter of Queen Mona Alastaire, princess of Lumen Lake, whip the head off a grasshopper and eat it raw. Nearby, a cricket chirps.

"Oh . . . ," she says through a mouthful of exoskeleton. She swallows, and her cheeks flush. "Blazes, I guess . . . most of your folk would consider that below them."

"Maybe, but not me." I reach for the nearest grasshopper. "Let me try."

Her eyes go unfocused. "Veran . . . it's times like these that I can't bring myself to believe I am who you think I am."

I don't know why, given her parentage, but it's times like these that I'm the *most* certain she's exactly who we think she is. Something inexplicable swells in my chest.

"Well, the good news is we'll have the luxury of confirming it now that we won't starve to death," I say. "Show me how you did the head."

With less gusto than before, she points out where to pinch the insect and pull it apart. I squeeze the guts into the grass and put it in my mouth. It's horrible, exactly the wrong kind of chewy, not crispy and smoky like the roasted ones on market day.

Still, I swallow and wipe my mouth. "We'd better gather more, before they warm up and start jumping, right?"

She nods and turns back for the flats. We progress a little way, pausing now and then to wring our bandannas into our mouths and pick grasshoppers.

"You know," she says after a while. "My life was a lot simpler before you showed up."

I spit out a thorny leg. "Yeah, Lady Princess, mine, too."

TAMSIN

I like Soe's house because it's quiet.

It's a different kind of quiet from the insulated glass bubble of Tolukum Palace—it's an open, breathing kind of quiet. The redwoods tower over the rough A-frame cabin and its little out-buildings, making me feel like a bug crawling around the feet of beings who have better things to do than notice me. The wind sighs through their lofty branches, easy to hear even from this distance because everything around Soe's house is soft, muffled. Her flock of turkeys drift here and there, pecking the dry walnut meal left over from the oil presses. The yard is carpeted with copper-colored evergreen needles, and the pitched cabin roof is so thick with moss and ferns it melds with the forest floor where the eaves touch. A sapling grows out of the northwest corner of the roof, its spindly branches reaching toward the happenstance light let through by the redwoods.

I've made it a point to visit Soe as much as I can in the three years since we shared a room in the Blows, but normally those

times were filled with chatter and music. The first time I visited
I brought her a beautiful new dulcimer, with opal inlays, as a
thank-you gift for the old boxy instrument she gave me when we
parted ways—the one I played onstage for Iano's parents to earn
the title of *ashoki*. She still has that dulcimer, wrapped in flannel
in the cedar chest. I let my fingers drift over it this morning,
sliding them along the strings. But I don't dare to pluck them,
and that's because I'm here alone.

It took several hours for Soe and Iano to agree to this, and
that was only after Soe showed me how to get into her hidden
root cellar where she stores her wines and oils. With a door covered in the same deep duff as the forest floor, it would be nearly
indistinguishable to an outsider, but the hole itself is dark and
too shallow to stand in—and I have a sudden urgent need to
avoid going into places I'm not sure I can get out of. Still, I gave
in to Soe insisting I check to see if the space she cleared for me
is big enough, and I attempted to smile at Iano as he earnestly
arranged a few items inside—a blanket, a canteen, a box of nut
biscuits. But inwardly, I imagined sitting or lying under the skin
of the earth, listening to people prowl around outside, looking
for me, and I held back a shiver. I don't plan on getting into that
hole if I can help it.

And this means being as quiet as I can—no dulcimer or
humming or too much moving about. An approaching horse's
hooves would be muffled on the thick redwood carpet, and a
single traveler barely noticeable. Even the mule and cart that Soe
drove away, with Iano at her side (looking back worriedly every six seconds), was lost to the deep swallowing silence of the
forest. But it's for the best—this way Iano can watch the road
into Giantess while Soe collects the salal berries and walnuts

she needs for her next round of pressing. Her last market run was two weeks ago, and we've unfortunately caught her when her supplies are low.

She lives simply here, with only three sets of clothes, and I'm wearing one of them, a work dress that would have fit me snugly several weeks ago but now hangs off me like a sack. Iano had to change back into his traveling gear—between that, his new stubbly beard, and his hair braided and tucked under a cap, I hope he'll go unrecognized as the face on the copper coins should someone pass by. I reach for another well-buttered nut biscuit, determined to reclaim some of my curves, and study the parchment balanced on my knees.

I've started notes from our conversation last night. Kimela's connection to the plantations on Ketori, her attention to symbolism and ceremony. Queen Isme's desire to see some order restored to the rollicking court, and her seal on the bounty sheets.

I've added Minister Kobok, but his name spurred half a dozen others who are equally outspoken about preserving Moquoia's slave-based industry. The only things that make Kobok stand out more are his management of the quarries at the edge of the Ferinno, and his determination to keep the country's industry safe from banditry—hardly insignificant motivations.

The *whos* and *hows* are exhausting, so I've moved on to a growing to-do list, the beginnings of something that could be considered a plan.

It feels good to write after so long. I organize things best this way—left in my head, my ideas jumble and hide, but on paper I can lay them out straight, connect them, label them, list them. Two pages now are filled with straggled text studded with arrows, circles, and underlines.

I take it back. It feels good to see my ideas on paper. It does *not* feel good to write. I rotate my wrist, trying to ignore the hot pain spiking in my joints. Nine hours a day for three solid months spent at a drafting table, recording the vital statistics of slaves passing through the illegal distribution ring—I carry that work as a penance in my right wrist, reminding me that I got off easy. I shake my arm, trying to will away the stiff curl that my fingers want to take. Mami had scribe's arthritis, too, her fingers so gnarled by the end of her life that they barely flexed at all. But there's more I want to write, there's more that needs doing. I swish another sip of Soe's astringent vinegar tonic around in my mouth—she says it will help my tongue heal—butter another biscuit, and take up the quill again, missing the ink pot on the first dip thanks to the stiffness in my fingers.

I've covered nearly every point of interest I can think of regarding our enemy in Tolukum Palace, so I move on to the next urgent matter weighing on my mind.

Veran and Lark:
Whereabouts???
Investigate South Burr for signs of activity
Check Pasul for return west—posthouse, prison, inns
Check Snaketown for journey east
Send letter to Callais; inquire after Eastern Ambassadors &
Lark's camp
If no news???

My quill pauses on the page, the whirl of my brain momentarily blotting out the throbbing in my wrist. If no trace can be found of the Silverwood prince and the Lumeni princess, what then?

Draft letters to Silverwood monarchy and Lumeni queen/ Cypri ambassador

Organize search & recovery of bodies

I swallow.

Prepare for collapse in diplomatic rela—

"Ah!" I drop both the quill and the nut biscuit, which lands butter-side down on the top half of my page. I suck in a breath and cradle my wrist to my chest. My fingers are curling in on themselves, my tendons tightening uncontrollably. I sniffle around the pain, carefully set the spoiled parchment at my feet, and lay my wrist on my lap. With my left hand, I uncurl my fingers one by one, biting my lip. Fire races up my arm, into my shoulder, all the way to my back. An hour spent writing, and already my body rebels.

"*Kuas,*" I say, the curse deadened by my inability to pronounce the *s* at the end. Clutching my right arm to my stomach, I stoop and lift the biscuit off the parchment. It's a dual tragedy—butter smears the neat lists on the top half of the page, and the biscuit itself is splotched with black ink. I almost throw the biscuit in anger, but I don't want to hit any of Soe's empty glass bottles or buckets of walnut meal. I consider balling up my parchment in frustration, but it feels like such a waste of effort, and anyway, I'd need two hands to do it satisfactorily. I want to shout, but I think again of the faceless enemy prowling around outside Soe's windows, waiting for a sign to burst in and end me.

I slump forward on the bench, winding my good arm over my head.

No speech.

No song.

No writing.

An image comes to me of a life lived in fragments, single words and short phrases scratched out on a slate. Gestures and points. Yes-or-no questions. Plucking a tune on a dulcimer and singing the lyrics only in my head. I may have learned to live with limited speech if I still had the ability to pour out the contents of my head onto paper. But this—robbed now of the written word . . .

My last weapon is gone.

I'm still in prison.

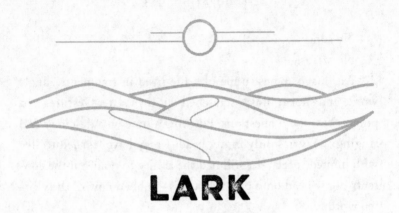

LARK

As twilight falls on the hillside above Tellman's Ditch, Veran collapses again.

He was sitting down this time, at least, and merely slumps to one side, spilling his lapful of chicory roots we had gathered. I'd been shushing Rat—he was whining—and so I don't have time to break his fall. I lunge forward and roll his head out of the grass, padding his cheek with my palms as he shakes.

"Rat!" I call. He's nestled down a little way from us, which is odd given that we're bivouacked under a hanging rock, and the ground here is damp and cool. He pokes his head out of the hot grass, batlike ears tilted backward.

"Come here, Rat! Come!"

Tentatively he gets up and lopes to me, skirting around Veran's seizing body with his nose down. I grab his ruff and drag him down behind Veran's back to keep him propped on his side.

At the last minute I think about yanking his trousers off to keep him from wetting them—he doesn't have a spare pair like last time—but I don't have the chance before his shaking slows. His body relaxes, and he retches, spraying spit into the dirt before he goes still.

I let my breath out through my teeth and brush his hair off his forehead. He didn't seem to hit anything when he went down—there are no fresh scrapes or blood, only the old bruise from his last seizure, now barely more than a greenish splotch near his hairline.

It could have been worse.

Still, he takes longer to come around this time. I wipe his mouth with his bandanna and dabble the other one in the seep we took turns digging through the afternoon—being closer to the river meant we didn't have to dig quite as deep, and we've spent the past few hours sipping the murky water in the basin. I make several passes between the seep and his mouth before he finally coughs, groans, and rubs his eyes. He pitches haphazardly off his side, and I grab his shoulder to roll him back. He cranes his head to look up at me.

"Hi," I say. "Welcome back."

"Ugh." He blinks several times. "Whuh . . ."

"It's me—Lark. We're in the water scrape above Tellman's Ditch. We have no gear, we're both filthy, our only water is in a mud seep, and the only things to eat are chicory roots and raw grasshoppers."

His eyes drift closed. "Oh, right," he says weakly. "Damn."

"Are you okay? I tried to keep you in place, but you hit the ground before I could stop you."

His fingertips creep experimentally over his cheek. "Yeah . . . I think so. Blazes." He scrubs his face. "What a pair we make."

"At least you didn't bring yours on out of stubbornness and spite. Want to sit up?"

He grips my arm and struggles upright. Rat sits up at the disturbance, and Veran scratches him behind his ears.

"Thanks, Rat." He glances over himself, letting out a relieved breath at his dry trousers. He wipes the back of his hand over his mouth.

"Three seizures in less than two weeks," he murmurs. "That's closer than they've come since I was fifteen."

"You're treating your body pretty rough," I say, wetting the handkerchief again and handing it to him. "No sleep, no food, no water, miles of walking. I don't blame our bodies for pitching a fit." As soon as the words leave my mouth, I regret them. "Sorry—I shouldn't joke."

"No, joking's okay. It makes it less terrible. And you're right. I'm pushing myself too hard." He squeezes the handkerchief into his mouth, swallows the pitiful dribble, and leans his head over his knees. "I just worry because we're not done yet. We still have to get out of the water scrape and into Moquoia. And once we're there—who knows what we'll find. If Soe's isn't safe, or if Tamsin and Iano aren't there, we're going to have to think of something else."

"First we have to get in and out of the compound," I say. "What's the thing your ma says?"

"One crisis at a time," he says.

"Yeah, I'm starting to see the wisdom in that." I gesture at the compound below us. "If we can't make off with something useful, it might not matter if we can't find Tamsin or Iano."

He gazes at the compound, his arms around his knees. The first yellow lights are starting to twinkle in the rows of barracks.

"I know what it means for you to go back in there," he says quietly.

"It's just headquarters. I wasn't there that much. It would be worse if it was—" I wave vaguely downstream, toward the quarry and the tents.

He looks in that direction, the giant raw gash along the river lost to the dim light. No lanterns in the tent city—only a straggle of lights circling the perimeter of the camp.

"How long were you there?" he asks.

"It's hard to remember. There was no sense in keeping track of time."

"Well, you're nineteen now. You escaped from the rustlers' camp—three years ago?"

"Four."

"Four years. And you were there for how long?"

"Three years, I think." I remember three drunken festivals to celebrate the Alcoran holiday Starfall, mostly because it meant Rose and I could sleep in the next morning.

"That puts you at—twelve years old, when you escaped from the slave wagon. And you had just turned five when you were—when you disappeared in Matariki. Which makes it . . ." His gaze settles on the near-invisible river. "Seven years."

A breeze, carrying the night's chill, slinks through the grass. My stomach is tight, but not turning like I might expect. Yesterday, hearing him methodically piece together my life—with spare parts borrowed from that other life that still doesn't feel like it belongs to me—would have sent me into a panic. But now it only feels surreal.

"I don't think I was here the whole time," I say.

"No?"

"They don't typically toss little kids into the quarry. They're not strong enough to dig sand. I started out cleaning glass in a factory." I can still smell the reek of the cedar-oil solution they had us use to wipe down the panes.

"Vittenta, probably."

"Probably. Then they shuffled me over here after a few years to run empty carts. I was only in the quarry for a year or so."

He rubs his bleary face. "And you're *sure* we can't just set the compound on fire while we're down there?"

"No," I say. "One of the workers will get blamed for it."

He heaves a sigh. "What about setting all the mules loose?"

"Why don't you rest for a little bit?" I say drily. "We're both going to need strength just to pinch a couple of canteens."

He grumbles but settles back down on the dirt, lacing his fingers over his chest. He takes a few deep breaths.

"It just makes me want to *destroy* something," he says.

The corner of my mouth lifts, and I scratch Rat's ears. "I'm telling you, you make a bad outlaw. You have to choose your destruction more strategically."

He heaves another sigh. "Oh believe me, I'm making a damn list. First up—the entirety of this mysterious Port Iskon. I'm burning that place down."

A swoop of some strange emotion pitches through me. It would be easy to needle him, to chide him for being a clueless, privileged prince, but I'm caught off-guard by how comforting his indignation is. How much it sounds like he actually cares about . . . well, me, potentially. I remind myself that caring is just a step away from pity, and I don't want his pity. I remind myself that I can't rely on him, or anyone—whether by choice or chance, people don't always mean what they say. People don't always stick around. Especially not gently bred princes with hero complexes.

Still, it's hard to ignore that little seed of gratitude. That he might care.

I shake myself, and he slits open one green eye. "You okay?" he asks.

"Yeah, just—uh, cold." I flush at the stupid comment—sweat still prickles the back of my neck.

He closes his eye again. "I'd offer you a coat, but I haven't got one."

"Thanks a lot."

"Anytime. I live to please."

"As long as you don't die for it, too."

"Nah," he says. "That part's out of my control."

My smile from earlier twists anxiously.

Joking might make things less terrible, but I wish it didn't hit so close to reality.

VERAN

We creep along the perimeter fence of the headquarters compound. It's a cursory construction, the pickets only just clearing our heads. Lark already described the double wall, twelve feet high, thick with guards, that surrounds the tent city. This fence exists more for the look of security.

Rat pads along with us. We couldn't be sure where we would leave the compound, so we couldn't leave him behind. But Lark pointed out that he also might serve as a decoy—if someone hears a stray noise, all they might see is a curious coyote nosing around camp. I just hope it won't end in crossbow fire.

We reach one of several wide openings in the fence for carts and clamber easily over the gate. A few dozen yards away sits a large log-hewn building, its glazed windows spilling light. All the other buildings in the compound are dark and hushed, and we're well hidden by the shadows. Lark leads us to the right, toward a long, low structure sitting against the far end of the compound. The stables. I follow, trying to control the jellied feeling in my legs.

Our hasty plan, based on Lark's memory of the compound and our observations throughout the afternoon, is to scavenge a few small necessities from the mule drivers' storage shed and then make off quietly with two mounts, exiting through the corrals. Unfortunately, this spits us out downstream of the compound, between the barracks and the tent city, but it's better than trying to sneak two mules past the guard quarters and out the main entrance upstream. We just have to hope any guards patrolling the quarry will be focused inward, not out on the corrals.

"*Sst,*" Lark hisses, touching my arm. I stop and follow her gaze. A few paces away, faintly outlined in the light from the main building, is a watering trough.

We crouch and scramble quietly toward it. There's a skim of grass and dirt over the top, and it gives off a horsey smell, but neither of us pause. We dip our heads toward the water and drink in short, deep bursts, trying not to gasp too loudly between each draw. Rat laps at the puddles around our knees.

When I've had as much as my stomach can hold, I lean my weary forehead against the cool metal. I'd be happy to just sit here for the next hour, drinking deeply whenever the urge rises, but Lark sits back on her heels and wipes her mouth. She looks out toward the stables.

"Blazes," she whispers. "What's that?"

I look up. Just where the circle of light from the main building melts into the night, a dark, hulking shape sits, stationary, outside the wide stable door. On its far side, illuminated by two lamps burning in the driver's box, are the shifting backs and flicking ears of a two-horse team. The sound of idle teeth mouthing their bits reaches us.

"A coach," I whisper. "Two in hand."

"There's a guard," she says.

I see him now, standing a few paces from the door of the coach, still but alert. He's facing the main building.

"Whose coach is it?" I ask.

"What does it matter?" she replies. "We have bigger concerns."

"Like what?"

"Like the fact that they're in our way."

We crouch silently, peering over the water trough.

"I suppose we could try to go around the back side," she murmurs. "Circle the compound and come at the stables from the other end."

"Will we be able to grab the mules without the guard hearing?"

"I don't know," she says. "But the other option is to wait and hope they go away."

We consider for a moment. I'm just about to suggest we retreat farther into the shadows, when a bright rectangle of light blazes from the main building—a door has swung open, and a shadowed figure appears on the threshold. We duck instinctively behind the trough, but as soon as we do, the door slams shut, dousing the light. Hurried footsteps crunch toward the stables. A few murmured words are exchanged. When we peek over the trough, a second guard is conversing with the first.

"Different uniforms," I mutter.

"The new one's a quarry guard," Lark says. "I don't know about the other one."

The quarry guard finishes his conversation and hurries into the stable. A moment later, we hear the thump of hooves on packed earth, and he reappears, mounted.

"Get back," Lark says suddenly. "Back toward the fence. Rat, *come*."

We shrink backward—practically crawling—into the deep shadows along the fence line. The mounted guard urges his horse straight past the trough, mere feet from us, not stopping to water the horse. He reaches the gate, dismounts, opens it, and clambers back into the saddle. And then he kicks the horse into a canter and takes off, leaving the gate wide open.

"Where would he—"

"The tent city," Lark says, her back flat against the fence. "He's taking a message to the guards—he'd have stopped to water the horse first if he was going anywhere else."

A second door in the main building bursts open, and another guard hurries in a different direction, half-jogging toward the shadowy peaks of the barracks.

"Lark," I whisper. "Something's going on. Whatever we're going to do, we should try to do it now and get out of here."

"I know. Let me think." She lets out a breath, her gaze flicking over the compound. "Why don't we forget the stable for the moment. I think the kitchen is on the far side of the main building. We can grab a few things there and then head toward the river. We may just have to walk."

The thought of more walking makes my aching body groan, but there's nothing to be done. "All right."

"At my word, we'll break for that hitching post over there—keep to the edge of the shadows. Ready?"

"Yeah."

Another door swings wide, and we startle—but it's on the stable side again. It stays propped open, illuminating another guard as she strides toward the one by the coach. In the light, I can finally make out their uniforms.

"They're from the palace," I say in surprise.

"Go!" Lark says, and takes off. I stifle a gasp and break after her.

My joints are loose and shaky, and despite my best efforts my footfalls are hardly silent. I focus on keeping inside the arc of shadow. Rat follows at my heels, his panting mingling with mine.

But when we're halfway to the hitching post, the door on our side opens again. Lark thinks fast, not bothering to swear or stop—she merely pivots and plunges toward the main building, keeping to the line of shadow thrown by the edge of the open door. I follow her, my heart in my throat. She runs into the very lee of the door just as another quarry guard emerges, fitting her cap onto her head. The guard's gaze would have fallen on me instantly if she weren't partially turned back toward the interior, listening to muffled words from a superior. I put on a burst of speed as quietly as I can and practically slam into Lark. She throws her arms around me and claps a hand over my mouth. Separated from the guard by only the angle of the open door, we shrink against the side of the building. I lean into Lark, my legs trembling. Rat slinks around our knees.

"Get Captain Ertsi, too," the voice inside is saying in Moquoian. "Tell him to have his squad in ranks in fifteen minutes. And leave that door open—the others are going to need the light."

"Yes, ma'am." The guard leaves the threshold of the door and runs toward the distant barracks. Already lanterns are twinkling in a few of the windows.

Lark moves her hand from my mouth but doesn't let go of me. I'm grateful—I probably would have collapsed on the spot. We stay squashed together in the dark corner made by the open door. I can feel her heartbeat thudding against my back.

"We can't stay here," I gasp. "There are more coming."

"I'm working on it," she replies.

She needs to work quicker—our safe patch of darkness is shrinking.

What is going on here? Why would a palace coach and team of guards be at Tellman's Ditch in the middle of the night?

Voices are still talking inside, though it's difficult to hear them. Gingerly I pat Lark's arm, and she obliges by loosening her grip. I ease off her shoulder and toward the crack between the door hinges and the frame.

". . . and a cadre to the western perimeter. Don't waste time with daily schedules—workers will stay on lockdown until they're sent for."

The deep, unpleasant timbre of the voice stirs my brain.

"It's Kobok," I whisper in surprise. "Minister of Industry. He's in charge of all the quarries."

"Can you tell how many people are inside?" Lark asks.

I strain my ears. Someone else is responding to him, but his voice is easily the loudest.

"Then leave it!" he booms. "I'm telling you, there's no time to parse over details. We're facing the likelihood of a coup, and until the prince is found, we must preserve Moquoia's industry."

"I'm not sure," I say to Lark. "But it sounds like they're talking about Iano. They haven't found him yet." A puff of relief flickers in my chest, but it quickly disintegrates.

Slowly Lark eases off the wall and slips toward the window. She tilts her head so just one eye peeks over the sill.

"Pull all the headquarters guards off their usual posts," Kobok continues. "As well as those on days off. We're operating on full staff, no excuses."

"Four quarry guards," Lark whispers. "One's the overseer. Plus three palace guards, and then your minister. Damn, that's a mustache."

In the lane between the barracks, a lantern starts to bob steadily closer. Someone shouts—it has a bounce to it, like they're running.

"Lark, we need to move," I say. "Folk are starting to come this way."

"Okay, grab Rat's ruff." The corner of her face is still thrust into the light from the window. "On my word, run with him to the other side of the door."

"What about you?"

"Go!" she says.

My heart rate spikes, and I snatch the fur on the back of Rat's neck. He yelps, but the sound is lost in the next round of indignation from Minister Kobok. Hurriedly I haul him around the door and into the flood of light on the far side.

Rat doesn't want to come with me—I hiss through my teeth as he twists under my grip. I dare a glance into the open door— Kobok is gesticulating at a parchment-littered tabletop, surrounded by a cluster of uniformed people looking bewildered, almost reticent. I drag Rat toward the shadows, his claws leaving gouges in the dirt. For one horrible moment, I think Kobok is going to look straight at us, but he only lays into one of the guards, his thick finger thrust in the other man's face. With a final burst of strength, I muscle Rat into the darkness on the far side of the door and pull him deeper into the shadows.

Lark sidles to the edge of the door. Her nose and cheek come into barest light as she peeks around the edge. I hold my breath. She watches for an opening and then, in a burst, she breaks from the door and flashes across the lighted ground.

Without pausing, she stoops and picks up Rat in her arms and then kicks my calf as an indication to move farther down the length of the building. We half-run, half-tiptoe toward the corner. Kobok's shouting grows muffled.

We reach the corner and slip around it just as the crunch of running boots reaches us. We watch breathlessly as a soldier comes barreling into the light and disappears into the open door.

Lark turns, her arms tight around a wriggling Rat. Her gaze sweeps the compound behind the main building.

"*Blazes*," she says fiercely.

The small outbuilding that I assume to be the kitchen is flooded with light—two big hearth ovens along the outside are just kindling with roaring fires, and people are rushing this way and that—hauling cast-iron pots to and from a line of water barrels, and shouting about coffee and jerky and how many pounds of cornmeal are left.

"What is going *on*?" Lark whispers emphatically, adjusting her grip on Rat. "This place was dead silent and dark not twenty minutes ago. We're going to be lucky to get out of here with *nothing*, let alone supplies . . ."

"There's a cadre coming," I say, peering back around the corner. "Go—move farther down the wall . . ."

"We're going to hit the light from the kitchen!"

"At least get around the chimney," I say frantically, pushing her. "If they line up lengthwise, they'll be able to see around the corner . . . go, go!"

Like snakes crawling sideways along the building, we flatten ourselves against the wall and slither around the bulge of the chimney. There's a window on the other side, cracked open and spilling light, but there's also a rain barrel and a few splintery timbers leaning against the wall, creating a jumble of shadows. We slip behind the barrel and try to recover our breaths as silently as we can.

"I don't care *how* it gets done, as long as it *does*!"

We both jump, nerves frayed. Kobok's voice is as loud as if he's standing right over us—I realize we're now at the opposite corner of the building that we started on, putting us right below the minister and his cluster of guards.

"This is not a question of doing things cleanly or strategically," Kobok continues. "This is a question of time. Moquoia is under attack, and if we want to keep from hemorrhaging six centuries of economy away, we have to act swiftly and decisively. You—blue cord—did you raise each of the cadre captains?"

"Yes, sir."

"They'll be ready to enter tent city within the hour?"

"Yes, sir." There's a helplessness in the guard's voice—she probably knows there's no other acceptable answer.

"Good. I want two cadres assigned to each quadrant."

"With respect, sir, quadrant four is a huge sector, two cadres will barely—"

"Then split the quadrant!" he says impatiently.

"You must understand, sir, doing so could split up families, people on the same bond ticket . . ."

"There's no time to spare on such things, Lieutenant. It will be dealt with later. I want everyone with Port Iskon in their records pulled."

Lark goes unnaturally still beside me.

"Are you sure sunrise is strictly necessary—"

"By the colors, how many times must I repeat myself?" There's an unsteady thump, as if a table corner has been bumped in agitation. "Listen to me, all of you, because you *must* understand the nature of our situation. The prince is missing, vanished with one of the Eastern ambassadors. My call for jailing the remaining two ambassadors was overruled. My sources tell me they are now en route back East, and I will be *very* surprised if they do not collect the prince along the way from wherever they spirited him to. In their minds, Tellman's Ditch and Redalo still operate illegally, and the East has seeded a coup right under our noses while we were bothering about hospitality. Do you understand? *War has begun.* We have a workforce topping five hundred able workers here, and we *will not* lose it to Eastern meddling. I will not repeat myself again. Pull every Port Iskon record on file. I need clear records of how long each one of them has worked. Set aside anyone who has been at this facility for more than ten years. They'll be redistributed to the islands by the end of the week. Leave the rest."

Lark is clutching Rat so hard he's trying to squirm free. She's staring straight ahead, into the shadows on the back of the rain barrel.

"My Moquoian isn't great," she says without looking at me,

her voice shallow in her throat. "So tell me if I'm wrong. They're pulling workers from Port Iskon—*only* Port Iskon."

"It sounds like it."

"They're redistributing them to the island plantations."

"I think so."

"They're splitting up quadrant four," she continues, her eyes glassy. "The quadrant that's extra big because it's where all the families, married couples, and partner bonds are housed."

"I think so," I whisper with trepidation.

"They're scrambling records," she whispers. "They're covering something up—something about Port Iskon. They're rushing those workers away before their records can be checked."

"Is there someone outside the window?" asks a voice inside.

"It's just the kitchens getting coffee ready," says another.

"Lark," I breathe.

She shifts, and with a heave, she thrusts Rat into my lap. I clamp my arms over him before he can wriggle away.

"All right, we're getting out of here," she says. "Your job is to get Rat and yourself inside the coach."

"What coach?"

"No, I think there's someone outside the window," the first voice says again, growing a little louder. "Is one of the cadres lining up in the back?"

Lark stands up, heedless to the glare of the window that pours over her. "Follow me, and don't stop."

"Lark!" I scramble to stand with Rat, still unhappily pinned in my arms.

She turns and runs for the corner of the building just as the windowpanes hinge open. A woman in the white uniform of Tolukum Palace stares straight at me. There's no chance to hide—I'm standing just five feet away in full lamplight, clutching a whining coydog in my arms. Her shocked eyes hold mine for a single heartbeat, and then in the next breath, I plunge after Lark.

She's running out of the light cast by the main building and into the dimmer glow coming off the now-lit stable lanterns. The pale sconces are still burning on Kobok's fancy two-horse mud coach. The guard shifts toward us when it's clear the footsteps are coming toward him, and not into the stable beyond.

"Guard!" I hear Lark call in terrible Moquoian. "I have a message!"

"Whu-huh?" the guard begins, tensing at her rapid approach but clearly unsure whether this is just part of the growing chaos. Barely slowing a step, Lark raises her fist and clocks the guard across the jaw so hard he spins in a circle. His crossbow drops to the ground. Before he can recover, she grabs his shoulders and slams his head into the glazed window of the coach. Glass shatters.

"Flying Light!" I gasp, squeezing Rat.

She wrenches the guard out of the window, simultaneously opening the door. "Get in!"

Another rectangle of light floods behind us. The side door in the main building flies open.

"What's going on out there?" barks a voice.

"In!" Lark orders, scooping up the fallen crossbow and scrambling into the driver's box. The horses twitch nervously at the commotion.

I throw Rat inside the coach and hop up into the open door, leaning out to keep her in sight.

"Lark!" I call. The coach lurches, and I grab the doorframe, swaying. "I thought—you didn't want . . . won't they blame the workers?"

She scoops up the driving whip and snaps it through the air. The horses leap forward, their tack jingling haphazardly.

"What the—what is this?" Kobok booms, his silhouette filling the doorway. "Surot! Is that you?"

Lark stands up in the driver's box, stamping her foot over the reins to keep them in place. She shoves the whip between her teeth. Wrenching her arms backward, she sheds her vest, swipes up one of the lanterns swinging on its post, and wraps it—still burning—in the fabric. Gripping the corners of the bundle, she smashes it against the side of the coach. Oil soaks the fabric. Flame bursts in her hands like a be-damned miniature sun. The horses break into an unguided canter, the coach swinging wildly toward the main building.

"Hey!" Kobok shouts again, leaping from the threshold. "What the colors do you think you're doing?"

"Lark!" I shout, desperately clutching the carriage frame.

She hurls the burning bundle. It arcs upward, streaming flaming oil, and lands on the timber-and-brush roof of the building. Fire bursts into the sky. We fly by the door, well within sight of the cluster of soldiers pouring from within. One grapples for a crossbow.

"Screw you!" Lark yells, swaying on the driver's box, as we thunder past Kobok. He stares, open-mouthed, as the leaping flames illuminate both our faces.

One of the coach wheels jounces against the corner of the building. I reel my head inside just before I can be decapitated by the corner. The carriage sways violently on its straps, and I'm thrown to the floor.

"LARK!" I bellow.

The teetering coach steadies itself, its swerving line corrected. Rat thumps against the interior bench, paws splayed and ears back. When I finally scramble to my feet and look out the flapping door, Lark is sitting, reins in one hand and whip in the other, urging the horses across the packed earth of the compound. Soldiers leap out of our way as we canter by—they turn in circles first to stare at us and then at the burning building and then at the howling knot of superior officers barreling around the corner, shouting a cacophony of orders.

It's too late for them. Lark has reached the open gate and careens through it. She arcs the horses to the right, onto the wide track leading west toward the Moquoviks, their black rippled peaks blotting out the stars.

I check to make sure Rat is all in one piece, and then I climb out onto the teetering running board. I shut the door firmly behind me and carefully clamber up the hand- and footholds to the driver's box.

When Lark sees me approaching, she sets the reins under her boot heel again and gives me her arm. I hoist myself up into the box, gripping the handles against the rollicking of the coach. I glance over my shoulder, the blazing orange of the inferno growing fainter and fainter behind us.

We sit for a moment, the space between us thick with the sound of beating hooves, clattering wheels, and squeaking braces. The gibbous moon hangs low on our left side, casting long, pale shadows in the grass. The single lantern not used for a firebomb swings crazily on its hook.

Finally I turn to Lark.

"What the *balls*, Lark."

She gives something like a triumphant grimace. Without her vest, her shirt blows open over her collarbones, revealing the beginning of the flowing river tattooed down her arm.

"Do you even know how to drive a two-in-hand?"

"Of course. I'm driving one, aren't I?"

"You nearly ran us into the side of the damn building."

"That's just because I was trying to get close enough to throw the lantern." She flicks the air with the whip. "This road's well used, and we have a moon. No problem. I had to help drive the chuckwagon for the rustlers, and that was with no moon and a rock ton of cows in the way."

"Right." I snatch at the handrail again as the coach lurches off a divot in the track.

"Rat's okay?"

"Scared spineless, probably, but yeah, he's okay."

She glances at me. "You're okay?"

"I dunno, I think I left my sanity somewhere behind that rain barrel. You know they're going to be after us like flies on rot?"

"We'll ditch the coach," she says. "Run the horses until we get some good distance, then unharness them. We can leave the track and ride toward the mountains. We should be able to get pretty close by sunup."

"Minister Kobok," I say, "will destroy us both."

She grimaces again and flicks the whip.

"If he can catch us," she says.

TAMSIN

I have something stuck in my head.

This happens a lot, especially in the dead of night—like now. These deep, secret hours were frequently some of my most productive times as *ashoki*, when I would jolt out of sleep with a phrase or melody drifting at the very edge of my brain. In Tolukum Palace, I broke more than one bedside candlestick in my rush to throw off my covers and stagger to my writing desk before the thought could pass.

I haven't been woken by an idea since my capture outside Vittenta. The time in my cell was so grim, so thick with pain, that the creative well inside me seemed to have vanished. The times I did lie awake at night, it was because I hurt too much to sleep, and those times were filled with the squeaking and leathery swooping of bats swarming in the darkness.

But now an idea has woken me up again. I lie on the floor of Soe's workshop, tucked between Iano and the small press. The bags of walnuts and baskets of salal they collected earlier today sit just a few inches above my head, filling the room with the scent of tart berries.

Rain cannot soak dry ground.

I don't know where this line came from, but it's hanging right there in my head like a ripe fruit. I prod it, the shape of it, the feel of its syllables. I repeat it a few times. I taste its cadence.

Rain cannot soak dry ground.

Unlike those times in Tolukum Palace, though, I don't rush to write it down. Why should I? What am I going to do with it? There is no court waiting to hear it. There is no song waiting to be written.

I shift on the floor. Soe's scratchy winter rugs tickle my skin. I reach up until my fingers bump the nearest basket of salal berries. I sneak a few and pop them in my mouth. They burst over my sore tongue, their tart sweetness hinting at the deeper flavor they'll carry as wine. It'll be weeks before they're ready—Soe plans to mash and cook them tomorrow, but then they'll have to sit and ferment, transforming from sweet summer fruit to something with a bite.

I grimace. My transformation, on the other hand, has done the reverse—a journey from someone with a weapon to someone both harmless and useless. The salal will ferment. I am just rotting.

I wriggle back down next to Iano. He shifts, sliding his arm around my waist. He smells like berries, too—Soe roped him into picking with her along the road. He came back with stained fingers and a flush of sunburn over his cheeks. I set my head down beside his.

The string of words nudges my brain again.

Rain cannot soak dry ground.

I shut my eyes, turn my head into Iano's shoulder, and try with all my might to ignore them.

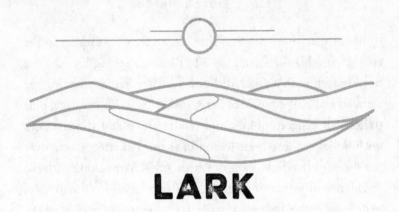

LARK

The North Burr is not like the South Burr.

I've seen it before, but farther downstream, toward Pasul, where it's the same kind of muddy, shallow river as the drainage below Three Lines. But here it's a foaming, rocky current, with white-frothed rapids and sudden pools so clear it looks like there's no water inside at all. I stand at the edge of the bank, staring at the bright golden-green riverbed under the rushing, glassy surface.

Veran sits back on his heels, his chin wet from his drink. The horses are watering a little way downstream, their sides dark with sweat. We abandoned the mud coach just before dawn, leaving it slouched tiredly behind a rocky outcrop. We unhitched the team and fitted them with the halters under the driver's box and guided them off the road. We walked until the sun rose, took a short rest under a stand of pinyon pine, and then mounted and continued northwest, toward the towering blue line of the Moquovik Mountains.

I shift, rubbing my backside. There were no saddles in the coach, only blankets, and my sit bones are aching like they've been beaten with a pike. Still, the minister had a fancy leather canteen and half a bottle of berry-red wine in his carriage, plus packets of ginger cookies and tender jerky and three scones with honest-to-goodness lemon in them. I'm still getting over the shock of that light, tangy taste on my tongue, along with the decadence of something baked with flour instead of cornmeal and sweet butter instead of lard, so that now, at the edge of the crystalline North Burr, I'm very close to being overwhelmed.

Veran wipes his mouth. "That's good water. Are you going to drink?"

I crouch down and dip my fingers in the water. It's shockingly cold. I cup my hand under the surface and bring a scoop to my mouth. It's sweet and bright and makes my teeth ache.

"So the good news is, I think we're pretty far north," Veran says, shading his eyes against the midmorning sun. "I expect it's nearly a straight shot west to Giantess at this point. The bad news is, we have to go over the ridge, of course, and I don't know if there's a track."

I let the last handful of water seep through my fingers. Down near the stones are tiny rock-colored fish, beating their little tails to stay in one place in the current. Imagine that—fighting every second of your life just to stay right where you are.

"Lark?" Veran looks down at me. "You're being awfully quiet. Are you all right?"

I stand up, reach to adjust my hat, and remember I don't have it anymore. For lack of anything else to do with them, I shove my hands in my pockets. "Yeah. West, you think?"

"I don't know how far we'll make it without a track," he

says, still watching me. "The understory gets pretty thick once you cross the rainshadow, and the loose slopes can be tricky up near the summits. Maybe we ford and follow the river a little while to see if we find anything promising?"

"Okay," I say.

"Okay?"

"Okay," I repeat.

I don't know what he expects me to say. We're well outside my range, miles and miles away from anything I could call familiar. I don't know why, but the North Burr feels like a boundary. On this side of the river is all the stuff I ever was—slave, runaway, rustler, outlaw. The Sunshield Bandit. I've left a trail of all the bits of myself—hat, eyeblack, sword, buckler. Jema—blazes, I wonder if I'll ever find Jema again. My eyes travel to Rat—with a sickening swoop I remember how close I came to losing him, too.

The space between my shoulder blades prickles, as if I can feel the eyes of the distant Ferinno watching me hesitate. Back there, back behind me, is everything I ever was. I look across to the far shore.

Over there is nothing.

"All right, well." Veran runs his fingers through his hair. "I guess we should get going. Unless you want to eat something?"

"Nah." The instinct to save what few provisions we have kicks in, despite the rising hills thick with promising greenery. I turn for the horses. Without any more words between us, we mount and urge the horses across the broad, stony ford, Rat splashing along behind.

It soon becomes clear that my urge to conserve our supplies is wasted—the riverbank is thick with late-summer berries.

Veran exclaims over each new thicket—"Oh, whortleberries! Look, a hackberry"—like it's the greatest damn delight of his life. We dismount and adopt a leisurely pace to eat what we find.

We also find bears—two of them, to be exact, gorging themselves on the same berries we're plucking. They're black bears, thankfully, not grizzlies, but I pull up short at the sight of them sitting on their haunches, delicately slurping berries off the branches with their lips. Coyotes and cats I know how to deal with, but there are no bears around Three Lines. Rat stops and growls, his hackles rising, but Veran barely blinks, merely lifting his arms over his head and giving a sharp, "Ha!" that sends them lumbering into the brush.

"You can come back after we pass through," he calls after them, then catches me staring. "What?"

"Don't tell them that," I say incredulously.

"Oh, sorry." He cups his hand to his mouth and calls, "Give us a few minutes, and then you can come back."

I shake my head, wanting to tell him off for making fun of me—but I'm not sure he is.

We go on.

Around noontime, we come to an old ramshackle hut by a bend in the river. Several tanning frames stand out in the sun, where beaver pelts are stretched to dry. A stooped man comes to the door of the hut with a crossbow and a wary glint in his eye, but Veran talks politely to him in Moquoian, and after a moment, the man points up the river a little way. From their conversation I gather we're approaching a footpath that leads up the mountain slopes. Veran thanks him and offers the last of the minister's rich wine in return for the promise that the man will deny seeing us if anyone comes inquiring. We come to the path just a few minutes later, marked with a stone cairn, and we turn our horses' noses west, toward the soaring Moquoviks.

We climb.

The canyons around Three Lines are steep and rocky, but they conveniently slope off right around the time you get really tired. These mountains soar up and up, turning the distances blue and blurry. The scraggly trail switchbacks this way and that, passing through dense copses of fir and pine, breaking apart to reveal sudden rock fields that ring with the squeaks of an animal Veran calls a pika.

It gets cooler. The track joins the course of a noisy stream, and soon its chatter fills our ears as it rushes down the mountainside. Two days ago, we were nearly dead of dehydration in the water scrape, and now there's a torrent of cool, clear water splashing right by our feet. It feels indulgent, selfish, wasteful—a luxury I haven't earned. Veran, Rat, and the horses take full advantage, stopping to drink whenever the fancy takes them, but I can't make myself do the same. I think of the couple hundred folk being separated out of Tellman's Ditch, and the ones farther south in Redalo, all the ones with Port Iskon in their records— like me. Soon they'll be marching inland with the dust in their eyes and throats, and then loaded on ships, parched by the salty breeze. I keep the minister's canteen full, but I only sip when my throat prickles. Stored in the canteen, the water is lukewarm and leathery.

There are birds, and bugs, and pikas, marmots, martens, and three more bears. I do have the crossbow from the minister's coach, and I suppose if I was feeling up to it, I could attempt to shoot something. The fat, golden marmots are especially bold, watching us from atop rocks so close I expect I could reach out and grab one with my bare hands. But I don't—I feel like an intruder here, and it feels too much like breaking into someone's pantry and making off with their canned goods.

Which, upon reflection, I have done in the past, so I don't understand why I should be so bothered now.

Late in the afternoon, when the mountains are throwing long purple shadows behind us, we reach a small, flat grove of spicy-smelling fir. We're walking at this point, resting the horses and our butts. For no particular reason I turn and look behind us.

"Blazes," I say—the first word I've spoken in hours.

The land ripples away from us, first the falling blue-green of the mountain slopes, and then the dull brown of the water scrape, and beyond it, barely more than a golden smudge on the horizon—the Ferinno. It flashes like a line of fire, ignited by the sinking sun.

Veran comes to stand at my elbow, letting his horse nose in some grass. "We've come a long way," he says.

"A lot of it was in the coach," I say.

He gives me a funny look. "We still came a long way."

I shrug. "I guess."

He keeps watching me for a moment, like he did down by the river, and then he looks around us. "What do you say we camp here? We'll lose the light in an hour or so, and it's only going to get colder the farther up we get."

"Okay."

We don't have much camp to set up—just fluffing around in the fir needles to find a soft place to lie down. Veran blankets the horses and collects some of the downed branches for firewood, and I occupy myself for a good twenty minutes with hollowing out a fire ring and coaxing a spark from my knife and flint. Once the blaze has caught, I hold the rock in my palm—a tiny chunk of the mesa behind Three Lines. It's completely unremarkable—when I picked it up it was only because it had a good surface for striking. If I had realized it would ultimately be the only thing I'd have left from the Ferinno . . .

I'd probably have scoffed at myself for being sentimental.

I close my fingers over it.

Veran, meanwhile, opens the jerky pouch, tosses a strip to Rat, and then hands me the bag.

"So," he says, chewing on his own strip. "Another day or so over the mountains, then we get our bearings and make for Giantess. If Iano and Tamsin are there, we tell them about Kobok and try to make a plan."

"Yeah." I take a piece of jerky but don't eat it.

"Lark, are you okay?"

"Yeah, are you?"

"I'm fine. My stomach hurts—I'm not sure if it's from all the berries or all the bad water we drank out in the scrape," he says, rubbing his middle. I know how he feels—I've been cramping too. "But I'm feeling a lot better since crossing the Burr." He nods at the jerky in my hand. "We might as well eat everything we have left—we don't have a way to hang our food up high, and chances are good some critter will chew through the bag during the night."

I take a bite of jerky. We eat in silence for a moment, watching the light fade. The eastern sky over the distant Ferinno turns dusty blue, speckled with stars. At one point, Veran cranes his head, as if to see past a few of the branches.

"What?" I ask.

"Oh, just looking. We have a summer star called Suitor Firefly—he's higher than I thought. I lost track of the stars in Tolukum Palace." He finishes off his jerky. "Do you know any star stories?"

"No." The rustlers only ever used the stars to navigate.

"The Alcorans have a blue-zillion of them—it's where they see the Light. But my folk call them fireflies, because they're what first coaxed my folk out of the ground. So every summer, instead of dying, the fireflies go up to take their place in the sky. We have a sending-up ceremony in September."

"What's a firefly?" I ask.

He throws back his head and laughs—but it's a laugh at himself, not me, evidenced by the palm he smacks to his forehead. "Oh, earth and sky, I'm sorry. They're a beetle that lights up. That pin you stole from me—blazes, that feels like years ago, doesn't it? That pin was a firefly. This is, too." He holds out his hand, where his seal ring sits, imprinted with a bug with spread wings and an oval abdomen. "It's a sacred symbol to my folk— one of the places we see the Light."

I remember him calling it a firefly, but I thought it was a fancy name for the jewel itself. "What's the other place you see the Light?"

"Foxfire—glowing mushrooms." He looks around. "Those aren't limited to just the Silverwood Mountains—we might see some after crossing the rainshadow."

"When you say . . . ," I begin, and then stop, considering my words. "When you say it's where you see the Light . . . I know a lot of people who swear by the Light, and I know the Alcorans have that holiday with the shooting stars, but I never really . . ."

"Ah. Okay. I'll tell you what my folk think, but you have to remember that every culture understands the Light differently—even people within the same country." He bends his knees and wraps his arms around them, looking out at the dark horizon, where the belt of stars is materializing in the darkness. "The Light is a—a force, I guess, that guides. It pulls plants up and turns the seasons. It tells animals when to forage or shed or hibernate. When my folk began, under the ground, we were called up to the surface by the sky Light, and given the courage to stay there by earth Light—the fireflies, the foxfire. The Light reminds us that we're small, but strong—the two sides of our nature, and that means that we should be humble, but brave. Does any of that make sense?"

I think of the light out in the Ferinno—like fresh water, it was frequently all or nothing. Burning sun, or cold, empty darkness.

"I guess," I say.

"Now, the Alcorans, like I said, see the Light in the stars. They think of the Light more in a tangible sense—that it can actually give messages and visions, sometimes prophecies. The Moquoians have sort of a distant view of things—the Light is out there, but doesn't do much to impact daily life. They see it in the rainbow, colored light—sort of like decoration. It's nice and pretty, but the things it does are mostly inconsequential."

I nod, even though both of those seem foreign to me—there have never been any colorful decorations in my life, and I've always associated visions with hunger or eating the wrong plant.

"Then the Cypri—I guess I should have told you about them first—the Cypri are different from almost everybody else. They see the Light as an internal force." He touches his chest. "The Light is a spark inside everybody, something intimate and individual. Something that burns even when everything else seems dark. They see the Light in fire." He nudges one of the burning logs in the ring, and a cloud of sparks goes up. "So the Light is a tool, as well—a means of creation and destruction, just like our own impulses."

I like that a little better—the idea of a flame inside me, threatening to break loose and burn everything to the ground.

"And Lumen Lake?" I ask. "Where do they see the Light?"

"Water," he says. "Well—sort of. Reflections. Their pearls are a big part of that—the way each one reflects light and color differently. The way the lake shifts and moves, the way the waterfalls change throughout the day, the way the sun filters on the lake bed. They see the Light as something so big and broad that we can only understand it by way of change—we can't perceive it as a whole, but we can see when it shifts and guides the things around us. Kind of similar to my folk—makes sense, since we're neighbors—but for us it's small and physical, while for the Lakefolk it's huge and intangible."

I purse my lips. He had me at the first mention of water, but then he lost me. "That sounds . . . overwhelming."

"Yeah, I think that's why a lot of Lake folk believe in the tradition of the Light more than the actual nature of it," he says. "Not everyone, of course—these are big generalizations. There are even differences from island to island." He scratches his chin, dark with stubble, and then he gives a little laugh. "Actually, it's kind of funny, if you think about it—you, the Sunshield Bandit, flashing that buckler around. Reflecting all that light. Kind of similar."

I can't tell if he means capital-letter Light or just plain old sunlight, but the thought makes me uneasy. I think of something watching over my shoulder, pushing and pulling me in different directions—why would it push somebody *into* slavery? Why would it separate a child from a family? For that matter, why would it separate hundreds, thousands of children from their families?

Suddenly, the Light doesn't seem like such a peaceful, spiritual force. "I don't know if I believe all that—about it guiding and stuff."

He shrugs. "Not everybody does." He pokes at the fire again and smothers a yawn. "Are you as beat as I am?"

"Yeah."

He rummages in the small bundle of items from the minister's coach. "There's just the one cloak. What do you think—back-to-back?"

We first slept back-to-back out in the water scrape, both fuzzy and disoriented from dehydration, our shoulders and waists pressed together for warmth. For some reason it feels stranger tonight, when I'm fully lucid. But there's no other option—we'll freeze if we lie separately, and any other position . . .

"Back-to-back, yeah," I say quickly.

"You want to face the fire?"

"No, you face it," I say. "I'll curl up with Rat."

We tidy up camp, check on the horses once more, and then settle down. I wait until he's situated himself where he wants by the fire and then lie down on his other side, pressing my back up against his. I pat the ground for Rat to come curl up beside me. He smells a little better after a day of romping in the crystalline water gushing down the Moquoviks. Veran shifts to spread the thick wool cloak over both of us.

"G'night," he says.

"Night," I reply.

He wriggles down and goes silent.

I wrap my arms around Rat and hug him close, burying my fingers in his fur.

I can tell when Veran falls asleep, the way the rise and fall of his back slows against mine. I listen to the crackle of the fire, the scurrying of a few nighttime animals. Twice Rat raises his head, ears forward and nose twitching, but each time he lowers it back down, assured of our safety.

I take a long time to fall asleep, which only unnerves me more, because normally I have no problem sleeping on any given patch of earth. But tonight I lie on my side, staring out at the stars slowly turning in the sky beyond the trees, thinking about the Light and culture and lines drawn in the sand. One country believes this, another believes that. What does it mean to be raised nowhere, with no strings tying you to a set of festivals or traditions? What do Veran's books say about that span of rock and sun, the wild country that belongs to Alcoro only in name, that celebrates the shooting stars mainly for the chance to drink and holler around a campfire?

Vainly I try to reach inside, to that kind of spark Veran said belongs to one half of me—my father's half. I don't know what it feels like, though, or how to find it. In the desert I always felt like I was made of dust; out here it feels like nothing, like I'm just a tent of skin over bone, with nothing but empty space inside.

The night cools. Rat twitches. Veran presses a little closer in his sleep.

I finally sleep, but don't dream.

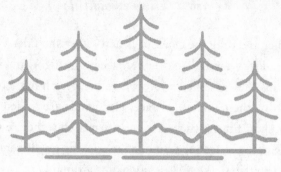

VERAN

When I wake, the fire is cold and the blackened logs are frosted white. My breath curls in front of my face. Frost in August—not even on the highest balds of the Silverwood do we have frost in August. I frown, and wiggle a little—my back is warm, but so are my shoulders, and the backs of my knees. Small puffs of warm air move against my neck. I go still when I realize what it is—Lark turned over in the night. She's facing me now, curled against my back. I can feel her forehead pressed against the back of my head. On her other side, I hear Rat snore.

I hold still, unwilling to wake her up, when a curl of cold air against my calves rouses me a little more. I carefully lift my head, and my fears are confirmed—I stole the cloak. The reason Lark is molded against me is because I bunched the fabric around myself, leaving only a small corner flopped over her hip. How long has she slept uncovered in this frosty night?

Prickled with guilt, I ease to my back, putting my hand on her shoulder to keep her from rolling over. I prop on my side facing her and drag the cloak back across her shoulders. Two of her dreadlocks have fallen over her face in the night, and in front of her lips they're rimed white where her breath has frozen on them. I lift them out of her face. Her hands are folded up under her chin, fingers tucked in for warmth, but they're still icy cold. Tentatively, feeling a bit like I'm sticking my fingers within range of a rattlesnake, I close my palms around hers.

She doesn't wake. I cup her hands, trying to share warmth. With our noses inches apart, I can count every freckle. Eloise's are clustered around the corners of her eyes, crinkling when she smiles, but Lark's are dusted more over her cheeks and nose— places usually hidden by her eyeblack and bandanna. There are sun lines around her eyes and worry lines on her forehead, but no lines around her lips—not from smiling nor frowning.

A tendril of cold winds between us, and I inch forward a little more, until our knees and chests touch. My stomach does a funny little wiggle, being so close. I lower my mouth to our hands and blow warm air between them, trying not to think about her fingers against my lips. It only just begins to strike me that maybe I should be worried about her being half-dead of hypothermia when her eyes snap open.

Every line in her face tenses.

"What are you doing?" she blurts out.

"I was just—"

"Don't touch me!" She snatches her hands out of mine and rolls over, flattening Rat, who yelps. She plants her feet and stands. "Were you watching me *sleep*?"

"I dragged the cloak off you during the night—your hands were freezing. I was trying to warm you up." I sit up. "I'm sorry."

"Why were you facing me?"

"You were facing me first."

She stares, flexing her hands at her sides. The breeze ruffles her old shirt.

"Here." I get up and hold out the cloak. "Look, I'm sorry I made you uncomfortable. Really. I was only trying to share some warmth."

"I don't need you to do that," she says, her voice staccato.

"Okay. I won't do it again." I shake the cloak toward her. "Take this, please. I've got my tunic over my shirt—you need the extra layer. Things are going to stay cold until the morning gets on."

She hesitates, and then reaches forward and flicks the cloak out of my grasp. She swings it around her shoulders.

We stand for a moment, silent. The fir trees sigh around us. Off to the right, our horses stamp and blow, their breath steaming.

Lark turns on her heel, the cloak swinging, and begins to stride off into the trees.

"Where are you—"

"I'm going to pee," she says. "Don't follow me."

"I'm not going to follow you," I say incredulously.

She disappears. I rub my hands over my face, feeling a little silly and a little irritated and also still a little wobbly, which I tell myself is from the gut memories of getting hit in the face with her buckler or stabbed in the sternum with her sword hilt or twisted by the arm after getting too close. And then another memory hits me, the vivid image of her face an inch from mine, slanted with sunlight, before she pressed a crushing kiss to my lips, her bandanna bunching between us.

It wasn't a kiss, she clarified a few days ago.

No, it had been a distraction to steal my firefly, and anyway, she'd apologized. We'd both apologized, for the cascade of hurts—intended or otherwise—that we'd caused the other.

So many apologies.

I remind myself to remember the consequences of getting too close. A rattlesnake was the wrong comparison. A rattlesnake is reluctant to bite. It rattles to warn folk away.

Lark bites first.

Have to remember that.

Rubbing my hands together, I head into the trees to begin preparing the horses.

TAMSIN

Soe's oil presses are like any other—a large screw holds a broad wooden plate suspended over a basin. A long wooden arm is fed into slots in the screw and cranked to pull it downward. The arm is drawn out, set into the next slot, and cranked again, until the plate applies the desired pressure to the goods in the basin. A spout opens out into a bucket, catching the runoff—in this case, salal berry juice.

"Your job is to have a bucket ready to swap out when one fills," Soe tells Iano, hefting the first basket of berries. She glances at me standing close by, as if I can be useful by proxy. "Tamsin, if you like, you could fit the strainer over that big pot there."

This task takes all of three seconds. I look around for another job, but I'm not familiar with the intricacies of pressing, and I'm not sure what would be helpful. I stand, frustrated, at the edge of the room while Soe pours the berries into the basin of the largest press and picks up the wooden arm. She fits it into the first divot in the screw and hauls it toward her, like a row-boat oar. The screw cranks down. She removes the arm, fits it into the next slot, and hauls again.

After a few more pulls, we're all rewarded with the first stream of burgundy berry juice trickling from the spout. The trickle turns into a stream, filling the bucket with dark, frothy liquid. Iano crouches with an empty bucket at the ready. He swaps it out, but not fast enough—a jet of juice spatters the floor, already stained a rich purple from previous splashes.

He hoists the bucket to the pot and pours the juice through the linen strainer. I hold the pot steady, though it's not needed. Soe keeps tightening the screw every minute or so. Iano swaps out three more buckets. I busy myself with mopping up errant splashes of juice—at one point, some spatters across the parchment Soe uses for labels. I trace it with my pinkie nail, drawing a shapeless design, as if pulling a quill through ink.

"Hey," I call to Soe as she starts to wind the screw back up. She looks up to see me holding the square of parchment—not parchment, I realize. I test the word.

"Paper?" I ask gingerly.

"Yeah, paper," she confirms, fitting the arm in the screw again. "I get it from the ragpickers at the mill in town. Linen scraps, you know. Cheap. It's good for the labels because it doesn't buckle like parchment. And it takes the stamps well." With the screw lifted, she works the cake of crushed berries out of the basin, emptying them into the slop bucket for her turkeys.

I rub the paper with my thumb. It's less smooth than parchment and vellum, but I can see what Soe means—rather than puckering up like parchment sometimes does under ink, the grain of the paper almost sucks up the berry juice. Growing up running around the scribe's office my parents worked in, I've seen paper before, prized for its low cost, but usually passed over by rich patrons, who prefer the look and durability of vellum. Paper is used for woodcuts, the only way to make a proclamation or advertisement that needs to be stamped over and over again. Cheap. Quick. Easy.

I look at the shelf where Soe keeps her label stamps, flat wooden blocks carved with mirror images of words like *walnut* and *pine* and *huckleberry*. I pick up the one for *ground*, perhaps because it appeared in that line that came to me in the middle of the night. *Rain cannot soak dry ground.* I dip the stamp into the puddle of juice drying on the wood.

I press it to the linen-rag paper—*ground, ground, ground, ground*—until the ink runs out.

LARK

I never thought anything could be as big as the canyon walls of Three Lines, until we rode into the shadow of the redwoods.

"By the Light," Veran breathes. He's been repeating the phrase for the past half hour, craning his head this way and that, not even bothering to hold the reins, twisting to stare up the soaring trunks. I did, too, at first, squinting up at the treetops swallowed by mist, but now I keep my head down. A feeling of being closed in—netted, caged—has been growing in my stomach, and I can't shake it.

"And these are—*alive*?" I ask dumbly.

"*So* alive," he says. And then—"Blessed Light!"

He pulls his horse up short and slides off, making for a massive, sweeping trunk, the biggest one we've seen yet. I grab his horse's dangling reins before it can amble off. Veran approaches the tree with both hands cupped toward it, as if receiving a gift. His head is thrown back, searching for the crown hundreds of feet above us. He reaches out and touches the trunk with one set of fingers, and then begins to circle it—he disappears around one side, and it takes a full twenty seconds for him to materialize around the other.

I stoop my head. It's raining, something I would normally welcome, but it's been raining since we crossed the ridgeline of the mountains yesterday, and I can't remember the last time I've been so wet for so long. I pull the hood of the minister's soggy cloak farther over my head. I miss the protective brim of my hat.

"Veran," I say. "Come on. They said the house is supposed to be this way. Are you talking to that tree?"

He turns reluctantly back for the horse. "Thanking it."

"Thanking it for what?"

"For just—" He mounts and gesticulates emphatically, waving his arms first between him and the trunk, and then all around, like that's an answer. "The very air breathes—can you feel it?"

"You're weird, you know that?"

He grins and nudges his horse. "Ah, Lark—ethnocentric bias. Don't let your uncle hear you."

The knot of anxiety in the pit of my stomach grows a little sharper, a little colder. "What?"

"Ethnocentric bias—thinking your worldview is the only, or best, worldview. It's something your uncle Colm hammers in to all his students on the first day of class. Skies forbid you ever use a word like *weird* in his discussions." He barrels his chest and exaggerates what I can only guess is a Lumeni accent, bearing down hard on his *r*'s. "*Never allow yourself to devolve into a dichotomy of right and wrong, of normal and not normal.*"

There are two words I don't know in that sentence—the two that started with *d*'s—but that's not what makes me uneasy. Normal and not normal? A *worldview*? I picture that man I attacked in the stagecoach, weeks and weeks ago, back when things were all in their right places. I remember his well-made clothes, his crisp tattoo, the casual way he encouraged me to take his money, his matches.

I must have looked so pathetic to him, a feral, cultureless outlaw. Someone to be pitied. And now my campmates—except for Rose—are heading to his house. They might already be there. And when the ambassador and the princess get there a few days later, the news will be out—that the professor is related by blood to the dirty, ignorant bandit who wrecked his stage and stole his shoes.

And if that's *his* outlook, what will his sister—

The queen.

My mother.

What will *she* think?

Veran must mistake my daunted silence for remorse. "It's okay," he says. "Think me weird all you want—my folk consider it good policy to offer thanks to your environment." He's in a jolly mood—the giant trees have brought out a kind of bouncy excitement. He gives his horse a little kick. "Come on—I think I see a light up ahead."

We plod down the track, the horses' hooves muffled on the wet redwood needles. Shockingly green ferns press thick around us, growing as tall as I am and drooping with rain. Rat keeps plunging into the brush, despite me calling him back—I can't help but feel that if he were to get too far away, I'd never find him again in this dense, skyless maze.

I catch a tendril of smoke, and I lift my gaze from the horse's mane. Through the trees peeks a squat cabin made of unfinished logs, its mossy roof a slice of green against the red-brown trunks rising around it. The windows gleam yellow through the rain, and smoke curls from the clay chimney. A few outbuildings are scattered here and there—a coop of turkeys, a woodshed, and a one-walled stable surrounded by a small paddock, where two horses and two mules cluster around a trough of hay.

We don't get much more than a glimpse, however, before a figure leaps up on the porch. There's a flash of metal, and I tighten my hold on the reins, causing my horse to throw its head up. My gaze darts around for cover, a place to fire from—and then an escape. My hands have closed on both the stock of the crossbow and a handful of quarrels before Veran urges his horse ahead, his arm raised in the air.

"Iano!" he calls, relief flooding his voice. "Iano—it's us!"

I stop plotting escape routes and look back to the figure, who's standing sideways in the rain. As we get a little closer, I realize it's because he has a long, bone-white bow drawn back to his ear. I stare at the old-fashioned weapon—the only ones I've ever seen are a splintered old thing collecting dust on a shelf in Patzo's general store and depictions in petroglyphs.

Iano lowers the bow, his face split with shock. Words tumble out in Moquoian, too fast and too muddled by rain for me to catch.

"I know! We weren't sure we would make it a few times, but here we are." Veran kicks one leg over his horse and jumps off. "Is Tamsin here? Is she all right?"

The answer comes in the form of the front door opening in a wedge of golden light. Two figures crowd on the threshold. Veran runs forward eagerly, calling greetings and questions. I follow more slowly, dismounting and once again gathering up the reins of his horse, leading them both forward.

Tamsin looks a lot healthier after several days of food and rest. Her skin is less gray, and her cheeks and eyes aren't quite as hollow. She gives Veran a short hug, patting his back, before looking past him to me. Next to her, a girl about our age stands wearing an oily apron, her long black hair in a thick braid. Veran immediately starts chattering to her, introducing himself and me, with a whole string of titles and accolades that go sailing untranslated past my ears. I stand between the horses, inexplicable dread rolling around in my stomach like a round of bad meat.

Silently, Tamsin detaches herself from the fray and comes down the steps.

"Hi," she says.

I swallow and try to find my Moquoian. "Hello. You, um, look more good than you did."

She nods in thanks. "You okay?"

"Yes—I am okay, yes."

She smiles wryly, knowing it's a lie. She says something, and I have to ask her to repeat it, which I feel bad about. She says it again slowly.

"I wa'n sure you' come."

"I . . . was not sure also," I acknowledge. "How—how is your mouth?"

"Shi'," she says, the *t* at the end unpronounced but suggested. I laugh nervously, and she smiles again and takes the lead of one of the horses. Waving a hand, she beckons me toward the little paddock.

"No' much room," she says, opening the gate. We turn the horses inside, looping their halters on a peg under the stable roof. They mill with the others, bumping and jostling in the small space. One of them—the only other mare, I realize—sets her ears back at the presence of a new female. Herd mentality. There are a few agitated snorts.

Tamsin leans against the paddock fence. I break my attention from the horses back to her. She looks me up and down, and I wonder what it is she wants to say. The last time she saw me, I had turned tail and run away into the desert, leaving the rest of them to face a mountain of trouble alone.

She is pursing her lips, as if considering her words, when Iano jogs toward us, his breath misting in the rain.

"I'm sorry, Tamsin, I'd have done that," he says. He gives me a slight bow, a baffling gesture, and switches to accented Eastern. "I'm glad to formally meet you, Princess Moira. From what Veran says, it sounds like you've both been through a lot." He motions toward the house. "Come, let's all get inside."

I stand with my ears ringing as he loops his arm around Tamsin's shoulders and begins to walk back toward the house. That name sticks to me like sap on a tree. I want to shout for Veran to tell him, prince to prince, not to use it, but I'm already so mixed up and turned around and hollowed out that I don't see how I can. I follow them numbly through the rain and climb the steps to the porch.

Before I reach the door, there's murmuring inside, and Iano looks over his shoulder at me.

"My apologies, Princess," he says. "But Soe is requesting the dog stay on the porch. She says she'll fix a bowl of scraps for him."

I'd like to request that I stay on the porch, too, scraps or no, but I only nod and tell Rat to stay. He drops onto his haunches, watching me until I've slipped through the door and closed it on him.

The house is warm and bright, and filled with cooking smells and steam. A fire burns in the hearth. Iano helps Tamsin to a bench close to the flames, and she looks around him to me, patting the seat next to her. I pretend I don't see her and instead shove myself into the shadowed corner by the door.

Veran is flitting around, helping the girl with the braid put bowls and spoons on the table, hopping back and forth between Moquoian and Eastern once he sees me come in. I realize his twang comes through no matter which language he's speaking.

"Lark, this is Soe, she's Tamsin's friend. Oh, I can reach that. It sure smells good. Yes please, I'd love some cider. Lark, do you want cider?"

"Uh, sure," I say, not exactly sure what I'm agreeing to. I press a little farther into the corner. Soe turns to regard me while stirring a simmering pot. Her eyes are two different colors, like my old campmate Voss's were—one dark brown, one as blue as the desert sky.

"The Sunshield Bandit," she says, looking me up and down. "I admit, I half-thought you were only a myth. You're not at all like the stories, though—they always put you on a big black horse, with a big black hat and black grease on your face, and carrying that mirror shield, too." She shakes her head and turns her attention back to her ladle. "I guess tall tales always do get embellished."

By the fire, Tamsin shifts, as if uncomfortable. She ducks her head, fumbling with something, and then she looks up. "Hey," she calls to Veran. She holds up a small black slate with letters scrawled in chalk. I squint at them.

YOU SAID SOMETHING ABOUT KOBOK?

"Oh, right," Veran says, bringing me a mug of something

hot. "He was at Tellman's Ditch, ordering them to separate out all the workers from Port Iskon. It sounds like he did the same in Redalo. He's moving them from the quarries out to the islands."

Tamsin's brow creases in confusion, and she wipes her slate and starts to write another question. Before she can finish, though, Iano cuts in.

"What on *earth* were you doing in Tellman's Ditch?" he asks, setting a mug of cider in front of Tamsin and sitting down beside her. I lift mine to my lips—the drink inside is tart and spiced, but so hot it burns my tongue.

"Trying to find a way not to die," Veran says, holding his bowl to Soe to accept a ladle of stew. "We were hoping to steal some supplies, but we ended up—uh, we ended up sort of stealing Kobok's coach."

Iano reels back from the spoon he was about to put in his mouth. "Stealing his—?"

"Yeah, uh." Veran's gaze flicks to me. My fingers tighten on the hot mug, and I fix him with a stare that I hope conveys how much I don't want him to tell this group of strangers how we hijacked a court minister's two-in-hand while setting his property on fire. We might all be momentarily hiding under the same roof, but that doesn't change the fact that I have a bounty set by the government run by one of the people in this room. If I've learned one thing in my dealings with town sherrifs, it's that nothing unites two squabbling political factions like a common, dirty outlaw.

Iano sets down his spoon. "I think you must have gotten your translation muddled—surely you mean you *borrowed* the minister's coach? That word you used—stole—it implies you took it without asking."

"I know what it means," Veran says defensively, looking from me to him. "We stole the coach. Well—Lark stole it." My stomach lurches. I think he's trying to be modest, but all I can see is the reward money on my bounty sheet jumping higher with every word. I might already be worth double my old amount.

Veran doesn't stop though, despite my attempts to set him on fire by mental power alone. He continues, not seeing my gaze, "We drove north across the water scrape and left it a few miles from the North Burr. Those horses we rode here were the team."

Tamsin gives a great shout of laughter, slapping her knee. Iano, on the other hand, blanches, his pale face going bloodless. Soe comes to me with a bowl of stew, keeping the amusement on her face turned away from Iano.

"I'm sure . . . I'm sure you know that wasn't strictly appropriate," Iano says hesitantly, his gaze jumping to Tamsin, who's now clutching her stomach with laughter. "I'm sure you and Moira were only doing what was necessary to survive and reach us. As long as . . . there was no damage done, I suppose . . . one can always plead the necessities of survival . . ."

"We're on the run," Veran says with some surprise. "*You're* on the run. We ran from the palace together, Iano. It was inevitable that we'd have to break *some* rules."

"I'm on the run from an enemy in the palace, *not* the entirety of my court," Iano replies with a dignified air that puts me on edge. "We didn't break any rules by leaving the palace. We didn't even break any rules by coming here. You'll forgive me if I prefer to keep it that way. Perhaps it doesn't matter as much to you, but I'm not thrilled at complicating the relationships with my political allies by stealing from them."

Kobok's not your ally, I think, but I can't bring myself to say anything. Because if this prince says he's on the same side as that minister . . . then I'm not sure what we've just walked into.

Veran obviously shares my thoughts, but not my reticence. "Kobok might not be your ally, though!" he says. "He was in a rush to cover something up in Tellman's Ditch, and he was always badgering me in court. What if he's your blackmailer?"

"You don't know that he is," Iano says. "And if he's not, I need him on my side. He's one of the most influential people in my court. I won't antagonize him before I have all the facts."

Royalty protecting their own. *Of course.* I was stupid not to expect this. My stomach is now so jumpy I set down the bowl of stew—and I'd been looking forward to it. Veran looks like he's about to say something else—something that will probably bump my bounty up another fifty or sixty keys. I jump to speak first.

"Port Iskon," I blurt out. "Where is it? Why are the workers from there so important?"

"Oh, yes!" Veran twists to face Tamsin again. "Yes—Kobok was only interested in redistributing the workers from Port Iskon. Why would he be so concerned about that one place? Where is it?"

"Port Iskon?" Iano cocks his head, confused. "There's no city by that name in Moquoia."

"That's what I thought—but, Tamsin, surely you would know, or Soe, since you were part of the trade for a while . . . is it a secret place? A secret name?"

Tamsin shakes her head and shrugs apologetically.

"Not at all? You can't recall any mention, from any of the documents you copied?"

"You have to understand, the black market runs differently from the state trade," Soe says, taking a seat at the table. "The ring Tamsin and I worked in never used the resources of the government contracts."

"There weren't folk who bounced between systems?" Veran asks. "Folk who—"

He never gets to finish his thought. The jumble of Moquoian is finally starting to settle in my head, and as it does my whole body flushes with shock, hotter and sicker than when Iano was dancing around calling that trafficking minister his ally.

"Tamsin," I bark, "was a *slaver*?"

The room goes silent. Every head turns to me. Tamsin's earlier laughter ghosts away.

Veran tilts his head. "I thought I told you that a few days ago, in Three Lines."

I slide back to Eastern, unable to organize my thoughts in Moquoian. "You said she *got caught up* in the slave trade—Veran, what did you expect me to think that meant? I thought she'd worked under bond." I lean forward off the wall. The brand on my right arm stings. "You mean to tell me I tore my life apart and dragged your ass and mine across the Ferinno to rescue a *slaver*?"

Veran's face goes red, and he glances at the others. "Lark, I'm sorry, I didn't realize that's what you thought—but all the same, it's not quite what you think—"

I look past him to Tamsin again. She's staring at me, her lips pressed together.

"Were you a slaver?" I prompt in Moquoian.

A storm of voices erupts around the table.

"You don't understand—"

"She was as much a captive as the others, Princess, I'll thank you not to presume—"

"And anyway, it was *ages* ago—"

I keep my eyes fixed on Tamsin. Through the clamor of folk all rushing to defend her, she holds my gaze and nods.

I turn on my heel, unable to breathe in the hot, airless kitchen. I wrench open the door and storm out onto the porch. Rat lifts his head from his paws, and then hops up to follow me down the steps. Over in the little paddock, the horses are still agitated—the two mares are at odds, nipping and squealing at each other. The geldings are crowded together, skittering here and there to avoid the clash. I move toward them—the second time, I realize, that I've run off into the rain from the crowd inside.

Veran seems to think the same, because he comes after me like a shot.

"Lark!" He grabs for my wrist and then immediately drops it, jumping out of reach like he's afraid I'll hit him, which is fair, since it's how I've reacted all the other times he's touched me— except for this morning, when I woke up to find him an inch away, hands around mine.

"Lark, please don't leave. Please don't ride away."

I spread my arms. "Where would I go?"

"Blazes, I don't know. Please, won't you—"

"I'm not coming back inside. It's all just parlor games to you, isn't it?" I wave at the house. "It's just politics, just talk. You'll jump to defend someone who profited off human lives, because she's one of you, and because she could be worse. But some of my friends are *dead* because of people like her, and because of that prince, too—protecting his powerful friends to keep things from getting *complicated*. And you're the same, Veran." I shove my finger in his startled face. "You are *no different*."

"I—"

"Maybe you're not the one making the laws in this country, but you benefit from them, and you're *just* as clueless as Iano is."

"I know," he says quickly. "I'm sorry. You're right to be angry."

I stop, breathing hard, and drop my finger back to my side, clenching my fists. He takes his own breath and goes on.

"You're right. I didn't think about how it would feel to find out about Tamsin, or how it would feel to join up with Iano. I know it's not the first oversight of mine that you've had to take the consequences for. Lark, if this isn't right—if you want to leave—we can. *You* can, I mean—if you don't want me to come, I won't come. You don't have to join forces with Iano and Tamsin if you don't want to, and this doesn't have to be your problem to fix. I'll do whatever you need me to do, but, please . . ." His forehead creases under the bruises and sunburn and grimy rain tracks. "Won't you . . . won't you just stay until morning? Please. We've been running for so long."

I release my breath. I can't stand the helpless look on his face, the rain flattening his curls that had just started to dry, so I drop my gaze to his feet. But that doesn't help, either. My eyes immediately travel to the hacked fringe and missing laurel medallion on his boot.

I rub my forehead and turn away from him, toward the paddock.

"I'm not going to leave tonight," I say, "but I'm not coming back inside. I can't deal with it right now, Veran—I can't. Those people . . . No. Not after everything that's happened this week. Just . . . leave me alone."

"Where are you going?"

"I'm going to walk our mare down to graze somewhere—she's stressing the other one out."

"Won't you . . . eat something, or—"

I head away from him without turning back. "No." I put as much finality as I can in that one word.

His dejected response comes after the barest pause. "All right."

I'm a few more feet away before I call back. "Veran."

He hasn't moved. "Yeah?"

"Tell Iano not to call me Moira."

"I will." Perhaps there's a bit more life in his response, a bit more hope, but I don't turn back.

I dip my head against the pattering rain and head off to find a shred of something that makes sense.

TAMSIN

It's well after dark when Lark returns, treading silently into the workroom. Through half-lidded eyes, I watch her stand in the doorway, looking over the rest of us bedded down on the floor in an array of quilts, woolen blankets, and old grain sacks—Soe is nearly at the end of all available cloth in the house. Lark's gaze lingers on Veran, who's crammed as close as possible to the large press, leaving a generous space with the nicest of the three quilts empty for her. If she had come back twenty minutes ago, she'd have found him awake, his head lifting at every creak and sigh of the house, but now he's still and silent, his head pillowed on his arm.

Lark steps quietly past me, gathers up the blanket left for her, and disappears back into the kitchen. I hear the front door drift open and closed again.

Gently, I ease Iano's arm off my waist, pick up my blanket, slate, and the bundle I'd wrapped up earlier, and follow her out to the porch.

Her head snaps up when I open the door. She pauses for half a breath, and then goes back to determinedly arranging the quilt on the wooden slats of the porch.

"I cannot sleep in there," she mumbles in her rough Moquoian.

"*Uah.*" I smooth a corner of her blanket for her and then sit down an arm's length away, leaning against the boards of the house. Her coydog Rat comes to me with his nose in the air—I scratch him behind his giant ears and then open the bundle in my lap. I toss him one of the meat pies that Soe put together with the last of the stew, and then pass the rest of the bundle to Lark.

She takes it hesitantly, looking at the lumpy pies inside. Slowly she removes one and then hands the bundle back to me. I shake my head.

"For you," I say.

"*Lu'étci*?" She lapses into Eastern—*all of them?*

"*Uah.*"

"What about tomorrow?"

I touch my chalk to the slate. WE'VE PLANNED A MARKET RUN. THERE WILL BE MORE FOOD

She peers at it, her gaze moving slowly at the letters. Her lips silently form a few of the words.

"Market . . . ," she says. "Who? I and you, we are both wanted. Bounties. This is a stupid idea."

I write again, trying to keep it as neat as possible so it will be easier to read. SOE, IANO & VERAN WILL GO. SOE IS LOCAL & THERE'S NO BOUNTY FOR IANO OR VERAN

"It is still very stupid."

I shrug. IT'S A RISK, BUT WE NEED FOOD. GIANT-ESS IS SMALL. NO SOLDIERS, NO SHERIFFS

She huffs her disapproval and sets the bundle of meat pies down next to her, looking away from me. I hold back a sigh. Maybe this was a bad idea. This would be a difficult conversation to have even if I had a mouth that worked and we could easily speak each other's native language. I begin to wipe the chalk off my slate.

"You are all *so stupid*," she says.

I pause, looking up at her, surprised that rather than sounding angry, she sounds frustrated. She sighs, scrubs her face with her palm, and then lifts the meat pie and takes a bite.

She waves between us. "We are funny," she says without any trace of humor. "One girl who cannot talk in Moquoian and another who cannot talk at all."

"Your Moquoia' okay," I say. Better than my Eastern—now more than ever, since it has so many quick, tipped consonants.

"My reading is bad." She finishes the pie in another few bites and brushes crumbs from her fingers, but she doesn't take a second from the bundle. She rests her wrists on her knees, gazing out at the rain.

I squint into the darkness, where I can just make out the glint of a wet horse's back. Did a horse get out? And why are there so many *s*'s, *d*'s, and *t*'s in that simple question?

I scribble the question on my slate instead.

"I build a hitching post," she says. "The girl horse is making the other bad. Mad." She waves over her head. "I try to tie together the branches so she is not wet, but it is not so good."

THAT WAS A LOT OF WORK, I write. THANK YOU

She shrugs. "It is good to work—it makes me forget for a small time."

I nod. That I can understand. ME TOO

She glances at my words, and then looks away. Rat creeps on his belly toward the bundle of pies, his nose twitching. She pets him absently, still staring off into the dark.

"When were you a slaver?" she asks.

"A few year' ago," I say. My *th*'s are still thick and spitty, but I go on anyway. "Three year. For three mo'th."

"What did you do?"

I tap my slate, and she reluctantly looks back at my letters. SCRIBED. HEALTH RECORDS

"Yes? Does it pay you good?"

She means it to be hurtful, and I can't blame her. I shake my head. NO PAY—THEY BROKE CONTRACT

This surprises her. She studies my letters, probably trying to be sure she has the meaning right. "*T'oit* . . . you are under bond?"

WAS, I write. I've noticed that the most common errors for Eastern speakers is saying everything in the present tense.

"You have this?" She pulls back her right sleeve to show the scarred concentric circle brand—only hers doesn't have the usual release line down the middle.

I shake my head. BLACK MARKET RING—NO BRAND. I wipe the slate. SOE & I WERE LOCKED INSIDE

She looks from my slate to me. "For three months?"

I nod.

She turns back to gaze out at the rain. In a furtive movement, as if thieving, she reaches into the bag of meat pies and pulls out another. The corner of my mouth lifts—I'm glad she's eating.

"Why do you not try to protect yourself?" she asks, then waves a hand. "I mean—*ä puirle* . . . defend. You are not saying things to defend yourself. Everyone else is fast to defend you."

I shrug. THEY'RE MY MISTAKES. I HAVE TO OWN THEM. I wipe the slate. CAN'T DO BETTER IF I DON'T ADMIT TO THEM

She stares at my words, and then up at me. Then, as if realizing what she's doing, she turns back to her meat pie and takes a too-big bite. Rat slurps up the crumbs that fall.

I rotate my wrist—already it's starting to twinge. I clear the slate again. VERAN TOLD ME ABOUT THE FIRE AT TELLMAN'S

She swallows the bite of pie. "He did?"

ONLY ME. NOT THE OTHERS. He pulled me aside as they were cleaning up dinner—I got the sense he wanted me to be aware of the possible consequences while not casting Lark in too bad a light to Iano and Soe. I let her see my grin.

WISH I COULD HAVE SEEN KOBOK'S FACE, I write.

The corner of her mouth flickers, but she smothers it. "I probably should have not." She rubs the back of her neck uneasily. "I do not . . . think of all the things . . . I do not know of all the things I am supposed to know."

YOU MEAN AS PRINCESS?

She glances at the slate and then flings her gaze away, as if the word hurts to look at. She leans against the wall of the house and sighs.

"What in the damn," she says.

I smile.

She frowns. "Swearing is not so fun in another language."

"Mm," I commiserate. I write on the slate. NOT AS FUN IN WRITING, EITHER

Another brief grin, and then another sigh. "I do not know what to do." She waves her hands in her lap. "I think I . . . know myself, understand myself, and then . . . nothing. I know, I understand nothing. Inside of me, there is nothing." She touches her chest, and then pauses with her fingers pressing her shirt. She puzzles at the rain, and then looks sideways to me.

"Maybe you know how that is feeling?"

I nod. "*Uah.*"

"This thing you were, you are not anymore? And cannot get it back?"

"*Uah.*"

She purses her lips.

BUT THAT'S NOT ALL THERE IS, I write. WE'RE ALIVE. YOU HAVE A FAMILY

"I did not want a family," she says—wearily, not angrily. "I do not know how to be in a family. Veran is telling me things about this family, and I—how do I be with them? What are they thinking about me?"

THEY'LL PROBABLY BE SO HAPPY, SO RELIEVED

"Maybe outside. Maybe at first. But after time . . ." She spreads her hands helplessly. "My camp is my family because we understand each other. We have the same history, the same experience. But, *lu'tuw*, we are all breaking apart now. And my . . . new family, blood family . . . I do not understand them—they do not understand me. I have . . . done things." She turns to face me. "I kill people. I attack people—I have attack my own family. I have run away from my family. I have steal things. How am I to be in a good, good, *royal* family?"

I purse my lips in thought, holding her gaze. I turn my chalk in my fingers, and then set it to the slate.

DO YOU PLAN TO KEEP DOING THOSE THINGS ONCE YOU DON'T NEED TO?

She reads my question, slowly. "No. But I still worry. I have still done this things. I cannot change them."

No, that's true. And I'd be naive to argue that a person's past is of no import to their present.

HAVE YOU TALKED TO VERAN ABOUT IT? HE KNOWS THEM

She looks away. "Veran . . . I do not think he understands. Not all the way."

MAYBE NOT. BUT HE CARES ABOUT YOU

She glances at my letters, and then sighs and rubs her eyes, muttering something in Eastern that I don't quite catch.

I flex my wrist again—the fire is starting to flicker up my forearm, needling my elbow. But I have something else I want to say. I just wish I wasn't limited to eight inches of slate to convey it.

HERE IS SOMETHING I'VE LEARNED, FROM MY TIME WITH THE SLAVERS, AND IN COURT:

I let her read, and then wipe it clean.

NOBODY CAN BE FAULTED FOR NOT KNOWING SOMETHING, I write, then erase. IT'S NOT A CRIME TO NOT KNOW EVERYTHING. Erase. THE CRIME COMES WHEN YOU KNOW, BUT DON'T ACT

VERAN DOESN'T KNOW EVERYTHING ABOUT YOU—HE CAN'T

YOU DON'T KNOW EVERYTHING ABOUT HIM
OR HIS WORLD

I DIDN'T KNOW HOW MY EARLY LIFE BENE-
FITED FROM SLAVERY

IANO DIDN'T KNOW HOW THE SYSTEM EX-
PLOITS BOND LABOR

THAT'S OK. IT'S OK NOT TO KNOW

IT JUST MEANS THAT ONCE WE LEARN, WE DO
BETTER

WE WORK TO RIGHT WRONGS WE'VE PROFITED
FROM

WE WORK TO BUILD A WORLD THAT'S BETTER
FOR EVERYONE

THAT COMES FROM GENUINE LOVE

AND I THINK YOUR FAMILY WILL UNDERSTAND

I set down my aching hand, my wrist coated in chalk dust.
Lark stares at my slate, transfixed. I realize I probably used some
words she doesn't know, but I didn't have time to refine them.

She leans back, her face not exactly lighter, but quieter—less
anguished. "You are very smart, Tamsin."

"No'alwaysh," I say.

"Maybe not. But I am thinking a lot of people could be good
to hear those words. Might help some change its minds."

"Hm." I allow a chuckle. "I have a bad mouth an' a bad
wris'. You thell everyone for me."

"Bad wrist?"

I roll my right wrist, grimacing at the pain.

"You cannot write a lot?"

I shake my head. "From bon' work."

"Oh. That is too bad. I am sorry." She gives a dark, humorless laugh. "I am wishing we could trade—you take my talking and go be princess."

"Pff," I snort, picking up my chalk. AND YOU CAN JUST BE A SILENT HERMIT IN THE WOODS?

"It is sounding like a good idea, *uah*."

I laugh, and she does, too. She digs in the cloth for another meat pie. Rat lifts his head. She breaks it in half and gives him a piece. We go quiet, listening to the rain hushing through the soaring boughs and the peeping of frogs down in the ferns. She savors the meat pie, eating it more slowly than the others and licking her fingers once she's done.

"I am sorry I run away," she says.

I don't know if she means tonight, or last week. IT'S OKAY. THERE'S BEEN A LOT OF BIG CHANGES

"*Uah*." She sighs. "Veran is okay?"

"*Uah*." HE SAT UP FOR YOU FOR A WHILE. FELL ASLEEP JUST BEFORE YOU CAME BACK

"I wish he is sleeping good. When he is tired it makes him worse—his thing I tell you about, the fast shaking. *Lu'tuw*, I don't know how your word is."

SEIZURE, I write. I'VE READ ABOUT THEM

"Oh?" She raises her eyebrows. "Anything to make them better?"

I scrunch my lips. NOT THAT I'VE SEEN

She goes silent again, a more profound silence than the easy quiet a moment ago. Her gaze is unfocused, neither here nor there.

"I am tired," she finally says.

I nod. Wrapping my blanket back around my shoulders, I stand. She hands me my slate.

"Tamsin—thank you," she says. "For talking with me. I am

not so angry as I am before. I am only . . ." Her lips move sound-lessly, as if searching for a word, in either language, and finding none appropriate. "Tired," she finishes. "I am very, very tired."

"*Uah.*" More tired than just a late night's tired. More tired than just a day's ride tired. Life tired. World tired. I understand. I reach down and squeeze her shoulder.

"Have a goo' nigh," I say.

"*Uah*, you, too." She kicks off her boots and lies down on the quilt with the air of someone used to sleeping on hard ground. Rat wriggles until he's sprawled against her legs.

Quietly, I pass back into the house, tiptoeing among the others sleeping in the workshop. I slither back down against Iano, who curls against me but doesn't wake.

Veran shifts in sleep, nudging the big press. I stare at its sil-houette in the darkness, its big arm and stained clamp. I listen to Iano's soft breathing, to Veran's quiet snores, to the rain and frogs outside.

I'm glad Lark and I could ease the tension between us. But I'm not as relieved as I should be. Following me from the porch is the realization that I've finally put into concrete words what exactly my future consists of.

A silent hermit in the woods.

I wrote the words to make her laugh, but they crowd in on me now. I can't lie to myself. If Lark wanted to trade, I would happily switch fates with her. The title of princess may terrify her, but I would take it in a heartbeat—not for the gilded society she's worried about, but for the platform it comes with. A posi-tion of influence, with the power to change.

A position with a voice.

VERAN

I'm the last one awake. Rubbing my eyes, I lift my head and realize I'm alone in the workroom. The dappled morning sun streams through the window.

I scramble to my feet, wincing at my stiff neck. The door to the kitchen is closed—from beyond comes the sound of murmuring. I stumble toward it and find the others sitting around the table with empty breakfast dishes in front of them.

Everyone except Lark, that is. My eyes sweep the room once, wondering if she's holed up in a corner, when Tamsin sees my look. She points toward the window.

"Outside?" I ask.

She nods and mimes a swinging motion, like an ax. From the yard, I hear the faint chop of a metal head hitting wood.

"Splitting wood?" I repeat. "Why is she—"

"She said she wanted to," Iano says. "I expect it was an excuse to get out of the house. Are you still planning to come into town with us?"

"Yes. Have you asked Lark?"

"She wants to stay," Iano says. "It'd be too dangerous for her to come in with the new bounty posters up, anyway. She's asked for a sword, though it's going to be hard to find one. She turned up her nose when I offered my rapier. She called it a word I didn't recognize—*otieni,* I think."

I smile. "Toothpick."

"Hmph." He maintains a princely facade, though Tamsin grins. "Well, she wouldn't take it."

"She's used to a broadsword." I look at Tamsin. "Are you sure you're ready to be here with . . . just her?"

She nods and waves a hand. "We're goo'," she says with conviction.

I take a small sip of air. It's not that I don't believe Tamsin— but I want to hear it from Lark. I can't think what could have changed in the short time between last night and this morning to make Lark move past the realization that Tamsin used to scribe for slavers.

"I'm going to talk to her," I say.

"Here, eat something," Soe says, handing me a sticky bun studded with walnuts. "We'll leave once we clean up."

I thank her and head out onto the porch. It's an absolutely gorgeous morning, cool and damp, the sun filtering through the mists hanging between the trees. Birdsong rings through the lower branches. I pick out the clear call of a meadowlark before again hearing the telltale crack of an ax head in wood. I descend the porch and round the house to the woodshed.

My steps slow as I near the splitting log. Despite the cool of the morning, Lark has stripped off her shirt, wearing only her breast band. I remind myself that I've seen her in less than that at our first real meeting in Three Lines, but nonetheless I try to focus on the glint of the ax head as it arcs downward, splicing easily through a short length of hardwood. Rat jumps up at my approach, brushy tail wagging eagerly. I scratch him behind the ears, keeping my bun out of his reach, and clear my throat.

Lark looks up, the ax above her head, the sunlight gleaming off her ropy muscles. I expect I could count every ridge lining her stomach, but I'm not going to because I am going to focus on her eyes. I am *intensely* focused on her eyes.

That doesn't exactly help though—she has nice eyes.

Really nice eyes. The sunlight makes them gold.

She lowers the ax. "Hey."

"Hi, hey," I begin, too loudly. I clear my throat again. "How, uh, how did you sleep?"

"Pretty good, actually. It's nice listening to the rain without being stuck out in it. What about you?"

"Good, yeah, good." I gesture to the bun. "Did you eat?"

"Plenty. We've been up for a while." She leans on the ax. "You're going into town with the others?"

"Yeah, if that's okay."

"I'm still not convinced it's a smart idea, but the others don't think anybody will recognize you or Iano, and Soe can't purchase everything we need while she's selling at her table." She straightens from the ax and lifts it again. "Besides, I have a job for you."

"A job?" My nerves fray a little more—I can't get a read on her this morning, and it's unclear whether she's going to request I do something helpful or direct me off the nearest cliff.

The sunlight on her bare skin isn't making things any

clearer. Since that first conversation in Three Lines, I had for-gotten about the howling coyote tattooed on her rib cage. I can barely think of anything else now as it ripples when she brings the ax down to quarter the hardwood she's working on.

Eyes.

"Yeah." She tosses the quarter onto the pile. "Keep your eyes open. Check the town sign boards, listen to the gossip. Maybe there will be something that could help us. News, or mention of Port Iskon. *Somebody* has to know where it is, even if the prince and Tamsin don't."

I don't miss her use of the word *us*. We're a team again. A flush warms my stomach.

"I will. And, Lark . . . about last night. I'm sorry I didn't make it clear about Tamsin . . . I didn't really think about it . . ."

"Oh, the *shock*," she exclaims, and to my utter surprise, she smiles. It's fast—a flash, quick as a bird wing, and then it's gone. She shakes her head. "The number of things you don't think about could fill a book."

"I won't deny it," I say, trying to contain my surprise at her easy mood. "But I'm thinking about things now, and I just want to be sure you're okay with being here—"

"We're good," she says with conviction, echoing Tamsin. "We had a chance to talk, as much as we could with my crappy language and her crappy mouth. I'm not as mad as I was before."

"No?"

"No." She places another log on the block and hoists the ax again. "She may have made a stupid mistake—one that made things worse for a lot of people—but then . . ." She swings the ax down. "So have I. Way more than one, in fact. At least *she* didn't know what she was getting herself into." She jerks the ax head out of the splitting block.

I think quietly of her campmates, the ones she's lost—Pickle, in the wagon chase. Rose buried back in Three Lines. My thoughts travel east, toward Callais. The rest of her campmates must be almost there by now, if everything has gone all right. Rou and Eloise are probably only a few days behind them—if the worst hasn't happened to them, either.

"I'd argue that you didn't know, either," I say, and if my voice was louder than I meant it to be before, it comes out too quietly now.

"I knew enough, and I made bad choices anyway." She stares at the now-empty splitting block, the ax drooping in her hands. "Over and over again. I did my best to get the easy ones back home—Bitty and Arana and all the rest. But I didn't even make an effort with the rest. Lila, and Rose, and Little Whit . . . Saiph. Pickle. They needed things I couldn't give them, but I kept choosing Three Lines. I kept telling myself they were better off with me than out in the world."

"It *wasn't your fault*," I insist. "The world hasn't made itself an easy thing for you to trust. You can't blame yourself."

She shakes herself. "Well, I'm gonna, and I'd like to see you try and stop me."

I draw myself up, matching her brassy tone. "Challenge accepted."

She tilts the ax in her hands, just an inch. The head dips into a patch of the slanting morning sunlight and beams a flash of it into my eyes. Unprepared, I jerk my head and swear. She grins. In retaliation, I toss the last two bites of my sticky bun at her, which she deflects easily with the ax handle. Rat lunges for the fallen pastry and inhales it.

Lark laughs then—not a snort, an honest-to-goodness laugh. I quit rubbing my eyes to watch, stopping just short of actually gawking. Her laugh sounds like Eloise's—if you maybe dropped it an octave and roughed it around the edges. It's warm and bright, like the flashes of sunlight she throws around.

"Wasting food." She shakes her head, still grinning—this is a record. "I keep telling you. You're a *terrible* outlaw."

I return her grin, my brain tripping over itself to think of something funny to say back, something to make her laugh again. But I'm too slow—over my shoulder, I hear the cabin door open.

"Veran! Are you ready?"

Suddenly I don't want to go into town. What worthwhile thing will there be in town, anyway? At the moment, it seems much more pressing to stay right here at Soe's splitting block and make Lark laugh again.

Her grin has melted away, though hints of it remain in the rounds of her cheeks. She jerks her chin over my shoulder. "You'd better go on—they could probably use help hitching the cart."

Reluctantly, I turn. Fat lot of help I'll be—I've never hitched a cart myself.

"Veran—hang on."

I look back.

Lark sets the ax head on the block and wipes her forehead. She opens her mouth, and then hesitates. First a laugh, now a hesitation. I raise my eyebrow. She sees the expression and shakes herself.

"Look, what I'm trying to say . . . because, see, I'm trying to be less mean."

"Less mean?" I ask, bewildered.

"Yeah, you know, just . . ." She gestures vaguely to herself, her skin dewed with sweat and mist over her muscles. "What I meant to say a second ago was, thanks. For getting them out. My camp. I keep thinking about what would have happened if they'd all been there when the soldiers came."

"I should have asked you first," I say.

"I'd have said no, on principle," she says. "That was well before I trusted you."

"Which suggests that you trust me now," I say, hoping for a laugh again.

I don't get one. She nods. "Well, yeah."

The answer hovers between us for a moment. That warmth I was feeling in my stomach blooms into fireworks, snapping and crackling around my rib cage.

"Veran!" Iano calls again.

"I've never hitched a cart," I blurt out to her. I point toward Soe's tiny paddock. "I've only ever seen it done."

She rolls her eyes and gives one of her usual snorts. She sets down her ax, picks up her shirt, and starts to move past me. When she's in range, she reaches out, grabs a handful of my hair, and gives my head a little shake.

"Knucklehead," she says. She lets go and bumps my arm. "Come on."

I follow her. Her shoulder blades bunch together as she works her arms through her sleeves. Before she flips the shirt over her shoulders, I see a tattoo I've missed before—a bird on her right shoulder, vaguely larkish with its dark collar and long open beak. I want to ask her who gave it to her, and when. Who gave her the others? When did she decide she needed them inked into her skin? And—are there more I haven't seen?

I want to see them.

I want to know them all.

LARK

I head back up the steps of Soe's cabin with an armful of split wood. The last creakings of the mule harnesses are being swallowed by the giant trees and dense ferns, along with the sight of Veran bobbing in the back, his face turned toward the cabin. Iano looked back several times, too, probably hoping to make his final words to me stick.

"I appreciate you staying here with Tamsin, Princess," he'd said. I'd ground my teeth against the honorific but didn't say anything. "Try to keep her from doing too much. Soe left her with the paper and stamps to make labels, but she doesn't have to do them if she doesn't want to. If it seems like she's tiring, try to get her to rest."

I'm not her nanny, I wanted to say. *She's a grown woman—she can make her own decisions.* But I just waved him away, perhaps a little more curtly than I should have, and headed back to the woodpile while Veran hurriedly called good-bye.

Now they're gone, and they'll be gone all day. I push open

the cabin door with my hip and bring the load of wood inside. Tamsin is sitting at the kitchen table, turning one of the stamps in her fingers. A piece of rag paper sits in front of her, blank.

She offers me a smile when I come in.

"Hi," I return, unloading my wood into the rack.

She leans forward and taps the table next to a plate of left-over walnut buns. A pitcher of that piney *urch* tea sits beside it. I can't get used to this—the idea of just eating whenever one feels like it. This morning, Soe apologized to me for not having butter for the buns. I'd just stared at her blankly. What ordinary person eats butter? In Three Lines, we were lucky to have grease left in the pan to mix into our cornmeal.

"Thanks." I brush off my hands and take a seat. I pour myself a cup of tea. Tamsin offers honey, but I wave it away. We sit for a moment in silence. I curl my fingers around the hot mug.

Tamsin sets her chin gingerly in her hand and regards the sheets of blank paper. She nudges one of the stamps, with *tul* burned on the back. There's a set of other words—*walnut* and *oil* and *huckleberry*—plus a tray of individual letters that can each fit into the slot of a wooden handle to form new words.

Tamsin glumly inks the *tul* stamp, rocking it into a leather pad coated with sticky ink, and presses it to the paper. It leaves a perfect imprint behind.

She sets the stamp down. Clearly, stamping labels is not what she'd like to be doing at the moment. Despite my irritated thoughts about Iano, I ask her if she's tired.

She shakes her head, her brow furrowing.

I cast around, trying to think how normal people who do normal things like sip tea whenever they feel like it might act toward a friend.

"You play the dulcimer. Yes?" I ask.

She nods, her chin still in her hand.

"You want to play now?" Soe had pulled the instrument out of the cedar chest this morning, perhaps to entice Tamsin to play.

But she shakes her head, scrunching her mouth.

"You want to go for a drop?" I ask.

She frowns at me, looking puzzled. I run back through the words I just said.

"Drop," I try again.

She shakes her head and tilts her thumb upward.

"Drop? Dro—*walk*."

She smiles, and then nods, pushing back from the table. I hadn't expected her to agree, but I can't back out now. I get up, too. She limps around the table, clutching the backs of the chairs for support. I offer her my arm to cling to, and we head out the door. Rat jumps up excitedly.

I plan to keep our route short, just accompanying her around the yard, but when we reach the back of Soe's house, Tamsin points down a narrow, ferny path. From this morning, I know it leads to Soe's latrine, so I expect she must need to use it. But when we reach the little shed, Tamsin determinedly tugs my arm, her gaze on the straggly trail beyond it. Wordlessly, I follow, my anxiety building with each step. I hadn't thought we'd go out of sight of the house. I don't have anything with me— not the crossbow, not a canteen, not even my bandanna. Tamsin doesn't have her slate and chalk. But she seems to have a destination in mind, placing her steps purposefully, if not quickly, on the needle-covered ground.

The trees loom over us. The brilliant green bracken crowds

the path. Birds call and swoop through the understory. I've never gone for so long seeing so little sky.

After another five minutes, there's a noticeable change in the forest. The trees, which were already big, swell. Their bark becomes rippled and cracked, some scarred black from past fires. The bracken becomes less thick, unable to find sun in the impenetrable shade. One blow-down lies half-buried in the earth, its exposed girth still twice my height.

The meandering path narrows and disappears just as we enter what must be the heart of the grove, where an incomprehensibly massive redwood stands. It's easily thirty feet around, perhaps more, and its crown disappears into a wreath of mist hundreds of feet above our heads. I tilt my head backward, flabbergasted.

"Cow," Tamsin says, gazing upward, and she grimaces. "Cowy."

"What?"

She rubs her face in frustration, and then gestures to the tree. "Cowy . . . Heg. *Hee . . . eh . . . oh . . . you . . .*"

She gives a little shake of disgust at her inability to even pronounce the letters, and takes my hand. She turns over my palm and traces the letters there instead. I concentrate as hard as I can, first on interpreting the letters she's drawing, then on ordering them in my head, and then on turning them into words.

"Cloudyhead?" I say.

She sighs in relief and nods. She gestures to the tree again.

"That is its name?"

She nods and limps toward the tree. She places her hand on the bark and, one careful step at a time, begins to make her way around its base. I follow her—the bark and roots are buckled and uneven, providing no easy path. But Tamsin persists, slowly circling the tree. I trail my fingers on the rough bark, trying to convince my brain that this thing is growing, alive.

Veran, I think. *Veran* needs to see this.

I remember his astonished rush to show his gratitude in the first few groves we passed through, turning his palms over and offering them out to the trunks, as if giving them a gift. The corner of my lips flicker. I still can't get over the lack of sky, but I'm starting to understand a little better now. It doesn't seem so weird to simply be grateful for such a thing, centuries upon centuries old, burned and broken, but still standing upright.

It takes a few minutes to loop around the tree. When we reach our starting point, we simply stand and stare. Tamsin's hands flutter. I glance at her. She twists her lips.

"I," she begins. She takes a few steps back from the base of the tree. She points to a crook in its roots, carpeted with years of fallen needles.

"I wro'," she says again. She mimes writing in an invisible journal. "A . . . de . . ."

She gestures again, this time to her lips, letting her fingers burst from them. Frustration creases her face. She can't pronounce the *s*.

"Song?" I say.

She nods, and points back to the roots. "Here. The one I play' . . . be . . ." She mimics the strumming of a dulcimer, and then waves hopelessly at herself.

"The one you sang to become *ashoki*?" I ask.

"*Uah*."

I look at the little crook in the roots, and then back up at the soaring trunk. "It is a nice tree." It's a stupid thing to say, especially to a poet in the shadow of the biggest living thing I've ever seen, but other words, particularly in Moquoian, fail me.

She sighs. "*Uah*." She gives the bark another pat, and then turns away. She takes a few steps back up the trail on her own. I hurry to give her my elbow again, and she takes it.

We've gone a few paces when I decide to voice the thought nudging my mind.

"You know," I say. "My friend Arana—she was a slave also, but now she is in Callais—she cannot hear in her ears." I gesture to the sides of my head. "When she is a little girl, she is working in the sand blaster, and the big noise makes her ears go quiet." I hope I'm explaining this well enough, or at least not being offensive. "She talks with her hands."

Tamsin eyes me sideways.

"We have to learn how to see it," I acknowledge. "Rose and me. We have to learn what she is saying. It takes a little time. But it is not so hard, after some practice. It is just normal."

Just Arana. That was when we had Bitty, too, and a slew of little ones—Meissa, Lefty, Clariet, Voss and all his little sisters. It became our typical routine to get all the young kids to sleep and then sit up around the campfire, signing in Arana's language so we didn't wake them. Those were some of the best times— everybody was healthy and reasonably well-fed, thanks to my forays into Snaketown. And we had a destination for the little ones. Voss and his sisters had family in Teso's Ford, and Clariet in Port Juaro. Meissa and Lefty had been stolen from Bitter Springs. Of them all, only Little Whit had nowhere to go, and so with me she stayed. My stomach twists as I remember her slow slide into silence. Now that I think about it, she used to sign with Arana, too, to avoid talking through her cleft lip. I wonder if some of her illness didn't come about because Arana and Bitty left to rejoin their families in Callais once we'd brought the others back home.

I should have made more of an effort to sign with Whit. I hope she's getting the care she needs in Callais, along with the others. Maybe she'll find Arana again, and they can sign together.

"That word, *song*," I say, bringing my thoughts back to Tamsin. I wave my hand back and forth in the motion that always looked like water to me, but that Rose insisted looked like someone conducting music, a phenomenon I've never seen. "This is the sign Arana is using for song. And for write . . ."

"*Uah*," Tamsin suddenly says firmly, cutting me off. She looks pointedly away from me.

I fall silent. My hand stills in the air, and then I drop it.

I've made her mad. My face heats, and I curse myself for prattling about something she doesn't want to hear. We walk, our footsteps muffled on the needles. The trees shrink from monstrous to simply massive as we leave the grove of giants behind.

As we near the latrine, Tamsin halts. I stop with her. Her breath hitches, and she covers her face with her hands. Through her fingers come a few muffled sobs.

I blanch—I've never known what to do with someone crying. I could handle the little ones in camp all right, but facing someone my own age or older leaves me perplexed. But Tamsin doesn't give me the chance to wonder what to do—she simply turns into my shoulder, her palms over her face, her shoulders shaking. I give her a few awkward pats.

It passes. Her crying slows. She leans back, red-faced, and waves a hand.

"You are okay?" I ask.

She nods and wipes her eyes with the corner of her sleeve. Gathering her skirt, she crouches down and brushes the ground to clear the redwood needles, then traces her finger through the dirt. She writes some letters and looks up at me.

I get the feeling she's trying to tell me something important, but I can't make sense of the lines in the dirt.

"Sorry, I cannot understand?"

She nods at me, gestures inexplicably. We both pause. I give her a look of trepidation. She clears the ground again and tries to write more clearly. But I'm terrible enough at reading Eastern, let alone Moquoian—even last night, reading the letters on her slate made my head ache. It takes several more tries of writing, rewriting, and gesturing for me to understand what she's asking me.

WHAT IS THE SIGN FOR SORRY?

"Oh." I rack my brain, trying to remember those times around the campfire. We didn't apologize to each other a lot. I pore back over the language Arana used, dredging up half-forgotten signs. Finally I recall the time she dropped a full bucket of water onto the campfire, engulfing us in clouds of smoke and steam. When our coughing finally let up, it turned into laughter.

Sorry, she'd signed, her laugh overly loud and lovely. *Sorry*.

I form a fist and rub my chest in a circle.

"Sorry," I say.

She repeats the gesture, once to mimic the motion, and a second time while looking me in the eyes.

"It's okay," I say.

Her hand drops from her chest, unfurling in a manner I recognize. It's not exactly the same as Arana's gesture for thanks, but it's a perfect copy of Veran's.

"You're welcome," I say.

She nods and clears away the last traces of tears from her cheeks. She points up toward the cabin, just peeking through the boughs. Without waiting for me to offer my arm, she starts back up the path.

TAMSIN

The walk to and from Cloudyhead has left me shaky and exhausted, but the inspiration that came from Lark's attempts buoys me up the steps. Once inside, I wolf down a walnut bun and half a cup of *urch* tea, and then I drop back down with the stamps and papers. Lark follows after telling Rat to stay on the porch. She takes a walnut bun with the same kind of sneak-thievery as last night and sits down opposite me.

Soe's blank stamp block is small, but big enough for me to cram on the letters I want. I fix them the way I want them, then rock them over the sticky ink pad. Lark watches as I press the block to the paper.

YOU HELP ME SIGN

I pop out the letters and slide in the next ones. There are only two of each letter, making repetition a challenge. Writing would be easier, but my wrist needles me, and I want to test this method. I stamp again.

I HELP YOU READ

I look at her. She raises her eyebrows in surprise and shrugs.

"If that is what you want. I am not sure Arana's signs are ones everyone uses. And it is maybe different in Eastern and Moquoian. But I can show you the ones I am remembering."

I nod and gesture for her to watch, hoping she'll catch on. I make the fist she showed me earlier and circle it on my chest. Then I push the stamps toward her.

She frowns, staring, and my hopes sink. I jump to try to explain.

"You pick . . ." I point to the stamps, but she waves at me.

"I understand. But I have to . . ." She taps her head. "Go from Eastern to Moquoian. I am not so fast as Veran. Give me a time."

"Ah." I nod and sit back. She studies the stamps, then selects a few and slides them into the block. She inks it and presses it to the paper.

SORY

I take the block from her, pop out the *y*, add an extra *r*, and slide the *y* back in. She stamps it again.

SORRY

I nod. I gesture for the block back and change out the letters. I stamp them for her to read.

SUN

She grins almost immediately—she knows this one. She cups her hand and hangs it above her head, moving it in an arc like a sunrise. I copy her.

We dive forward. At first, we have no discernable strategy beyond taking turns. Sometimes she stamps a word, I correct the spelling, and then she gives me the sign. Sometimes I stamp a word, she tells me what it is, and then gives me the sign. Sometimes we point at an object. Sometimes she gives me only a sign and I have to guess. When she doesn't know the sign, I stamp it on another piece of paper to learn later. When she doesn't know the translation, and if gestures fail, we put it on a third piece of paper to ask Veran.

At first, we choose things within sight and easy to understand with this patchwork language. *Cup. Fire. Paper. Table. Sword. Tattoo. Eyes.* After a while, I begin signing back to her, to be sure I'm remembering them—she reverses the process and stamps the word I'm giving her. We delve into harder, more ephemeral words. *Please. Give. Time. Music. Strong. Love.* She shows me fingerspelling, giving me the alphabet to spell out signs I don't know. We spend almost two hours on that alone, practicing until I can reliably call up the letters I need. I know it's not going to stick—I'm going to be practicing in my sleep, feeling these signs in my dreams. But I'm too excited to slow down. I press her to show me how to string words together into sentences. I learn to drop articles, to rearrange words, to corral an unruly phrase into a succinct gesture. *What is your name* becomes *name you*? *How do I sign that* becomes *how sign* and a point.

It's visual poetry.

I realize it as she shows me the differences between *should* and *must*—the same gesture, only with different emphasis and expression. It's lyrical, it's theatric, it's a thousand times more nuanced than I thought it could be. My excitement builds. I'd considered the idea of hand signing during the long, dismal hours in my cell, but only briefly. At the time, I told myself it was because I didn't know anyone who knew the language. There was a scribe in my parents' office who was deaf, and one of the mail couriers in Tolukum Palace was, as well. But I expect the first is dead now, and the courier nearly as unreachable in our current state. But this wasn't the only reason I couldn't bear the thought of signing for long. Dwelling on the concept made me feel the same way Lark's casual offering did on the trail back from Cloudyhead. I didn't mean to turn her down so sharply, but the more she talked, the more it felt like the linchpin in my fate. The truth. That my tongue doesn't work, and won't work again. That verbal speech is out of my reach forever.

It was an ungracious reaction, and I hope she understands that I'm sorry for it. I repeat that word, the first sign, *sorry*, several times, until she finally counters with *it's okay*. Then she grins and gives me a string of satisfying curses that I can easily imagine being tossed around her campfire.

We continue well into the afternoon, until we've filled nearly all the paper on the table and the plate of sticky buns has been polished off. I could keep going, but eventually she groans and rubs her temples.

"No more," she says, laughing. "It is more words than I have ever read." I brighten—already her tenses are getting better. "I am not so smart for all this."

I laugh and repeat her word back to her, one she showed me an hour ago. *You are smart.* Damn, it feels good to have the letter *s* back!

She shakes her head and rises from the table. "Not enough for this. If we ever fix things in Moquoia and in the East"—she gives me the signs for both places as she says them— "you should meet my friend Arana. She shows you them much better."

Maybe. But you are a good—

I flounder. She hasn't shown me *teacher*. I fingerspell it instead, asking for the sign. Lark screws up one eye in thought, first arranging my letters in her head, figuring out what Moquoian word I'm spelling, and then translating it into Eastern.

She shakes her head. "Teacher. I don't know the sign."

You are a good one, I insist.

"Well, you had a good idea. This is smart." She taps the stamps. "Makes me think of the letters better. If the block was bigger, we can write longer sentences."

Need more stamps, I suggest.

"True." She stretches her arms toward the ceiling, popping a few joints. "With enough you can write a whole page. You can write out all those smart things you are telling me last night. *Stamp, stamp, stamp*—put them on lots of paper and let everybody read them." She laughs at her own joke.

I smile. Then, in the blink of an eye, it slides away, and I'm left staring.

Stamp, stamp, stamp.

I reach across the table and pick up the block, studying it more closely. It's such a simple tool, just a length of wood with grooves to hold the letters.

Make it a little longer, have multiple sets of letters, and you could write a complex sentence.

Make it bigger, add more grooves, and you could write a whole *page*.

And then—and *then*—you could *change the page*.

A buzz jolts through me, prickling the short hairs on my scalp.

Woodcuts are normal. Woodcuts have been normal for hundreds of years. Carve a picture or a set of words backward, ink them, and press them to parchment. It's slow work, unadaptable.

Mess up a block, want to change a word, and you have to start over. Scribing, especially on the scale my parents worked, is faster and more flexible.

But what if you could *change the letters*?

Lark drops her arms from her stretch. "Lunch?" she asks. She signs the word to me. "Soe says there is cheese in the dairy jar."

I stand up, knocking the table. The stamps rattle.

"Hey," I say.

"Hey," she repeats, raising her eyebrows.

My brain is turning. I hold up the block.

Do you think, I sign, stumbling back over words we just spent hours learning. Even with all that work, I don't have enough words. I muss around on the tabletop, but we've used every scrap of paper. I unearth my slate from the pile.

DO YOU THINK THAT KIND OF STAMPING COULD BE DONE? I write.

"What kind?" she asks.

MANY STAMPS ON A BIG BLOCK, THAT YOU COULD STAMP MANY TIMES? SENTENCES? PARA-GRAPHS?

She scratches her head. "It can probably work, *uah*? Though . . ." She mimics pressing down. "A block so big . . . it will be hard to ink, hard to press. Hard to get all the letters down. Actually tough work, I think, to press that big block over and over."

She's right. I look at our paper again, riddled with patchy words where the ink wasn't strong enough, or where one of us didn't press hard enough. Smudges where the paper shifted, misshapen letters where the stamps wiggled in their grooves. It

would be hard to press a page-size block full of individual letters and still make it readable.

"Need a giant arm," she says, laughing again. She flexes and
palms her bicep.

My mouth drops open.

A giant *arm*.

To *press with*.

"Ah!" I shriek.

Lark jumps. "What?"

I hurtle from the table, knocking a leg and sending papers
flying into the air. Ignoring them, I lunge for the workroom. I
kick aside the blankets we all slept in last night and swoop down
on the big press.

"Tamsin, what is it?" Lark follows me to the door.

I turn just long enough to sign something she showed me.
Hot damn!

"Hot damn?" she repeats.

I drag out the heavy wooden arm that fits into the screw of
the big press. I hoist it over my head like a trophy.

"Ah!" I shriek again.

Her face widens. "Hot damn!"

Then it's just yelling.

We just yell.

VERAN

Giantess Township is teeming on market day. The town proper is set in a grove of redwoods, dominated on one end by the Giantess herself, a tree so tall the top becomes blue and hazy even without a mist. Turquoise streamers stretch from the trunk—Soe tells me the color is changed to coordinate with each month's new *si*.

In the center of town is a large clearing, left when one of the massive trees must have fallen. Its stump remains in the middle of the town square, set over with boards to form a central stage. Soe explains that most of the time, the stage is free for public use, but on market days, merchants can rent it out to sell their wares. Right now, it's being dominated by a stock tender auctioning off goats.

Most of the other stalls are set up around the periphery, selling everything from candles to quilts to briny crocks of seaweed. Only a few vendors look permanent—a blacksmith's shop pouring acrid smoke, a furnace boiling molasses, and a small mill. The rest of the stalls are cloth or canvas stretched over temporary frames, some right off the backs of carts. Soe sets up her awning under a redwood with a split trunk, and almost immediately, people materialize to purchase a quart of walnut oil or to bring goods for her to press. Soon she hands Iano and me a bag jingling with crescents and coppers, along with a list of the things we need at the cabin. Shouldering an empty hamper, we set off into the crowds.

The food stalls are teeming with summer produce, and we fill the hamper with knobby squashes, meaty orange mushrooms, and baskets of plump berries. While we stand in line at the dairy stall, we hear a woman buying the same number of squashes we did for half the price. Iano frowns.

"We've been marked as newcomers," I remark.

He looks down at the copper coins in his palm, stamped with an approximation of his profile.

"It *is* my first time in the market," he says. "Yours?"

"Sort of. If my parents or siblings want to visit the market, a special afternoon is cleared for them, and a squadron of the Palace Guard makes a perimeter. Vendors would never overcharge the king and queen, even though they're the most able to afford it. My ma always overpays."

He turns a few of the coins. "We don't go into the city much, and when we do, it's always in litters lined with mosquito netting. But I remember my grandmother saying they used to go a lot when she was a child, often to visit the soup kitchens. They stopped once the fever started to climb."

I can't help myself. "You mean once the palace atriums were built?"

"And all your little birds started hitting the glass, *uah*," he says, matching my barbed tone, but his gaze is still serious, on the coins. After a moment, he closes his fist on them. "I guess . . . I never really thought about how that might have impacted relations between the monarchy and the populace."

I open my mouth to reply, but I cut off abruptly. The woman standing in line in front of us has turned her head—as if listening. Iano sees my frozen expression and glances, too. He goes still and silent. I realize how loudly we were speaking.

There's a long, awkward pause as the woman waits for the dairy maid to fill her order. The very edge of her face is visible, enough to see that her eyelid is twisted and lashless with a faint scar. We try to stand nonchalantly and act as if we weren't just chatting about our lives as pampered princes. After a long, breathless moment, the customer collects her goods, pays her fee, and moves away, giving us room to conduct our business.

When we finally make it back to Soe's table, her stock is almost gone and her coin box is rattling.

"Where have you *been*?" she asks. "I thought you'd be back an hour ago."

"We're market beginners," I say, setting down the hamper. "Took us a while."

"Well, give me your change, and I'll see how much more you need—"

"Uh, no change," Iano says.

Soe tosses up her hands. "What'd you do, let every granny swindle you? *Colors.*" She opens her coin box and counts out a few handfuls of crescents. "Here—you're going to need to split up, if we want goods of any quality. Iano, why don't you go to the herbalist, she's over there by the well. Veran, you go get the blankets and clothes. Most of the clothiers are by the stage. If someone asks about your accent, just say you're from the islands."

With some trepidation, we do as she says, splitting up. I poke through the coins in my hand, trying to orient myself. Despite my grasp on the language, I haven't had to spend much Moquoian coin, and the rate is different from Common Eastern silvers. I spy the quilter and head her way, trying not to look like an easy target.

It goes better than I expected, as does the men's clothier, where I buy a few changes of clothes for Iano and myself. I'm tripped up at the dressmaker, not sure how to estimate Tamsin's size. I choose two that look like they'll be short enough for her, and then move to the women's work shirts and trousers.

"What size are you looking for?" the vendor asks.

"Uh . . ." I stare at the shirts, suddenly realizing what I'm doing. Picturing a garment to go over Tamsin was one thing. Picturing one to go over Lark . . . I'm hit suddenly with the memory of this morning, of the muscles bunching and sliding under her bare skin, her shoulder blades drawing together.

I break into a cold sweat.

"Well?" the vendor asks.

My gaze falls on a pile of vests, not unlike the one she ripped off in Tellman's Ditch to make a firebomb. A glint of thread peeks out from a fold, and I shift a few aside to get a better look.

"That one," I say, pointing. The vendor pulls it out, and I can't help it—I grin. I couldn't have found something better if I'd commissioned it myself. As blue as any Lumeni flag, the vest has golden embroidery on either side of the lapel, bursting outward like unmistakable sun rays. The buttons flash bronze, like her eyes.

"Definitely that one," I say.

"It'll cost you," the vendor warns.

"I don't care. I'll take it," I say. "And two long-sleeved shirts—those'll do."

She wraps up my picks and charges me a whopping seven crescents for the bundle, but I couldn't care less. I pile my finds with the quilt and turn away from the stall, satisfied. I poke down the final row of stalls, rounding out my purchases with several pairs of stockings and a few handkerchiefs. Hefting the massive quantity of cloth in my arms, I'm about to pass by the last vendor when I see what his wares are.

Hats.

Most are straw sunhats, but there's a small selection of broad-brimmed leather hats. EASTERN DESERT HATS, GENUINE ALCORAN LEATHER, says the sign beside them. My gaze falls on one sitting above the others, a handsome work of brown-and-white patch cowhide. At first glance, it looks too large, but then I remember how big Lark's old black hat was to fit over her dreadlocks.

"I'd like that hat, please," I say.

The hatter looks me up and down. "That's twelve crescents."

"I'll take it for seven." I only have eight left, plus a few odd coppers. *Please sell it for seven.* I could always go back to Soe and see if she's made any last sales today, but something tells me both she and Iano wouldn't technically approve of this purchase.

"The hide in that hat alone is worth nine," the hatter says, disapproving. "If you can't do better than twelve, you can move along." He looks over my shoulder at a customer drifting up behind me.

"No! Um . . ." I shift my pile of cloth onto his table, which makes him *tsk* in disapproval. "No, here. I can do eight crescents, and this." I dig in my pocket for the laurel-flower medallion, the one I hacked off my boot in the water scrape. I hold it toward the vendor.

"That's genuine Silverwood silver," I say. "Not sterling. It's worth another eight crescents, at least."

The hatter blinks in surprise, perhaps at my desperation to buy his hat. He takes the medallion and turns it over, studying it. I watch, drumming my fingers anxiously.

"Very well," he says, rubbing his thumb over the metal. "Eight crescents, and this silver piece."

Victorious, I hand him the rest of the money. He lifts the hat from its stand and rests it on top of my bundle. I breathe in the scent of clean leather. I gather it all up and turn.

Then I stop short.

The customer standing right behind me is the same woman who was in front of us at the dairy stall, the one with the scar twisting her eyelid. I stare at her. She stares back. Her eyes narrow.

"Desert hats are selling real good right now," the vendor comments behind me. "Thanks to that Sunshield Bandit. You from out East? Is that where you got foreign silver?"

I swallow but don't turn back to face him, still holding the gaze of the woman. "No," I say with what I hope is conviction and not fear. "The islands."

And then, without another pause, I step around the customer and walk away as fast as I can without appearing to be running. I start to head back toward Soe's cart, but veer off at the last second—if the woman is watching me leave, I don't want to make it too easy for her to find me again. Instead, I circle toward the central stage built over the redwood trunk.

The stock tender has been replaced by a chemist hawking some miracle cure to a small crowd. I sidle around the edge of the stage. There's a signboard tacked with adverts and notices, flanked by a few little saplings springing from the base of the long-dead tree. I shuffle close to them to screen myself from view and draw a few breaths.

"Hey!"

I start at the quick shout.

A man is at the signboard, tacking up a new piece of parchment. He takes the nails out of his mouth and angrily brandishes his hammer at me. "Get off the roots!"

"S—sorry?"

"Get off the damned roots! Where were you raised, under a rock? Have some respect for your environment!"

I look down, where I'm standing in the space between two small redwood saplings. Their roots crisscross under my feet.

"Oh—sorry." I step sideways, rattled. The man shakes his head, hammers a final nail in the board, and then moves off, muttering about soil compaction and careless youths.

I lean against the signboard, taking a few deep breaths. The bundle in my arms is getting heavier by the second—I need to get back to Soe. Hopefully I can cross through the crowded square without being picked out by that woman with the eye twist.

Maybe I'm just imagining things. It *is* market day after all—

why should it be unusual to bump into the same person at two different stalls? Maybe she needed a new hat. That's all. Maybe she didn't actually hear me chatting about palace life with Iano in my accented Moquoian at the dairy stand. Maybe she didn't hear me boasting about Silverwood silver to the hatter.

I swallow.

We should get going.

I pick myself off the signboard. At the last second, I remember Lark's suggestion to check the news, and I skim the notices on the board.

My gaze is drawn immediately to her bounty sheet, and I suck in my breath. Iano and Soe hadn't exaggerated. Two hundred crescents, dead or alive, plus an extra fifty for accomplices. Still, the portrait is out of date. Lark doesn't have her sword and buckler, or her big black hat and eyeblack anymore. Next to hers is Tamsin's, but it's partially hidden by a newer sheet, one of many with the same bold text riffling in the breeze.

My jaw drops.

COME OUT TO WITNESS
TOLUKUM'S NEWEST ASHOKI
KIMELA NOVARNI
ON HER
DEBUT CIRCUIT

Below it is a list of town names and the dates of each performance. Giantess Township is in the middle of the pack, listed for *Mokonnsi* 31—the last day of August. The day before Iano was originally supposed to be crowned—and Kimela officially instated as *ashoki* with him. What's she doing on a debut tour the week before?

I whip my head around. The man who just tacked up the notices is standing in front of the stage with the crowd, listening to the hawker shouting about his miracle tonic. I rip one of the pages from the board, stuff it in my tunic, and hurry his way.

"Excuse me," I say breathlessly. He turns to face me and frowns. "That notice you just put up—about the *ashoki*. Where did it come from?"

"From the printer's, didn't it?" he says in irritation.

"No, but I mean—where did the news come from? Tolukum? Who gave the order to put them up?"

"The palace," he says. "A messenger brought the woodblock this morning."

"Did the order come from the queen?"

He shrugs. "I 'spect so. The royal seal is right there at the bottom. It's not up to me to nose about palace orders." He squints at me. "You're not from these parts, are you?"

Too late, I see the woman with the eye twist standing a few paces away, looking up at the stage with a faraway expression, as if not actually focused on the hawker's presentation.

I clamp my arms tighter around my bundle, and without another word, turn and rush back across the square, not caring whether I've come across as rude. I weave in and out of buyers and sellers, children and carts, until I spy Soe's stall. She and Iano are just finishing breaking down the table. They both look up as I join them, panting and sweaty.

"Where have you *been*?" Soe demands. "We thought you'd been mugged."

"We need to go," I gasp, flinging my bundle into the cart. "There's someone following me around—that woman who was listening to us in the dairy line, Iano. And that's not all. Kimela will be coming through Giantess on a debut tour in just a few days. She's been appointed *ashoki* without you."

Iano's face pales. "*What?* When? By whom?"

"I don't know. I have the notice here. Let's get on the road, and I'll show you."

We rush to get the last of the goods packed into the back of the cart. I keep looking over my shoulder, expecting to see the scarred woman materialize from the crowd. But she doesn't appear. Soe rouses the mules, hitches them back to the cart, and guides them out into the busy causeway. Iano and I hop into the cart, he into the seat and I into the back. I wriggle down between the hamper of groceries and the pile of clothes, trying to keep my head low as Soe drives the team through the crowds. I chew my lip, pondering what the appointment of the *ashoki* means—for us, for Tamsin, for Moquoia, for the East, for our doomed alliance. *Ashoki*, after all, is a lifetime appointment.

After several minutes of lurching, the towering trees start to close in over us again. The clamor of the market fades away, replaced by the squeaking of the cart and the call of birds in the distant branches. I lean my head against the balled-up quilt, staring at the sky peeking through the dark boughs. Between the stuffy glass interior of Tolukum Palace and the blazing, wide-open Ferinno Desert, I've forgotten how much I miss being cradled in trees. I breathe through some of the tight apprehension in my chest.

Iano turns in his seat. "All right. What's this about Kimela?"

"Here's all I know," I say, handing him the crumpled notice from my tunic. "The fellow who put it up said the woodblock came from the palace this morning."

Iano takes it, but he hesitates before turning around to read it.

"What is *that*?" he asks, laying eyes on the patch cowhide hat.

"A risk," I say. "But I'm beginning to think it was a good one."

"What does that mean?"

"I'm not sure yet," I admit. "But I think I might have a plan."

TAMSIN

I'm standing on tiptoes to hang the latest sheet over the rafters to dry when Rat starts barking. Lark lunges from her place at the table, swathed in a drift of wood shavings, and unearths the crossbow from a pile of papers. By the time she has it free of wood shavings and the crank wound, the door has swung open, and Soe stands on the threshold, her arms full of parcels.

Her gaze sweeps the kitchen. Her lips part.

"What," she says, "are you *doing*?"

Iano and Veran crowd behind her, their attention flickering between Lark—filmed in sawdust, with the crossbow in one hand and a carving knife in the other, a bloody rag bound hastily around the base of her thumb—and me, standing on my highest tiptoes to reach the rafters, my hands, dress, and probably face smudged with ink.

I don't blame them for staring. We've turned Soe's kitchen into a cross between a mad chemist's lab and some kind of library catastrophe. Ink boils heartily on the hearth, thickening down to the stickiness we need for the stamps. Next to it, resin melts in a pan, filling the room with the scent of burning pine. Paper and parchment litter the table and floor, all stamped with meandering lines of letters, many nonsensical or overlapping. In the center of the table stands a bowl packed with damp sand. Wood shavings coat the floor, and in a walnut basket sit piles of thumb-size wooden blocks.

This is nothing, though—she's going to have a fit when she sees the workroom.

Veran looks around. "Had fun, did you?"

"Tamsin! Be careful!" Iano leaps forward, stretching out his hand to help me off the chair.

I don't take it, though—I reach up and pull down one of the dry sheets and hold it outward, grinning.

"Ha!" I exclaim.

His gaze flicks over it. "'*Rain cannot soak dry ground*'— what does that mean?"

I shake the paper and then look at Lark. I tip my finger toward my chin, and then at Iano, in the motion she showed me this morning.

Tell him, I sign.

"We're printing," Lark says. "Putting words onto pages."

"Stamping labels?" Iano asks, looking around at the wreck of the kitchen, bemused.

"No—stamping sentences." She gestures at me. "Tamsin's sentences."

He looks again at the sheet I'm holding out. "Why?"

I pretend that he's asked *how* instead of *why*. I point to Lark and start to sign all the relevant words we've worked on today, fingerspelling the ones I can't remember—*letters, sand, resin, blocks, ink, paper, press . . .*

"What are you doing?" Iano asks, looking at my fingers.

"I teach Tamsin some hand signs," Lark says.

Veran swivels his head to her. "You taught Tamsin sign language? You *know* sign language?"

She rubs the back of her neck and answers in Eastern, explaining about her deaf friend. She nods back at me. "I am not remembering all of them, though."

"I don't understand," Soe says, looking at the nearest scrap of paper, with a crisp line of *E*s stamped out like a written screech. "How are you printing sentences? I only have two sets of each letter."

"Yes, we—we are pushing the stamps into the sand." She points to the bowl of damp sand on the table. "To make . . . holes. *Lu'tuw—itsk*," she says to Veran.

"Imprints."

"*Uah*, the shapes of the letters in the sand, then we pour in the resin." She points to the pan full of bubbling sap by the fire. "They get hard and make the letter shapes. Then we put them on blocks, so—new stamps."

That was your idea, I sign to her.

"*Uah*, that part is my idea," she agrees hesitantly. "It is how, uh, how the rustlers are forging their brands." She switches back into Eastern again, explaining what she already described to me— that the rustlers would build a bootleg kiln, melt pig iron inside, get drunk around it all night, and then cast the melted metal into shapes in the sand. It meant they could forge new, unregistered brands on the go without the bother of finding a blacksmith.

Veran is listening to her with a mixture of surprise and awe on his face. Iano is still watching me worriedly. I finally step down from the chair.

Soe picks up one of our new resin stamps. "So . . . are you just stamping a few words at a time? Wouldn't writing be faster?"

I lift my hands, then hesitate. I still don't know enough signs to explain, and Lark would have to translate my words anyway. Instead, I beckon them to the workroom. Silently, they follow me from the trashed kitchen into the equally trashed workroom, where the big press sits in the middle of the floor, surrounded by inky leather pads, dishes strewn with stamps, and drifts of crumpled paper. I urge Iano and Soe closer, so they can look into the basin of the big press, where the big wooden block sits, carved with ten rows of grooves, plus a splash of blood from where Lark's knife slipped while she was carving them. Filling the top two rows are tight lines of letter stamps, facing up.

Iano starts to speak, but I hold up a finger and pick up a leather pad. I smear it in a blob of tacky ink, then pat it over the letters. Soe and Iano watch as I hunt for a scrap of paper that still has some clear space, then set it carefully over the letters. When it's in place, I pick up the long wooden arm, fit it into the screw, and haul it down. Lark has been doing this bit for most of the day, but I'm determined to do it now, pulling the clamp tight until my arms tremble with the effort. When I can't pull it anymore, I reverse it, lifting the screw until I can slide my hand underneath and pull out the paper, stamped perfectly with two lines of crisp, uniform text.

Iano takes the page, the sentence identical to the one he already saw. Soe looks at it, too, then at her press, the sides now smeared with sticky black ink. Veran and Lark watch from the doorway. I catch Lark's eye—she leans against the doorframe and gives me a tired but satisfied half smile. She's been an absolute machine today, hauling and carving and teaching me good Eastern curses and adding every sign she knows to her speech. There's no doubt in my mind that this beast we've created would never have come about without her.

It's not perfect yet. We're still finessing the ink—too wet and it runs off the resin, too sticky and it pulls them off their wooden backs. The resin takes a long time to harden, and many of the letters are misshapen or fuzzy with sand. And the wooden backs aren't right either—they tend to splinter after a few presses. Metal—something soft like lead—would be ideal. A letter and block cast entirely in metal. With the right equipment, I don't see why it can't be done.

Iano looks up at me, back at the page, then up to me again. He doesn't seem to know what to say.

"Don't get me wrong," he begins. "This is . . . clever. Very inventive, to make rows of stamps. But . . . I still don't understand. This is all so much *work*. If you want to write out a sentence, why wouldn't you just . . . *write* it?"

A spark of indignation flares in my chest. I face him fully and give him a series of three signs that should be obvious even to someone who doesn't know them.

My. Wrist. Hurts, I sign, adding what sounds I can make with my mouth.

"I know," he says, taking my right hand. "I know your wrist gives you trouble, but . . . surely you can write a few sentences, take a break, and write some more later? And if you want to make several copies, why not commission a woodblock?"

The spark turns into a flurry at his questions. How am I

to dictate a woodblock, Iano? Why should I be content with scratching out just a few sentences at a time, while the rest tumble and wheel inside me? What if my thoughts go beyond one block? What if a different word strikes me halfway through? Don't you see what movable letters can do? Don't you see what we've *done*?

"Oh!" Veran says from the door. "That reminds me—the notice we saw in town."

"Right." Iano digs in his pocket and pulls out a folded sheet. He opens it and hands it to me, worry creasing his face. "Kimela Novarni has been officially instated as the *ashoki*. I don't know how, or why—perhaps she threatened my mother, the way she threatened me. It would have been easy after I'd already named her to the court."

I jerk my gaze up to him, my brow furrowed.

"Tamsin said a few days ago she didn't think Kimela was behind it all," Soe says. She's right, but my irritation builds again despite her good intentions—I'm tired of people having my conversations for me. I pull my index finger across my chest.

"We," Lark says from the doorway. She's leaning against the frame and watching me. "Don't," she continues as I splice the air with my palms. "Do that."

"Just because *you* wouldn't do these things as *ashoki* doesn't mean others wouldn't," Iano says.

Veran shifts in the doorway. "Either way, if we can confront her, this could be a perfect opportunity to either get a confession out of her, or see if she has any better sense of who's behind the blackmail."

Get a confession?

"How?" I ask.

"Well, she'll be traveling by coach on the circuit there on the page." Veran's face takes on a kind of wry excitement. "And it just so happens that we have a professional bandit in our midst."

Behind him, Lark furrows her brow. "What?"

He half-turns to her. "Think about it, Lark—we stop the coach just like you stopped all those others, somewhere outside Giantess. You and Tamsin could get in and confront her, like you did me. Stuck in that little space, facing both the Sunshield Bandit—who she framed—and Tamsin—who she had attacked . . . don't you see? She'll have to confess, or give us the information we need."

I raise my eyebrows at the optimism—or, more bluntly, naiveté—of his conviction. Lark looks past him to where Iano is nodding his head. Her gaze slides to me. I frown and give her two quick signs, the opposite of what we've been telling each other all day.

Bad idea.

Soe catches my movement and watches me complete it. The boys are watching Lark. She stays quiet a moment longer, and then says something to Veran in Eastern, jerking her head for the front door. He hesitates, then hurries after her. We hear the door open and close, followed by the murmur of voices on the porch.

Iano turns back to me. "I know you don't think it's Kimela. Veran isn't entirely convinced it's her, either—he's more suspicious of Kobok. But even if it's not her, we may still be able to get some answers. And—you may be able to share your ideas about policy. If she's not guilty, then there's no other option—she's Moquoia's *ashoki* for the rest of her life."

"Tamsin isn't dead," Soe points out. "*Ashoki* is a lifetime position, and she's still alive."

A flash of trepidation crosses Iano's face, and then he meets my gaze and the expression is replaced with guilt. "I know, but . . ."

I make a flowery, agitated gesture to my lips to show that my thoughts are the same as his. Dead or not, I'm hardly going to sit onstage and silently strum my dulcimer for perplexed audiences.

"I'm not saying we can't work something out," Iano says quickly. "You'll always have a place in court, Tamsin, whether you're onstage or not. Perhaps you can serve alongside Kimela, compose music that she performs. Maybe she can be convinced to adopt our ideas."

Kimela Novarni would sooner ally with an Utzibor bat than me, I expect, and even if she did, my professional hubris balks at the thought of writing lyrics for her to sing.

My thoughts must show on my face, because Iano waves at the workshop, the press, the paper in my hand. "At any rate, we have a few days to strategize. You can use what you've started here today . . . write something that might sway her. It could be the best chance we have."

I look away, in part to avoid his searching gaze. I stare at the press, the stamps, the ink, the half-formed thoughts pressed into paper.

"Maybe we can still print it, whatever you come up with," Soe says, clearly trying to find some compromise. "We can keep making the stamps if you'd rather write it out that way. But . . ." She nods apologetically. "I am going to need my press back. I have orders from town I have to fill."

I sigh. Then I point to one of the scraps of paper, and, looking between the two of them, bring my fingertips together.

"More," I say.

"More paper?" Soe asks. "I can get you more. I'll have to run back to town in a day or two for deliveries. I can get more from the ragpickers then."

I nod, trying to force myself to look on the bright side. I don't think Kimela set up my attack. But chances are good she'll have more current information than any we've been able to glean so far. If she's the *ashoki* now, she'll have already started her scrutiny of the court. Surely chaos this big has to have left some trail.

I look back to Iano. He gives me a placating smile.

"I know you want to aim bigger," he says. "But I think it's best to stay within our means. Stay small. That makes sense, right? Kimela first."

I force everything I have into returning a half-formed smile.

He nods and gets up to help Soe with their parcels. I stare absently at the cluttered tabletop.

Stay small.

For whatever reason, instead of the piles of paper and ink and words teetering around me, I get a vision of that empty room in Utzibor where I was locked for six weeks. Four walls and a bucket, with only a tiny airhole to the world outside.

Stay small.

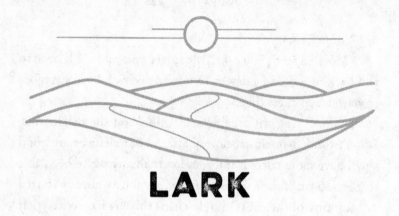

LARK

"I don't know."

"But just think, Lark, think what we could do. This could end everything—the quarry marches, the trafficking rings, work bonds, abductions . . ."

I open my hands. "Me threatening one person could do all that?"

"It could be a start, at least."

I look down, where Rat is sitting between my knees. He's been exiled to the porch all day and happy to have company. I scratch him absently behind the ears, my stomach still turning at the thought of Veran's plan. He's taken a seat across from me, on Soe's overturned cast-iron cauldron, and he's watching me anxiously.

I drop my gaze to my hands, spotted with ink, sticky with resin, and sliced with the carving knife. I turn my palms over, studying the tattoos along my wrists. *Perseverance. Strength.*

I've been thinking of them a lot today—they've been right in front of my face as I hauled the screw press down or whittled the next wooden block or pressed a line of letters into the sand. Never in my life have I been so saturated with *words*—I've never been good with them, or needed to be. Silence was a preferred trait among both the slavers and rustlers—no chatter, no talking back. Reading was even less useful than talk.

But today, this day filled to the brim with words and letters, broken apart and put back together, shaped by our fingers, cast into sand . . . while it's worn me nearly to the bone, there's the oddest feeling of accomplishment whirling around in my stomach.

I *did* something—something beyond just scrapping to survive, or swinging a punch, or stealing a loaf. I *made* something. It's not done, and it's not perfect, but if anything, that's only building this little flare inside me. I did a useless, frivolous thing. Tamsin had most of the big ideas, but I—I made them work.

Veran's clearly bursting with impatience. His fingers fidget on his knees. The fringe twitches on his boots. "Are you worried about not having your sword and buckler? We might be able to find something in town."

"It's not that. It's just . . ." I rub my face. So many things come to mind. There will be guards—lots of guards, if these *ashokis* are as important as everyone says. This isn't my terrain. I don't know the land, I don't know the road, I don't know where the angle of the sun will help me or hurt me. I don't know my horse. I don't know my new companions like I knew my campmates. I don't know that Iano or Soe will fall into line behind me. I don't know that Tamsin's physically strong enough. I don't know what Veran—knuckleheaded, heroics-obsessed Veran—

might do in the heat of the moment. With a lurch, I think of Pickle, his last impulsive fight on top of the stage, and the fall that broke his body and let his life out.

My stomach clenches. "I just don't know, Veran. I don't feel good about it. I get the feeling more things could go wrong—really wrong—than right. And . . ." I rub my face. "I don't . . . I don't know that I'm the same person who stepped up in your stage a few weeks ago."

Don't feel like the same person.

Not sure I *want* to be the same person.

It's been a slow slide, starting with the decision to leave Three Lines and travel into the desert with this stranger—someone I'd never have said yes to back in the days of Arana and Bitty, when we were at our highest. And then came that trek across the desert, that fight at Utzibor, that killing strike to Dirtwater Dob. The ride into Pasul—that was the last little slip of normalcy. After that came the posthouse, the man, the girl—my father, my sister. The blind race back to Three Lines, and then the gutting feeling of finding it empty. Losing Jema. The water scrape. Tellman's Ditch.

And then today, this weird, upside-down day, when for the first time I was up to my ears not in sand or sweat or blood, but words.

Maybe *that's* why I've been so absorbed in my tattoos today. Before all this, they were my identity—a sun, a sword, a lark. Now they seem like a record. A diary of a past life. Petroglyphs, carved in old stone.

Veran's fidgeting has stilled.

"You *are* still the same person, Lark," he says quietly.

I shake my head—I hadn't meant it to be a dig at myself, that

I'm not the same as the bandit who held a knife to his throat out by the South Burr. But before I can speak, he turns, reaching for one of the many parcels they've brought in from town.

"I have something for you," he says. He pushes a quilt aside and pulls out a bundle of clothes. He hands me two long-sleeved button-down shirts and a new handkerchief, bright red. I rub the stout fabric between my fingers appreciatively.

"Thanks," I say. "That was nice of you."

"Oh." He waves a hand, still rifling through the bundle. "Those are just the basics. Have a look at this."

He shakes out a vest and holds it up so I can see. In the fading light, it looks blue, with bright gold threads shooting outward. He watches my face, his eyes dancing.

"Wow," I say. "Uh . . . that's something. How much did that cost?"

"Bah—I don't remember." He drapes it across my knees, and Rat snoots the fabric with his nose. The buttons flash as they move. I lean back, almost unwilling to touch it.

"And," he says, with an air of anticipation, reaching into the sack.

"And?" I repeat, looking up. "Veran, how much did you spend?"

He doesn't answer. He slowly straightens, bringing out a crisp, clean-edged cowhide hat.

I stare at it. It's a thing of beauty, with brown and white patches and a rolled brim, and a leather braid running around the base. It's the kind of thing I'd swipe off a traveler in a stage and slap down triumphantly for Patzo in Snaketown, winning me a sack of beans and a pound of bacon and a night spent comfortably in the woodshed.

"Since you lost your old one," he says, holding it out between his fingertips.

Hesitantly, I take it, since that's clearly what he wants. I set it on top of the fine vest. I can't think of anything to say. I've handled clothes this nice before, but it's always to pass them on to my campmates or trade them in town. I can't imagine myself actually *wearing* them. Suddenly I feel dirtier than ever, the sweat and blood and ink from today all sitting heavy on my skin.

Veran leans forward, his wrists draped off his knees. "Lark, listen . . . I know a lot of things have happened in just a few weeks. And I know a lot of it was my fault. Sending your campmates away, losing your horse, bringing the soldiers after us. But . . . despite all that, despite being here in Moquoia, you're still the same person. You're still the Sunshield Bandit. Whether or not you still have your old sword or your old hat or any of that doesn't matter—it's still who you are. And you can still use it to help those people in Tellman's Ditch."

He's speaking gently, sincerely, trying to reassure me without realizing that he's doing just the opposite. That title, *the Sunshield Bandit*, given to me by sheriffs and angry posses across the Ferinno, plastered across bounty sheets, settles deep in my gut like a stone. My thoughts flicker to my tattoos again, and I realize—they're not a diary. They're a proclamation, sunk into my skin, the same as my slave brand. Past life or not, I've still marked myself as the outlaw who terrorized the Ferinno.

The little burst of pleasure from a minute ago over a day spent on a fanciful word machine crumbles away, leaving guilt in its place. In the excitement of helping Tamsin, I forgot Tellman's Ditch—*literally* forgot the people being marched inland.

I didn't think of them once. I sank into a day of distraction without a single thought, while they're getting parceled out and forced onward, over the dusty plains and into the cold mountains, into a life beyond anybody's reach.

I let out my breath, my fingers tightening on the brim of the handsome hat. As Veran watches, I tilt it to check the size, but it looks large enough to go over my hair. My dreadlocks are bound up in a thick bun—I reach up and unwind the cloth holding them there, and then pull them back into my old ponytail. I lift the hat and settle it over my head. It's a good fit, snug enough to stay on without pinching.

I'm not sure why that should disappoint me.

Veran's smiling, his eyes agleam in the light coming from Soe's windows. I take a breath.

"You're right," I say. "I got carried away today. We shouldn't waste any more time."

"Don't get me wrong," he says quickly. "I think what you and Tamsin did is amazing. I can't believe you thought of casting the letters in sand. Everyone at the university is going to lose their minds—your uncle Colm—"

"No," I say, straightening up and spreading out the vest over my knees, my fingers tracing the rays of the sunburst embroidery. "I shouldn't have gotten distracted. This is too important." I pull out the bandanna from the work shirts and knot it around my throat. "Get me a sword—not the toothpick one Iano has, but something broad, single grip. I don't need anything else."

"Not a shield?"

"There's hardly any sun for me to use, anyway. It'll be fine. Can you get me a sword?"

"Soe will have to go back into town in a day or two—I'm

sure she can buy something from the metalsmith if you're not picky."

I nod. "Good. Do you know where you plan to confront this *ashoki*?"

"She'll be traveling from Ossifer's Pass, so she should be coming in from the north."

"Tomorrow you and I'll go out and scout the road—figure out the best place for the ambush."

His eyes flicker in excitement. "Got it."

I'm reminded again, uncomfortably, of Pickle. "You sure you'll be up to this?"

"You tell me what to do," he says confidently. "I'm all yours."

I'm not sure I like that, either.

Nothing good seems to come to the people who get tied up with me.

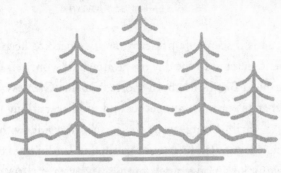

VERAN

Four days. We have four days to solidify our plan to confront Kimela and get some answers—maybe all the answers. I'm still placing my bets on Minister Kobok's involvement, but I can't deny that Kimela has the most tangible reason to want to get Tamsin out of the picture, and I can't forget the sly way she insulted my country and my folk at the *Bakkonso* Ball. I think of the way Lark stepped up in my stage a few weeks ago, how she filled the little space, menacing with purpose, and how I babbled like an idiot when faced with the point of her knife. I have no doubt that Kimela, when faced with the same threat, will give us whatever information she knows—and as she's the new *ashoki*, I'm hoping it will be a lot.

The big thing will be making sure any guards are detained long enough to let Lark and Tamsin get in the coach. So the day after our foray into Giantess, Lark and I ride out to the road leading into town. She's wearing one of her new work shirts, but none of the other purchases—we both agreed they'd be too conspicuous if seen by a passerby, and we need to keep her involvement secret until the day of the attack. If word gets out that the Sunshield Bandit has been spotted outside Giantess, Kimela might change her route altogether and spoil everything.

It's a thrill riding through the countryside with Lark, weighing the merits of various terrain and landmarks. For two days, we poke among outcroppings and weave through redwood stands, fluffing up duff and debating hiding places and escape routes. She clambers into embankments and has me ride by, studying the angle of travel and the confines of the space. She rides ahead with instructions for me to wait ten minutes, then follow and try to pick out her hiding place. It's rough, satisfying work, and we arrive back at Soe's exhausted but grimly satisfied with our decisions.

Lark doesn't stop to rest once we're back at the cabin, though. She goes right back to teaching Tamsin sign language in between whittling little blocks for their resin letter stamps. Tamsin still seems determined to write out her essay using her co-opted screw press, and none of us are brave enough to contradict her. While we sit in the kitchen—Lark in the corner in a pile of wood shavings—Tamsin bends over the grooved wooden plate, painstakingly sliding letters into the grooves with her lips pursed in concentration. It makes my head spin to watch her—she has to compose each word backward, and near the bottom all her sentences are full of gaps where she and Lark haven't finished making enough stamps. At the end of each day she gives Lark a list of the letters she needs, and Lark obligingly uses her bootleg branding-iron technique to cast more in the sand.

I'm hoping that perhaps the novelty of seeing all those letters printed in neat, even rows will work in our favor. We're all getting better at recognizing Tamsin's most frequent hand signs, but without her voice, our plan hinges on Kimela taking the time to read the essay in full. The lines of stamps—more crisp and compact than a woodblock, more precise than handwriting— might not be fast, but they're certainly different. The fragments that Tamsin has managed to get out of one of the small presses— the big one being reclaimed for pressing the goods from town— are so unusual in appearance, it may be just the extra hook we need to keep Kimela's attention.

On the third day, Soe goes into town with her newly pressed goods. We spend the day around the cabin, hashing out the finer details of our plan. I'm halfway concerned that she'll return with word that there are bounties up for Iano and me, or that soldiers have poured in on the report of that woman with the twisted eyelid who shadowed me on market day. But Soe returns with news that everything seems normal. From her cart she hands Tamsin a giant stack of rag paper, more than she could possibly need, and to Lark she hands a burly, fullered sword with a squat hilt.

"That's the only thing he had that matched your specifications," Soe explains as Lark tests its balance. "He offered to forge something more to my liking, but I told him this one would do."

"It'll do," Lark confirms, giving it an experimental swing.

To me, she hands over a long, toothed crosscut saw and several wedges, the kind my ma has her scouts and sawyers use for timbering. I handle them as if they were relics. Never have I been allowed to help fell or buck a tree, whether it's an infested pine to be taken down or a timber oak bound for the Paroan shipyards. Now that I think on it, examining the teeth of the saw, I don't know why. These saws are meant for two people to operate, so if I were to collapse on the spot, my partner would know right away. I'm hardly going to lie around unconscious while trees fall without anyone knowing. Felling, limbing, bucking, hewing . . . they're all inherently dangerous jobs anyway. There's an endless well of tragic tales, some true, some not, that scouts tell around their fires about deadly mishaps brought on by a hatchet or a handsaw.

I turn the wedges in my hands, suddenly stung by a sense of injustice. Why should my parents, after all, keep me from such a task? Why should they keep me from *any* of it? Mama knew how much I longed to be in the woods. I begged, I pleaded, I tried every treatment she researched and several more I unearthed myself for slowing or stalling my seizures. Anything for the chance to earn my florets, the first and most basic badge signaling the transition from trainee to scout. Instead, I was kept back, kept inside, kept in bed, while my mother leaned over me, her own silver florets worn from their decades on her uniform collar.

I close my hands on the wedges. I'm done letting my parents' overcaution keep me from the things they always warned me against. I've already proved I can travel cross-country, even if I did collapse twice along the way. I even dug a seep and revived Lark. Why should I be any more afraid of timbering, or ladders, or walkwires?

I ignore the tiny voice in my head, speaking incongruously in my older brother's voice, reminding me of how I nearly fell apart when Lark collapsed in the water scrape.

Shut up, Vynce, I think furiously. *You're just worried I'll finally beat you at something.*

So, on day four, Lark and I take the mules and cart back out to the place she's chosen to stage the attack. We've been calling it that—*the attack*—but we're hoping the landscape will do most of the work for us. After crawling over nearly every inch of road and bank for three-quarters of a mile, Lark has picked the spot. It's a hairpin curve set into a steep slope, hemmed in by dense bracken and redwoods. On one side, the bank rises up toward a squat summit; on the other, it falls sickeningly into a deep ravine, so choked with sword ferns and sorrel that the stream at the bottom is apparent only by the distant chatter of invisible water. Any coach team is going to take their time going around this bend, and, most useful to us, it's impossible to see around it.

"Okay," Lark says, standing hip-deep in bracken on the uphill embankment, surveying the road. "The coach comes in on the straightaway. Tamsin said she usually traveled with three guards—one on the coach, one in front, and one behind—plus her maid."

I nod eagerly. The main subject of our kitchen discussions for the last three days has been how to get as many guards as possible away from the coach and held up. Iano had suggested he simply step into the road and give the royal order to stop, but Tamsin reminded him of how we're still unsure if his mother had a hand in the attack on her stage, meaning we have no way of knowing what the palace guards' orders might be should they encounter him. I offered a series of attack formations, moving our little group around in an array of swords and crossbows, with Rat thrown in. Iano got hot and bothered, and was arguing against any injury to royal guards when Lark finally cut in and offered her simple, elegant solution.

"The coach stops," Lark continues, stepping back onto the road and striding toward the hairpin. "A guard rides forward to check the way." She rounds the blind curve, ducking around ferns hanging into the road. She stops. "And then they see the tree."

"And there's a lot of swearing," I say.

She nods, looking from the empty road up to the redwoods reaching to the sky. "It's too steep and narrow for the coach to turn around. The guards will get out their tools—if we're lucky, they'll only have hatchets, but in this terrain they'll probably at least have a bow saw—and they'll get to work clearing the tree while the coach waits."

"The curve will hide us, and the noise from sawing should cover our sound," I say.

"Again, if we're lucky," Lark says, staring darkly at the road. "Chances are high they'll leave at least one guard with the coach, and if Kimela or her maid screams, the others might hear over the noise of their saws. That's where the rest of you come in."

I nod again excitedly. We've parceled out the weapons we have among us—Soe with her crossbow, Lark with her knife and broadsword, Iano with his rapier . . . and me with his longbow. He'd reluctantly handed it over yesterday, and I've been practicing with it since then. I was surprised—it's not nearly as hard to draw as I thought it might be. My folk use shorter flatbows, and I'd failed to realize that my ma's stubby hedge-apple bow is ten times stiffer than Iano's willowy yew bow. I'm hardly the archer my sister Ida is, but after a day of practice, I'm at least hitting the target as many times as I'm missing it.

"You'll stay upslope, and Soe will be down the road," Lark says, looking up the bank again. "That way you can snipe from the trees if you need to. You'll be at that rock we found, so you can see around both sides of the bend and use those birdcalls you taught us to keep everyone coordinated."

My excitement spikes. This was my best idea—using the scouts' long-distance whistles to run our attack. I've been practicing them since I first learned to whistle, tiptoeing around our family's wing at Lampyrinae and letting them ring out when things got too quiet. When I got older, I was able to use the excuse that I was helping Vynce practice them for his rise through the Guard ranks, but in reality it was so I could internalize what little scout culture I had access to.

It only makes sense to use them now. Golden-crowned sparrow for a warning. Cardinal for all clear. Goldfinch for location. Towhee for aid. We've added a few more to suit the needs of our plan. Soe's cabin had rung with experimental whistles and chirps as I'd taught them to the others, making Rat finally slink out of the kitchen with his ears back.

Lark goes to the edge of the narrow road, looking down into the steep-sided ravine. "Iano and I will detain any guards that hang back. When we're sure they're secure, Tamsin and I will get into the coach with Kimela. I'll help her say her piece, and then we'll hand Kimela the essay. If she seems ready to ally with us, she can have her guards stand down, and we'll all have a long chat. If she doesn't . . ."

This has been a sticking point for us—what to do if Kimela isn't swayed by Tamsin's appearance and composition, or what to do if she just caves and gives us a confession right away. Would the guards follow Iano's orders if it turns out that Kimela has been our enemy? Or will they attempt to fight their prince?

We tossed around the idea of trying to take Kimela away with us, but none of us liked that plan. Lark pointed out that the guards would be after us like a shot, while Soe pointed out that we had nowhere secret or secure to keep her prisoner. In the end, Tamsin convinced us all to simply retreat, making sure we all got away in one piece, so we could make a new plan with the information we had gathered. To me, it seems like a loose end, a place where our plan simply stops. But Lark agreed, insisting that we need to be more focused on our safety than doing anything too rash.

"All right," she says, scuffing a few rocks experimentally with her boot. "We've covered everything we can think of." She nods to the cart, where the crosscut saw and wedges are. "Ready for the hard bit?"

"Ready," I say.

"Are you sure?" she presses. "You know what this means, don't you?"

"'Course," I say with forced indifference, reaching into the cart for the canvas-wrapped saw.

But when we've struggled up the steep bank and reached our selected tree, I hesitate. The redwoods here are small for their kind, practically tiny compared to ancients like Giantess. But their trunks are still three feet across, strong and healthy, their roots weaving through the soil to hold this hillside together. I check to make sure Lark is occupied around the far side of the tree, and then I rest my palm on its bark.

Mama has seeded a deep culture of forest conservation in the Silverwood, though she argues against folk who say so. She counters that she didn't start it at all—that it's always been in the blood of our folk to protect our forests the best ways we know how, and that she simply codified it again after the bad practices employed by my grandfather. I've seen the scars on the landscape from overharvesting and unchecked pests and disease. I've seen the barren hillsides, burned right down into the soil by roaring wildfires that raced across the ridges where scout-controlled burns had been neglected. The Silverwood's legendary forests are a joint product of both forestry and deep respect, and nowhere is that more evident than my ma's eye on the mountains.

Rule number one—don't cut anything without a good reason.

Fire management and pest control are good reasons.

I'm not so sure staging a bandit attack is.

I run my fingers over the crevices in the cinnamon-colored bark. I wonder how old this tree is, what creatures call it home, what it's seen, what it's survived.

I'm going to kill it.

Lark comes around the other side before I can pull my hand away. She pauses.

"We can try to think of another way," she says.

I shake my head. "No, we've made our plan. The only other possibility is a full-on attack—better to cut down one tree than have one of us get hurt."

"We could call it off," she says lightly. "There's still time. We could see if she'd meet with us once she gets into town."

I lift my eyebrow at her, forcing bravado. "Is the *Sunshield Bandit* arguing for diplomacy over an ambush?"

"Yeah, the Sunshield Bandit just might be," she says with an edge. "It never hurts to think twice about these things."

I sigh. "I've thought a lot more than twice, and I know you have, too. If we were sure Kimela wasn't behind the blackmail, maybe we could meet with her in Giantess. But if she is, the lot of us waltzing right into her entourage would put Tamsin exactly where she'd want her. It would put *all* of us exactly where she'd want us. This way at least there's a chance to get away." I look up at our doomed tree, trying to push away my guilt. At least it will die for a cause. "Have you ever done this before?"

"Not on anything this big," she says.

"The hard part's going to be knowing when to stop so it doesn't fall until tomorrow—we don't want somebody else coming along and clearing it away." I roll up my sleeves and start to unwrap the saw. With some reluctance, Lark unrolls the wedges, ax, and sledgehammer. When all our tools are in order and there's no more stalling to be had, I pick up one end of the saw. Lark takes up the other end, but she doesn't move toward the trunk with me.

"You sure?" she says again.

My irritation—and guilt—flare. "*Yes*, Lark, I'm sure. I know you think I rush headlong into everything, but I've actually thought this one through." I try to shift toward the trunk. "Anyway, what's made you so sentimental about one bitty redwood all of a sudden?"

"I just know you'd probably like to not kill this tree," she says shortly, not giving in to my tugging. "And I'm telling you we can find another way."

"No, we can't! Not one that makes sense, anyway. Quit trying to talk me out of it."

"I just want you to think . . ."

"I am thinking! I did think!" I jerk the saw handle in my fists. "And how come suddenly I have to be all careful and reasonable, when you've crashed a dozen-odd coaches? Did you hem and haw before you turned over Professor Colm's stage?"

"Is that what this is all about?" she asks quietly, still holding the other end of the saw loosely at her waist. "Getting to play outlaw for a while, like there are no consequences attached?"

"I just want to do something that's going to make a difference," I say hotly. "And you suddenly feeling bad about stuff you've done isn't going to stop me."

As soon as I say the words, I wish I hadn't. She stares at me, her face tense and guarded—almost sad. She doesn't look like Eloise, or Rou, just now. She looks more like Queen Mona than ever. The cold, steely stare is familiar, but . . . I hadn't been expecting the sadness.

I almost say something to walk back my callous words, but before I can, she steps up to the tree. Adjusting her grip on the saw handle, she places its teeth against the rippled bark and pulls. I stagger as the saw moves. With a long, raw *scrape*, the metal makes the first bite into wood.

I straighten and set my footing, and then haul the saw back toward me. Within a few pulls, we settle into a stiff, silent rhythm, the only sound the fitful *whrzz, whrzz* of teeth slicing through living wood.

TAMSIN

Rain cannot soak dry ground. When met with arid soil, it runs off and races onward, becoming destruction, pulling land and root and creature with it. For rain to penetrate the earth, that earth must already be damp. Rain must find its likeness on its plunge from the sky—it must find its own blood reaching for it. A sibling to a sibling, a friend to a friend. Only then can it seep gently downward, fueling life and yes, change, without destruction.

So, too, is the manner of people, and of the perils Moquoia faces. We find this country at a breaking point, when there exists not so much a spectrum of humanity, but a gulf between two extremes. Those with means stand on the backs of those without. Climbing out of the grips of the bond system is not only barely possible—it is purposefully kept that way by generations of asho-kis, ministers, and monarchs within the comforts of Tolukum Palace.

For too long has the cry for change been met like rain on dry *ground—rolling off unwilling ears, channeling instead through exploitive practices that continue to wash away the scaffold of our society. For too long has the self-interest of politics hardened itself to this country's dark storm of slavery and bond servitude . . .*

I look up as Iano sits down across the table.

"How's it coming?" he asks.

Done, I sign. I turn the pamphlet around so he can read it. By this point he's seen enough drafts to know the gist from start to finish, but he reads it all the way through anyway. Observing it upside down, I take the time to appreciate the precise, even lines of text turned out by the stamp press. I've switched over to using Soe's medium-size press, which I thought might not give me the same quality given its shorter screw, but I found that printing was much easier with the fewer turns required to clamp the plates. I admire, too, the title font, which Lark carved a little bigger and bolder, in all capitals:

THE PATH OF THE FLOOD

Iano reaches the end of the three pages. He takes a breath, nods, and slides it back to me.

"It's a good essay, Tamsin. Kimela's got to see the truth in it."

I pull my slate toward me, because while Soe has caught on to many of my signs, Iano still struggles to interpret them.

I PLAN TO PRINT MORE TO HAND OUT IN COURT

He chews his lip. "Well . . . perhaps, once we've set things straight. Small steps, you know?"

There's that word again—*small*.

There's thumping on the porch, and through the door come Lark and Veran, both looking stiff and exhausted. Sawdust flecks their clothes and hair, and they bring the smell of green wood and sweat with them. Neither of them sit at the table—

Lark eases onto the potato bin, groaning, while Veran sinks to the floor in the corner, resting his head on the wall and closing his eyes. Rat comes in after them—Soe's gotten more lenient about letting him in the house—and trails around the kitchen, sniffing hopefully at the stove. Soe flicks him a bit of venison from her skillet.

"Hey." I rap the table. Lark opens her eyes. *How did it go?*

"Hard," she says, rubbing her face. "I am never wanting to fall a tree so big again."

"Did you bring it down?" Iano asks.

"Not yet. We have the—uh, things, *lu'tuw*—"

"Wedges," Veran says, his eyes still closed.

"*Uah*, wedges, we have them inside the cut, holding." She makes a shallow *v* with her palms. "So tomorrow it is not too hard to finish."

"We hope," Veran says. My gaze darts between the two of them—is it just me, or are they acting a bit stiffer toward each other than usual? Only yesterday Veran was making doe eyes any time Lark's back was turned.

Maybe they're just tired.

Nobody else seems to notice. Iano picks up my pamphlet. "Tamsin finished the essay."

"Oh, can I see?" Lark stretches her hand out and takes it. She studies it, holding it close and furrowing her brow as she concentrates on each word. She slowly turns the fold and similarly scans the interior. After a moment, she turns it around.

"What is this word, *economy*?" she asks, pointing.

Iano translates for her. "That section goes into the practical implications for Moquoian infrastructure." He scoots his chair forward—Rat is still circling the kitchen, his claws clicking on the wood floor.

Important for people in court, I say when I see Lark frown. I reach for my slate nearby. WE HAVE TO MAKE IT AS EASY AS POSSIBLE FOR PEOPLE TO CHANGE THEIR MINDS

Lark opens her mouth to say something, but she's cut off by Rat, who barks. She looks at him and clips a few words in Eastern, scolding his bad manners. She goes to the door and opens it for him. He stands on the threshold, looking not outside, but up at her, his head cocked to the side. After a moment, she curses him and closes the door again. He goes back to pacing, treading over Veran's splayed feet.

Lark sets the pamphlet back down on the table. "As long as the money isn't becoming more important than the people."

I shake my head. *No. But if people—important people—I* need to learn the sign for lawmakers. I turn to my slate again. IF THEY DON'T SEE STRATEGY, THEY'LL THINK IT'S ALL TALK

That it can't be done, I finish.

"I understand. Rat, *durst*," she says, grabbing his ruff and trying to get him to sit. He flops his rump down on her foot, panting agitatedly. She scratches his ears, but as soon as she takes her hands away, he's back up again, this time going to Veran and thrusting his nose in his ear. Veran turns his face away without opening his eyes.

Soe taps her spoon on her skillet and looks over her shoulder at me. "Do you think the *ashoki*'s maid will give us any trouble?"

I shrug. This had been a troublesome point a day or two

ago, when I described how my maid, Simea, had jumped to my defense when my coach was attacked. She'd thrown herself across me, shielding me from the loaded crossbows, and had died as a result of it. The terrible thing is, I may have been able to escape through the opposite door had her body not pinned me to the seat, but I can hardly grudge her brave action. Once I had the space to think about it, her sacrifice had surprised me. Simea had been recently assigned to me, and I wouldn't have thought she'd be so loyal. My throat closes up. I owe her my life.

If Kimela's maid is just as protective, we could have trouble. But I'd like to think that Lark could keep such a person in check.

Rat stops in front of Lark, his ears and tail up, and barks at her again. She swears at him and tosses up her hands.

From the corner comes a short, sharp groan.

Veran slides sideways and hits the floor with a dull thud. His body stiffens and starts to shudder, rigid.

We all move at once—Iano and I jump from our seats and Soe leaps back from the stove. Lark vaults from the potato bin and hauls him from his stomach to his side. She waves toward us, and despite my own heart having sprung to my throat, her voice is pointed and calm.

"*It'sko*—a shirt, a cloth, or something," she says.

I shrug off the shawl from my shoulders and pass it to her. She folds it a few times and settles it under Veran's knocking head. While she's situating it, Rat paces around behind her and flops down on the floor behind Veran's bowing back, still panting heavily.

Iano grips the back of his chair. "What do we do?"

"Wait for it to stop," Lark says. "Get some water."

Soe obediently skirts the pair of them and heads out the

door for the water barrel. Iano bends over and scoots a pot sitting on the hearth just a few inches from Veran's feet, the fringe
on his boots swinging. I stand at the table, watching all three of
them—Veran, Lark, and her dog.

"Hey," I say, and when Lark looks up, I point to Rat. *How
did he know?*

"Know what?"

I gesture to Veran, whose seizing is starting to slow. Lark
looks at me, puzzled, and then at Rat. "I have made him lie down
behind Veran before—maybe he thinks he is supposed to now?"

I shake my head and reach for my slate. BUT HOW DID
RAT KNOW HE WOULD COLLAPSE?

Lark studies my words, frowning. "What?"

HE BARKED AT YOU. HE POKED AT VERAN

Lark stares at the slate again, and then turns back to Rat.

"I don't think the dog knew," Iano says. "How could he?
Veran wasn't doing anything except resting."

I throw my hands up. *I don't know. But the dog was upset—
about what?*

Veran's final tremors slow, and his body loosens. He retches
deeply a few times but doesn't come around. Lark checks him
over, from his lap up to his neck and head. She arranges one of
his wrists into a less awkward angle.

I rap on the table and sign with conviction. *The dog knew
something was wrong.*

"It must have been something else," Iano says, just as Soe
comes back in with a full water pitcher. "Soe, is there anything
outside? A creature? Are the horses acting up?"

"What?" Soe says breathlessly. "No—why? It's raining now.
Has he stopped?"

Lark looks back to me, consternated. I go for my slate again.
HAS RAT BEEN UPSET THE LAST FEW TIMES
VERAN'S COLLAPSED?

Lark's eyes go distant as she searches her memory. Her gaze
drifts down to Veran, lying partway in her lap, breathing shallowly through pale lips. After a pause, her head jerks up sharply.

I raise my eyebrows at her.

"The first time," she says slowly, "Rat was whining. He was
under me, pressing under my legs. I did not think of it until
now."

Any other times? I ask.

"Outside Tellman's Ditch . . ." She scrunches her eyebrows.
"He stayed far away from us, in the sun, outside the shade. And
he whined again. I was thinking he is only tired."

We all stare at each other around the kitchen.

"But there was nothing to see," Iano insists. "Nothing to
indicate . . ."

My hands jump up. *To you. Dogs smell things, hear things
we don't.*

"But I've never heard of a dog . . ." Iano's words die on his
lips as he stares at me. I can feel my face contorted at him, and
I hope he's realizing that his own limited experience isn't the
truth of the world over. I thought I'd shown him that when I
first walked onstage as his parents' *ashoki.*

Lark shifts, adjusting Veran's head. "I am going to bring
him into the workroom. He is going to be confused when he
wakes up." She nods at Soe. "You can get his feet, and bring the
water?"

Soe nods and crouches down, linking her arms under Veran's
knees. Lark lifts his torso, steadies his head, and together they

move him toward the workroom. Rat, in the absence of Veran or his oncoming seizure, rolls onto his side and sprawls leisurely on the hearth, at ease.

The door to the workroom closes, and for a moment the only sound is muffled murmuring and the shifting of presses. We're still standing on either end of the table. Iano looks at his chair, then at the fire, and then back at me.

"Tamsin," he says slowly. "I get the feeling that you're angry with me, but I don't know what for. Ever since Pasul, it seems like . . . like I just keep doing and saying the wrong things."

I drag my slate toward me. I don't want to have this conversation like this, but thanks to *everything*, I don't have a choice. WHY ARE YOU TURNING DOWN ALL MY IDEAS? I write.

"I'm not," he insists.

YES YOU ARE

"I just haven't ever heard of a dog . . ."

I smack the table. NOT THE DOG. THE PRESS. KIMELA. OUR PLAN

"I just want you to be careful," he says. "You're still healing. We don't have many answers. I don't want you to get hurt again. I just think it's better to stay small."

My next words are huge and uneven. THERE IS NO SMALL

"Yes, Tamsin, there is," he says. "I know you've always thought big, aimed big, but look at what's come of that."

I stare at him, gripping the chalk in my fingers, repeating his phrase in my head. Look at what's come of that? Of *what*?

I'm struck by a sudden, staggering realization.

Iano never believed in what we were doing.

Slowly, I scratch the chalk over my powdery slate again.

WHY DID YOU AGREE TO END SLAVERY? I write.

He stares at my slate. Whatever he expected me to write, it wasn't that. He looks back up at me.

"You helped me see it was wrong," he says.

WHY THOUGH?

"What does this have to do with the dog?" he asks almost pleadingly, gesturing to Rat lounging by the fire.

I point at the question on my slate.

"Do you want reasons?" he asks. His fingers twitch almost imperceptibly toward the pamphlet with my essay, still folded on the table. "Do you want me to recite your words back to you?"

I shake my head. That's exactly what I *don't* want. *Was it just because you loved me?*

Confusion flares on his face as he tries and fails to interpret my signing. "What?"

The words burst from my mouth, perfect in my head and nearly unintelligible on my tongue. "Was it just because you loved me?"

He jumps at the startling sound of my voice. "Just because I loved you?"

WERE YOU SO DESPERATE TO IMPRESS ME THAT YOU JUST AGREED TO WHATEVER I SAID? I palm the slate, smearing the chalk. IF I HAD SUGGESTED WARRING WITH THE EAST, WOULD YOU HAVE GONE ALONG WITH THAT TOO?

He has to squint to read this last tirade—by the end my words are a tiny scrawl.

"Tamsin . . . ," he says.

Think, I demand, jabbing at my head. *Think before you speak*.

He bristles, angry. "Tamsin, none of it was a walk in the park. None of it was without consequence. If I'd just been out to impress you, do you think I'd have stood by our policy once the blackmail started?"

DID YOU STAND BY IT? I scrawl. WHEN I DISAPPEARED, YOU LET ALL DIPLOMACY FALL. YOU DIDN'T GET A THING DONE WITH THE EASTERN DELEGATION

He lifts his hands. "Because I was trying to keep you from being murdered!"

AT THE EXPENSE OF THIS! I slap my pamphlet, which flutters feebly.

"Yes!" he shouts. "Yes, I admit it. At the time, I cared more about getting you back alive than our policy. Would you rather me have left you to die?"

I WOULD RATHER YOU HAD SOME BELIEF IN SOMETHING OTHER THAN ME

I toss the slate down with the words facing him, and he stares at them as if they're incomprehensible. I take a long breath, clenching and unclenching my hands at my side, and then I lift my fingers.

I'm not your ashoki *anymore*, I say, using the sign Lark and I made up for my old title. *Kimela is. You can't make your decisions based on me. You have to make them because you actually believe in them.*

"I *do* believe in them," he says. "I just want them done carefully."

I push back from the table, the chair screeching on the floor.

I stand for a moment, glaring at him, a flood of words piling up behind my lips. In the workroom, things are quiet—I'm not sure if Soe and Lark are still tending to Veran, or if they're waiting for us to finish.

I turn on my heel and pick up my cloak from the back of the chair.

"Tamsin," Iano says heavily. "We talked about Kimela. I can argue to reinstate you."

I swing the cloak around my shoulders angrily, wondering what exactly his vision of my future as *ashoki* looks like—just me onstage, silently strumming a dulcimer? I wrench the door open to the falling rain. I want to say something cutting, something poignant over my shoulder, but I can't, so I merely pass through and slam the door behind me.

I head down the cabin steps, keeping one hand on the porch rail until I round the corner and have to manage on my own. Slowly, I head toward the path Lark and I walked a few days past, the damp redwood duff swallowing the sound of the rain. The drizzle mists down, diffused by the distant canopy, beading on the fibers of my cloak. I plod through the vibrant shocks of ferns and splashes of moss, breathing in the darkness of the forest.

After I pass the outhouse, my steps slow, my breath catching in my chest. I have more strength than I did a week ago, but I still feel unsteady, like a bad footing would send me flying. I place my feet more carefully, my head bowed against the damp. As the trees swell and close in, the patter of rain stops, no longer able to reach the ground. I sink into the feeling of being swallowed by the forest.

Mist gathers in the crevices and hollows of the roots. A gray fox darts across the path, casting one glance at me with its sharp black eyes before plunging into the bracken. Ahead, Cloudyhead looms among the other trees, its rippled bark stained deep red.

I settle into the wings of its roots, the same place I wrote the audition song that won me the position of *ashoki*. I was no one then—no title, no job, no prospects. Bold enough to dream big, and naive enough to think my life could only get better.

I stare into dark space, my thoughts a jumble, my knees drawn up to my chest. After a few minutes, a figure melts through the gloom, and I turn over what I'm going to do if it's Iano. I'm surprised by how much I don't want to see him right now. He doesn't know about Cloudyhead—not because it's a secret, but because it never occurred to me to tell him.

But it's not Iano. It's Soe. She shuffles forward with a thick woolen blanket clamped under her arms.

She doesn't say anything. Not *I knew I'd find you here* or *You'll catch your death* or *You shouldn't wander off*. She silently settles down beside me, unfolds the blanket, and tucks it around our knees. Then we just sit.

We sit long enough that the forest forgets we're here. An owl swoops by on pale wings. A pine marten lollops across the duff. Songbirds—ones with names Veran could recite but that I don't know—call through the growing evening.

The mature part of me should find a silver lining in having a better appreciation for silence, something I was never adept at before.

But I don't want silence.

I want to talk to my friend.

I pull my fingers out from beneath the blanket. If I knew more signs, if I thought she could follow them, I would dive into an explanation on how Iano and I fell in love in secret, how it thrived on the stolen moments, the thrill of discovery.

How I'm not sure that was as strong as I thought it was.

Soe's watching my fingers where they're frozen in the air. I twitch.

I don't understand what I feel for him anymore, I finally say.

She leans against me, her shoulder warm.

"Feelings change," she says.

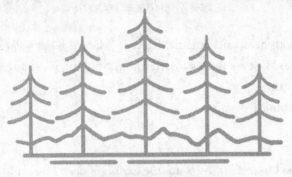

VERAN

When I crack open my eyes, it's night. The world makes a bubble around me, distorted even in the darkness. Shapes blur and bend at their edges. One detaches from the others, leaning forward.

"Ma," I croak. It only makes sense—unless she's out in the wood, she's always the first to me.

"Veran?"

The voice isn't Mama's, and once I place it, and the dim outline of the face beside me, I can't think why I'm in Lumen Lake. When did I get to Lumen Lake?

I crane my head. "Lady Queen?"

The person stiffens, and the more I blink, the more things fall into place.

"Oh," I say. "Eloise. Sorry." We must be at school, then. Blazes, I hope I didn't collapse in class.

There's a sharp inhale, and Eloise's face disappears. There's murmuring outside my line of sight. That's okay—my body is outrageously heavy. The muscles in my shoulders burn.

I can hear rain outside. Rain in Alcoro! That's a welcome change. My eyes flutter closed again, bringing no change in the darkness.

I think I sleep?

The next time I lift my head, the sounds of deep breathing combs through the rain. Eloise sits on the floor a pace away, her knees drawn up to her chest. I squint. What did she do to her hair?

She turns her head. "Feeling okay?"

"Yeah," I say automatically, a complete and utter lie, but I don't like to worry Eloise. "You?"

She snorts, a sound I can't recall her making before.

"You knew all that time," she says. "From that first time you collapsed on the way to Utzibor. You recognized me then. Those were some of the first words out of your mouth—*Lady Queen*. I must really look like her when you're hallucinating, huh?"

"What?" I ask.

She's silent.

Rain patters. Something warm and oddly furry presses against my hip. I nudge my fingers through a coarse coat.

I want to rub my face, maybe sit up—I feel like there's some urgency just out of reach, something I can't quite pin down. But sleep is clawing at me again, hooking its smoky fingers into my skin.

"I liked your curls," I say drowsily, intending to go on that I also like whatever she's done to them now.

"I don't give a damn what you like," she says, as I'm drawn

reluctantly back into sleep, trying to remember when I've ever heard Eloise curse.

"Veran. Veran—can you wake up? It's time."

Who the balls is speaking Moquoian to me? With a huge effort, I slit open my eyes. Bending over me is Iano, looking pale and haggard.

"We tried to let you sleep as long as you needed, but we have to get to the road now—everything's all packed up."

I groan and drag my hand over my face. A familiar ache squeezes all my muscles, along with an unfamiliar race of pain down my back from working the crosscut saw.

"I seized?" I ask, pressing my palm over my eyes.

"Last night. You didn't hit anything. How are you feeling now?"

"Murder." I roll onto my side, pressing my forehead to the quilt. "Is there water? Or something hot?"

"I've got both. You might have to drink them fast."

I push myself up on hollow arms. I roll my neck a few times.

Iano holds out a mug of *urch* tea. I sip it, letting it scald my throat.

"Lark rode out before dawn to check the road. The tree is still up. Do you think you'll be able to finish felling it yourself, or do we need to change our plan?"

"No, we can't change it now. All the rest of you need to be down by the road." I don't add that I can't stomach the idea of any of them being the one up top, coordinating the activity below. I've played it all out in my head so many times it feels like I've done it already. I'm not going to hand it off to someone else.

I rub my face again. "Let me eat something, and then walk around a bit—I'll be okay."

"All right, if you're sure. The others are almost ready, though." He hesitates and then says, "Have a care—I think Lark might be mad at you. I know Tamsin's mad at me."

"Why?" I ask, at the same moment I recall the curt things I said to Lark across the saw as we prepared to fell the redwood. We'd worked for hours in determined silence, relying on the demands of the work to absorb any need to talk. Her silence persisted throughout the ride back to Soe's.

"I don't know about Lark." Iano looks away. "Tamsin . . . she's saying I don't trust her decisions anymore."

"You need to let her make her own choices," I say, feeling wise and worldly. "Let her be the person she believes she can be, not the one you want her to be."

He eyes me sideways, almost shrewdly. He looks like he's about to say something when there's a rap on the doorframe. Soe sticks her head in the room.

"Feeling okay?" she asks.

"I'll get there," I say. I down the rest of the tea and push myself to my feet. "Sorry about last night—I didn't break anything, did I?"

"No. It's fine. We're all glad you're okay. There are huckleberry cakes here on the table."

I make my way into the kitchen with my hand on the wall and wolf a few down without taking a seat. From outside comes the continuing patter of rain. We'd factored the possibility of rain into our plans, but I can't help but worry that I've glossed over something. The fuzzy cobwebs in my head don't help. I shake my head a few times to clear it. Surely the rain won't change things. It may even help, masking our noise and making the work of clearing the fallen tree take that much longer.

As I throw back another mug of *urch* tea, the door opens, and on the threshold stands Lark. If I'd been writing a script, this is where I'd throw in a flash of lightning and a roll of thunder, but the skies don't comply—the rain continues to drizzle behind her.

Still, I have to bite back a triumphant grin. She's wearing the blue vest and the cowhide hat. Her red bandanna is pulled up around her chin, and she's even smudged soot from the fire over both cheeks. The broadsword hangs in a loop at her belt. I *wish* I'd been able to find her a buckler to complete the picture.

Her gaze lands on me for only the barest second and then skirts away.

"Ready?" she asks the room.

Soe and Iano nod and swing their cloaks around their shoulders. Lark steps aside to let them pass through the door. Out on the porch is Tamsin, wearing one of the new dresses, carefully closing the top of an oilcloth pouch under her cloak, where her essay must be tucked inside.

I pick up my own cloak and Iano's bow and quiver.

"Lark," I say as she heads for the porch. She turns halfway back, offering me her ear, but not her eyes, which remain fixed on the doorjamb. If Tamsin is mad at Iano, at least I can remedy things on my end.

"Listen, I'm sorry about yesterday," I say. "I shouldn't have snapped at you about cutting the tree. I appreciate your help."

She frowns at the door, and then shakes her head, still not looking at me.

"You're dense," she says.

"What? Lark—I just said I was sorry."

"Veran—" She glances out the door at the others. "Look, let's get this thing done. We can talk after, okay?"

"What's there to talk about? I *said I was sorry.*"

She turns fully away from me, hitching her bandanna up over her nose. She whistles to Rat and together they descend the porch steps, heading out into the rain.

I throw up my hands in frustration, pull on my cloak, and stomp out the door after her.

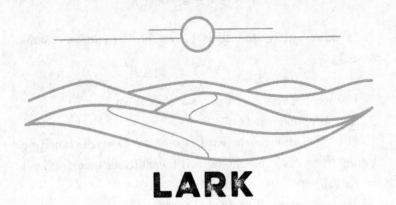

LARK

Tamsin and I huddle in the ferns.

"You okay?" I ask.

She grimaces. *Wet.*

"Yeah." I tip my hat, letting a stream of water sluice off the brim. It's been over an hour since we first took our positions, and I'm stiff with cold and from crouching on the steep slope. Iano and Soe are spread out down the road, and Veran is up the hill with the redwood tree, the wood straining against the metal wedges keeping the slice open.

Tamsin sighs and shifts in the leaves. *I want this to be over.*

I nod. "Me, too. I just hope this gets us some answers. That we can stop Kimela."

"Hm," she says. *Or at least that she listens.*

"*Uah*, that is what I meant. That she sees how smart your writing is and changes her mind."

She sighs again. *What will you do after?* she asks. *If it all works.*

"Find a way to go to Callais, I guess. I have to find my camp-mates."

And your family?

I pause. "I guess . . . I will have to see them."

You still don't want to?

"I . . ." I look up the road, where the carriage should be coming from. "Is it making sense if I want to see them but I am worried about . . . them seeing me?"

She looks at me. *We talked about that.* She pats the pouch at her side, where her slate is hidden. *The first night on the porch. That when we learn . . .*

Her fingers fumble, and she waves as if to clear the air.

I nod and finish her statement. "We do better." I do remember her writing that. It made a lot of sense to me, brought me a lot of comfort.

I gesture to the hilt of the sword on my hip.

"And here I am anyway," I say. "Not doing better. Doing exactly the same thing I've always done."

She purses her lips, but she doesn't get a chance to go on. From down the road, ringing through the trees comes a distinct four-note chirp. Both Tamsin and I perk up.

"Soe?" I whisper.

She nods. *Here they come.*

I cup my palm to my mouth and give my best whistle, mimicking the sparrow Veran taught us as a warning. It's wobbly and sounds far more like a person whistling than a bird singing, but a second later, we hear the same call repeated back in an affirmative. After another few silent beats, we hear the first metallic *clang* of a sledgehammer against a wedge.

I draw in a breath. This part is the most crucial to get right.

If Veran doesn't drop the tree quickly enough, there's a chance the oncoming entourage will hear him, or that they'll pass by before it falls. Tamsin and I both lie, tense, in the underbrush, waiting to hear the crackle and groan of the falling redwood. *Clang, clang, clang.*

A flash in the wet underbrush across the road catches my eye. I prod Tamsin and point. She looks. Iano and Soe are hurrying into position. Tamsin takes a small breath and looks back toward the crest of the hill, still ringing with the sledgehammer. *Clang, clang.*

I grind my teeth. Iano had wondered last night if I should switch places with Veran to fell the tree, but I talked him out of it. Now I'm wondering if I should have insisted, even if it made Veran go to pieces. *Clang.*

From down the road trickle the first sounds of clopping hooves and squeaking braces. I chew my lip, my mind racing. If I'm going to rush across the road and up the hill to help Veran, I have to do it now. In another moment, the coach and riders will round the bend, and the chance will be lost. I shift my feet to a ready position underneath me.

Then, the sound—a tremendous groaning, and the splintering of wood. Through the ranks of trunks, we see a bundle of branches suddenly shudder and whip. With a sound that shakes the whole hillside, the tree arcs downward, disappearing behind the curve of the road with a muffled smash.

Tamsin lets out her breath. I release my white-knuckled grip on the hilt of the sword.

Hope they didn't hear that, she signs grimly. I nod.

Veran cut it close. Less than a minute later, the foremost rider comes around the far bend, dressed in palace livery and riding a chestnut horse made sleek and dark in the rain. Another rider flanks him, and then comes the coach, pulled by a four-in-hand and rumbling ponderously over the road. Two guards sit atop the coach with the driver, and as they roll nearer, we can see the hooves of two more horses bringing up the rear.

I inch my fingers toward Tamsin. *Six guards.* Plus the unknown threat of the possible maid inside.

The first riders reach our hiding place and pass us by, followed by the stamping and jostling of the horse team. The driver and guards sway on top of the coach, its iron-shod wheels throwing up mud and pebbles. Tamsin and I both hold our breaths.

The horse team slows at the hairpin curve.

The coach stops, its rear wheel just a few feet up the steep slope from us.

"What is it?" calls the driver.

"A tree!" one of the front riders shouts back.

"How big?" asks the driver.

"Damned big," replies the guard.

There's a coordinated round of cursing. On the coach window, a curtain flutters. Tamsin grabs my wrist.

That's her, she says, her fingers moving sharply.

Good. I study the woman's face in the window, accented by colored powder and framed by large jeweled earrings.

"What's the trouble, Uerik?" she calls.

"A tree down around the bend, my lady," the driver calls. "We'll have to clear it."

The *ashoki* sighs and withdraws from the window. Tamsin and I watch as the guards dismount and situate their horses on the narrow road. The ones in the front edge around the coach, their boots sliding in the soft earth and sending trickles of mud skittering past our elbows. They confer with the rear guards and begin to unpack their tools from the luggage compartment.

The group's commander singles out one of the coach guards to stay behind, and with a lot of grumbling and squelching of boots, the rest trudge back up the road and around the bend. The guard clambers back up to her post, idly checking her crossbow. The driver reclines, hooking the reins and setting his boots up on the edge of the box. He draws a pipe from his pocket.

We wait. Across the road, I can just barely see the shifting of Soe's boots, the glint of Iano's rapier. A few horses snort and stamp. The rain drums on the carriage roof.

Finally, there's a piercing call. Veran said it was a pewee, and that his folk use it for *attack*. We decided to use it for *go*.

I draw in a breath.

"See you in a minute," I whisper to Tamsin. She nods and gives my arm a quick squeeze.

I loosen the sword at my hip, seeing the ferns part around Iano and Soe across the road, and rise like a ghost from the bracken.

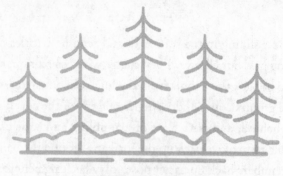

VERAN

The attack is swift, quiet, and amazingly efficient. With no sound, Lark makes two hops up the far side of the carriage. One moment the guard on top is sitting with her crossbow in her lap, the next she's facedown in the guard box, clutching her forehead. Lark catches up the fallen crossbow with her toe and flings it into the swallowing bracken, while in the same motion brings the flat of her sword around to connect with the driver's head. Iano's up by that point—he springs to pin the guard's hand as she struggles to find her sword hilt. Soe climbs into the driver's box with crossbow cocked and pointed at the cowering driver.

Then, it's just a matter of binding both their hands and mouths. As Iano stands over the guard, and Soe over the driver, Lark swings off the coach. She reaches down into the bracken, and Tamsin appears, sliding on the steep slope. Lark adjusts her sword and knife, hitches her bandanna a little higher, and moves to the coach door. Tamsin follows. After that, my view is blocked by the carriage.

I lean against the cold rock and wipe my forehead, my arm trembling with effort and anxiety. My hands are still stinging from the blows of the sledgehammer. I thought the tree would never come down. But it did, mighty and tragic and falling exactly where we wanted it to. Now the guards swarm around it, their hoods up against the rain, pointing at different places along the trunk and lopping off a few small branches, completely unaware of the plight of their comrades just around the bend.

I try to calm the butterflies in my stomach. Things are working. Now it's all down to what Lark and Tamsin can glean from inside. I shift on the rock, my vantage point, checking the bow and quiver of arrows for the dozenth time.

These guards are slow to begin their work, noodling around the trunk, peering here and there. There's not much sound from the coach at this point, but I'd like them to start sawing—it would keep them all the more preoccupied.

My gaze flicks between the two scenes. The coach, still and silent, with Soe and Iano standing over their wards. The tree, where the guards cluster around the trunk, their tools at their sides.

What are they *looking* at?

Slowly, one by one, their faces turn up toward the hill.

My heart vaults to my throat.

I'm hidden well enough that they can't see me from the road, but I shrink against the rock all the same. I watch with horror as two of them detach from the others and begin the tedious, slippery work of toiling up the hill, along the length of the tree. The others begin their work a little half-heartedly, trimming off a few skinny branches here and there.

I race through my options. If they reach the base of the tree and find it cut, what then? They won't be able to see the coach from the stump, but it will definitely make them wary. I glance down at the carriage again. No change—but have Lark and Tamsin made any progress inside? Will Kimela tell the guards to stand down?

The two are getting closer to the stump. I wet my lips, making a decision. At the very least, I can warn the others that something's amiss. Trying to beat away the same panic that crept up on me when Lark collapsed in the water scrape, I purse my lips and blow. The first whistle is only air, and I rush to try again. I give the rising two-note call of the cardinal. *What cheer!* Danger.

Through the trees, I see Iano's head shift, but he doesn't react beyond that. At least I know he's heard. The two guards climb closer. With fumbling fingers, I pull an arrow from the quiver and set it to Iano's bowstring. I'm not sure what I plan to do with it, but it's there.

The two guards stop short, their gazes up the slope. They've seen the smooth, purposeful cut at the end of the trunk.

I purse my lips again. *What cheer!* I don't dare take my eyes off the soldiers to see how the others react at the coach.

The guards close the last few feet to the stump and see the saw, the sledge, the wedges. They look around their immediate vicinity. I'm above their line of sight, but any closer and I won't have much cover to depend on at all. This rock was convenient because it was high above everything else, with little to block its view down to either side of the road. But it's a perch, not a hiding place.

I whistle again, trying to inject urgency into the call. *What cheer!*

Best case scenario, Kimela will pop out and holler for everyone to stand down. Worst case, Lark and the others are planning their retreat. I throw a glance down at the coach.

They're just standing there! Iano and Soe, standing immobile, the same as before. No movement from the coach. Didn't they listen? Have they forgotten the calls I taught them?

The guards are alert now, their hatchets replaced by their sword hilts. They're looking around, back to back, searching for the culprit. With real panic now I clamber sideways along the rock, hoping to find somewhere with better cover. There's a cluster of trunks nearby that should hide me—if I can get to them.

When no attack bursts from the underbrush, the guards must realize the danger isn't right here at the stump. They turn back down the hill. One shouts to the guards clustered around the tree.

I take another breath and give one more desperate attempt to warn the others. *What cheer!*

My whistle cracks on the final note, sounding more like a person than a bird. The rear guard halts in his tracks and pivots back up the hill. His gaze locks on me.

"Hey!" he shouts.

As sure as if his shout was a crossbow quarrel, my foot slips on the wet rock. I slide toward the ground, losing sight of the carriage.

It's only as I hit the brush and scramble in the opposite direction that I realize what I've done.

The cardinal isn't *danger*.

It's *all's well*.

TAMSIN

The interior of the coach is dim and thick with the scent of perfume. Lark enters first, her sword up. There are two high gasps.

"Quiet," she growls. "All we need is quiet, and you will not be hurt."

I step up behind her. It's a tight fit, but both Kimela and her maid have shrunk against the far door, leaving the middle of the coach clear. Lark edges to one side to give me space, blocking the maid from my view. Kimela's gaze falls on me. At first, there's only the same terror as for the Sunshield Bandit, with no flicker of recognition.

"Hi," I say flatly.

"What do you want?" Kimela asks sharply. "If you want the jewels, you can have them. But I warn you—the palace will not rest until they've tracked you down—"

"Quiet," Lark orders again. "Your job is to listen to Tamsin."

"Tamsin?" echoes Kimela faintly. "Who . . ." Her gaze

travels to me again, and her eyes nearly pop from her head. She straightens up, staring through the dim light. Her rouged mouth drops open.

"Tamsin . . . *Tamsin Moropai*?"

I thin my lips as her gaze roves over me, from my homespun dress to my shorn hair. I'd like to think I look a little healthier than I did a week ago, but all the same, I'm certainly not the same person she remembers—I'm the face on the bounty sheet, the accomplice of the Sunshield Bandit.

"How did you . . . where . . . *you died!* Everyone said you had *died!*"

I shake my head grimly.

"But I . . . I saw your *si-oque* myself—they locked it in the case by your pedestal. It convinced Queen Isme to rush my appointment. She hoped it would draw out the prince's kidnappers . . ."

I frown and hold up my wrist, where my *si-oque* rests just above my sleeve. Her gaze falls on it.

"But . . . ," she says. "But then . . . how did the minister produce it? Whose did he have?"

"Who?" I ask.

"Minister Kobok—he received your *si-oque* in the mail anonymously. He presented it to the queen and suggested that expediting my appointment would encourage the kidnappers to come forward."

Lark and I exchange a glance. Kobok, always an opponent of mine, miraculously produced a forged *si-oque* and claimed it was a sign to rush Kimela's confirmation?

That seems *awfully* convenient.

"But there were other people who saw you die!" Kimela protests. She turns to her maid. "*You* said she had died!"

I crane my head to look around Lark. Kimela's maid is shrunk against the seat, a look of dread on her face.

My next thoughts fizzle out.

It's Simea.

My maid.

I go to declare her name and end up only sputtering on the *s*. She draws a deep, trepidatious breath.

"My lady Tamsin?" she whispers.

"I . . ." I begin. Lark cuts her gaze to my fingers as I move them numbly.

"Tamsin says she thought you died in the attack," Lark translates, then glances back to me. "This is your old maid?"

I nod. I remember her body, heavy and stifling, as she collapsed against me, pinning me in the coach outside Vittenta.

"You said she'd died!" Kimela insists.

"I thought she had," Simea whispers.

A creak of the coach and an angry mutter from up top whips me out of my thoughts. I can dwell on Simea later, but we have to buy ourselves time first. I shake myself and lift my hands again. Lark and I have practiced this part, and she barely has to take her gaze off Kimela and Simea to give them my words.

"Tamsin didn't die, and she is not here as your enemy," she says. "She commends your appointment to *ashoki* and hopes your career will be long. But Moquoia and Prince Iano Okinot in-Azure are in very great danger." It does seem ironic to say this when Iano himself is just a foot above us, brandishing his rapier, but I go on.

"Tamsin needs to talk to you about the threat to the Moquoian court, and how it can be stopped—"

"I beg your pardon, I'm sure, but why are *you* doing all the talking then?" Kimela asks, her voice high but resolute. She's regained some of her poise, a steely glint in her eye.

"Tamsin, if you did not know, had her tongue split in the attack outside Vittenta," Lark says, shifting her sword the barest inch. Kimela's eyes dart to its point. "She is speaking to you with hand signs. I am telling you her words."

Kimela looks back to me again. Simea is sitting rigid in her seat, her lips parted in a sort of permanent, soft scream.

"Tamsin needs you to listen to her now," Lark goes on. "We ask that you tell your guards to stand down."

"I most certainly will not!" Kimela exclaims. "Not with the world's most notorious bandit waving a sword in my face!"

I have to give Kimela credit for pure nerve, but I need her to understand what we're here for. Despite her new career in theatrics, her shock is real, and with the news of Kobok's miraculous possession of a forged *si-oque*, I'm now certain she's not our blackmailer. If I can get her to calm down, we can all sit and think rationally about this. I dig in the pouch on my belt and come out with my pamphlet.

"This is an essay Tamsin has written," Lark says as I hand it over, "explaining the root of the problem in Moquoia and the steps the court can take to fix it."

Kimela's gaze flicks to the pamphlet, then back up to me. She seems to gather herself to say something, but stops and looks again at the paper. She takes it, staring at the text.

"What on earth—who wrote this? Who can scribe like this?"

Oh, bless the colors, a lucky break.

Lark glances at my hands. "Tamsin says read it, and she'll tell you."

Kimela clucks her tongue in irritation, but nevertheless her eyes begin to dart down the page. Furrows form around her mouth, but I use her momentary distraction to turn back to Simea.

What happened outside Vittenta? I ask, and Lark translates.

She's sitting pressed firmly against the seat, with her hands buried inside her cloak. "I was pulled out of the coach and bound by the attackers. I didn't see what happened to you. When they said you'd died, I believed it."

You fell on me, I say, lifting my eyebrows in surprise. *I thought you'd been shot.*

"I was trying to protect you," she says.

I struggle to make sense of this, but as I'm placing her story alongside the events I remember, a distant, shrill whistle pierces the air. Lark and I go still, straining to hear. It's that two-note birdcall, the one Veran told us is the cardinal. We exchange a quick glance, frowning.

All is well, I sign, and she nods. He must be merely keeping us updated about the guards around the bend.

"Wait just a moment," Kimela says, now skimming the second page of my essay. "Look here, Tamsin, you completely gloss over the impacts that reducing bond labor would have on our social services, our health care system—you act as if it's just going to create a dip in our economy, not undo centuries of social infrastructure . . ."

I jump to move my hands.

"Tamsin knows there are more considerations than are named in the text," Lark says. "But the point is that these things are . . . *lut'uw* . . . sorry, Tamsin, I do not know . . . they are in to being fixed," she stumbles, and then, on a whim, she goes off my signs, locking sights on Kimela. "And these things—people services, health system—these are not so important as the lives of slaves, the lives of families and children."

"Not so important!" Kimela exclaims, her grip creasing the paper. Outside, the cardinal call comes again—Veran is being overcautious, it seems. "You were on this nonsense before, Tamsin, when you were *ashoki*. Do you know how it sounds to your colleagues in court, when you dismiss their industries as unimportant? I come from the rice families of Ketori. How dare you suggest dismantling such a pillar of Moquoian trade by wrapping it all up in laborer welfare?"

Just read the rest of the essay, I say, and Kimela flicks her hand at Lark as the words come out of her mouth.

"No, I will not. I can see where this is going. I am the *ashoki* now, Tamsin, not you, and I will inform you that I have brought some balance back to the court you rocked. Moquoia in danger, indeed! *You're* the one who went and tipped it on its head!"

She closes the pamphlet with a curt slap and holds it back out to me. From outside, Veran shrieks the cardinal's call again. My anger flickers briefly in his direction—if he's not careful, he's going to give away his position.

"Bond labor is wrong and has no place in Moquoia anymore," Lark says carefully, watching my fingers. "But there are ways to undo it without destroying the country."

"A fanciful dream of the unpatriotic and overemotional," Kimela says firmly. "Moquoia wouldn't be half what it is without bond labor. Blessed Light, do watch where you're putting that thing!" she cries, leaning away from Lark's sword, which has jumped toward her.

Lark drives it into the quilted seat back just a few inches from Kimela's left ear. She leans forward, her teeth gritted over her red bandanna, and Kimela has the wherewithal to remember her terror. Lark spits a few words in Eastern. Veran whistles a fourth time, his call cracking on the final note—by the colors, what is wrong with him?

There's a sudden shout from up top, and the whole carriage rocks. Something that sounds remarkably like a crossbow quarrel thumps the side of the coach.

"Tamsin!" Iano calls, his footsteps hitting just overhead. "Lark! Get out of there! The guards are coming!"

Lark reels back from Kimela, jerking her sword out of the seat back. At exactly the same moment, Simea flings herself from her seat toward me.

She'd have made contact if Lark hadn't moved—instead, they collide, and all three of us ricochet in the cramped space, our legs tangling. I land against the door, and it hinges open, swinging over the empty space just off the road. Rain pelts my face. There's shouting outside. I struggle to free my feet from the pile of us on the floor. It's only as Lark gives her own yell, twisting awkwardly toward Simea, that I see the knife.

It's wrapped in Simea's fingers, and it's arcing toward me. Lark launches herself off the bench and plunges the end of her sword into the dark folds of Simea's cloak. She spasms and gasps. The knife falls. Kimela screams, high and long. The coach rocks, and the far door bursts open. A crossbow is thrust into the space, and Lark rushes to deflect it—but misses. Her fist swings by it ineffectively, as if she'd forgotten her shield wasn't on her left hand. The quarrel fires, missing her head by inches, but the mistake has thrown her off balance—a black-liveried body barrels into the coach, slamming her against the edge of the seat. She gives a snarl; there's a horrible groan as their grappling bodies land on the bleeding Simea. Kimela is still screaming.

Lark twists in the guard's grip, his burly arms wound under her shoulders. Her eyes find mine. Her last movement in the tiny space, filled now with the tang of blood instead of perfume, is to kick.

Her boot hits my calf so hard I can feel the worn tread of her soles, and I slip backward, my fingers just missing the door-frame. One of my feet lands on the soft, perilous edge of the road—the other swings out into open air. The rain-soft mud gives way beneath me.

I fall, first through air and then through brush, rolling and tumbling uncontrollably into the fathomless forest below.

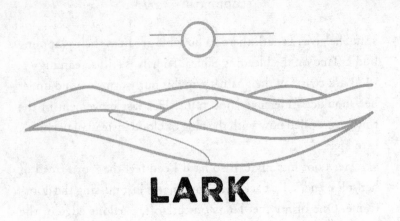

LARK

I hit the wet road face-first. On principle, I start to roll over, but the guards are expecting this. A reinforced toe flies in from nowhere and connects with my ribs, bringing a shocking flush of pain in my lungs. I gasp, dizzy, trying to drag my sword out from under me, but someone puts a knee on my back, crushing out the last of my breath. One by one, my fingers are pried off the hilt, and then my hands are planted firmly behind my back. I feel the rub of a rope.

"She killed my maid!" Kimela is shrieking. "Look at her—she's dead! The Sunshield Bandit murdered her!"

I give a feeble buck, my cheek grinding the dirt, but there are hands all over me now, and the race of pain up my side only grows worse. Someone grabs my ponytail and lifts my head—the fancy cowhide hat must have fallen off in the coach—and pulls my bandanna into my mouth, knotting it tightly behind my neck. A bag that smells like wood shavings and rusted metal goes over my head. My boots drag against the mud in a final attempt at a kick, but it takes only seconds for my ankles to be bound together, too.

Following that comes a kind of stunned silence from everyone—me, the *ashoki*, the guards, the woods.

"What . . . what should we do, Captain?" asks a voice, sounding like she's still trying to process what just happened.

"There were more bandits—they must have fled into the forest. You two—stay here with the coach. Lock the doors. Uerik, work on clearing that tree. You, and you, make a sweep of the banks. Lieutenant, you and Portis ready your horses." Someone nudges me with their boot. "You'll take the bandit back to Tolukum."

There's a murmuring of affirmations and a rush of crunching boots and hooves. The rain spatters the cloth sack over my head, seeping down my face.

Veran, I think hazily. *If you ever wanted to play the hero, now would be a great time.*

But the woods remain silent.

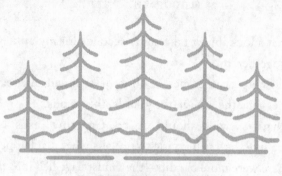

VERAN

By the time I'm sure the guards have made their final sweep of the forest and given me up as lost, it's edging past the afternoon. The rain has let up, and the air is heavy and warm. The distant sounds of chopping and sawing have stopped, so the tree must be cleared from the road. My legs have cramped from staying tucked up inside this rotting, half-buried redwood log, and I'm painfully thirsty, but I still don't dare to move from my hiding place. I'm hoping, perhaps, that I'll simply die inside this tree. Maybe I'll seize again and it will be my last, my brain's final misfire.

But the minutes slide consciously on. It's only as the heat reaches its peak that I hear a sound I've been dreading. A goldfinch, inexpertly whistled. *Per-chick-o-ree.* A call for location. One of them remembered.

I let the call pass twice before I answer. I hear footsteps hurrying through the bracken, and finally I crawl out of the log and through the sword ferns. I emerge coated in sweat and grime just as Iano and Soe push through the foliage. Soe has a strip of her cloak bound around her wrist.

"Veran!" Iano gasps. His eyes flick around. "Where's Tamsin?"

"What do you mean, where's Tamsin?" I ask. "I assumed she was with you. She was in the coach under you."

His face splits with panic. "No! We fled the coach when the guards came back, like we planned. Is she with Lark?"

"Lark is gone," I say, the words thick and distant. "They tied her up and put her on a horse and rode back toward Tolukum." My stomach turns as I remember the pile of guards holding her down, the rib-breaking kick to her side, the tool bag pulled over her face.

"Tamsin wasn't with her?"

"Not that I saw. I figured she must have escaped with you. I only saw what happened after you had left."

Iano stares at me, his eyes wide and blazing. "And you just . . . you just *watched*?"

"Yeah. Until the guards started searching the woods," I say. "And then I ran."

He gives a shake. "Where's my bow?"

"I lost it," I say. "Back at the rock."

"What *happened*?" Soe asks, cradling her arm. "We heard you whistling the all clear . . ."

"I messed up," I say. "I whistled you the wrong bird. I meant to warn you that the guards had realized something was wrong, but I panicked. It's my fault."

For a moment, there's only the thick, stifling silence of the forest around us.

Then Iano lunges.

His hands close on my collar. I trip over a tangle of ferns and land on my back with his knuckles jamming painfully under my jaw.

"You stupid fool!" he shouts down at me, shaking my collar. "You damned idiot! This was *your* plan, *your* idea, you demanded that *you* be in charge, and look what's happened!"

"Iano, stop!" Soe drags one-handed at his shoulder. "Keep your voice down—the guards might still be around!"

Iano does drop his voice, to a gritted hiss, but the pressure from his knuckles doesn't let up. "Tamsin could be dead! She could be hurt! And you got Lark captured—do you know what will happen to her at Tolukum? Do you know what the sentence is on her bounty sheet?"

"I know," I say, my voice a dead thing. "I know. I know. I know."

"You ruined *everything*, you've undone it *all*—"

"I know," I say, my words cracking from the pressure of his knuckles against my throat.

"Iano," Soe whispers fiercely, still pulling his shoulder. "Stop it. Let him up. We have to think about this."

His fists tighten, his eyes just inches from mine, and if he'd only squeeze a little harder, I might slip into blissful unconsciousness. But he reluctantly lets go and leans back. I stay where I am, breathing shallowly, staring up at the towering crowns of the redwood trees. They crowd in, seeming to peer down at me, perhaps knowing I killed one of their brethren for no good reason. For less than no good reason. I killed one of their brethren and it only brought more pain, and more death.

We're quiet, the three of us—me on my back, Iano and Soe standing over me, Iano's hands still clenching and unclenching.

"Do you think they found our horses?" Soe asks, when it's clear neither of us is going to speak.

"It's likely," Iano says curtly, still looking daggers at me. We'd left our horses a few hundred yards down the small track leading from Soe's house to the main road, in a copse of sugar pines. "Which leaves us stranded with absolutely no food, money, or gear."

That sounds familiar. I've done that before. These conifer forests aren't nearly as harsh as the water scrape. But I had Lark in the water scrape. I hadn't gotten her captured in the water scrape.

I hadn't ruined *everything* in the water scrape.

"We're not stranded yet," Soe says, obviously aggravated at the two of us. "Why don't we head in that direction—it's the way home, anyway. If the horses aren't there, at least we're a little closer. Come on, Veran, get up. Are you hurt?"

"No," I say. Not at all. If I were, it might have given me a reason to have run, to have panicked and dropped the bow and left Lark and the others at the mercy of the guards. But I'm unhurt. The guard I ran from at the rock didn't even have a ranged weapon—only his sword. I managed to slip him using the age-old habit of simply being quiet, but he never would have given up his pursuit so quickly if the other guards hadn't needed help subduing Lark down at the coach.

Soe helps me up, and we start out, weaving in silence through the thick trunks. We have to stay within sight of the road, or risk getting hopelessly lost.

My ma wouldn't get lost. She'd have her compass. And if she didn't have her compass, she'd have thought to memorize the position of Soe's house in relation to her direction of travel.

She'd be able to navigate the forest without running the risk of being seen.

But she wouldn't need to, because my ma would have kept her head up on that hillside.

She'd have given the right warning.

And she'd *never* have run.

I trudge after the others. We find the stand of sugar pines after a half hour. The horses aren't there.

"*Kuas*," Iano says darkly.

"Maybe we could go down into the valley and try to find Lark's," Soe suggests. She and Tamsin had both ridden hers downhill of the road, so they wouldn't have to cross to get to their hiding place. Rat was told emphatically to stay, bribed with a generous ham hock Lark tied to a rock.

"A great help one horse will be to the three of us," Iano says.

"I don't deny it, *my prince*," Soe snaps. "But I'm trying to think of options, instead of just glowering about the things we can't change. I'm worried about Tamsin and Lark, too."

Iano opens his mouth, perhaps for a royal reprimand, but falls silent as a new sound reaches our ears. From the junction with the main road comes the quick thudding of hooves and jingling of tack. We immediately retreat into the undergrowth, burrowing down among the ferns. I wedge myself into a brushy hollow and wince at a flash of prickly pain. I look down to find I've backed into a mat of greenbrier. The little barbs sink neatly into my skin.

At this point it just feels like mockery.

I don't have time to free myself, however. All three of us go still, peering through the barest gaps in the foliage, as a party of horses and riders appear, trotting smartly down the road.

"It's the guards," Soe whispers, but Iano peers closer.

"They're different guards," he says.

Soe frowns as they come closer. "Wait . . . that one in the front . . . that's Osti—the blacksmith from town. He sold me Lark's sword, and the saw."

"Who's that behind him?" Iano says suddenly. "Is that—?"

"Who?" Soe says, alarmed.

"That woman who was following us at the market."

"I don't know, is it? I never saw her."

"I'm almost certain it is. Yes, look there's the scar on her eye."

They don't ask me to verify. I don't blame them. The long-familiar feeling of being a burden settles thick around me, only now I don't have the excuse of seizing at some inopportune or embarrassing moment.

I pick my head a few inches out of the clutch of the green-brier. Sure enough, riding behind the blacksmith, dressed in the black livery of Tolukum, is the woman with the twisted eyelid. She trots smartly at the head of five soldiers, her face grim.

"What else is down this track?" Iano whispers to Soe after the party has passed.

Soe grimaces. "Besides my house? Not much. A few other farmsteads, the charcoaler, and the old caved-in lead mine."

"Not much reason to go that way."

She shakes her head. "No. I think we have to assume they're here for us. That woman must have gone back to Tolukum for reinforcements and then asked around Giantess. People know me—asking for a sword and timbering equipment would have stood out a mile."

"So we can't go back," Iano says.

"Not unless you trust that those people aren't out to do you harm."

They go silent. I lay my head back against the greenbrier. Barbs prickle my neck. The world swirls around me, like the swollen South Burr the morning after I tailed Lark back to Three Lines. Words and choices and failures tumble by like the debris in the flood. Shame coats me inside and out like thick, cloudy silt. I struggle for breath, drowning in misery.

An ant—or something else, I'm probably buried in mites and chiggers at this point—bites me through my trousers, right on the soft spot beneath my knee. I shake my leg, earning myself long scrapes from the greenbrier. I rest my boot on a pile of bracken, trying to get my leg out of the brush. The fringe droops, muddy and limp. These used to be my best boots, back when they'd only ever seen the shiny interior of palaces and houses of state. Now the embroidery is stained and ragged. The one remaining medallion rests cockeyed, the threads loosened.

I gaze vaguely at the laurel flower stamped into the silver, distantly thinking of its partner and how I traded it for Lark's hat—the hat she didn't want, to do a job she didn't want to do. The truth doesn't so much hit me as bubble up from my subconscious—it's something I knew all along. Lark didn't want to carry out the attack. How many times did she tell me it was a bad idea? How many times did she try to talk me around it, talk me out of it? I thought she was trying to coddle me. But now I realize she was trying to protect herself, not me.

And I didn't let her.

They're going to execute her at Tolukum Palace. Because of my mistake.

Another ant bites me near my wrist, and as if hitting a magic button, tears spring to my eyes. I lift my palms and crush them against my face, digging them into my eye sockets. My breath catches in my chest, and then bursts out in a choked gasp, then another, and another.

I've killed Lark—brave, good, mighty Lark, and in killing her I've killed Moira Alastaire. The impossible happened, the lost Lumeni princess appeared alive out of the desert, and now I've destroyed her—and I've destroyed her father, and her sister, and her mother, and her uncles, and her folk. Her campmates, waiting for her in Callais. My parents, who loved her, too.

And I've destroyed myself, because I will never, *ever* forgive myself for what I've done.

Iano and Soe don't say anything while I sit and shake, sobbing into my palms. I sink farther into the nest of greenbrier, the epithet I chose because it's tenacious and tearing. I thought it was the opposite of me, but now I think I saw its nature in me all along—that it grips something bigger than it is and won't let go, tearing it apart in the process.

Another ant bites me, and another. I gasp and shake my arms, overwhelmed. I beat my legs and slap my boots. This is too much for my weary medallion, and it pops off its threads. It falls into the dense underbrush, and with a flare of panic, I plunge my hand after it. My fingers close around it, and with it I bring up a few strings of bright green moss.

Moss and silver and laurel. I swear, all I need is a firefly and I could probably summon my mother by magic ritual. The thought guts me—what she would say to me in this moment, what she would say in the face of what I've done to Lark. I bend my head toward my knees, still fighting for breath through my tears.

Her old phrase, the one scouts have adopted as lore, comes back to me.

One crisis at a time.

I shake my head. She wouldn't say that, not now. The crises were of my own making, and they're gone, passed on by.

One crisis at a time, Veran.

I made the crises myself, Mama. They're my own doing.

One at a time.

They're done now.

Always remember what's important, and what's urgent.

Lark's going to be killed. Tamsin's missing. People are searching for us.

Start with what you have.

The horses are gone. We've got nothing.

What do you have?

I look back down at the medallion in my palm. My seal ring glints on my finger.

You have more!

Iano and Soe murmur beside me, their voices low and serious. The smell of damp, rich earth, of water and growing things, of rot and life, rises up around me. The buzz and click of insects, the calls of birds overhead. I pick out a goldfinch, a real one. *Per-chick-o-ree! Per-chick-o-ree!* A scout calling for location. *Where are you? Where are you?*

Another ant bites, adding to the stings and scrapes and bruises webbing my skin. And then, in place of the mantras Mama drills into her scouts, up comes the whisper she repeats only to me, clutching my face.

Listen to your body, Veran. Listen. Listen.

My body hurts, lying in this hollow. The greenbrier, the ants, the shame.

Listen to it.

I place my hands beneath me, feeling the fuzz of moss and the sting of two more ant bites. And then I push. Briars tear at my clothes and hair, but I rip free of them, heedless. I shoot out of the brambles like a rabbit out of a warren, jumping a foot in the air and landing with a forceful *thud* on the earth, trying to jar the ants free.

Soe and Iano abruptly go silent, staring at me. I beat my clothes and hair again.

Soe lifts an eyebrow. "Bugs?"

My hands drop to my sides, and I face them. My cheeks are still wet, but my tears have stopped.

"I'm going to Tolukum," I say.

Iano's forehead creases in anger. "How? We have no horses."

"Then I'll walk," I say. "But we're not out of options yet. I have this." I hold up my medallion. "It might buy me a ride on someone's wagon."

"They'll arrest you at the front gates, if you get that far," he says.

"Then I'll go quietly, and I'll tell them who I am, and who Lark is. The worst has already happened. They're going to execute her for banditry. If I can get there beforehand, I might be able to delay them long enough for her family to step in. If not . . . then I'll be in place to contact Rou, and tell him what I've done."

"They might kill *you*," he says. "If they think you're an accomplice of hers."

"I don't care," I say firmly. "I really don't. But I can't do nothing. I already did nothing, and I've sent her to the execution block. I have to try. And I have my parents' seal—it might give me some leverage."

"What about Tamsin?" Iano presses.

"She might have been brought back to the palace, too. Maybe they locked her in the coach, or took her away before I got back to the road."

"Or she might be *dead*," Iano says, with the crisp edge of panic.

"Maybe, but maybe not—and if she's not, she may need help. You stay. Stay around here and look for her. Even if she's not hurt, she can't go far. Then you can find somewhere safe to hide for a while. But I'm going to Tolukum. If she's at the palace, I'll find a way to send you word."

They both stare at me. I lift my hand, scratched and studded with bites, and open my palm toward them.

"Thank you, for what you did today," I say. "I'm sorry I ruined it all. The rest of you were amazing."

They still don't answer, and with nothing left to do, no pack to shoulder or weapon to sheathe, I start to turn toward the track.

Iano gives a loud sigh. "Hang on."

I look back. He's working at the clasp on his *si-oque*. It opens, and he slides the heirloom bronze band off, the lapis winking.

"*Don't* pawn this," he orders. "Use it at the palace. The guards will recognize it, and it'll let you speak in my name. It may get you out of trouble, or secure you an audience with my mother. It may help Lark. Don't lose it."

"I won't," I promise. I slip it on my own wrist, cover it with my sleeve, and lift my palm to him again. "Thank you."

"You're welcome. Good luck."

"Good luck," Soe echoes. "Be careful."

I nod and turn away, but it's a lie. I'm not going to be careful. I'm going to do whatever it takes to get into Tolukum and to Lark, until I can't do anymore.

I push through the ferns, hit the track, and turn toward the main road. I walk slowly at first, easing my sore body into movement, but then I pick up the pace, my mother's words finding their place in my stride.

Listen. Urgent. Start.

TAMSIN

I open my eyes to the twilight, the purpling sky slipping through the distant treetops. Not so different from that little bit of sky in my cell window. Only instead of one tiny square, these are shards, fragments, wisps.

I shift, testing my body. It's still aching, but nothing screams as if sprained or broken—a miracle, I suppose, or the luck of the piles of duff and redwood needles carpeting the ravine slopes.

I look down at my side, where Rat lays half on me. I scratch his ears. I'd probably have grown dangerously cold if he hadn't found me a few hours ago, snuffling me out in this nest of bracken. He settled down against me, lending me his warmth.

"Goo' boy," I rasp. He stretches against me, giving a little hum of satisfaction.

The stream trickles nearby. I've already drunk from it once today, when I crawled from my original landing spot. I must have left a trail in the underbrush three feet wide all the way down the hillside, and I didn't want to make it too easy on anybody who might come looking. But nobody did. I don't know if they didn't see me fall, or assumed I'd died instantly.

I haven't died, though. I've lain, silent, dozing in and out, and thinking. My slate is broken, cracked into pieces by the fall. And the carriage and guards on the road are gone. I'm not sure where anybody is, or whether Lark escaped the coach.

But I have figured one thing out.

Kimela was the wrong audience.

The *ashoki* has been the most influential position in Moquoian politics for centuries. Tales are told of how they seeded wars, or ended them . . . how good ones made poor monarchs great, and how bad ones brought the greatest monarchs to their knees. This country has been run, tugged, lofted, and buried, not by its monarchy, but by its *ashokis*.

I had great visions for my career. I envisioned myself lauded and praised, my statue raised alongside the others in the Hall of the *Ashoki*, my words carved into marble and set down in Moquoian lore. I envisioned my name in history books, my achievements written out by scribes as they told the story of our country.

And I used Iano to get there. I can't deny it. If he was blinded by his adoration for me, then I was all too ready to accept it as a stepping stone to greatness. A monarch and an *ashoki* at odds has never gone well. A monarch and an *ashoki* smitten with each other, as evidenced by the last six weeks, is a recipe for disaster.

What a dangerous amount of power for one person.

Which made me realize who I should have been talking to all along.

I pat Rat again and push myself up, my battered muscles protesting. I take things slowly, crawling again to the stream for another drink. I'd slipped a few of Soe's huckleberry cakes in my pouch this morning. They're crumbs now, ones I've been snacking on throughout the day, and now I allow myself a meal of the biggest piece. I swallow, wash it down with another drink, and then get slowly to my feet.

"Okay, Rat," I say. "Come."

We follow the stream, moving slowly through the darkening woods, until the valley sides grow less steep. I turn upslope, breathing heavily, but it's not far until we reach the place Lark and I left Rat this morning. Her horse is still there. Kobok's horse, rather. I grin painfully.

The horse has been grazing all day, so I bring it down to the stream to drink, and then I clamber onto its back. I nudge it uphill. Rat follows.

There's evidence of a lot of activity on the road, churned earth and trails of hoofprints all crisscrossing each other, but we meet nobody. By the time we reach Soe's house, it's fully dark. I turn the horse into the paddock, and then I realize that the two mules are gone, along with their tack. The cart is still there, though. I'm not sure what to make of this until I get to the cabin door and go inside.

The place has been—not exactly ransacked, but at least searched thoroughly. Cupboards are open, furniture is moved, and rugs are peeled back and piled in corners. Soe's bed is pushed along one wall, and her wardrobe and cedar chest thrown open, the contents strewn over the covers. The dulcimer lies under a pile of shawls. I clear them away and pull it out, setting it on the bedspread.

In the workroom, my scattered papers have been moved

into piles so that the presses could be shifted around. But nothing seems to be broken or taken. If anything, whoever was here seemed to be looking for places in the floor that might hide a door. They were looking, not for goods, but for people. Me, probably.

Well, they missed me, and now I have Rat to sound an alarm. Still, it adds to my sense of urgency. Hastily, I turn up the lanterns and shove the big press back into the middle of the room. I warm the jars of tacky ink in my hands and neaten the stacks of blank paper. I unearth the three big blocks Lark carved, set with their lines of stamps, painstakingly cast and crafted, from the tidy rows of text to the bold title font. THE PATH OF THE FLOOD. So much work for one meager little pamphlet. So much effort, to be read by only one person.

But not for much longer.

Rain cannot soak dry ground. When met with arid soil, it runs off and races onward, becoming destruction.

My metaphors had been good, but slightly off. Tolukum Palace has always been the dry ground, but the destruction doesn't have to be just its making. It's the rain, after all, that strikes the unyielding surface and then goes tearing off, joining forces, becoming rivulets, then streams, then floods. And it's the flood that destroys—reshapes the arid land to something of its own making.

The enormity of what I'm about to do—what I'm about to *undo*—strikes me, and I stare at the hulking wine press. If my idea works, am I turning it into a machine of creation, or a machine of destruction?

It's both, I decide. Such is the nature of justice. Iano and I had been focused so much on the *creation* that we ignored the fact that something had to be destroyed first.

The achievement of justice relies first on the destruction of injustice.

I push up the sleeves of my dress, eat another of Soe's cakes, and get to work.

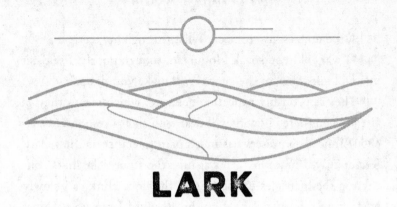

LARK

Footsteps sound on the stone, and keys ring against the metal door. Hinges groan. My closed eyelids redden with new light, so I keep them shut. I'm lying on my side, my arms stretched out to accommodate the manacles on my wrists. I breathe only deeply enough to keep air flowing in my lungs. Anything deeper and my cracked rib slices with pain.

"So," says a voice. "The Sunshield Bandit."

I don't say anything. From the shuffling of feet, I gather there are several people in front of me—probably not friends.

"Open your eyes," the voice demands.

I slit them open and immediately blink them shut again—the light is offensively bright, brighter than just a standard lantern. Someone snickers.

"Can't take your own medicine, I see. I said *open your eyes*. And sit up."

I don't move. Lying on my side helps contain the pain from my rib.

A toe nudges my stomach. I hiss through my teeth.

"I was told you speak Moquoian, though poorly. I said, sit up and look at me, or the guards will make you sit up."

They're probably expecting defiance, which means they've already considered how they'll deal with such a response. I suspect I'll need to preserve as much pain tolerance as I have left. Reluctantly, I brace my arms against the stone. The links connecting the manacles to the ring in the floor clink as I slowly push myself upright. I hold my breath until I can lean against the wall, and then I let it out slowly, opening my eyes.

Before me is the man from the headquarters building at Tellman's Ditch—Minister Kobok. He's flanked by four guards, one of whom has a lantern half-cased by angled mirrors, intensifying the beam while shielding the rest of them from its glare. A power tactic. There's one more figure—a servant, I guess, her head bent over a scribing board, a charcoal stick in her fingers. She doesn't look at me, but she doesn't seem to be looking directly at the paper, either—her eyes instead seem far away.

Kobok's boot moves forward again, so shiny the light reflects off it, but he doesn't go for my ribs. His toe drags at a few of the chain links on the floor, pulling my right arm sideways. The hems of my sleeves had been chafing under the metal cuffs, and I'd tugged them partway up my forearms with my teeth. Far enough for my brand to show.

He gives a humorless snort. "You seem to be missing something, I see. The rumors did say you were an escapee. Redalo or Tellman's Ditch? Or were you perhaps in one of the factories?"

I don't answer, don't shift. He releases the pressure on the chain, and my arm rolls back over in my lap. He regards me with disgust.

"You burned down my quarry compound," he says with venom. "You injured my guard and stole my coach and team. You attacked the royal *ashoki* and murdered her maid. And I have my suspicions that you know where our crown prince is. And that's just your list of crimes from *the past week,* without even touching on your reign of terror in the Ferinno. You are in a very, very bad position. Would you agree?"

I shrug as much as I can given the pain in my side. I have very little energy to spend worrying over the dwindling time left to me. The hours-long journey from Giantess to what I assume is Tolukum prison was excruciating, first draped over a horse, where I didn't get a good breath for about three hours, and then locked in a cramped prison coach with my wrists chained to a bolt in the ceiling. By the time they took the bag off my head and my handkerchief out of my mouth and closed me in this cell, my main life goal had simply become drawing one breath after another.

"The queen would like to give you a public execution," he says to my persisting silence. "She thinks it necessary to show the people of Moquoia that you are no longer a threat to them, and I am inclined to agree. However." He bends forward. "She could perhaps be persuaded to afford you a more private and, shall we say, less gruesome end to your life—if you cooperate."

I lean my head against the stone wall, marveling vaguely at the fact that he really seems to think I care.

Kobok sweeps the scribe forward. She curls over her board, her head down, but her eyes flick up to meet mine before settling back on her parchment.

The minister waves a hand without looking at the girl, as if turning on a machine. "You might start by confirming my suspicions that it was Prince Veran Greenbrier of the Silverwood Mountains, second son of King Valien and Queen Ellamae Heartwood and erstwhile translator to Eastern Ambassador Rou Alastaire, who was your accomplice in the attack on Tellman's Ditch?"

That was a damn lot of titles—Veran would be pleased.

"Well?" He twitches my chain with his toe again, jerking my wrists. "Confident in our pain threshold, are we? Shall we test it? Was Veran Greenbrier your accomplice or not?"

"No," I say. "He was not."

He's expecting a lie, and he frowns almost triumphantly. "I have three separate officers who personally vouched for seeing him with you—"

"I didn't say he was not there," I say. "I said he was not my accomplice."

"But he was—"

"He was my hostage," I say. "I was using him for protection. I knew you would not kill him."

Kobok stares at me. Beside him, his servant's charcoal stick scratch-scratches on the parchment. "And how did he happen to fall into your hands?"

"He came looking for me," I say. "He thought I could help him. Instead I took him prisoner. I meant to ransom him in Moquoia, but he got away."

"How?"

"Slipped his rope. While I was robbing the *ashoki*'s coach."

"He wasn't assisting you with the *ashoki*?"

I squint up at his face, washed out in the glare of the lantern. "Have you met him? Do you really think he could rob a coach?"

Kobok considers this for a moment, his scribe still dutifully recording my words erasing Veran's crimes.

"No," he acknowledges. "I suppose not. I admit I was surprised to hear otherwise—particularly as my sources tell me he has a weak constitution."

I think of Veran slogging across the Ferinno, sunburned and exhausted, hauling me toward cover and hand-digging a twelve-inch hole for water. I think of him felling a redwood, and of how much he *didn't want* to fell that redwood. I think of him navigating his world every day of his life, all the tiny choices and tethers.

You think he's weak?

I'm struck with how much I'd like to punch Minister Kobok.

I link my fingers in my lap, forcing my tensed shoulders back down.

"But there were others with you during the attack," Kobok continues. "Who were they?"

I shrug again. "Just other outlaws."

"From the Ferinno?"

"I don't know where they were from. It's not hard to find desperate folk in tavern corners, ready for a chance to earn some income."

"*Ashoki* Novarni is convinced it was Tamsin Moropai inside her coach with you."

I fight to keep my face smooth. "Who?"

"Tamsin Moropai, the former *ashoki*," he snarls. "The one you attacked in *Iksi* outside Vittenta. She was thought to have died. Did she join you, instead? Or . . ." His voice tenses with a kind of new excitement, as if something just occurred to him. "Has she been in league with you all along? Spouting anti-industry rhetoric, infiltrating the court, influencing the prince—have you been partners this whole time?"

I almost raise an eyebrow at the absurdity of this story—that Tamsin would work to become the country's *ashoki*, the most influential position in Moquoia, only to give it up before the work was done and go back to being a nameless outlaw robbing coaches.

Kobok must mistake my silence for guilt. "Well? Have I struck a grain of truth?"

"No," I say.

"Don't lie to me."

"I'm not," I say, marveling that he'll believe a lie about Veran being a hapless victim but not the truth about Tamsin being unconnected to a grimy, dirt-poor criminal.

"Consider that this bit of information might ease the final hours of your life," he says curtly. "Tell me that Tamsin Moropai was operating with you, and I will advocate for a private hanging."

"No," I say. "It's not true."

He moves forward, and I flinch despite myself. He sets the sole of his boot against my stomach and leans on it, pinning me against the stone wall. I spasm, tears springing to my eyes at the race of pain. My fingers jump to his ankle, trying to relieve the pressure, but he doesn't let up, setting one elbow on his knee and drawing his face close to mine. The chain clinks, betraying the shaking in my linked wrists. Behind him, the guard with the lantern shifts to be sure the beam still hits me around his shadow.

"Tell me Tamsin was in league with you, that you infiltrated this court through her."

"That's the stupidest thing I've ever heard," I say through teeth gritted so hard they're making my head pound.

He pries one of my hands off his boot and holds it—loosely, gently, like someone might hold a child's hand. With his face still close to mine, he bends his thumb and digs his nail under mine. My head swims at the new pain.

"Where is Tamsin now?" he asks.

"I don't know."

"Where is Prince Iano?"

"I *don't know.*"

The pressure on my ribs and under my nail increases. The light from the lantern burns my eyelids. I shut my eyes to block out his looming face.

"What *do* you know?" Kobok asks, so close his breath puffs on my cheek. "Anything could help you. Who assisted you in the desert? Who sheltered you in Moquoia? Who were your accomplices?"

I stay silent and silent and silent, my mind shrinking to a bare rock. Silence and stillness have always been security, they've always been a means of control in a world moved by other people. I don't know where that notion came from—that with an identity formed around fighting, silence has always seemed the real strength.

A spike of pain creates a flash of movement in my mind's eye—an image of cloth fluttering idly, as if in a breeze. The angry lantern becomes the soft play of sunlight. The clinking of my chain morphs into something I can't place, but I don't have time to wonder at it. The strange moment is over in the next breath, overtaken by the sensations of now. My rib crackles beneath his boot. My thumbnail bends.

We hold our positions for an eternity, my head dizzy with the lack of breath in my lungs. Finally, Kobok straightens, his motion causing one more deepening of pain, and then his boot disappears. I draw a terrible breath, both agony and relief. Kobok neatens the creases in his dark gold jacket.

"You have tonight to do the remainder of your thinking," he says. "A cell guard will be posted outside—feel free to inform her if you have second thoughts. Otherwise, you will be executed at midmorning tomorrow on the outer ramparts. There will be quite an audience by then—do not expect things to be done swiftly."

He thinks a slow death is somehow different from the rest of my life? The only change he's making is getting other people interested in it.

I don't reply, slouched against the wall, the stone cold against my back. Kobok gives one final look of disgust, and then turns for the cell door. A guard opens it for him. The servant with the scribe board tucks her charcoal into a pouch, shuffling after the others.

I unlock my clenched jaw.

"One question," I say.

The minister doesn't turn around, but I hear the sneer in his voice. "You hardly have the leverage—"

"Not for you," I say flatly. "For her." I point with the toe of my boot toward the servant, and she looks up, startled.

"For who?" Kobok asks, following my gesture as if seeing the girl for the first time.

I tilt my chin at her. "You have the brand?"

She blinks at me, frozen. Kobok snaps back toward me, his face twisted with anger. He takes one step forward, his hand raised. I'm too tired to brace for it, so I let my limbs go loose to absorb the blow. His palm strikes my cheek, and my head whips to the side. I stay that way, my gaze locked on the damp stone wall, while Kobok turns on his shiny boot heel and strides to the door. His entourage follows him, all moving quickly to match his pace.

All except one.

Without turning my head from the wall, I slide my gaze to the door. The servant is following the final guard with her head down, moving just a half-step slower than the others. With her gaze on the floor, her finger hooks the hem of her sleeve.

As she slips silently past the guard, she turns her forearm just barely toward the lantern light, showing me the pale, ridged scar curving under her sleeve.

TAMSIN

Giantess Township is busier than I'd have thought first thing in the morning, but perhaps I'm out of touch with village life. People, adults and children alike, bustle through the mist breathed out by the redwoods, clutching shawls and coats against the cool damp. I hitch the horse to the post by the massive tree stumps in the center square. Reaching into one of my bulging bags—I thankfully managed to unearth Soe's traveling saddle from the paddock shed—I withdraw a short stack of folded papers. From another sack I draw Soe's dulcimer. Tucking my cargo under my arms, I climb the steps to the stage.

I stop short at the top. Two children are there, standing at one of the corners. They glance at me when I've climbed the steps, and then go back to their task. One fumbles at the fastening to the *si* pennants fluttering from the corner post. The second holds a bundle in her arms. While I watch, the first finally pulls down the turquoise pennants, which drop in a limp heap on the stage, and takes the end of the new string offered by the second child. She loops it over the hook and it begins to unfurl, the threads catching the early morning light. The fabric is a dark burnished yellow.

Dequasi. Gold.

Mokonnsi is over. It's the first of September.

My stomach gives a funny jolt. I've been so out of touch with the passage of time that I hadn't even realized the new *si* was approaching. During my brief career as *ashoki*, the end of each month meant a rush of new composition, of delicately twining my messages in with the concepts associated with the upcoming color. I'd been attacked at the start of *Iksi*, July, the deep green of the forest and the *si* of kindness. I spent *Mokonnsi*—friendship—in the cell and then on the run. Now it's *Dequasi*—the *si* of new beginnings.

This morning, all across the country, townspeople will be celebrating with music and food, and replacing the old colors with the new. In Tolukum Palace, this feat is achieved the night before by the army of servants and bond slaves, climbing teetering ladders to switch out massive wall hangings, removing dyed fish from the fountains and replacing them perhaps with sparkling lanterns or falsely colored water lilies. Tiles are pried up and relaid, lantern glass is exchanged, food and drink are curated and colored to be marveled at the next morning by courtiers dressed in their finest interpretation of the month's colors.

But outside the bubble of the palace, the changing of the *si* is done by people in the first light of morning. Children replace baubles in windows and scatter petals over house stoops. Adults take down hand-stitched banners, bundle them carefully away for next year, and replace them with new ones, sewn together during long nights in front of the fire, or at stitching bees and gatherings. Every town has their favorite recipes, motifs, and traditions to herald the start of the new *si*, but it's always a town event, the chance to gather with neighbors and regroup to face the joys and challenges of this shared life.

I look through the gauzy mist to where the Giantess looms across the common, her trunk swallowed fifty feet up by the swirling mists. Down around her girth, a cluster of people hold the base of a ladder while another fixes the end of a new *si* banner to the rope around the bark. As I watch, the person on the ladder shifts carefully, the fabric bundled to their chest, and then they fling it into the air. Gold unfurls in a shining stream.

There's a frustrated murmur at the corner of the stage. The children are at the last post, but the hook is higher than the others. Both are on tiptoes, trying to hook the pennants to the nail. I take a step closer and finish the job for them.

"Thanks," says one. They gather up the old turquoise pennants. "Bright *Dequasi* to you."

"*Uah*, an' you," I reply.

They scamper off. I look again at the new pennants fluttering on their hooks.

Dequasi—the color of new beginnings, of harvest, of changing leaves, of the sun.

I'm not *dequasi* gold. I am Tamsin in-Ochre, the *si* given to me by my parents, and the *si* I chose to keep upon gaining a right to title from Iano's father. Ochre is a narrow color, a finicky color, difficult to match, difficult to wear. A color that needs just the right circumstance to shine.

Maybe this is the time.

Maybe ochre, anyway, is just gold in the ordinary world.

I set down my papers, laying them carefully at the edge of

the stage. I lay Soe's dulcimer over my lap, giving the strings a few experimental plucks. The cool mists have thrown them out of tune, and I take the opportunity of fiddling with the pegs to change my plan of attack. I'd planned to simply play some background chords, something to get people's attention, but now I file quickly through the tunes sung at the beginning of *Dequasi*. I settle on my favorite, one that emphasizes new beginnings by forming a round, the opening melody circling back time and time again.

I give a few experimental strums on my strings. They're the first notes I've struck since the attack on my coach. My fingers are stiff. My body aches from the fall down the hill yesterday; my back protests from the hundreds—possibly thousands—of times I ratcheted the screw press up and down last night. I'm fuzzy with exhaustion after only a few hours of sleep. But the melody of the song is bright in my head, and pushing my aches aside, I begin.

At first, it's mostly children who flock to the stage, recognizing the opening lines of the round. They sing happily and chaotically, missing the harmonious off-set lyrics. I smile at them to keep them going. They hop around, singing. After a few times through, two young women pass behind them, wearing wreaths of black-eyed Susans in their hair and carrying baskets piled with goldenrod. They smile at the children, too, and add their own voices, giving a sweet backbone to the recurring rhythm. A man with a hammer is next, using the excuse of counting the nails in his pouch to stop and hum along. A few parents drift over to check on their children, and soon their voices join in.

Finally, after another round, one of the adults spots the

pamphlets. She moves for a closer look. She picks one up, examining the title.

She frowns.

But she reads.

I watch, doggedly continuing the tune, adding a few flourishes to spice up the repetitive melody. The woman's partner joins her, looking curiously over her shoulder. The hammer-carrying man comes to pick up his own pamphlet. Soon the adults are clustering around. More people drift from their morning tasks, drawn by the singing. More people pick up the papers. More read them. Some walk off, their gazes still fixed on the page. I watch one young man carry one to the porch of the public house and rap pensively on the door—he misses and hits the lintel first because his head is tilted toward the paper in his hand. The mistress appears in the door with a dishrag. He shows her the pamphlet, their heads crowded together in discussion.

My tired heart jumps.

Two people, a man and a woman, look distinctly scandalized. They peer around at their neighbors, give me dark, furious glares, and storm away. But most stay, or else hurry off purposefully, some after grabbing a handful of pamphlets. A few return bearing others, shunting them to the front of the stage. My stacks dwindle, but I don't stop to get more out of my saddlebags. I'm going to need every copy I have, and besides . . . the seeds have been planted. It's better they share, anyway. Share and discuss.

I play until my fingers sting, switching tunes halfway through to the one about the man who finds a gold piece and gives it away, only for it to return to him in his time of need after fourteen stanzas. By this time the mist is burning off. Gold winks all around the square, and my crowd is thinning. A long table has been set up in front of the public house, laden with honeycomb cakes and mead, and what's left of my audience heads toward the small crowd gathered. I see my pamphlet change hands.

I strum the last few chords of the final stanza and rest my hands on the dulcimer. My pamphlets are all gone. A few people tossed coins, mostly spare coppers and one thick silver crescent, placed on the stage by a man who read my essay in full, lifted his stunned gaze to me, reached into his pocket, and purposefully pulled out the coin, holding it out for me to see before he set it down. I loop the dulcimer by its strap around my back and crouch to sweep the coins into my palm.

When I reach the public house table, several people crowd around me.

"Look here, miss, I have a few questions for you—"

"My sister had to take a bond for six years, she says exactly the same as this here . . ."

"I've always said bond service is a curse, haven't I, Ham? But will anything come of it, that's what I want to know . . ."

"Who *scribed* these? They're practically identical!"

I wave all the commenters away, gesturing mournfully to my throat. I make a few sad rasping noises. A few people look concerned, and then turn back to themselves when they realize they're facing a mute. The snub that would have wrecked me a few weeks ago—cut out of the buzzing conversations around me—only fills me with satisfaction now, to the point that I have to fight off a grin.

I've given them my words.

Now let's see what they do with them.

I use the copper coins to buy five honeycomb cakes and a bottle of mead from the pub mistress. Then I fetch my horse, and, munching one of the cakes, turn toward the post office.

I take the silver coin passed on by the man who so intently read my essay, remembering the puckered scar that just showed on his wrist beneath the hem of his sleeve. I bring six neat stacks of my pamphlets inside, tie them up with string, and trade the coin for shipping to every town along the south coach road.

Buoyed by honey and a kind of furious excitement, I return to the horse and carefully pack away the dulcimer and the rest of the pamphlets. Then I mount and turn her head north up the track—toward Tolukum.

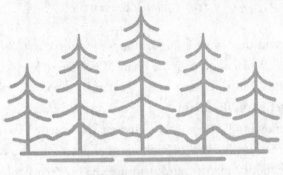

VERAN

My medallion gets me as far as the town of Ossifer's Pass in the back of a hay cart. The farmer driving isn't going into Tolukum, but perhaps feeling guilty about the high value of the silver in return for dropping me off short of my destination, he gives me a crescent, enough for a meal and a bed at the town inn.

"It's another five miles to Tolukum," he says, nodding up the track. "With the day getting on, you'd best stay the night—a crescent won't get you far once you're in the city."

I thank him for the advice and the ride, watch as he trundles off toward the nearest livery, and promptly start walking, leaving the inn behind. I spend the crescent at a street cart selling hand pies, pocket the change, and then continue on.

I know what Lark and the others would say about me skipping the offer of a meal and a bed, but for once I'm not actually pushing myself. I planned for this. After leaving the others behind yesterday, I walked and walked, through Giantess, up the road beyond. I passed several travelers but only one with a cart, and they were going in the wrong direction. So I kept walking. When night crept up on me, I wanted to keep going—I wanted so badly to keep moving, step by step, toward Tolukum and Lark. But Mama was in my ear, and I was in my own head, knowing I'd be no use to anyone if I seized in the middle of the road in the dark of night. So I slipped into the cover of the redwoods, burrowing down into the bracken flanking the roots. And I slept. Wrapped in my cloak, a mere insect at the feet of giants, I slept better than so many other fretful, purposeless nights. I slept like I had a reason for it.

At the first cold, misty touch of morning, I woke damp and stiff and rested. I thanked the tree and got back on the road. Fifteen minutes later, the hay cart rumbled up behind me. After another five minutes, my silver was in the driver's pocket and I was tucked into his prickly, musty-smelling cargo. And even though I'd had a good night's sleep, I made myself rest more. I spent several bumpy hours dozing under the thinning redwood branches until they cleared into open sky.

I'm ready to walk now.

Five miles to Tolukum.

Five miles to Lark.

It's only as I leave the last buildings of Ossifer's Pass behind that I notice the old turquoise pennants that had been hanging in shop windows a few weeks ago have been replaced with fluttering gold. It's the first of September. This shouldn't be particularly noteworthy, except today was supposed to be the original end date for our diplomatic trip. If things had progressed as we had planned, Rou, Eloise, and I would be climbing into coaches right now, with our sights set for home. Instead, I'm putting one foot in front of the other, heading back to Tolukum. And instead of Rou or Eloise, I'm tracking down the lost princess of Lumen Lake.

Not lost anymore.

But definitely in trouble.

A week ago I might have been wrapped up in visions of heroically storming the castle and saving Lark from the gallows at some critical moment. My stomach turns at the thought. My fingers stray absently to Iano's *si-oque* under my sleeve, then to my seal ring. I stowed it deep in my tunic pocket lest some street thief see it and demand it. The firefly insignia is the same as the one on my father's crest, and my mother's badge, and my sister's ring. It's the same as the insignia pressed into wax, alongside the crests of Lumen Lake, Cyprien, and Alcoro, on the letters we sent through the desert on the desperate outlaw road—the letters that started this whole tumbling mess. My hope is that between these two symbols, I can channel enough authority to at least stay the execution order. Then, somehow, I'll have to get in touch with Rou or Colm in Callais. That's my real power—a conduit for bigger voices than mine.

But first, I have to get to Tolukum in time.

I pick up my pace.

TAMSIN

I get through three more towns by the time the first of *Dequasi* is waning. I've made some good coin throughout the day, which has gone toward a full meal in each town and then to the mail carriers, arranging for pamphlets to travel to all the hamlets in their jurisdiction. My supply is dwindling, with only a dozen or so left in my saddlebag, but much of my work is done. My essay is slowly traveling outward like tendrils from a vine.

I'm sitting on the porch of the inn at Bearberry Crossroads, just south of the outskirts of Tolukum, enjoying a cheese bun, when two figures on mules come trotting purposefully up the track. I don't recognize them at first, wrapped up oddly tight in their cloaks despite the warmth of the evening. Then I see the edge of the rapier peeking out from a hem, and my gaze goes back to their faces. I set down my bun in surprise. They don't see me at first, studying the signpost and its many markers, when Soe looks toward the inn and does a double take. She exclaims to Iano, and when he sees me, he spurs his mule in my direction.

"Tamsin!" He hikes his leg over the saddle and jumps to the ground. Unlike our last such reunion in Pasul, however, when he ran straight for me and gathered me in his arms, this time he stops short a few feet away. Like Pasul, though, he doesn't seem to know what to say.

I take him in as he does the same to me, almost seeing him for the first time. Three weeks away from Tolukum have changed him. Where I've finally gained some of my weight back, he's lost a little, pinching his cheeks. His beard has officially filled in, accenting the angled line of his jaw. He has scratches on his face and hands from rough travel, and his hair is loose and wind-swept. His clothes are plain and muddy, and both earrings are gone.

Soe comes to join him, leading both the mules. "Tamsin—are you all right?"

"*Uah.*" *Where's Veran?*

"He left for Tolukum yesterday, and we haven't heard from him since," she says. "You heard Lark was captured?"

I nod grimly. *I hoped she might get away, but when Rat came to me . . .*

We all look down at Rat, stretched at my feet.

How did you find me? I ask, though I think I already know the answer.

Iano digs in his pocket and pulls out my pamphlet, creased in half.

"We followed your trail," he says, sounding almost stunned. "We spent the whole morning searching the woods for you, until we decided to chance Giantess for news. And we found the place buzzing over your pamphlet. We asked which way you'd gone, and they pointed up the road. It was the same in Purituka, and Ossifer's Pass, and Blue Joy."

I look back to the mules. They're unfamiliar, not the two Soe uses for her cart. *Where did you get these?*

Iano suddenly becomes guarded, almost sheepish. "Giantess."

I squint at him, hardly daring to believe it. *With what?*

"Well, my earrings paid for one . . ."

"He *stole* the other," Soe says with undeniable pride in her voice. "Orchestrated the whole thing. Right out from under the ostler's nose."

My mouth drops open in delight, and I use the sign Lark taught me back during our first session in the cabin. *You're an outlaw!*

He winces and looks at his scuffed, muddy boots. "I'll pay them back. But . . . what was I supposed to do?" His gaze jumps back up to me, anguished. "Our horses gone—*your* horse gone, no sign of you or Rat, and we couldn't go back to the cabin . . . once we realized where you'd gone, we had to follow you." He glances at the pamphlet. "But . . . I don't understand. When did you make all these? *How* did you make all these?"

Last night, I say. *Same way I did the first.*

"Where . . ."

I gesture to Soe.

"But the guards were there . . ."

I got there later, I say. *They'd left.*

"How many did you print?"

I wave my hand. *About two hundred.*

He stares to be sure he's reading my signs right. "Two . . . two hundred?"

I would have done more, but the stamps kept breaking.

Iano turns the paper delicately in his fingers, as if it's a dangerous item, a shard of glass. "I . . . I had no idea . . . I just thought you wanted a way to write without holding a quill . . . I didn't think about . . . just *how many—*"

My fingers move sharply, accompanied by an appraising look I can't hold back.

I know.

There's a heavy silence. Soe pauses for a breath too long, and then blurts out, "I'm going to water the mules."

She turns and guides them away toward the trough at the far side of the porch, leaving Iano and me alone.

The silence persists for another few moments. He rubs the back of his neck. Finally he gestures again to the pamphlet.

"Have you given them all away?"

Almost. The last few are going to . . . I point up the road toward the city of Tolukum.

He absently reads the first few lines on the paper, lines he must know by heart now. "There's powerful stuff in this, Tamsin . . . people are going to feel it. Already people are feeling it, all through the towns we passed through. I expect if they'd known who I was I'd have been mobbed." He rustles the paper. "You've given them a weapon."

I am not sorry, I say firmly.

"I know." He finally looks me in the eyes. "And I'm grateful for it. You were right, the other day. I was beginning to worry we'd created something too big, too wild. Something out of our control. But . . ." He looks at the paper, his face equally bleak and relieved. "That's your point, isn't it? It's not meant to be controlled. We do it or we don't. And this—you—you've gone and pushed the rock over the edge. We'll have people howling at our gates come tomorrow morning. Weekly petitions are going to be chaos. There'll be riots. Half the court will be calling for my blood before my reign has even begun. I was afraid of all that, before." He lifts his gaze—not to my eyes, but to my lips. "But I let myself forget that you'd already spilled blood for it. You took the first blow. I'm sorry, Tamsin. I wasn't as brave as you. But I think I can be now. Can you forgive my doubt?"

I take a breath. *I'm not done yet*, I say. I want him to understand, to realize what I'm going to do to his palace and his court—and his country—before he comes looking for my forgiveness. *There's still the* ashoki *to consider.*

"You think you can convince her?"

No. But it doesn't matter. I'm going to . . . oh, there are so many words I'd like to use here, if I only had more poetic signs. Undermine. Dismantle. Deconstruct. I sigh. *I'm going to take her power, and I'm going to give it to our people.* I wave to the pamphlet. *I'm going to work on a new press. I'm going to set it up in the scribes' shop, and I'm going to write more of these. And I'm going let other people use it, too.*

"Use it . . . to write . . ." He struggles to comprehend. "Just . . . whatever they want? In these kinds of numbers?"

I nod.

"But . . . that kind of power . . ."

It's the power of the ashoki, I say. *Too much for one person.*

"It was *your* power. It still could be, with this kind of technology. You could write instead of sing. I could argue to negate Kimela's appointment on those grounds."

I shake my head. *She's been appointed. Let her stay. It won't matter. I'm giving the power of her position to the people of Moquoia. This country has been at the mercy of the* ashoki *for too long.*

He blows out a breath, looking weary. I wait for his anger, or perhaps his sense of betrayal. The painful protestation that once upon a time I was on his side. The decisive declaration that he and I are through now.

He closes his eyes. "Okay."

I cock my head. "Okay?"

He nods. "Okay, let's do it." He opens his eyes. "I trust you."

"Why?" I blurt out before I can stop it.

"Well, for one thing, because I know whether or not I agree with you isn't going to stop you from doing it anyway." The corner of his lips twitch. "And all told, if this is your plan, I'd rather be on your side than against it."

The wryness disappears from his voice, and he looks again at the pamphlet. "And because I know you have Moquoia's best interests in mind. And . . . because I know you see things I don't see. You've lived things I haven't lived. It's no different from when you first started singing for the court, Tamsin. Once you showed me the problem, I wanted to help make it right. We were partners then." He folds the pamphlet and meets my gaze again. "I know things are different from what they were before, that our emotions have changed. But that doesn't mean this work has to change. It *shouldn't* change—too many lives are at stake to rest on whether you and I are in love. So, I guess what I'm trying to say is . . . I'd like to still be partners, if you would. Professional partners. And partners trust each other."

I smile. *Yes, I like that idea.*

He takes a breath and holds out his hand. But before I take it, I sign again.

You know I will always be grateful to you searching for me, I say. *For sending Lark and Veran to rescue me.*

"I know," he says. "But it's not a debt."

And there it is, that strange feeling I haven't been able to identify, that unsettling mixture of guilt and helplessness and singleness of purpose—he moved mountains to find me. And I felt that I owed him my heart in return.

I take his hand with one of mine and then wrap my other arm around his shoulders. He hugs me back, with no awkwardness where we touch. As I lean against him, I'm surprised by the surety I feel—a different beast from the heady infatuation we operated on before. The times we met alone to discuss policy or draft letters were the only times we could touch, or kiss, or romance the other, and so they were laced with a feverish excitement. This—this feels different. Where that felt like a bonfire, this feels like a forge.

Something useful.

We share one last squeeze before breaking apart. Soe has finished her conversation with the innkeeper and is heading our way.

"Are we okay?" she asks.

"We're okay," I confirm.

"Good, because we need to get going." She nods toward the signpost. "The innkeeper says it's just a half hour to the city gates, but they lock them at nightfall."

The urgency of Lark's plight hits me again, and I start to bundle up my things. Iano helps me finish.

"I suppose we'll have to try to go straight to the palace," he says, stuffing the last few things in my bag. "None of us have the money for room and board in the city. But . . . aside from trying to halt Lark's execution, I don't know what we can accomplish. We still haven't found our enemy."

I have a lead, I say.

"You do?"

I nod. *Inside Kimela's coach was my old maid, Simea.*

"Simea? I thought she died in the attack . . ."

I did, too. She fell on me. She said it was to protect me, but now I realize it was to keep me from escaping. I gesture to his rapier. *She attacked me again in Kimela's stage. Lark killed her.*

He pauses with my bag in his hands, his face paling. "By the colors . . ."

Even if Simea wasn't the mastermind, she knew about the attack, I continue. We head toward the horse and mules. Rat gets up and lopes after us. *We'll need to talk to her colleagues, to Fala. She must have left some kind of trail behind. If she was working alone, then our threat is gone. If not, we're a lot closer to finding out who it was.*

"Or you put yourselves right back in their reach again," Soe points out.

I nod reluctantly. *Or that.*

"But if we're the only ones who know Simea may have been behind the attack, and Lark killed her in front of witnesses, then the ministers will be all the more anxious to execute her," Iano says. "Even if it puts us in danger again, we can't afford to abandon Lark."

There is Veran, I point out.

He winces. "Not that I don't think Veran's heart is in the

right place, but if we get to the palace and he's not sitting in the next cell over, I'll be *very* surprised indeed."

"Well, let's get going, then," Soe says.

But as we're still a few paces away from the mules, someone steps around the corner of the porch, blocking our way. We halt. It's a woman in a dark palace cloak, stained with mud from the road. Brass glints beneath her hems.

Her eyes narrow, one lid rumpled by an old, puckered scar.

"Not so fast," she says.

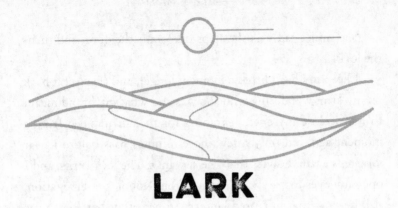

LARK

No one enters my cell again until several hours after Kobok has left. The quiet snick of the lock on my door nudges me from my doze. I open my eyes, expecting the minister again, or maybe the guard coming to take me to an early execution. But it's neither. It's a small woman, oldish but not too old, in a neat black servant's uniform. She holds nothing in her hands besides the key, which she tucks on a chain into her pocket.

I lift my head, surprised. "Who are you?"

She doesn't answer. She just stands, looking me over, her face unreadable. Then, like Kobok, she steps forward and draws my chain to the side, baring my forearm. She studies my brand. Unlike Kobok, though, she doesn't say anything, or react at all.

"What do you want?" I ask.

She sets my arm down, stands back, and goes back to the door.

"Are you a slave, too?" I ask.

She smiles sadly as she steps out, shuts the door, and turns the lock.

I keep my head lifted a moment longer, and then set it back on my arm, wondering who she was and what my brand meant to her. I close my eyes, searching for that fitful sleep from a moment ago, but only a few more minutes pass before I hear footsteps again, heavier than the servant's. The lock turns, and I open my eyes to see the cell guard from Kobok's interrogation, still bearing that mirrored lantern. In her other hand is a tray. She sets it down on the floor and steps to the ring fixing my chain to the floor. Pulling out her keys, she unlocks the manacles on my wrists and instead fits an ankle cuff to the chain. She locks it around my boot and steps back.

"Dinner," she says.

I look down at the tray, expecting swill, but I'm surprised to see a silver plate with meat and rice, and a cup of dark wine.

"Last meal?" I ask dryly.

She fixes the manacles on her belt. "The council of ministers has always sponsored the final meal for prisoners heading to the gallows. An act of goodwill."

I snort in contempt.

"Enjoy it," she says acidly. "You're lucky they held to tradition instead of letting you go hungry."

I turn my head away as she heads back out of the cell, her key ring jingling importantly. My stomach turns at the thought of food, but I think of all the times in Three Lines I checked a snare to find it empty, or scraped the bottom of a pot for the final burned flakes. I think of how often the only thing to offer my campmates was cattail powder and withered roots.

I massage my wrists, stiff from the manacles, and drag the tray toward me.

I eat without tasting, my thoughts drifting back toward Three Lines. Slowly, methodically, I start to neatly sever myself from the people who could be used against me, or could be drawn into my dangerous orbit and destroyed. I force myself to believe my campmates are safe in Callais, that Veran's friends have brought them into their circle of protection and are giving them the lives I never could. I say good-bye to Sedge and Lila, and Bitty and Arana, thanking them for helping me get through the toughest times. I say good-bye to Saiph, wishing him good fortune. I say good-bye to Andras and Hettie, praying they'll find their ways back home and into the arms of their families. I say good-bye to little Whit, wishing her a soft bed and good food and the voice of somebody gentle, somebody who can smooth away the demons she should never have had to live with. I say good-bye to Pickle, wishing him a death easy and free. I say good-bye to Rose, kissing her forehead and laying her back down to rest in Three Lines, the guardian of the South Burr. I apologize in specifics to each person, but I don't wait to hear their responses, relying on the whole span of the Ferinno to cut them off from me.

I say good-bye to the Ferinno, the flushes and washes and massive sky, the larks in the scrub and the dust and the snakes. I say good-bye to Three Lines, the water pocket and sun-hot walls. I say good-bye to my horse Jema and wish her a sweeter life with a kinder rider than me. I say good-bye to Rat. The food sticks in my throat at this point, and I fight away the headache that springs up at the thought of him. I wish him good hunting and dust baths and stretches of sun to lie in, and then I move on fast, before this headache breaks apart into something I can't stop.

I say good-bye to Soe and Iano. I don't know whether they would count themselves as friends to me, but they didn't turn me in or turn me out, and for that I'm grateful, I guess. I say good-bye to Tamsin. I liked Tamsin a lot, and I hate how good the world is at targeting our specific joys and turning them into pain. I don't offer her many words, though. Whatever I have to say to her, I expect she already knows. Instead a memory rises, unbidden, of the giant redwood tree she took me to on my first day at Soe's, a place of peace and purpose for her, and I wish her that, I suppose.

When the food is gone and I'm back to lying on my side again, when I've gone through everyone else I can think of, every incidental face, from Patzo in Snaketown to Cook and the rustlers to Dirtwater Dob decaying somewhere under the desert sun, I reluctantly turn to Veran.

I spend a long time staring vacantly, my mind slow and empty. I don't know what to wish him. I don't have anything to offer. Apologies seem pointless. Forgiveness seems trite. Well wishes of happiness and health seem almost offensive. The longer I think, the emptier I feel, like I've given away the last bits of myself that were still clinging under my exterior.

I find my thoughts instead simply settling on his face, the familiar copper of his skin, the black of his hair reflecting the sky in glints. I think of his sagebrush eyes watching me, drinking in the world in great gulps, determined to absorb as much as possible with each available heartbeat. Where the limits of my life have made me closed up and callused, his have made him wide open, hoarding all the highs and lows the world has to offer. I think of his excitement over gear, his enthusiasm for action, his regard for his family and his ma's forest scouts. I think of his soft, practiced footsteps and buoyant energy. I think of his funny habits toward the natural world—thanking trees, welcoming thunder, ranting about songbirds hitting glass.

I frown.

I try to find that funny.

It's not funny, though.

I think of the little birds in the sage throughout the Ferinno, wheeling through the open air. I know what it feels like now to slam into something you never see coming, to break your body on solid glass, and then to fall from the wide-open place you've always called home.

And then for that to happen dozens—*hundreds*—of times a day, every day, and for people to call it normal.

My mouth twists.

Veran's right to be angry.

In fact, it makes me angry, too.

This palace is a quarry of arrogance and death, breeding it both inside and outside its brilliant glass domes.

Impulsively I slap the tray that was paid for so generously by wealthy folk upstairs, offering me one last condolence for the life they created for me. The silver plate jumps from the tray, resting at an angle against the lip, and the empty cup tips. Flecks of wine trickle down the surface of the plate, trailing past the sudden reflection of my face staring back at me.

The image wobbles on the silver as I blink back at it. I scan my reflection for familiar details, but they're muddled by the dings in the metal and the guttering lantern light. Even my face has shifted, dissolved with all the other stuff that used to be inside me.

And then, in the next breath, I blink and find myself staring not at myself, but at that other girl.

Eloise.

I stare at the reflection. The metal distorts the razor edges I'm so used to seeing in my face and replaces them with softer lines. The darkness unlocks my hair and piles it over my shoulder. The lantern flashes on the tin studs in my ear, turning them to pearls.

Princess Eloise Alastaire.

She was sick, when I saw her just a few weeks ago. Weakened by that fever that's crept into Tolukum. Infected by mosquitoes purposefully drawn into her room, the insects turned unknowingly into weapons because there aren't enough birds to eat them.

Because the birds hit the glass.

Because the glass is impressive to powerful people.

Because the powerful people can force less powerful people to make the glass for them.

My fists close and squeeze, and in the metal plate, Eloise's reflection spasms with anger. I catch a glimpse of that other man, the ambassador, as he ran at me, wild-eyed. The princess's father, Rou. I only saw the two of them for a few minutes at most, but I can see his face in hers.

I wonder what else of him lives in her—what about his laugh? His smile? The way he bounces his leg while thinking?

My stomach goes cold.

Is that a memory?

I recall that patchy vision that came with the pain as Kobok loomed over me—the shifting cloth, the play of sunlight, the sound of clinking. My breath comes shallowly in my throat as these things grow sharper. The cloth is a tablecloth fluttering on an open terrace, lit with morning sun. The clink of the chain is the sound of cutlery on breakfast dishes. There's a giggle. Curly hair brushes wood as we crawl under the table. Voices murmur gently above. Two pairs of legs flank us in our cave, our fortress—on the one side, trousers and boots, with one knee bouncing. Movement and deep laughter, the smell of cinnamon.

On the other side, stillness.

Her leg didn't bounce. She always sat perfectly still, a rock, an anchor. Cool and quiet and *safe*.

I see Eloise's face next to her father's again, and even though there's sameness, there's difference, too, and I wonder—if some things came from *him* . . .

Which things came from *her*?

The reflection in the silver plate flickers again, and my own face returns to me—not Eloise's, not her father's, not her mother's. And then finally, *finally*, I recognize what exactly I'm looking at. Veran would have already spotted it, if he were here. His giddy voice filters back from the top of the mesa.

Start with what you have.

I push myself up from the floor, my ribs blazing with pain. Stiffly, I draw my ankle toward me and examine the lock on the cuff. It doesn't look complicated—all the manacles in the prison probably take the same standard key. I look at the cell door. It probably takes a different key.

I pick up the plate and wipe the last trickles of wine from it. Slowly, I get to my feet. Wincing, I shrug off the fine blue vest Veran bought me and lay it over my shoulder. The chain of my ankle cuff clinks as I step to the cell door. I crane my head against the bars and look down the corridor. About twenty paces away are the crossed legs of the cell guard, bathed in a circle of light from the bright mirrored lantern.

"Hey," I call. My voice echoes off the stone. The boots down the corridor twitch.

"What?" The guard's voice is annoyed.

"Did you send this message?" I ask.

"What?" she asks again.

"This message, in my food. Is it from you?"

A stool scrapes the floor. The circle of light swings as the guard snatches up the lantern. Her boots slap on the floor as she hurries toward me. I shift the plate in my fingers.

"What message?" she asks with alarm. "Where? Let me see."

She holds the blinding lantern aloft. I tilt my head against the bars so their shadows fall over my eyes. Her fingers stretch toward me.

I slip the shiny silver plate through the bars, tilt it, and beam the reflection right back into her face.

She scrunches her eyes shut, and I lunge, grabbing her outstretched hand and yanking it through the bars. She shouts in surprise as she stumbles forward, but the noise cuts off as I bend her arm awkwardly against the bars. She tries to swing the lantern toward me, but I meet her fingers with the edge of the plate. The lantern drops from her grip, landing mirror-side down on the floor. It shatters. The corridor goes dim. I trap her other hand and twist it through the bars as well, pulling her shoulder flush against the metal with her arms pinned through two different openings. Leaning against the bad angles of her elbows, I reach for her belt and pluck the knife from her hip. I let the edge brush her neck.

"Yell again and you'll wish you hadn't," I say against her ear.

She grits her teeth and struggles, but the angle is too awkward for her to pull away. I shrug the blue vest from my shoulder, praising Veran for his exorbitant taste—my old threadbare vest would have split apart with minimal tugging, but this one is thick, lined, and heavily stitched. Setting the knife momentarily in my teeth, I work the guard's wrists through the arm holes and then cinch it tight.

With her secure, I set the knife against her neck again and work the ring of keys off her belt—not an easy thing since I can barely get my wrist through the bars. She fights me silently, trying to keep her hips as far from me as possible, but eventually I hook her belt and manage to slide the ring off its clasp. The keys jingle as I pull them through the bars.

"You're nothing but a common outlaw," she snarls.

"I'm an *extraordinary* outlaw," I say, picking through the keys. "I am a *crowned queen* of outlaws."

I work through three of the smaller keys before I find the one that unlocks my ankle cuff. For good measure I close it around her wrist—even if she manages to get free of my vest, she'll still have one hand trapped inside the cell. The key to the door is easy to identify, being stamped with the same number as the lock, but it's not so easy to reach it through the bars. I wince as I press my cracked ribs against the metal, fighting to fit the key into the tumblers.

Finally, it turns, and I sigh as the door hinges open. I step into the corridor and shut it behind me.

The guard is twisting her hands viciously in my vest. I step toward her and slide her belt off—if she gets a hand free, I don't want any of her gear close by. I remove the gag from its pouch.

"You'll swing for this," she hisses.

"Nah," I say. "I'll swing for everything else. This bit? I doubt they'll care. Although *you* might get a reprimand."

I fix the gag over her mouth, give her an encouraging pat, and then step over the lantern and head down the corridor.

TAMSIN

Iano's rapier is out and pointed at the woman with the scarred eyelid, but instantly several other burly guards in palace insignia materialize behind her. A fight against just the one strong, well-trained guard would have been chancy. A fight against four others would be laughable.

But the woman doesn't reach for her weapon. She spreads her hands and her cloak, showing the short sword sheathed underneath.

"You can stand down, my prince. I'm not going to harm you. I'm going to reach into my pocket and show you something, all right?"

We watch dumbly as she does this, producing a small leather bag. She tips the contents into her palm. An elegantly cut ruby flashes in the late-afternoon light.

Iano stares at it, his rapier still raised. "That's from my mother's *si-oque*."

"Yes. I'm abroad on her orders. There's been some suspicion that someone forged her seal."

"Forged her seal?" Iano repeats faintly.

"*Uah.* A few weeks ago, a rumor went out that two rookie soldiers had been dispatched on a mission, but nobody seemed to know where the orders had come from. Any secret mission should have borne the queen's seal, but she'd never made such an order. So a moratorium has been put on all documents bearing it. For the moment we're back to the old-fashioned way of validating her orders."

The three of us stare at her, and then at each other. Iano is pale, no doubt reliving the deaths of the two soldiers that first night after we fled Pasul. My mind, however, is wheeling on what this means. A small thread of relief creeps through my stomach.

It wasn't your mother, I say to Iano.

He draws a sharp breath, and looks back to the woman. "Who are you?"

"My name is Enna. The queen placed me on this detail after you disappeared—I've been looking for you for weeks. Shall we talk?"

He shifts, looking at me again. "We . . . have urgent business in Tolukum. We can't delay."

"So I heard—at least, partially," Enna says. "And I believe I can answer some of your questions. We can talk and ride. But I regret to inform you that now that I have found you—you'll pardon my language, my prince—I'll be absolutely damned if I'm going to let you ride away without us."

I squeeze Iano's arm. He lowers his rapier, but otherwise he doesn't move.

"You saw us in Giantess Township," he says. "Why didn't you arrest us there?"

"I'm not arresting you, my prince. I am ensuring your continued safety. Granted—I wasn't sure that I *did* see you in Giantess. Forgive me, but you look . . . rather not like your usual self. And I didn't know your companions." She inclines her head to Soe. "I had to do some more asking around town before I was sure it was you."

She gestures apologetically to the horses. "I'm afraid I cannot give you the option to refuse. I will be happy to escort you through the city and into Tolukum, but I'm not unwilling to do it with you tied over the back of my horse. The queen will see me and the rest of my cadre hang if she knows I had you and let you go, and that is the plain truth. Shall we?"

The other guards have already brought their horses around. With reluctant glances at each other, we head to ours and clamber into the saddles. The guards take up position around us, circling us in a tight wall of horseflesh. Making a break for it would probably just look foolish.

Besides, this is what we want—I think.

Enna doesn't hesitate in providing answers to our questions. After only a few cursory questions about our whereabouts and activities the past several weeks, she launches into an explanation.

"I work as a coach guard for the Royal Stage Line," she explains. "I was a colleague of Poia Turkona."

"Poia!" I exclaim, remembering the surly, one-eyed guard who'd held me captive in the Ferinno with batty old Beskin.

Enna nods. "When she vanished from her duties around the time you were attacked, I was suspicious. When the prince disappeared, too, I decided I couldn't afford to give her the benefit of the doubt. I went to the queen and told her what I suspected."

"Why would you suspect Poia?" Iano asks. "I mean—you were right, but couldn't she have just gotten sick?"

"I checked the log books, and there was no indication that she was on ordinary leave," Enna says, narrowing her eyes at a passing potato cart as if the driver might leap and attack. "The head of staff usually keeps immaculate records about any illnesses or personal time, and there was nothing mentioned. I talked to a few others, and they hadn't heard anything, either. But the main reason I suspected her was—Poia was a Hire."

I nod. *"Uah."*

Enna glances at me. "You knew?"

I gesture at Iano, who fills in for me. "She found out, eventually—she saw Poia's tattoo."

"I'm not surprised she had one—but we knew how she leaned even without seeing it. I think a big reason we didn't report her missing right away was because we weren't sorry to see her go, always grumbling about how much she resented sharing the mess hall or wash duty with bond laborers. But when you, my prince, and the Eastern prince vanished, I figured I couldn't keep my concerns to myself. I requested an audience with the queen and told her that Poia had unexpectedly disappeared around the same time Tamsin did. At that point, it was our only lead, and she ordered me to take a small party and make a search."

I wave at Soe and twist to let her see my hands.

"But Poia wasn't the one to attack Tamsin," Soe interprets. "She was one of her prison guards, but not an attacker."

"I didn't say I'd have *all* the answers," Enna says. "But if it's true that Poia really was involved, my guess is you could start by checking with other palace staff to see if anyone else disappeared."

Did you know Beskin? I ask. *She was the other prison guard.*

Enna shakes her head at Soe. "Sorry, no."

I exchange glances with Iano.

Fala, I spell, and he nods. The head of staff is our best hope now.

Iano's face is still etched with anxiety. "I worry that once we get back to the palace, we'll be sucked back in court—healers will want to look at us, questions will have to be answered. It might be difficult to get hold of Fala right away, and our success—and helping Lark and Veran—could depend on mere minutes."

"I'm not letting you go anywhere else, my prince," Enna says firmly. "I told you, your mother will send me to the scaffold . . ."

"Hey," I say abruptly. *Can you get us into the palace a different way? Through a guard entrance?*

Soe passes the question to Enna. She frowns.

"I don't like the idea . . . it seems devious, and the queen . . ."

"I'll make sure no trouble comes to you for it," Iano says. "I promise. It could mean the difference between true danger and safety in the court, along with saving at least one life."

Enna purses her lips, but finally she nods. "We'll bring you in through a service entrance. But I'm still not letting you out of my sight until you're in the company of the queen."

"Very well." Iano looks at me and shrugs. I nod. We have a way in. We have a way to Fala.

I turn in my saddle to face the rising swell of the city. The clouds overhead are gathering with the promise of rain tonight, but the sun is slipping into that magic opening just above the horizon. The city is cast into vivid golds and purples. At the top shines Tolukum, the glass dome too bright to look at, a beacon of opulence for all who gaze on it.

Opulence and treachery.

I nudge the horse, hoping we're not too late.

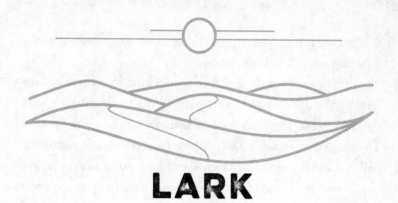

LARK

The key ring gets me out of the cell blocks and into the outer guard corridors. Nobody's about, but it doesn't put me at ease—I feel naked, unarmed, despite the tools in the guard belt. I hold my breath as I edge around a corner, my gaze drawn to a door spilling light. I see shelves beyond, stocked with prison gear—rolled blankets, wooden bowls, manacles . . . and *my hat*.

I slip into the empty room. Arranged together on one of the shelves are the things the guards took off me after my arrest— the patch cowhide hat, the red bandanna, and the broad fullered sword. I scoop them all up, fix them in their proper places, collect the key ring again, and head back out.

It's two staircases up to the main palace, and another key on the ring to unlock the outer door. Carefully, I poke my head through.

Dammit. The landing leads to a short hall that opens into a larger wing of the palace. Servants rush about with baskets, buckets, and lanterns, their voices kept to the barest whispers.

But between myself and the end of the hall are two guards, standing with their backs to me.

I ease out of the door and close it behind me. There's a lantern by the door; silently I turn down the wick until it snuffs out, then stand anxiously in the darkness, weighing my options. There are trees—trees? *Trees.* There are trees inside, across the hall. I shake my muddled head. They'll provide good cover, but even without the guards, it's going to be hard to cross the open hall without raising an alarm.

Maybe I'll just have to settle for raising an alarm, then—bolt straight between the guards and across the hall, and hope the trees will hide me long enough to get away.

I slip to the very edge of the shadows. I spread my feet, my weight forward, mentally and physically preparing to run. My ribs burn—not only is this going to be difficult, it's going to be painful. There's only about two feet of space between the guards, and a whole lot of open hall beyond them. It's a long way to run.

I blow out my breath.

My fingers stray to my sword hilt.

Because that's really the only other option.

In the muffled silence beyond the guards, there's a sudden resounding clang. I nearly jump out of my skin, my gaze skirting past them. Staring straight at me is the scribe slave who had accompanied Minister Kobok into my cell a few hours previously. A metal tray at her feet is still ringing.

We both freeze, our gazes locked together, with the guards oblivious between us. My knuckles tighten on my sword hilt. My ribs sear with my rapid breath.

One of the guards ruffles with irritation, still facing the girl.

"Pick that up," he says. "Get on with your work."

As if roused from a trance, she drops to the floor and begins to pile writing implements back on her tray. But when she goes to get back up again, her foot snags in her hem, and she falls—dramatically—and sprawls on the floor, flinging the contents of her tray even farther afield. Ink jars go rolling. Quills fly.

The guards make noises of impatience, reprimanding her for her clumsiness. They move toward her, batting loose items her way with their boots. She babbles apologies, scooping everything toward her. And then, when the guards are as close to her as it seems they'll get, her gaze jumps up from her tray, meets mine, and then darts unmistakably to the side.

There's now an eight-foot gap between the guards' backs and the corner of the hall. Without pausing for another breath, I slide forward, gripping my sword and the key ring so they won't clank. I slip around the corner, skirt a decorative pillar, and lunge toward a line of towering shrubs, their pots each the size of a wagon wheel. I slip into the shadows behind them and edge farther away from the guards, trying to catch my breath against both my ribs and the tension crackling through me.

I don't know where I am in the palace, but I don't have to wait long for answers. As I near another corner, this time to a much smaller service corridor, footsteps sound behind me. Into the darkness of the shrubs comes the scribe. She unceremoniously drops her tray into one of the giant pots and joins me, her eyes wide.

"Thank you," I say.

"You got out," she says in an awed whisper. "I never . . . I had no idea you might get out on your own. I was coming to try to break you out."

"You were?" I ask. "How?"

"I . . . I wasn't sure. I thought I could claim I was bringing supplies down to the record room."

"And then what? The keys? The cell guard?"

She twists her hands. "I didn't know. I thought something would come to me."

I lean back from her, grimacing. "Well, I appreciate your courage, but I'm glad we didn't have to rely on that plan. What's your name?"

"Irena."

"I'm Lark," I say. "Are you Alcoran? That's an Alcoran name." And she looks Alcoran—sandy skin and light brown hair like Sedge's.

She nods, and her shoulders sag, as if in relief. Her next words are in Eastern, their cadence more natural than the Moquoian she was just speaking. "My sister and I were captured four years ago. I could read and write, so I was sent here. My sister was sent to Tellman's Ditch."

"Are you under bond?"

"No bond," she whispers. "It's forever."

"And your sister?"

"She's free," Irena says breathlessly, her eyes fierce and bright. "You broke her out of a wagon when she was being moved to Redalo two years ago."

Silence rings between us.

"I heard the coach drivers talking about it after it happened," she says. "It wasn't hard to find the report and see her name on it. Meissa."

A sharp memory rushes back to me, of another little girl with similar straw-colored hair and round cheeks.

"Bitter Springs," I say. Arana and I had brought her back with the little boy, Lefty.

She nods. "So you see," she says, her voice tight, "I had to do something. I couldn't just leave you down there. I'll help you escape any way I can."

I spare myself a moment to think, but not for long. "I'm not going to escape. Not yet."

"Whatever it is, I'll help you," she says.

"You could get in trouble, Irena. You could wind up on the scaffold next to me. You've already helped me get away from the guards—you don't need to feel like you owe me something."

She straightens. "I don't. It's like that story where the stars leave the sky to follow Justice into battle, and the world goes dark until she wins."

I don't know that story, and I don't like the idea of drawing her into battle, but I don't think I can get through this place by myself.

"Can you get me upstairs?" I ask. "Without being seen?"

"You're in luck," she says. "The first rule for any palace staff is *don't be seen*." She turns and beckons for me to follow her, heading for the service corridor.

I start after her, instinctively pulling my bandanna up over my nose.

"I can't believe in this whole wide palace, I ran into the one person I've helped," I whisper as we turn the corner.

"Oh no," she says over her shoulder. "That's not surprising at all. You've helped a lot more than just me."

VERAN

This is what I have:

Iano's *si-oque*.

My parents' seal ring.

My chevron-fringe boots, sans their medallions.

The clothes I'm wearing.

One copper coin.

Half a sweet potato hand pie.

I check all these one final time, along with my surroundings. The sky is drizzly, hiding what must be a waning crescent moon. Before me, Tolukum Palace glows like a pearly orb, its miles of wet glass illuminated by the lanterns within. It splashes light over the wet plaza in front of the great double gates. Beyond it, the city is dark and quiet in the dead of night.

I take a short breath and step from the shadows. I walk purposefully across the plaza, keeping my arms away from my sides and my gaze on the guards posted above the gate.

The call to halt comes almost immediately, along with the

cranking of several crossbows. I stop. A beam from a lantern is concentrated through a lens. I blink against its light, but I don't hesitate.

"Greetings, and a bright *Dequasi* to you," I call. "I'm Prince Veran Greenbrier of the Silverwood Mountains, ambassador of the Eastern delegation. I have urgent news regarding Prince Iano Okinot in-Azure and a prisoner in your palace. I have his *si-oque* here," I raise my wrist in the air, "as well as the royal seal of the Silverwood. I request an emergency audience with Queen Isme Okinot in-Crimson."

There's a sort of stupefied silence. I bite my lip in an effort to keep from spouting more titles and demands. A few guards murmur, and then several disappear from their posts, leaving the rest to keep their crossbows trained on me. A minute later, the little contingent appears from the tiny guard tower door, eyeing me with heavy suspicion.

"Show me the *si-oque*," the ranking officer commands.

I do. He reaches toward my wrist, but I draw it back.

"I must request to keep it, until I am granted an audience with Queen Isme," I say. "The safety of Prince Iano depends on it."

It's not a lie, ultimately, but I plan to hold off mentioning Lark until I'm facing someone who can do something about it. If they think I'm in league with her, they might not be so keen to let me in.

"You're with the Eastern delegation?" the officer asks. "You're that one who disappeared with the prince?"

"I am," I say. "And I assure you, much of what you've heard about the past few weeks has been a misunderstanding."

"Where is the prince?"

"Please, grant me an audience with the queen, and I'll share everything I know."

The guards confer quietly, still keeping me covered by their crossbows. I shift on my tired, wet feet.

After an eternity, the officer nods.

"I cannot guarantee an audience with the queen," he says. "But we will bring you inside for the moment. You must submit to being searched."

I agree, and they lead me to the guard door. It's narrow and opens immediately into a steep set of spiraling stairs, so it takes some maneuvering to get inside while they continue to flank me. Once inside, they lead me away from the wall and to the guard room. They search me there. I don't protest, shivering in bare feet and chest while they prod me and paw through my clothes, inching along the seams and fringe for hidden weapons. They produce the coin and hand pie. They replace the coin but break apart the pie, perhaps checking for a minuscule knife. I watch mournfully—I should have finished it while I had the chance. I'm wearing the *si-oque* and seal ring again; they study them closely, consulting a box of musty paperwork that details the official symbols of important palace personnel. At long last, they hand me back my wet clothes, stand around watching while I get dressed, and order me to follow them.

They take me through a service entrance and into the palace. My hands aren't bound, but the knot of guards presses so closely around me I can barely see through them. When we finally reach the first public hall, I have to blink to be sure I'm recognizing the same place I left three weeks ago. The turquoise is gone, replaced by gold in every imaginable form, but what

throws me off the most is the absolute *chaos* of the formerly se-
rene halls. People rush about, clattering with buckets of gardening tools, hot coals, and cleaning supplies. Carts rumble by with
linens, lanterns, and firewood. The windows positively swarm
with ladders as glass cleaners methodically polish every possible
surface, filling the air with a symphony of discordant squeaks.
Below all this racket is the steady hiss of whispering—everyone
is whispering.

I gawk in the same way I did when I first arrived in Tolukum
during the day, marveling at the otherworldly glass and color
and light. This is the Tolukum I never saw during my stay, the
one I always wondered about. This is Tolukum at night, when
its aristocratic residents are asleep in soft beds, and the armies
of servants and bond slaves emerge to groom it back to elegant
perfection. Flanked by the guards and wearing no indication of
status, I go completely unnoticed by the servants, who jostle
past us in their effort to stay on task.

The guards lead me up several flights of stairs and down a
hallway I recognize as a guest wing for unimportant visitors,
one floor down from where Rou and Eloise and I stayed. It's not
the royal apartments, but it's not the dungeon, either, and I manage to hold my tongue until we arrive at a door.

"Please," I say, "do you have news of the Sunshield Bandit?"
I try to feign a gossip's awe. "Is she really here in the palace?"

The officer grunts as he opens the door to a room. "No
questions answered until we're sure you're telling the truth."

"But—but is she *alive*?" I ask, too rushed to cover my desperation.

"No questions," he repeats. He points into the room. "In."

I obey. The room is small and neatly furnished, but spare, with only a bed, a wardrobe, a washstand, and a tiny writing desk under a small window.

The officer holds out his hand. "Give me your tokens, and I will take your request to the queen."

I coil my arm against my stomach. "I told you—I won't give them up until I'm allowed to see—"

"I'm not trotting up to the royal wing and telling the guards to rouse her majesty without something to back it up," he interrupts angrily. "Give them to me, and I'll take them to records to be officially confirmed by someone who's allowed to do such a thing. If they're legitimate, *then* I will bring your request to the queen, and if she consents, *then* I will collect you and bring you to an audience room. Until then, you'll stay here, under guard." He bounces his open palm impatiently. "Give me the *si-oque* and the seal."

I hesitate—handing them over feels like giving up my only weapons. But I don't want him to think they won't be confirmed in the records. With a weight of unease in the pit of my stomach, I unclasp the bronze bracelet. Harder to hand over is the seal, the one remaining token that shows I have any worth at all. I grip it before the guard can take it.

"I need this back," I say, trying to keep my voice from cracking. "As soon as you confirm it."

The guard grunts and plucks it out of my fingers. He tucks the two tokens in his belt pouch and steps back into the doorway.

"Please," I say quickly. "About the Sunshield Bandit—"

"No questions," the guard says, pulling the door. "You're under guard. Stay."

The door shuts. Keys jingle in the lock. Boots shift into place outside, casting bars of shadow in the light under the door.

I waver in the middle of the little room. There's a tiny grate, but no fire lit, and without a moon in the window, the room is almost pitch black. I go to the door and crouch at the keyhole, but the guard outside is blocking any view into the hallway. I cover the short space to the window and peer out into an awkward view of half a brick pillar and the roof of a colonnade. I crane my head to get a look at the outside wall, but there are no ladders for glass cleaners—this less extravagant part of the palace isn't made of the soaring panels of glass like the royal wings. Servants probably just give them a quick polish from the inside.

I shiver, still wet, and go to the bed. I nearly cast myself on it, but a thought of Lark, somewhere here in the palace, deep down below in the even colder prison, or else . . . I vault off the mattress as soon as I touch it. No, I won't think of Lark already being executed, and I won't think of sleeping, either. The guard will be back soon. He'll have confirmed my tokens with records. I have to focus on what I'll say to the queen. These are the most important words I've ever had to say in my life.

I ignore the bed, and the door, and the window. I pace instead.

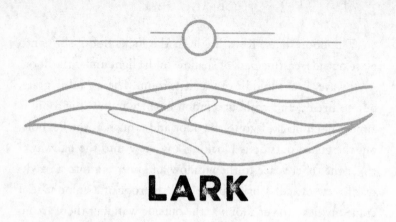

LARK

Minister Kobok passes by in a waft of steam, clothed in a silk dressing gown that would pay for a wagonload of grain. He sinks into the waiting chair with an appreciative grunt, sticking his feet out, clearly waiting for the servant bobbing nearby to put his slippers on, which are sitting mere inches from his toes.

I move forward and go for his arms, not his feet. Before he even thinks to open his eyes, the stout golden cord from his curtains is looped over both wrists. I pull it tight, cinching them to the armrests of his chair.

His bare, perfumed feet thrash. "What the—? What is the meaning of this?" The back legs of the chair thump against the floor, muffled by the carpet.

Standing behind him, I set the edge of my sword against his neck, and he falls still with a gasp. I bend down close to his ear.

"My turn," I say.

He gives a great start, his chest heaving in and out, and strains to look at me without turning his head.

"The Sunshield Bandit . . ." His face contorts with rage. "How *dare* you! I'll have your head for this before the night is out—"

"Not if I have yours first," I say, edging the blade just a hair nearer. It barely brushes his skin, and he goes still again, his lips moving soundlessly. I echo his parting words from my cell. "At the moment, you don't quite have the leverage."

He swallows.

"I have some questions for you," I say, still behind him. "And if you would like to see the sunrise, you'll answer them."

"Where are my servants?" he demands, a tremble below his bravado. "My guards?"

"Out and about," I say nonchalantly.

"You killed them, didn't you?"

"The longer you keep asking stupid questions, the more angry I am getting." In fact, the guards are only a few doors away, alive and at their posts, and I'm hoping I can keep Kobok quiet enough to avoid any suspicion. The servants were easily deterred by Irena whispering to them who I was and what I was doing—they merely eyed me, and then each other, and then disappeared without a word.

"Told you," Irena had whispered to me.

Still, relying on the unexpected goodwill of strangers has never been a habit of mine. An alert could be raised at any moment, as soon as someone heads down to my cell block. I have limited time.

I put one hand partway up the blade to steady it against Kobok's neck. He whimpers.

"You planned the attack on Tamsin Moropai," I say in his ear. "You blackmailed the prince to be sure you could keep your job. You made a fake *si* bracelet to make Kimela the *ashoki*. And then you stirred the country up against the East to make it seem like you are doing it all to protect Moquoia."

"What on earth . . ." His panicky gaze darts around the room, still straining to see me out of the corner of his eyes. "That's a lie, by thunder! All lies!"

"You hurt Tamsin and locked her up, and you blamed it on me." I press the sword until it makes a divot against his neck, just short of breaking the skin. His voice turns to a high rasp.

"It . . . it wasn't me! I didn't start the rumors in court. And I didn't know anything about Tamsin before today—I thought she died months ago, until the reports came in that she was with you in the *ashoki*'s coach!"

"Don't lie!" I snap. "You knew she was alive—why else would you make the *si* bracelet? When Veran and Iano left, you knew they might find her. You had to make people sure she was dead."

"I didn't—I didn't make the *si-oque*! It was delivered to me! I didn't know it was a fake—and I don't know who sent it!"

"That seems very lucky," I say. "Why would they send it to you? Why not to the queen?"

"I don't know!" He squirms in the chair. Sweat has broken out on his forehead and around his bushy moustache. "I . . . I thought . . ."

I jostle him and he gasps again. "You thought what?"

"I thought it might be a threat," he says quickly. "Someone trying to intimidate me."

"Why would the bracelet make you think that?"

"It was left in my room," he says. "Not with my mail, but

right on my mantelpiece. Someone was able to get into my room. *Without* murdering my guards," he adds in a high voice.

I ignore the last remark. "So *what*? You have servants."

"None of them knew where it had come from. None of the guards saw anyone come in. How did *you* get in?"

"I killed everyone, remember?" I remind him. I take the sword away from his neck and come around the front of his chair. "You're all by yourself."

He whimpers again, his gaze flicking over me. Fire and smoke, what an idiot. As if leaving a pile of dead guards outside his door would go unnoticed for more than a minute. I rattle his chair again. "You are not telling me everything. The *si* bracelet should have been what you wanted. It should have meant things were happening your way. Why get so nervous? Why think someone is threatening you—unless you have done something wrong?"

"I didn't attack the *ashoki*!" he insists again.

"You're lying," I growl.

"I swear, I didn't—"

I straighten my arm against the back of his chair and shove, tilting him on the back two legs. He jerks and gives something between a shriek and a gasp, his feet wiggling feebly in the air. I press the hilt of my sword—not the blade, just the hilt—into the fleshy part of his chin, underneath his jaw.

"I!" he pants. "I—the records. I thought someone knew, had seen the . . . inconsistencies . . ."

"Speak plain," I spit.

"The laborer records!" he babbles. "Some of them—a few . . . hardly any, but it might appear that some had been falsified.

Not . . . not *falsified*, just . . . filled in with—with the best guess as to where some of the . . . bonds had . . . originated . . ."

I glare at him, trying to line up his nonsense in my head. Records falsified with where the bonds had originated?

"You have three seconds to start making sense," I say.

"It's just!" he bursts. "A while ago—before your time—there was an incident, with a foreign monarch. Moquoia was accused of abducting the princess of a minor monarchy. Inquiries were made. I had to protect our industry."

There's a funny ringing in my ears, as if my blade had struck something metal while I was still holding the hilt. When I speak, my voice is dry and detached. "What does that have to do with Tamsin? What does that have to do with Tellman's Ditch? What does it have to do with *right now*?"

"There was a supplier, you see, a transient labor distributor . . ."

"Sorry, I don't know those words," I say acidly.

"A . . . well, a ring that operated, sort of . . . beyond the administration of the crown . . ."

I give his chair a thrash. He gasps again.

"A black market ring! There were many—still are many—and they tend to operate with code names . . . you know this is all classified information, highly volatile . . ."

Understanding hits me like a lightning bolt. In one swift move, I straighten and let go of the chair. It teeters and then arcs backward to the floor. Kobok groans.

"You mean Port Iskon," I say, standing over him.

"My head . . . ," he moans.

I lay my sword along his neck again. "You mean *Port Iskon, don't you*?"

"The Port ring," he says. "They'd change their name depending on the location. They couriered the laborers from the Alcoran sea routes to the Moquoian border. At that time they were using the name Iskon. When we started getting inquiries from the East, it only made sense to protect our industry from a possible audit . . ."

"How did you protect yourselves?" I ask. "Why is the name Port Iskon still being used in Tellman's Ditch?"

He struggles feebly against the silk cord. "That's . . . that's *highly* classified information, *extremely* sensitive . . ."

I put my foot on the rung of his chair and haul on the cord, heaving him upright. His head wobbles on his neck, disoriented. I take his face in my fingers like a vise.

"You have *much* more to worry about than exposing classified information," I say, my face inches from his. "Tell me, did you start using the name Port Iskon on more slave records?"

"Only the ones from the Ferinno," he says, his words ridiculous through his pouched lips. "Merely a way to consolidate files, to organize . . ."

"You used it to cover up the abduction of the Lumeni princess," I say.

"Only initially. Then it became a way to notate who might be a citizen, and more likely to have bond restrictions."

"You mean people who might know the laws, or who might have family that know the laws—know that there are always supposed to be term limits. You mean you started using Port Iskon as a way to label workers who never had to be released. As a way to do away with bonds completely. To *create* slaves."

He's silent, his eyes squeezing shut. I stay there for a moment, clutching his jaw, and then I straighten, releasing his face. His brow knits, but his eyes don't open.

"How classified is this information?" I ask. "Does the queen know?"

"Few people outside my department know," he replies. "It's for the stability of the industry. Voluntary bonds are at a historic low, while industry is at an all-time high. Something had to be done to . . . meet the demand. At least temporarily."

"It was never supposed to be temporary," I say. "You forging slave documents would have gone on forever if Tamsin hadn't started to look into it. That's what happened back in the spring, isn't it? She was coming to poke around Tellman's Ditch, to rustle up some truths she could tell to the court."

"I didn't attack the *ashoki*."

"If you didn't, and you didn't make the *si* bracelet, who did?"

"I have no idea!" he says, opening his eyes. "I told you, it was left in my room. I thought someone was threatening that they would finish what she'd begun—that they'd expose my department's methods. With the prince missing and war building with the East, my department can't handle a public relations nightmare on top of everything else."

I lift my sword, and he flinches, his breath rising shallowly in his throat. I set the point against his chest, my palm halfway up the blade. "So you decided to scramble your records in Tellman's Ditch? Tell me—all those years ago, when you realized you'd somehow trafficked a princess, why didn't you just return her?"

A look of sincere consternation crosses his face, as if the idea is absurd. "There were over two hundred people processed through the Port Iskon ring that particular month. We could hardly know which one she was—and if we returned her, there would be complaints about the others. We would have had to return the whole shipment."

My sword point drops back to the floor, and he draws in a deep breath with it gone. He fidgets against his cords—the longer I stand there, staring at him, the more anxious he becomes. Finally, his nerves get the best of him.

"So what now?" he asks, and despite the sweat on his brow and upper lip, he manages to sound angry.

"I'm thinking," I reply. "You've given me important information—not the answers I was hoping for, but good enough, I think."

"For what?" he prompts. "Even if you kill me, you'll never get out of the palace alive. Everyone from the ministers to the staff knows what you look like. You'll barely get to the atrium. And even if you do, what then? Knock on the queen's apartment door? Hope she'll sit and listen as the continent's most notorious bandit slanders her country's industry?"

"Hm," I say, tucking the blade of my sword under my left arm. "I think she might listen to me."

"Why? Because you have a sword?"

"No. Because it was me, all those years ago."

"What was you?"

I roll up my right sleeve. There's probably symbolism in baring my unsealed slave brand, but I'm not interested in that at the moment—I just don't want to bloody my cuff. "I'm not the Sunshield Bandit. I'm the damned princess of Lumen Lake."

His face creases in confusion. "What—?"

I make a fist and punch him in the face.

His head slams back against the chair, and then rolls sideways. He groans, his eyes blinking at different times. I sheathe my sword back in my belt and go to the large, gilded wardrobe in the corner. I rifle among the silk robes and nightcaps—he has a whole wardrobe just for *sleeping* clothes—until I find a stack of embroidered handkerchiefs. I select two and carry them back. He groans again as I get nearer, a purple mark in the shape of my knuckles blooming under his eye.

I ball up one handkerchief and stuff it in his mouth, then tie the other one around his head to keep it in place. He rouses just enough to struggle again as I take the long end of the curtain cord and tie his feet to the chair legs.

"You just sit tight for a little while," I say, patting him on the shoulder. "I'm sure someone will be in to check on you when you miss breakfast tomorrow."

He muffles something through the handkerchief, but I turn and head back to his adjoining parlor, closing the door behind me.

I go to the middle of the room and look up at the fancy glass skylight, a few drops of rain spattering my cheeks. Irena's anxious face appears in the opening. Getting in had been an easier job than I thought—the rivets around the glass panels came up easily, I suppose for quick replacement when one cracks. There were even anchor brackets for workers to tie harnesses to, which made things even simpler. Irena twitches the rope dangling over a small puddle on the carpet.

"Ready?" she mouths.

I nod and twist my fingers through one of the loops in the ropes, the kind the window cleaners use throughout the palace. The descent wasn't too bad, but I'm dreading the upward climb. I breathe as shallowly as I can, but I can't stop my ribs from searing against my sides as I labor up, the rope ladder swinging with each step. The worst part is wriggling back through the open pane—Irena helps me slide over the slick glass until I can lie, panting, on top of the skylight, my palms pressed to my sides. The rain drums around us.

Irena coils up the window-cleaner's rope and replaces the open panes on the skylight. Lightning flashes overhead, illuminating the tile roofs and glass skylights of the palace. Bad place to be right now.

"Did he confess?" she asks.

I shake my head, my eyes closed against the rain thumping my face. "It wasn't him—at least, he gave a convincing performance, and his story makes sense with his panic at Tellman's Ditch. But he did confess to something else. I just have to figure out how to get the information to someone who matters before they get me on the scaffold."

Distantly, a bell begins to ring. Irena pauses to listen. I open my eyes.

"I'm guessing that's not a good sound?" I ask.

Irena grimly shakes her head. "It's an alert. They've probably found your cell."

And the cell guard. Wincing, I sit up and hitch my bandanna over my nose. "What are our options?"

"To get you out? We have a few choices." She gets to her feet and holds out her hand. "This way."

I take her hand and get to my feet. Breathing carefully, I follow her back among the narrow roof walks. But we've only descended one flight, opening into a narrow staff hallway in the eaves, when footsteps thud around the corner. I wrench Irena behind me and am pulling my sword out, blinking away spots from the pain in my sides, when a young boy comes barreling around the corner. He skids to a halt mere inches from being spitted on my sword, his eyes wide as apples.

"You!" he gasps.

I adjust my grip. "Me."

"The Sunshield Bandit!" he exclaims.

"So they say."

"Wait!" Irena whispers, hurrying around me. "Wait a moment—it's all right. What are you doing up here, Rin?"

"Closing the hatches," he says, still goggling at me. "We're on lockdown—they say the bandit escaped her cell." He puts his hands to his forehead. "I didn't think you were real! My brother tells me stories about you when I have nightmares."

My sword drifts downward. I'd always assumed I was the source of nightmares, not the other way around.

"She has to get out of the palace," Irena says. "Which ways are still open?"

"Not many," he says. "You might try the cleaning ladders by the red gardens." We start to move past him, but he stops us. "That's not all, though. I don't think I was supposed to see, but I was waxing the floors in the guard wing."

"See what?" Irena asks.

"The prince," he says, nearly trembling with the excitement of the night. "Prince Iano is back."

I reach forward and take his shoulder. He gasps again, sagging like a rag doll in my hand.

"Was he alone?" I ask. "Or were there others with him?"

"There were others," he says. "I'm not sure how many."

That's all I need to know. I whirl back to Irena. "Let's go."

"The guards, though—they're looking for you . . ."

"If we can get to Iano and the others, it won't matter if they find me," I say. "Can you get me there?"

She bites her lip, but nods. "Follow me."

I sheathe my sword, and we charge back into the shadowed palace.

TAMSIN

Iano, Soe, and I huddle, dripping, under a stand of tree ferns. Enna snuck us into the palace through the west guard gate. We look so bedraggled that when she explained we're palace staff returned from a journey, her story wasn't questioned at all. Now we cluster between the ferns and the rain-streaked glass, wringing out our clothes into the garden bed. Enna and her cadre stand a few paces away, not doing anything to lessen the strange sight we make—three ragged travelers gathered conspiratorially at the edge of the public halls, flanked by armed guards and a wet coydog. Rat has already rolled in the rich mulch of the indoor gardens and is now digging under a doomed ficus.

"The problem is, we don't have enough *time*," Iano whispers, raking his wet hair behind his ears. "It won't be long before someone recognizes us, and word gets to my mother."

Or our enemy, I sign grimly.

"Right," he says. "So, the question is—what do we do first? Find Fala? Look for Lark? Ask about Veran?"

I purse my lips. *Lark is most important.*

Soe stirs. "But this enemy of yours—if you can't identify them, you don't know who to trust, or avoid."

"So should we go to Fala first?" Iano asks.

What about your mother? I ask. *If we go to her right away, she could stop any execution order and buy us more time.*

"Or it might give your enemy more time to strategize, or get away," Soe points out. "If they hear you're in the palace, it takes away our element of secrecy, and surprise."

Iano rubs his forehead worriedly. "If we could just take care of even *one* of our unknowns, it could make all the difference— who our enemy is, whether Veran's here, whether Lark is okay . . ."

In a moment so perfectly scripted it couldn't have been carried out better on a stage, lightning flashes across the glass, the branches above us shake, and the Sunshield Bandit drops like a meteor into our midst.

Soe shrieks. Iano stumbles backward and hits the glass wall. I clap my hand over my mouth. Enna and her cadre all draw their weapons and charge toward us. Rat, however, erupts from his progress on the ficus and leaps into Lark's arms. She grapples with him, squeezing him tightly.

"You're here—you're alive!" Iano exclaims, his back and palms flat against the glass. He quickly straightens and waves at Enna as she reaches us. "No, it's fine, she's fine—I just . . ." He shakes his head at Lark. "I swear every time I think you can't surprise me . . ."

"That is why you could never catch me," Lark replies.

He draws in a breath of patience but gestures at Enna again. "It's fine. Truly."

We'd told Enna about Lark's innocence—at least in the current affairs—on the road, but the guard still keeps her gaze warily on us as she guides her cadre back to their lookout post.

I turn to Lark, not bothering to hide my admiration. *You're not in prison*, I sign. *What did you do, kick down the door?*

She grimaces. "I maybe attacked the cell guard and stole her keys."

Iano groans.

Lark looks around. "Where's Veran?"

"We don't know," Soe says.

"You *don't know*?" she repeats.

"He was making for the palace last we saw him, but that was two days ago."

"Alone?" she asks.

"Alone," Iano confirms.

"We couldn't talk him out of it," Soe says.

Lark's eyes glitter above her bandanna, but before she can lay into us, the trees rustle again. With much more timidity and less fanfare than Lark, another figure comes clambering down the trunk, breathing fast. She drops to the ground and then freezes, eyeing all of us. She's wearing the plain, dark uniform of the palace staff.

"This is Irena," Lark says. "She helped me get past the prison guards, and find you. She will *not* get in trouble for this," she says fiercely, turning her glare on Iano. "If something bad happens to her, I'll kill you, I swear."

He gives her a pained look. "You have to try to stop threatening death to people."

"I will when they stop doing it to me," she replies flatly. "Promise me she won't get in trouble."

"I promise, but listen, we still don't have answers," Iano says. "Until we know who organized the attack on Tamsin, none of us are actually safe."

"It wasn't Kobok," Lark says.

How do you know? I ask, at the same time that Iano and Soe voice the same thing.

She shifts. "I asked him."

"You *asked* him?" Iano says incredulously.

"Yes, very nicely," she says without any hint of amusement. "He says he didn't make Tamsin's fake *si* bracelet. He said it was left in his room. It made him panic—he thought someone was threatening him about Port Iskon."

Did you find out where Port Iskon is? I sign quickly.

"It's not a place," Lark says, an ugly edge to her voice. "It's the name of an old black market ring. They started using it on Alcoran captives' papers fifteen years ago to sidestep bond limits—and to cover up the abduction of the Lumeni princess."

My stomach flips. Silence rings among us, our faces all frozen in shock and horror. Iano struggles to find a response.

"*How* is that possible?" he begins. "That kind of corruption . . ."

Lark whirls on him. "I swear I will kill you," she repeats, "if you can still defend him."

He ruffles in irritation, and to my surprise, he draws himself up, throwing his shoulders back in a mirror of hers. In a flash, she shifts her weight, dropping Rat and squaring toward

Iano, fists clenched. *Dammit.* We have barely minutes to spare, and I'm about to have to break up a fist fight between the prince and the Sunshield Bandit.

"*Hey,*" I say, putting a palm on both of their shoulders.

But Iano doesn't break Lark's gaze. "My esteemed political ally," he says in his addressing-the-court voice. "My lady princess of Lumen Lake and representative of the Allied East, I was going to say that that kind of corruption is grounds for prison, indefinitely."

My gaze goes from Lark's sparking eyes to his. Lark pauses, digesting his words, and then her lips bend into a half grin. She holds up her palm. Stiffly, with his chin serenely raised—but with a definite twitch at the corner of his own lips—he slaps his palm against hers. She resolves it into a firm handshake.

"Finally, something we agree on, outlaw to outlaw," she says.

I let out my breath and drop my hands from their shoulders. *Congratulations. Now—our plan.*

"Our plan," Soe echoes drily. "So far we know that our enemy probably isn't Minister Kobok, and that Lark isn't dead."

"Yet," Lark says.

We still don't know about Veran, and we still need to talk to Fala and the queen, I say. At my side, Irena stares blankly at my fingers.

"She's signing," Soe explains to her. "Talking with her hands."

But Irena doesn't take her eyes away. "I beg your pardon, but where did you get that *si-oque*?"

I twist my wrist to show the amber cabochons. *This? It's mine.*

Soe translates for her.

"But . . . if it's here, on your wrist, what's the one in the Hall of the *Ashoki*?" Irena asks. "In the display case beside the empty pedestal? It looks practically the same."

We all pause for a moment.

"The forgery," Iano says. "It must be. They must have put it in your display case, Tamsin."

"We should get it," Lark says. "If we can show it with Tamsin's real one, it proves someone has been working against the country."

"And," Soe points out, "it could draw out our enemy—once they hear we're in the palace, they might go to the Hall of the *Ashoki* to retrieve it."

We're quiet a moment, thinking.

"Okay," I say. I gesture for Lark to repeat my words, so I know everyone understands me plainly. *Here is our plan. Iano— you go to your mother with the guards. Tell her everything, and stop the hunt for Lark. Soe—you go find Fala. Bring Irena. Tell her we need to talk to her right away, to ask who she suspects may be with the Hires, and if anyone disappeared at the same time as Poia. Lark and I will go to the Hall of the* Ashoki. *If our enemy shows themselves, Lark can detain them.*

She winces as she finishes translating. "Not for long."

By then we'll have the guards back on our side, I assure her.

"I'll believe it when I see it," she says.

"Where can I find Fala?" Soe asks. "Does she have a . . . room, or an office?"

"She's in records," Irena says, so quietly I almost don't hear her. "At least, she was earlier."

"That's where her office is?" Soe asks.

"Oh no, her office is in the staff corridors, at the head of the main workroom. She was in records to validate something—she's had to do that sort of thing since Beskin left."

We all go still.

"Beskin?" Iano repeats.

Beskin was in records? I ask, my fingers fumbling.

"Yes, but she left," Irena says again.

"Was she a Hire?" Lark asks.

Irena's eyes drop, and she fiddles with the sleeve that covers her slave brand. "I don't rightly know. But it wouldn't surprise me. She wouldn't be the only one on staff."

Iano turns to Soe. "This makes Fala even more crucial. Tell her we need to see her *immediately*."

She nods and joins Irena. I move toward Lark, but to my surprise, she doesn't budge.

"Wait," she says. "We're still forgetting Veran. We don't have *any* idea where he is?" She looks at Irena. "Have you heard anything about him?"

"Who?" she asks.

"Veran Greenbrier—foreign prince with green eyes and a hero complex?" she says. "Real pretty hair?"

I snort, but Lark is being serious. Irena looks perplexed, so Iano adds, "The translator from the Eastern delegation."

"Sorry," she says. "I haven't heard anything. Though the guards did bring a ring with a foreign symbol on it up to records. That's what Fala had to validate."

"A ring?" Lark says quickly. "A silver one? With a bug on it?"

"I don't know," Irena whispers, twisting her hands—she clearly wants to have better answers.

I touch Lark's sleeve. *I don't think we can worry about Veran right now.*

She pivots to me, gripping her sword hilt. "I worry about that idiot *constantly.* Why should they have his seal ring if he's not in trouble? What if they're trying to identify his body?"

"Soe can check to see if it was really his, when she goes up to records with Irena," Iano says. "But Tamsin's right, Lark—we can't worry about Veran. We have to pinpoint our enemy first."

Her mouth twists. "And if our enemy decides he's a target, too?"

"I don't think they will," he assures her. "If the guards really did have his seal ring, and validated it, they'll know who he is—if he's here, he's being well-guarded. He's safer than we are."

Lark grinds her teeth, but I bump her elbow. *Please, Lark. We'll help Veran soon—but we can't if we don't catch our enemy, and we're running out of time.*

She blows out a frustrated breath, but finally nods. "All right. The Hall of the *Ashoki.*"

Soe turns to follow Irena. "See you all soon."

Iano clasps my shoulder as he moves past me. "I'll meet you at the Hall. Be safe."

"*Pff,*" I reply. *No time to be safe.*

"Try anyway," he says drily. He looks to Lark. "You, too. We can finish this thing tonight—nobody else has to get hurt."

She pauses, and then stiffly bends down and gathers Rat in her arms. She straightens and turns to Iano. "Take Rat with you. Find a safe place to put him—give him some water, and somewhere to lie down. I am afraid if he's with us in the palace, the guards will shoot him."

To my utter astonishment, Iano accepts the damp, muddy dog and bundles him in his own arms, his face grave at the responsibility just entrusted to him. "I will."

Lark presses her forehead once against Rat's, and then, with another sigh, turns back to me. With that, we part ways, our footsteps underscored by the drumming of rain and the dwindling descant of Rat's anxious cries.

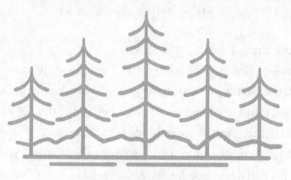

VERAN

I rouse from sleep at the sound of voices outside my door. Guilt washes over me at the realization that I dozed off, wrapped in the bed quilt and propped up in the desk chair. I hurriedly shake off the stiffness in my neck and jump to my feet, preparing for the guards to open the door.

But they don't. I hear muffled commands, punctuated with urgency. Boots tromp, brass jingles. The bars of shadow leave the crack under my door, and the keyhole glints with light again. I go to it and peer through. The hall is empty. There's a sound of rushing footsteps, and after a moment two figures run past, clutching the weapons on their belts to keep them from jostling. Then it goes silent again.

I wait a few more minutes, but no one reappears. When my knees start to protest, I stand up.

I rap on the door.

"Hey," I call. "Is anyone out there?"

No answer.

I test the handle. It's still locked.

I take a few paces backward and simply stare at the door. Did *all* the guards go to alert the queen? How long was I asleep? I'm thirsty and tired, but that's not much indication. My clothes are still damp, but the room is cold, so that's not surprising either. I go to the window and peer into the sky, but it doesn't help—it's still dark and cloudy. A flicker of light catches my eye, and I look down into the colonnade. Lanterns bob haphazardly between the pillars, as if a group of people are heading somewhere at a run.

At a loss, I resume the pacing I'd been doing before I fell asleep, interspersed with checking the window. As time passes, lamps are lit in all the windows I can see from mine, as well as the colonnade. Twice, a bell rings from somewhere outside, but I don't know what it means, and no one returns to my door.

After an unknown length of time, I can't stand it anymore. I knock and call again, to no avail.

I'm locked in a room in Tolukum Palace with no food or water, and the guards that had been outside my door have gone. Something is going on outside to draw them away. Has Iano returned to the palace? Has there been an attack? Has—my body flushes with fear—has the queen decided to conduct a late-night execution?

I stand still in the middle of the room, worrying my lip. What do I have?

Not much.

They took the *si-oque* and my seal. I have no real clout anymore. I have my battered boots, my clothes, and a single copper coin.

More! Mama calls. *You have more!*

I look around the room. The lanterns from outside have brightened things a little, and my night vision is sharp from the long hours of darkness. I move to the shadowy desk and open the single drawer. I creep my fingers through the contents, which are predictable and ordinary—a few sheets of parchment, two quills, a jar of ink, a blotter, a penknife . . .

I halt on the penknife. Memories flood back of Eloise's uncle Arlen sitting with us on the floor of the map room—he'd been supposed to be giving us a lesson in defensive cartography— showing us how to jimmy the lock on the door with a penknife and one of Eloise's hairpins. I picked the lock on Tamsin's door in Utzibor. If I can find a pin, I can do it here.

I grope through the rest of the drawer, but there's nothing else apart from some wax. The washstand isn't any more helpful, nor is the firebox. If only I had my firefly pin! I crab blindly through the room, hoping for inspiration, until I reach the door. I'm feeling along the frame, wondering if there's a nail I could work out of place, when my fingers hit a small metal object hanging on a hook. I pause, feeling the shape of it and wondering if I can bend the hook straight, when finally my brain catches up, and I feel exceptionally stupid.

This isn't a prison cell. It's a guest room. Nobody locks their guests up—of course the key would be hanging by the door. The only people with keys to the outside are probably servants and guards.

I take the key off the hook, my face hot in the darkness. I nearly throw the penknife back onto the bed in disgust, but the next moment I pocket it instead.

Stealing from the palace, I think, slightly giddy and disoriented. If I wasn't an outlaw before, I am now.

I fit the key in the lock and turn it. Carefully, I poke my head into the hall. It's utterly silent and deserted, with only a few lamps lit at haphazard intervals. I open the door wider and step out, straining my ears for noise. But there's nothing—not murmuring voices or quick footsteps or the distant buzz of the army of servants.

I make a hasty decision, heading down the hall toward the main atrium, hoping that if I run into the guards, I can bluster my way through with pompous royal affront at being locked up, wet and thirsty and under suspicion. But I meet no one in the atrium. Buckets and mops are strewn around, some in patches of suds. A bundle of linens lay draped over a railing, as if flung down in haste. I creep through the abandoned atrium, uneasy.

Where is everyone?

The boles of the indoor cedar forest rise at the center of the atrium. I'm in their midstory. The royal chambers are near the canopy, on the opposite side of the atrium. Without hesitating any longer, I start around the landing circling the trees. Rain drums on the dark glass, punctuated by lightning. The storm has grown.

I'm halfway around the landing, near a hallway I vaguely remember as leading to clerk offices, when a door slams. Footsteps hurry up the hallway. I tense, but as I recognize the person who appears, I sigh with relief.

"Mistress Fala! By the Light, I'm glad to see you."

She halts as soon as she sees me, her hands busy with a rag. "Prince Veran? I'd heard you were in the palace—I was coming to find you."

"Do you know what's going on? I was brought in by the guards, but they disappeared, and I need to speak to the queen.

It's about Tamsin, and Prince Iano. I'm worried the guards won't let me through . . ."

She shoves the rag into her pocket and beckons. "Come with me."

"Thank you," I say, holding my palms out gratefully as she heads to a service door. I follow her into a narrow, low-ceilinged hall, its bare wood and ungraceful hurricane lanterns a stark contrast to the lavish public halls. She leads me down it at a fast walk—I pant to keep up.

"What's going on?" I ask again. "Where is everyone?"

"The Sunshield Bandit is loose in the palace," she says without slowing down. "She broke out of the prison and is somewhere inside. The whole place is on lockdown."

My heart practically vaults out of my chest. "She's alive? She's in the palace?"

"Yes, and her accomplices may be here as well. If you don't want to be accidentally shot by the guards, you need to stay somewhere safe."

My joy freezes into terror. "Shot?"

"Of course—the guards have orders to shoot on sight. Anyone wandering about could be working with her." Fala's usually kind voice is emotionless, distracted, almost snappish. She's worried, I realize.

"But—but Lark—the Sunshield Bandit, that's her name—she's innocent! I mean, not *innocent* . . ."

"She murdered the last *ashoki*," Fala says sharply.

"No, she didn't!" My voice comes in gasps as I follow her brisk steps down a cramped staircase. "She didn't attack Tamsin outside Vittenta—and Tamsin didn't die, either! She's alive. We found her, Lark and I—we rode out to Utzibor in the desert and found her, and brought her back. That's where Iano and I went—"

Fala stops so abruptly on the landing below that I barrel into her. She takes one step to steady herself and turns to me, her face rigid with something close to shock.

"The Sunshield Bandit helped you find Tamsin?"

"Oh yes," I say. "Tamsin was drawing bats in her ransom letters—Lark knew right away she must be at Utzibor caverns. Lark didn't attack Tamsin—she *rescued* Tamsin."

Fala blinks in astonishment. Her hands, smudged with dark polish, grip her skirt.

"Who else knows about this?" she asks.

"About Lark? Prince Iano. And Soe—a friend of Tamsin's. No one else, I think," I say. "So you can see why I need to speak to the queen."

She stares a moment longer. "Yes, I do. Remarkable." She shakes her head, and her demeanor softens. "Truly remarkable, my lord Veran. Come sit down, and we can sort this out."

"With the queen?"

She waves me down a passage that joins with two others at the landing. I follow her into a wider hall lined with doors. Some are propped open to reveal storage closets or laundry chutes. The air smells of cedar shavings and window polish.

"Is this the way to the queen?" I ask as Fala shunts me toward the end.

"It's too dangerous to move about the palace right now," she says.

"But—"

"I'll send someone to alert the queen," she says.

"I'd really rather speak to her myself," I protest. "This is too important—what if the guards find Lark?"

"I'll have someone alert the guards. Your safety is more important." We approach the end of the hallway, which opens into a vast workroom scattered with long wooden tables. Doors ring the walls, some with signs for where they lead—the grounds, the laundry, the kitchens, the Hall of the *Ashoki*. At the end, like an overseer's platform at a mill, is a raised office fronted with windows. The glass panels are the biggest I've seen anywhere in Moquoia aside from the Tolukum atrium, and as Fala leads me up the staircase to it, I realize this must be her headquarters, the hub of servant activity in the palace. Her status as head of staff doesn't need to be mounted on a plaque when her office boasts glass that rivals any of the windows in the rooms of noble folk.

Despite the opulent glass, the office inside is cozy and homey, with well-organized stacks of parchment on a carved oak desk. A fire smolders in the grate, throwing our flickering reflections against the large, dark windows in the opposite wall. The pattering of rain and rumble of thunder returns—she must have a view out to the grounds during the day.

"Please, sit down," she says, guiding me to a chair beside the desk. Her motherly voice is back now that we're safe from the danger in the main palace. I sink into the chair, grateful for the chance to sit but wishing I was closer to the fire.

"Now," Fala says. "Tell me—the Sunshield Bandit reunited the prince and the *ashoki*?"

"Yes," I say. "But we were all separated again after Lark was recaptured—he stayed behind to look for her. I'm afraid she might have been hurt or—delayed. I don't know where—"

"The *ashoki* is alive," she interrupts with certainty. "And she's here in the palace."

I blink. "You mean Tamsin? Not Kimela? How do you know?"

She turns a sheet of paper around on her desk, one that had been sitting out away from all the others, and slides it toward me. I peer at it, recognizing the familiar title.

"'The Path of the Flood' . . . that's Tamsin's essay," I say. "The one she wrote for Kimela. How did you . . . did it come back with the *ashoki*'s coach?"

"No," she says. "It was one of about five dozen scattered around the Bearberry Crossroads. One of my drivers brought it to me this evening. They said similar pamphlets had been distributed up and down the north-south road."

"By the Light," I breathe, looking at the paper again. "She did it—she made it work. Her press, I mean. Tamsin. She made multiple copies of the same essay." I shake my head, aware I'm babbling. "But . . . how do you know she's in the palace?"

"I was informed," Fala says simply. And then—"You said this friend of Tamsin's was the only other one who knows about this?"

"Soe? I think so, aside from Prince Iano," I say.

"Does Tamsin know who attacked her outside Vittenta?"

"No," I say, my head spinning at the jumps in topic. "All she knew was that it wasn't the Sunshield Bandit."

"Anything else?" she presses. "Did she recall anything else at all?"

"I . . . don't think so. They killed her maid," I say. "Apart from that, I don't think she remembered anything specific."

"She said they killed her maid?" Fala asks sharply.

"Yes . . . forgive me, I don't remember her name."

"Simea."

"Yes! That was it."

"She was *sure* they had killed her maid?"

"I . . . yes, that's what she told us." I shake my head again, trying to tame the flicker of unease needling me. Whether or not Tamsin's maid was killed months ago doesn't seem like the most pressing concern at the moment—unless, I suppose, Fala knew the girl personally. Still, there would be time to mourn afresh once the current danger has passed. "Mistress Fala, please—you said you'd send someone to tell the guards to stand down. We can't let them find Lark, and if Tamsin is here, she could be in danger, too . . ."

"Yes. Of course." Fala stands from her desk and goes to the bank of windows facing the workroom. She closes the door behind her and descends the staircase. I watch through the glass as she disappears back into the hall we came through. I take the opportunity to get up and move next to the fire, shivering and holding my numb fingers out to the flames.

There's a tortured knot in the pit of my stomach. I'd envisioned returning to Tolukum and bringing everything to a screeching halt, but so far I feel like I've barely made a dent. I'm here, but . . . does the queen know? Have the guards found me missing? Or are they more focused on hunting for Lark?

Surely, if Lark broke out of prison—*Lark broke out of prison*! I flush with admiration. But surely, she wouldn't stay in the palace. Why would she? She's smart. She'd run.

But . . . Fala seems so sure she's still in Tolukum.

Important, and urgent, Mama says.

I bite my lip.

It's important not to be shot in the palace, I guess.

But . . .

It's urgent that Lark and Tamsin not be shot, either.

Perhaps I can write a note and ask Fala to send it up to Queen Isme. Maybe that's what I should have done all along, before they took my seal ring away. I turn from the fire to Fala's desk, arranged with neat files and lit with sweet beeswax candles. There's a blotter on her desk but no other writing utensils—I cast a quick glance through the glass, trying to shake the feeling of snooping. I open her topmost desk drawer. It's a collection of stamps and ink, with words like *Approved* or *Denied* and a collection of *si* names and numbers to indicate the date. There's even a small seal, similar to the Moquoian redwood cone, but with a concentric circle behind it. I give a small shiver . . . it reminds me of the brand on Lark's arm, and then I realize that's precisely what it's supposed to be. The mark of slavery, set right into the seal of the palace staff. I close the drawer quickly, reminded uncomfortably of the Hires and how they've adapted that concentric circle as their own mark, too.

What a little monarchy Fala is in charge of—almost a court within a court, with its own hierarchy and laws. From the highest-paid royal attendants down to the lowliest unbonded slaves.

I yank open the next drawer down and am relieved to find ink bottles and quills. Behind them, shoved oddly toward the back of the drawer, is paper, but it's all folded. I rifle for the top piece and have it halfway out when I realize it's not blank. Oops. I'm sliding it back into place when the corner catches on the ink bottles, and I get a better look at the writing under the fold.

An *M,* scrabbled with a flourish that looks like a bat.

The hinges on the glass door swing. I slam the drawer and straighten, my heart pounding. Fala stands in the doorway, a mug in her hand.

For a moment, there's only the sound of rain beating on glass as we stare at each other.

"I—" I begin. My mind is spinning. "Forgive me, I was looking for parchment. I thought I might write Queen Isme a note."

Her gaze flicks to the desk, and I will myself not to look down at the second drawer. In the folds of my damp clothes, I rub my fingertips together, recognizing the rough grain of the paper, made from desert sawgrass, so different from the smooth vellum used in Moquoia.

Fala smiles at me, the same kindly expression she's granted me so many times before—while doctoring my feet, or explaining the court to me, or guiding me out of danger.

She closes the glass door behind her. She takes out a key on a chain of others and turns the lock.

She gestures to the mug in her hand. Now that I look closer, the polish stains I saw her wiping from her skin earlier don't look quite so much like polish.

"Tea?" she asks.

TAMSIN

Lark and I pull up short at the corner where the staff halls open into the public halls.

"*Dammit*," she whispers.

Even though the Hall of the *Ashoki* sits just across the open atrium, there's a cluster of guards around the entrance, and more rushing about with loaded crossbows. Too many to distract, or fight.

Lark flexes her fingers in agitation. *Is there a different way in?* she signs.

I bite my lip. *There are terraces. But they may be locked.*

Her quick eyes scan the atrium, landing on the glass doors through the cedar trees. She nods at them. *Can we use those?*

I waver my hand in uncertainty. *They don't connect directly. We may have to use some service ladders.*

She grimaces but nods again. We start toward the trees, slipping through the garden beds. The atrium is dim, many of its lamps left unlit in the staff's abrupt retreat. Lightning flashes, lighting up the rain smearing the glass walls. We reach the doors to the exterior terraces, and Lark pushes the handle.

"Locked," she whispers. "Of course—they've sealed the palace." She digs in her pockets and brings out a ring of keys—they must be the ones she stole from the prison guard. She holds several up to the lock, but it's clear this won't work—they're all twice the size of the keyhole.

"Dammit," she mutters again.

I bite my lip. *There are service entrances, but I don't know the passages.*

From the trees behind us comes a call.

"Three of you—with me! There's a commotion in the clerks' offices!"

We jump at the voice and the sound of rattling weapons that follows it. In the next flash of lightning, I meet Lark's gaze.

Soe, I think.

"Irena," she mutters.

"Hey!" calls another voice. "There are tracks here, leading across the tiles."

We look down between us, where our muddy boots have left a line of prints.

"Go," Lark murmurs, pushing me along the glass wall. She slides her sword from its sheath and follows as I hurry along the curve of the wall, one hand on the glass. Behind us, foliage rustles and snaps as soldiers comb through the gardens, searching for our prints in the soft soil and shouting when they find them.

Ahead, the glass ends at a solid wall, where a service door sits ajar. We reach it just as the guards behind us break free of the foliage. They shout at us to halt; a crossbow crank winds. We swing through the door and Lark slams it shut, but there's no bolt inside, only a narrow staircase rising into darkness. With no other options, we thunder upward—I can hear Lark's ragged breathing, mine not much better, followed by the renewed shouts of the guards.

At the top of the staircase is a landing that stretches in two directions—with no inkling of which way to go, I veer to the left simply because it's darker. Lark follows, and we run. We turn one corner, and then another, and I pull up short just in time to avoid slamming into a door. Lark slows at the last second, throwing her sword wide to keep from skewering me with it. It drags a gouge in the wall. Around the corner behind her comes the clamoring of boots and voices.

The door has a bolt—I throw it and push it open. We're met with a curtain of shocking rain, icy and stinging. It sluices off the castle walls and splashes off the paving stones of a long terrace. Lark pushes me through the door and slams it shut behind us, keeping her grip on the handle. Squinting in the driving rain, we both look frantically around the terrace for something to bar the door. This must serve as a landing platform for staff— ladders stretch up the walls in intervals, and there are jumbles of gardening supplies stashed in alcoves.

There's a thump at the door, and Lark's wrist twitches as she fights to keep the knob from turning. She grits her teeth and nods at the nearest alcove, water streaming from her hat.

"There," she says.

I pull the tarp off a collection of empty stone planters. One by one I roll them to the door and prop them against the wood. A rake jammed against the knob and lodged into the pavers is the finishing touch—not exactly a fortress, but it might hold for a minute or two. Lark steps away from the door, watching as it strains against the planters, and nods.

"Good enough," she says, and then looks down the terrace.

"Ah," I say, pointing to the end of the platform. *There's another door.*

We hurry to it, and I grip the knob. I groan.

"Locked?" Lark asks.

I nod, and together we look blearily up at the ladders soaring into the darkness, their rungs ringing with rain.

We don't have a chance to pick one, though. The doorknob rattles under my palm, and I snatch my fingers away. There's the sound of a bolt sliding back.

Lark grabs my arm and drags me into the nearest alcove. We stumble amid a stand of shovels and broken bricks, falling clumsily against the alcove wall. I hear Lark hiss in pain as my feet slip and I press into her ribs, but she grips my arm to keep me from falling.

It's a terrible hiding spot—we're hidden by the darkness, but one lightning flash and we'll be neatly cornered targets to anyone on the terrace. Fish in a barrel.

We hear the door open.

With it comes the sound of someone wailing, a high, keening cry.

A knot of guards spills out, their backs to us. Lightning glints off their crossbow quarrels and sword points. They fan out into a half-circle, and the foremost throws a figure onto the wet paving stones.

It's Irena.

"It wasn't me!" she cries, curling up with her arms over her head. "I swear, it wasn't me!"

The guard raises his crossbow to sight.

Lark spasms with anger, and with a roar, she pushes me aside and barrels from the alcove, her sword up. Surprise saves her—the guards barely have time to whirl around in the darkness before she's on them. There are thumps and cries, and the sounds of splintering wood and winding cranks. A shattered crossbow clatters to the stones.

I scramble forward and grab Irena's arm, tugging her off the ground. She looks up, panicked, and blanches when she sees me. A crossbow fires, the quarrel whizzing overhead, and Irena stumbles to her feet. I drag her toward the now-unlocked service door, throwing a glance over my shoulder. On the other side of the terrace, there's a burst of clattering stone—the guards have forced open the other door. Planters go rolling across the terrace.

"Lark!" I shout.

She's broken two more crossbows and drawn a misfire from a third, leaving the little group scrambling to draw swords in the cramped space. She doesn't wait for them to finish—she turns and runs after me, swinging into the service entrance and hauling the door shut. With fumbling fingers, I throw the lock, and then I pull Irena down the narrow corridor. She's crying, her free hand clutching her face.

We reach a junction with two other hallways, an oily lantern burning on the corner. I slow to a halt, holding my breath and straining to hear, but there's no sound from any direction. Behind me, Irena puts her palms over her face again, this time to muffle her sobs. Lark hunches against the wall, gripping her ribs and wheezing painfully.

I turn back to the two of them, my heart thudding. In the dim light, I see dark streaks on Irena's face from her sleeve. I snatch her arm and hold it toward the lantern, but there's no rip or wound.

"I'm sorry," she says in an anguished whisper. "I'm sorry."

I stare at her. "Wha' happen?"

"Your friend," she says. "Soe."

Soe? What about Soe? She was right here. I grab her shoulders. "*Wha'?*"

"We got to records," she says unsteadily. "And went inside, and Soe told me to check that room for the seal ring while she looked in the other one. And she went in, and I could hear her talking to M-Mistress Fala, and Soe did just like you said, asking about the ring, and the Hires, and telling her you were here, and . . . I stayed in the other room—we're not supposed to speak to upper staff, so I just stayed in the other room, looking through the papers, and then there was a bump, and a cry, and then . . ." She covers her face with her hands, her whole body trembling. "And then moaning—a terrible moan . . ."

I shake her shoulders, ice coursing through my veins, trying to force her to continue. Lark is staring at her, still bent painfully over her ribs.

"Did you see her?" Lark asks, and her voice is calm—not at all like the whirlwind starting up in my head.

Irena nods behind her hands. "I heard the other door slam, and I went in, and there she was on the floor—your friend, and blood . . ." She takes a breath. "I screamed. I shouldn't have—it was stupid, but I couldn't help it. It brought the guards—they found me kneeling beside her, trying to cover the wounds . . ."

"Dead?" Lark prompts.

"I don't know—I don't think so, but they dragged me away. I'm sorry. I'm sorry."

I clap my hand to my mouth, reeling back from her.

Soe.

Fala.

Soe, my dearest friend . . . I sent her right into the heart of danger, I told her to say exactly the things that would put her in harm's way . . .

Fala.

My body flushes with shock. While Irena's sobs begin afresh, I lock gazes with Lark. Her eyes are creased in anger.

"Your head of staff is a Hire," she says. "And now she's trying to cover her tracks."

The guards would have killed Irena without question, thinking her guilty of the crime, and the secret of Soe's attack would have died with her. It would all have been pinned on the chaos of hunting down the Sunshield Bandit.

Shards of memory start to fit together, tiny things that didn't have a pattern before—someone was able to get into Iano's rooms to leave the blackmail letters, someone even the servants didn't see, because they didn't see anyone they wouldn't expect. Someone had to have access to the queen's seal to replicate it, and then use it to verify orders. Someone had to have access to records that would detail my *si-oque*, and the ability to anonymously deliver a forgery to an influential minister. Someone had to have spies, informants, muscle—not in the oblivious court, wrapped up in its own importance, but below, in the fabric of the staff. Someone had to be willing to risk everything to pre-serve the labor system—a system that created its own hierarchy under the stagnant, self-absorbed power of the palace. While politicians squabbled and bartered with human lives, another society quietly organized itself to take hold of the power be-stowed by a too-mighty court.

Fala coordinated the attack on my coach.

Fala ordered the cut in my tongue, the weeks in a cell.

Fala blackmailed Iano to appoint Kimela.

It was Fala.

I lunge forward and tug Irena's hands away from her tear- and blood-streaked face.

"Where?" I ask urgently. "Fa'—*where*?"

"I don't know," she whispers. "She left the records room, but I didn't see where she went."

"She's destroying evidence," Lark says grimly. "Where would she go? The Hall of the *Ashoki*?"

"I don't . . . perhaps there, or her office," Irena says. "Palace records are up with the clerks, but staff records are all in her office."

Beskin. Poia. Simea. How many other staff mysteriously disappeared around that same time?

I point at the different hallways.

Which way? I ask. Lark translates.

"This way to the main workroom, and her office," Irena says. "There's a corridor leading to the Hall of the *Ashoki* from there."

Up the hall, a door slams.

I nod. "*Go.*"

We run.

VERAN

"It's a Moquoian tea, you won't have tried it before," Fala says, pushing me down into the chair and handing me the mug. "It's invigorating for the cold, but it's best drunk quickly for full effect. It helps with the unusual taste, too."

She closes my hands around the mug and then returns to her desk. I stare as she sweeps her gaze over the drawers. I look down at the mug, my mind racing frantically. My thoughts crash back to the rock above the coach road just a few days ago, where I needed to think clearly and instead I panicked, where I needed to be brave and instead I fled.

You and your hero complex, Lark has said so many times now.

A few days ago I thought I knew exactly what a hero was.

A few days ago I figured out I wasn't one.

After a moment of silence, Fala looks back up at me, and without trying to make sense of my thoughts any longer I hurriedly lift the mug, not wanting her to grow suspicious at my hesitation. The tea inside smells familiar, like the high evergreen slopes of the Silverwood after a rain.

What do you have? Mama asks in my head.

Fala sinks into her desk chair, still watching me. She's here, and I'm here. She's wary of me now. And I have a full mug but no real answers yet.

Start with that, Mama says.

"Oh, I've had *urch* before," I say, tilting the mug toward my mouth.

"Good," Fala says.

I lower the mug and wipe my lips with the back of my hand.

There's another length of silence, and then abruptly she leans forward and taps Tamsin's essay, still lying on her desk. As she does, I see her *si-oque* peek out from the black hem of her sleeve, the first commoner's *si* bracelet I ever saw. I asked her why there were so many colors on it. She explained that she had no family to pass the beads on to.

She explained that her work had always come first.

"You know why this pamphlet is so dangerous?" she asks.

I shake my head. That scent of evergreen curls off the lukewarm mug. It's naggingly familiar—less like my mountain home than I thought. And certainly not *urch*. I know what larch and birch smell like. This is stronger and sharper. *Why do I know it?*

"No," Fala confirms. "You're a foreigner. You would not be expected to know. Let me explain. This pamphlet is akin to pulling a thread holding a tapestry together. It's the start of an unraveling."

Important, and urgent, Mama says.

With the barest turn of my head, I slide my gaze to the glass door she locked with a key, then to the other end of the room, where the rain hits the windows. There's a door handle there, too—there must be a landing outside. I can't tell if it's locked or not. I squint at it.

One crisis at a time, Mama says.

Fala sees my look. She checks the far door as well. The mug tilts in my hand, and when she looks back, I raise it hurriedly again to my lips.

"How is the tea?" she asks.

"Unusual," I reply. I show her the half-empty mug, shuffling my damp boots on the floor.

It seems to put her at ease. She leans back in her chair.

"You did a very bold thing, Veran, writing that first letter to Prince Iano last year. You pulled the first thread."

"Tamsin had already started pulling," I say.

"*Tamsin*—" she begins sharply, and then inhales. "Tamsin Moropai didn't pull threads. She set the tapestry on fire. There were many in this palace who hoped her messages would be too extreme for the young prince to take seriously—until pressure started coming from across the Ferinno, as well."

"Pressure was already building here in the country," I protest. "Just because it never penetrated the palace doesn't mean it wasn't there. Folk's lives are at stake."

"Oh yes, *folk's* lives are at stake," she says, repeating my careless Eastern word back to me. "But I don't think you realize just how much. I don't think you realize in what ways. You've tampered with an entire political system, Veran."

"Not the one up top, I'm guessing?"

She narrows her eyes at me, and I wonder how I ever thought

her motherly. The whole room smells of the sharp, pungent liquid in my mug. I'm flushed all over now with my own stupidity.

"I should have gotten you out of the way from the first moment you started bumbling around this court, complicating all my work," she says quietly. "Things would have been completely straightforward without you."

I struggle to order my thoughts. "Like you tried to do with Eloise? Putting that bowl of water on her windowsill and removing a pane to draw infected mosquitoes into her room?"

"I assumed *she* would be my main problem, not you," Fala says with a sour twist to her lips. "But you would have been even easier to remove—as easy as this. Who's to say it wasn't just one of your fits?"

Listen to your body, Mama whispers.

I finally place the scent of the remnants in my cup. Redcedar. It's mentioned in the scout handbooks, but only in the forestry sections, because it's considered a timber wood, not a medicinal.

In fact . . . it's the opposite.

Vague memories of footnote warnings slip through my head. Convulsant. Purgative. But I know the real reason it smells so familiar.

Glass cleaner.

The mug falls from my hand and hits the hardwood floor with a crack. I catch a final glimpse of Fala's stoic face as I slide off the chair and crumple to the floor.

LARK

Tamsin is ahead of me, racing across a long, shadowed room filled with worktables, the high ceiling lost to darkness. I grip my ribs in one hand, my sword bare in the other—drawing each breath is agony, but it's drowned out by urgency. This woman, Fala, just attacked a stranger who knew too much—who else might she deem a threat? She had no problem going after the high-ranking *ashoki*, no problem threatening the prince.

And Veran could be in the palace—and *she would know* if he was. If that ring belonged to him, she must have held it in her hands and known he was here, asking to speak to the queen.

Behind me, Irena gasps, "There!" She points to a short staircase at the end of the long workroom, where a glass-fronted office glows with firelight. Tamsin barrels up the stairs and lunges for the door handle. She rattles it and then pounds on the glass.

"Veran!" she shouts, her voice echoing through the cavernous space.

My stomach drops. He's in there?

With *her*?

I take the steps three at a time and arrive beside Tamsin. Through the glass I see the woman who came into my cell to look at me. She's standing behind a desk, staring at Tamsin with a look of shock. My gaze drops to the floor, where Veran is sprawled on his side, unmoving, his shoulders and head angled around the far side of the desk. A broken mug and puddles of liquid are scattered on the hardwood floor. My stomach dissolves away completely.

No.

Tamsin heaves on the door handle again, and then slams her palm against the glass, screaming her frustration at the woman inside. Fala, in turn, stoops to retrieve something in the desk, scattering quills in her haste.

"Move!" I push Tamsin out of the way and pull the patch cowhide hat off my head. I fold the thick leather around the blade of my sword, wind it back, and then arc the hilt toward the glass with the strength of a thousand swings at the firewood block. The hilt punches through the massive panel, spiderwebbing the glass and spraying shards inward. Inside, Fala shouts, but I wind back and swing again. Fragments fly across the room. Fala leaps back from her desk, cowering behind the chair. My third strike is the one that does it—with a sound like a stagecoach smashing on rocks, the entire panel shatters, crashing to the floor. Silica dust blooms into the air. Tamsin flings her arms over her head. Irena crouches by the stairs, shielding her face.

A reek of glass cleaner—the kind they had us wipe down panels with before shipping—billows out with the silica. I don't wait for the dust to clear—I jump over the doorframe, skidding on the piles of glass shards. Fala doesn't wait, either. With a panicked look, she lunges again for her desk drawer and thrusts her hand inside. She emerges with a bundle of papers and jumps backward toward the fire grate.

"Stop!" she shouts, flinging her hand out, her eyes wide, but I'm not going for her. She's cornered and unarmed—I'll deal with her in a moment. First I lunge down toward Veran. My boot slides on the glass, and I fall to one knee by his feet. I shake his leg.

"Veran!"

He doesn't moan, doesn't stir.

"Fire and smoke, Veran, *no*—"

"Fa!" Tamsin roars, struggling into the room behind me. And then, the *L* of my name deadened on her tongue, she cries, "*Lark!*"

I look up in time to see Fala fling the bundle of papers into the fire. Just as they land in the smoldering grate, Veran's boots thrash. Like a quarrel from a crossbow, he shoots off the floor and leaps for her, catching her around the knees. A penknife spins wildly through the air—I can't tell who it belongs to, but it doesn't matter. It falls uselessly to the floor and skids under the desk. Gasping, Fala topples sideways. Her head hits the wall, and she crumples to the floor. Veran rolls off her, tangled between her body and the far windows.

"The letters!" Veran cries, flinging an arm at the fire. "Lark, get the letters!"

I leap toward the smoking grate and hook the hilt of my sword over the burning pile, drawing them out, along with a trail of glowing coals. The bottom few are reduced to ash, but the top two are only scorched around the edges. I'm starting to stamp out the creeping flames when a trio of yells fills the little space, spinning in the chaos of desk chairs and fresh glass and smoke and bodies. Fala is up, and, though weaving from the hit to her head, steps on Veran's open palm as she rushes to the far windows.

Too late I see the latch. Too late I watch the door open and Fala flee out into the driving rain.

Tamsin, though, doesn't miss a beat. With another roar, she barrels past the desk and both of us, out into the dark night. Irena, still standing outside the shattered office door, gasps and turns. Without a word of explanation, she rushes back down the staircase and out of sight.

I set my boots to jump to my feet, but Veran yelps again, "Lark—the letters!"

The embers are still determined to claim the paper for themselves, and I hurry to crush out the final trails of flame. By the time I've beat the rest of the coals away with my hat, there are two mostly intact letters remaining, with all the writing visible, right down to Tamsin's familiar signature, with the bat she hid in the *M* of her last name to lead us to her prison at Utzibor.

A numb silence falls. The air curls with the scent of smoke and blood. Glass shifts under my knees, and I finally feel the bite of their sharp edges. Through the open door, the rain makes a constant hiss. I take what feels like my first breath in five minutes, my ribs searing in protest. I drag my gaze from the letters to Veran—he's slouched against the wall, clutching his palm to his chest. He's staring at me, too, his chest rising and falling with rapid breaths.

"Lark," he whispers.

I let out my breath but can't bring myself to say his name. I crawl over the glass-coated floor, shoving the heavy desk chair out of the way. He wriggles up to a sitting position, his back against the wall.

"Are you all right?" I ask. My voice feels distant, detached.

"I'm fine," he says. "Are you?"

"I'm fine."

"You're bleeding . . ."

It's an understatement. Little stings and pricks are starting to smart all over my body, from nicks on my arms and knees to two neat slices on each palm from the blade of my sword, despite the protection of my hat. A glance down at myself gives the impression that someone spattered me with red paint.

I look back up. "I'm okay. You're bleeding, too." There's a cut on his lip, and his cheek, and several along the backs of his hands. I grip the knees of my trousers, trying to still the shake in my fingers. "What happened? Did you seize?"

"She gave me poison," he says. He sounds just as stunned and surreal as I feel. "Glass cleaner. She said it was tea."

"Did you drink it?"

"No," he says. "I tipped half the mug onto my boots when she wasn't looking."

"But you fell . . ."

"I faked it," he says. "I figured . . . it's what she expected. If she thought she'd succeeded, it might give me an advantage. To do . . . something. I didn't know what." His gaze strays to the space under the desk, where the penknife slid. "I can't decide which I'm more angry about—that she tried to poison me, or that she thought I can't tell my evergreens apart."

He looks back to me, and we stare at each other for a moment. My heartbeat has never felt so loud.

"I thought you'd died," I say before I can stop myself.

"I thought *you'd* died," he replies in a rush. "Or at least, that you were going to die."

"I didn't."

"Me, neither."

We go back to just staring again, our quick breaths matching the shush of the rain outside. His sage-green gaze flicks over me, all the bloody, torn places on my clothes and skin. I go on staring at his face, the now-familiar little scar, the damp curl of his hair, the sweep of his eyelashes, the cut on his lip.

For one terrifying moment, I thought I'd lost it all.

I thought I'd lost him.

His lips part as if to speak, but nothing comes out. He wipes the blood off his cheek. Somewhere outside, past the rain, a faint bell begins to ring, a different pattern from before. We both seem to rouse from a trance.

"Tamsin," I say.

He nods. "We should go."

"Can you get up?"

"Yeah—can you?"

With a mutual amount of clutching and lifting, we heave ourselves to our feet, trying to avoid any more cuts from the treacherous floor. We stand for a moment, our fingers closed over handfuls of each other's clothes, absurdly trying to make sure the other is steady while brushing off our own hurts.

Then, without warning, we're just standing, our hands on each other and our faces just inches apart. Veran realizes it at the same time I do—I feel when his body goes still. He takes a breath, his face just a hair below mine, and looks up. A sudden memory materializes of that morning on the frosty slopes of the Moquoviks when I woke up to find him just as close.

402 EMILY B. MARTIN

He swallows.

"I left you," he says, his voice soft and strained. "I screwed everything up, and then I left you behind."

"It's okay."

"I'm sorry," he says. "I'm so sorry."

"It's okay, Veran." I don't know how to touch a person to comfort them—I awkwardly squeeze his elbows, and then his shoulders. He draws in a long breath, and his fingers jump to brush my wrist, and then drop, and then touch my sleeve, and then smooth his bloody tunic front.

And I want to catch his shaking hand and just press it, just hold it, keep it still between mine. I want something else, too, something more that I can't identify.

But that bell is still ringing, and the rain still drumming outside. And when I look out the open door, he twitches back a step, his expression almost apologetic. With another breath, he stoops and picks up the two scorched letters. He tucks them carefully in his tunic.

"Let's go help Tamsin," he says.

I nod, and we pick our way to the outer door, and though everything is rushing me to get back to Tamsin's side, I can't help but feel like I've left something behind.

TAMSIN

I tear down the outer landing, the rain driving against the side of the palace. Fala's feet slap unevenly on the wet tiles.

"Fa!" I call, though I know it won't do any good. In the darkness, a rectangle of dim light swings open and she barrels through another service door, casting one look up toward me before hauling it shut. I hit it just a moment too late—the bolt locks.

"*Fa!*" I shout again, pounding the door in anger. Screaming my frustration, I step back and sweep my gaze down the landing, but it's no use—even without the rain, it's too dark to tell if there's another door farther down. Should I go on, and hope one is close by? Should I go back up through her wrecked office? I don't know the staff halls at all. By the time I find my way back to this entrance, Fala will be long gone.

I've just made up my mind to continue down, when the knob rattles. The bolt slides. Slowly, the door cracks open, and an anxious face appears.

It's Irena. She steps back and pulls the door wide.

"When I saw you go through the outer door, I figured this was where you'd come in," she whispers. "It's the only landing until the boiler rooms."

I squeeze her arm in thanks as I step inside. She starts to close the door, but I wave at her to leave it open in case Veran and Lark come this way.

"She's going to the Hall of the *Ashoki*," she says, pointing down the hall. "It's up the left staircase. I think she must be trying to remove the *si-oque* before anyone sees you." She looks out the door to where the rain lashes the landing. "Where are the others?"

I point back toward Fala's office.

"Go he'p?" I ask her, walking backward down the hall.

She dips a short curtsy and disappears into the rain. I turn around and pick up my pace, but not the flat-out run I was using before. When I reach the left-hand staircase, I pause and slip off my wet shoes, leaving them at the base of the stairs. Then I steal upward, throwing long shadows in the light of the hurricane lamps.

There's a very small landing up top, with an undersize door—one of the hinged wall panels. There's an ingenious peephole set into it, disguised with a decorative wooden overlay on the far side, allowing servants to peer into the room beyond and avoid entering when there are courtiers about. Through it, the Hall of the *Ashoki* is dark and silent, with a slice of light spilling from the grand entryway. A shadow flickers—Fala is making her way across the hall.

I lift the latch and push—the hinges move noiselessly. Barely daring to breathe, I slip into the hall, placing my feet carefully on the cool redwood floor.

Fala is being cautious—certain that she succeeded in locking me out, she's being extra careful not to let the guards in the entrance hall hear her. They're standing in the open doorway, their backs to the room, murmuring to each other. Fala moves slowly, taking a halting path across the hall to where my pedestal must be. I choose a different route, hugging the very back wall, letting the deep shadows from the towering statues and display cases hide me. Thanks to this, I reach her destination before she does—the only empty pedestal in the whole hall. I place my palms on the cold marble—the place where my statue is meant to go. With a silent heave, I pull myself on top.

She doesn't notice me at first. So focused on the display case, where the light from the distant doors falls on my dulcimer and the forged *si-oque*, Fala creeps by the pedestal without looking up. But as she reaches for the lock on the case, she must get some kind of premonition. She freezes, her hand outstretched.

She looks up.

I'm standing with my bare feet spread on the pedestal, a mockery of the other grand statues in the hall. Fala gives a spasm of surprise that ripples through her whole body. I glare at her, my face contorted in anger and grief, my fists shaking at my sides. But I force myself to stay rational, as much as I want to throw myself at her. Slowly, I lift my finger to my lips, glancing meaningfully at the guards just outside the hall.

She licks her lips but doesn't move. "I can shout for them, and they'll shoot you as an accomplice of the Sunshield Bandit. They've seen your face on the bounty sheets."

The sheets she surely commissioned, using the painstaking description Poia must have reported to her. *Shorn hair. Mute.* Trembling with anger, I sweep my hand at the display case, illustrating her conundrum. They could shoot me, yes, but my *si-oque* is still on my wrist, and the false one in the case.

Her gaze flicks to the case and then back to me.

"You can . . . you can scream, but you can't explain." She seems to be weighing her choices to herself. "Poia described to me what your speech is limited to." She straightens up. "I can remove the *si-oque*, and call for the guards, and they'll see you as nothing more than a thief. And you *can't explain*."

I continue staring, letting my gaze bore into hers. She stares back, looking unnerved, and then shakes herself and plunges her hand into her pocket, removing her keys wrapped in her fist so they won't clink. Breathing heavily, she stuffs the master into the lock and opens the case. She snatches up the false *si-oque* and buries it deep in her pocket. She steps back, leaving the case open and me standing on the pedestal with the remaining *si-oque* on my wrist. Incriminating evidence, for sure.

She pauses for the barest moment, as if second-guessing her decisions, and then she does it—she opens her mouth and screams.

"Guards!" she calls, not taking her eyes off me. She expects me to run. "Guards! The Sunshield Bandit's accomplice! Here—she has the *si-oque!*"

There's a ring of answering shouts from the open doors. I bend my knees and drop down to my seat on the cold pedestal. As the guards barrel into the hall, Fala draws herself up, fixing me with a triumphant look. Nowhere to run now.

But I don't run. I lean over and reach into the open display case, closing my fingers on the neck of my dulcimer. I draw it out and settle it in my lap.

Fala's face flickers with confusion, but she remembers her role.

"Guards!" she shouts again, pitching her voice into a high, helpless shriek. She wrings her hands as they thunder nearer. Behind them is a knot of servants and onlookers. "Oh please—it's her! The Sunshield Bandit's accomplice! Quick—before she gets away!"

It's a laughable thing to say, and I do—I tilt my head back and laugh, an ugly, humorless sound. The guards spread into a half circle around us, raising their crossbows to sight.

"Quick!" Fala says again to the nearest guard, flinging her finger at me. "Shoot her!"

Enna's voice, when compared to Fala's, is even and calm. "Hands on your head, Mistress Fala."

Fala thinks they want her to get out of the way. She starts to move toward the end of their line, but Enna blocks her path, her crossbow still raised. "I said, hands on your head, please."

I press three fingers to the frets of my dulcimer and give a hearty strum. The sound blooms into the darkened hall, its acoustics designed down to the tiniest detail to amplify music. Fala gives a great start at the sound, whipping her head back to me.

Any traces of my laughter are gone now—I'm back to just staring at her with every ounce of hatred I can muster.

"You don't understand!" Fala insists, turning back to the guards. "This is the accomplice of the Sunshield Bandit! She helped her escape, she's a wanted criminal—there's a bounty!"

"A bounty I did not authorize."

The voice is cool and instantly recognizable to anyone who has spent any time at all in the halls of Tolukum. The queen, wrapped in a quilted dressing gown, steps forward, surrounded by a knot of guards and tousle-haired attendants. Beside her, looking tired and rough, but full of grim determination, is Iano. Anything Fala might have been preparing to say dies away. She looks past him to the palace guards whose orders have now changed, to Veran and Lark supporting each other, and to Irena clinging to the shadows behind them. Fala's gaze drops to the floor, her eyes wide and unseeing, perhaps with a dawning comprehension of exactly what she's put her foot into.

I pluck a clipped, minor-key arpeggio on my strings, letting the eerie sound fill the hall. Fala recognizes it, and her whole body shudders. The opening melody to "Gathering Storm"—I remember her face now, amid the others in this hall, when I first sang the song.

Iano studies her for a moment, and then looks to me. "We arrived at the hall just before Veran and Lark did. The physician is with Soe—she's lost blood, but she's holding on."

Relief flushes through my body—the hope I hadn't been able to face before comes crashing back. Soe is still alive. She could make it.

There's a flick and the sizzle of a match. One of the guards lights a lantern and proceeds to the next one. The warm light in our semicircle grows, throwing our faces into mixed shadow, with Fala at the center.

"You fed me a great deal of lies, Mistress Fala," Iano says, "and committed a growing list of crimes to accomplish your goal, nearly bringing this country to its knees. I will be curious to hear if it was worth it to you, in the end."

"Where is the *si-oque* you have spoken about?" Queen Isme asks him.

Check her right pocket, I sign.

Iano instructs a guard forward. Fala doesn't even twitch when the guard reaches into her pocket and comes up with her key ring and the false *si-oque*. He moves to her left side and produces a blood-stained handkerchief, and two more items—a small seal ring, and Iano's heirloom *si-oque*.

"I'll take that," Veran says acidly, swiping the seal ring out of the guard's palm.

Iano takes the two *si-oques*, slipping his over his wrist and studying the false one.

"It's a rushed job," he says, unimpressed. "The amber could be passable to a casual acquaintance, but nobody can forge personal *si* beads. You are fortunate I was not in the palace to validate it—but that was the point, wasn't it?" He looks up at Fala. "When Veran and I left, you must have been worried someone had a lead on Tamsin, and that news might slip that she was alive. You needed proof for the court that she wasn't."

And, I say, and Iano's gaze shifts to me. *She needed someone with the right convictions to send it to—someone who might use it as a sign to confirm a new* ashoki.

"Who was that?" Iano asks.

"Kobok," I say.

There's a snort from behind the queen. Lark, hunching painfully on Veran's shoulder, says, "If that is true, it failed. It made Kobok afraid someone is threatening him for faking records for Alcoran slaves. Thinking someone is pointing out that they will finish what Tamsin started."

The queen turns to her, a stiff line in her shoulders the only sign of her discomfort at being so close to the bandit she had been planning to execute, despite the line of guards separating them. "Faking laborer records? Are you quite sure?"

"Ask him yourself," Lark replies flatly. Perhaps she catches a smothered wince on Veran's face, because she hastily adds, "Lady Queen."

"I shall," Queen Isme answers evenly.

"Not quite to plan, I suppose," Iano says to Fala. "But up until Veran and I left, things had been going smoothly for you, hadn't they, Mistress?"

Fala still says nothing, her gaze on the shadows at Iano's feet. In the actual interrogation, she's going to be required to give yes or no answers, but for now she remains silent. Veran shifts carefully under Lark's weight and pulls out a few pieces of singed paper.

"She took great care to try to dissuade me from provoking you and distracting you from the letters she was sending." He hands the singed papers to Iano. "There are only two left, but the writing is all there. She was trying to burn them when Lark, Tamsin, and Irena showed up."

I slide the dulcimer from my lap. It settles on the pedestal with an ambient thrum.

When the threats failed, and you disappeared, I say, *she tried something else. She stole the queen's seal to send those two soldiers to hunt us down in Pasul, and to set the bounties for Lark and me.*

Lark is watching me and she translates this for the rest. Iano nods, and when he speaks, his voice is the gravest it's been yet. "That didn't go well for anyone, and I admit I am particularly grieved by it, because it cost the lives of two more people. A lot of blood was spilled for your cause, Fala. So again, I ask: was it worth it to you?"

Finally she stirs, raising her gaze just a few inches to Iano's knees.

"I have only ever served the interests of this country," she says. "I have only ever wished for its stability and prosperity."

"Ha!" My laughter rings out like my dulcimer chords after all the hushed voices. With a meaningful glance at Lark, I say, *You wanted a prosperity that doesn't exist. You wanted a prosperity that grants you power at the expense of others. And to gain it you almost tore this country apart.*

Fala stares at my fingers while Lark gives her my words, perhaps finally realizing the extent of what I can do with them.

You didn't take my voice, I confirm. *You just spread it around.*

She shakes herself and looks up at my face, hers creased in anger. "Who are you to speak to me about power? You force these ideas onto the court, you debate them with each other over tea and cake, you weave them into love letters as poetry, while we slip around you, invisible, making your world turn . . . and yet you don't even bother to understand the hierarchy you're trying to destroy! Give up *your* power first, Tamsin, give up *your* voice, and then tell me to give up mine! And you—" She turns abruptly to Iano, and then looks past him for Veran. "And you! Fighting to undo a system without giving up anything yourself—"

"Bullshit."

All heads swivel to Lark, who pushes herself off Veran's

shoulder. With one arm wrapped around her ribs, she unconsciously throws her shoulders back, her eyes boring down on
Fala.

"That is Hire bullshit." Lark waves stiffly to Veran and Iano.
"You are not wrong about noble folk being blind—sometimes
on purpose—to the people below them. Noble folk can be very,
very stupid, and greedy and selfish."

Next to her, Veran shifts, his gaze darting to the queen,
but Lark continues. "But that is not really what you are so mad
about. Tamsin was at one time a slave, so you think she is supposed to be below you—but instead she comes here and rises
over you, and then tries to make the other slaves equal to you.
Not take away your job, Fala! Just make them equal to you. But
to you that feels like an end of power.

"You want to talk about giving up power? You want to talk
about giving up a voice?" She waves to Irena behind her. "Talk
to your workers who are taken away from their families, whose
homes are erased and turned into nowhere, who are put into
the bottom of your system. Talk to the kids in my camp who
come from locked wagons—the tiny kids with the brand, the big
kids with made-up names because they do not know who they
are. Talk to me sometime. I will fill you in."

There's a ringing silence, much more profound than my
strums on the dulcimer. I grin at Lark. Veran's gazing at her
like he might get down on one knee right now. Queen Isme is
regarding her coolly, as if considering her for the first time, and
then she turns and addresses the gathered company.

"I think we'll leave it there for tonight. We shall delve into
plenty of other details later. Guards—please escort Mistress Fala

to a secure cell and order a watch, then you may take your leave. I will send someone else to place a watch on Minister Kobok's door—we can conduct that interrogation in the morning."

Enna's cadre busies themselves with the orders. Fala's gaze is back on the ground, no longer demure, but angry. She lets the guards secure her hands behind her back without a struggle, and doesn't look at any of us again as she's led from the hall. Their footsteps fade away.

Queen Isme rests her hand on Iano's shoulder. "I must draft notices to the ministers for emergency sessions tomorrow. I recommend you all take some rest while you can." She pats him tiredly. "Perhaps request a bath."

He grimaces as her swarm of guards and attendants turns with her for the door, but the queen pauses, her gaze falling on Irena.

"What is your name?" she asks.

Irena's gaze widens and rivets on the floor. "Irena, Lady Queen."

"You are the one who found the injured woman in records?"

"Yes, Your Majesty."

Lark stirs, as if preparing once again to jump to Irena's defense, but the queen only nods.

"You did a great service tonight. This monarchy has not served you well in the past—with guidance I hope to do better for you in the future. Please consider yourself and anyone else under bond on temporary relief until more permanent arrangements are made. I will put the order in to . . ." She pauses, remembering her head of staff is heading to prison. ". . . someone in Services. Thank you."

Irena curtsies low as the queen and her entourage pass by. She straightens but keeps her eyes on the floor, moving only when Lark claps her shoulder.

Once the queen is gone, Iano lets out a long, weary sigh and drags a hand over his face. "*Kuas*, what a night. Is everyone all right? Lark?"

She grunts, both arms hugging herself. "I am not too bad, if I am not having to do any more running and climbing. Bandages might be good."

"We'll wake one of the healers. Anyone else?"

"Just scrapes," Veran says, flexing his palm. "Maybe something worse in my hand."

"Tamsin?"

If Soe is okay, I sign, *then good. Very good.*

He looks past Veran and Lark. "Irena? Are you all right?"

She seems rooted to the spot, her fingers clasped at her waist. "Yes, sir."

"Good. I echo my mother's thanks to you."

Irena makes a sound like a cheep, wavering in the clutch of Lark's arm.

There's a silence while we all trade tired glances, our faces ragged in the lamplight.

We did it, I finally say.

Iano nods. "I admit, I doubted whether coming back to the palace was a good idea. But you figured it out just in time. If you'd told me yesterday, I wouldn't have believed you."

"I can't believe it was Fala," Veran says quietly.

"I can," Lark says with a grimace. "She is like so many others—thinking people being treated equal is an attack on them."

"I have a question," Irena whispers from behind Lark. "It's just . . . it was no secret what your message was as *ashoki*, Lady Tamsin. But—how did Fala know she could use you to black-mail the prince? This is the first I've heard of you being in love. How did she know?"

I think she told us just now, by accident, I say. *Poetry in love letters.* I look at Iano. *We may have been discreet in public, but we exchanged plenty of letters that would have made things obvious. Mine were hidden in one of my jewelry boxes. Where were yours?*

"On top of my wardrobe," he admits.

Both places easily found by someone cleaning. I shrug re-signedly. *A mistake.*

"One of many." Iano rubs his eyes. "It's going to be a night-mare to sort out. We'll have to be sure she has no more allies in the palace. Someone new will have to be appointed head of staff. And then we're going to have to figure out how to dissolve the labor bonds and get people either employed or back to where they want to go."

It would be best, I say, *to pass something quickly. Something decisive. Something that dissolves the bond system immediately.*

"It's going to be difficult to get past the ministers," he says wearily. "I guarantee you the first thing they'll pounce on is where the money will come from."

"The Ferinno Road," Veran says. He stares around at us as we all look at him. "Well—that's where the money was slated to come from before. We had it all laid out. If Fala hadn't disrupted everything, we'd probably be heading home with an official agreement in place. Though . . ." His eyes widen. "If Fala hadn't disrupted everything . . ."

We wouldn't have Lark, I finish with a smile.

Lark snorts. "Lucky for all of you."

"Blazes," Veran says shakily. He turns to her, obviously rattled. "By the Light . . ."

"Cut it out," she says, her palms pressing her sides.

"I'm serious. Lark—if it weren't for Fala, I never would have had to come find you."

"Tamsin also would not have gotten hurt," she says sharply. "Or Soe. Or any of us. Do not make Fala into an accidental hero. Things happened the way they did, and we can't change them. So what happens now?"

"You are welcome to stay as guests, of course," Iano says. "Once we all recover a bit, we could make good progress on the road."

"I don't have the authority to make decisions for the East— not on my own," Veran says. "But more important, it's September. *Dequasi.* The reason this was our end date was to beat the autumn floods that wash out the trails in the Ferinno. That means if Lark and I don't leave for Callais soon, we could be stuck here until the spring."

"Of course," Iano says. "It's just—the road, the funding . . . even after I'm crowned, we can't make decisions without the collaboration of the East . . ."

"*You* could come with *us,*" Veran suggests. "Come to Alcoro. All the right people will be in Callais. From there, we can go forward with everything we planned before."

I rap the pedestal for their attention. *I think going to Alcoro is a good idea. But not yet. Like you, if we travel now, we will be stuck there for the winter, and Moquoia needs to regain its balance after the last few months. What if we plan to meet in*

Callais once the desert is passable again in the spring? That way you can go home to your families, and we can steady things here. Iano can be crowned. Then we can meet again—and start over.

There's something like a collective sigh of relief.

"*Uah,*" Iano agrees.

Veran nods. "That's a good idea."

Lark has a pained look on her face—I'm not sure if it's from her ribs or the thought of what awaits on the far side of the Ferinno.

Are you okay? I ask.

"*Uah,* yeah, um—the talk of leaving just reminded me." She rubs the back of her neck. "Someone . . . should maybe go up to Minister Kobok's rooms and see if he is okay."

"Why wouldn't he be okay?" Veran asks.

"I—tied him up."

"You *what?*" Iano barks.

"And I punched him in the face," she says.

I break out into a peal of laughter. Iano claps both his hands to his face in agony.

"*What* am I going to do with you all?" he groans.

But Veran's lost the last of his restraint. After a heartbeat of just goggling, he takes two steps toward Lark, clasps her face, and crushes his lips against hers.

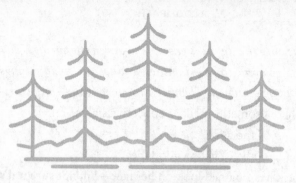

VERAN

The world shifts underneath me, rollicking like a boat on choppy seas. But there's too much jostling and clattering to be on a boat. I slit open my eyes and find a sky of canvas stretched over arching timbers, the sunlight piercing through the weave. The air has a dry, sandy taste to it.

"Hey."

I tilt my head on my stiff neck—not far, because my head is in someone's lap. They're silhouetted against the bright canvas.

"Lark?" I croak.

"You're okay. You seized about an hour ago while we were stopped to water the animals."

"Did I fall?"

"No. You were sitting. Rat warned us." She reaches behind me to scratch Rat's back. He's sprawled out leisurely among teth-ered crates. "He got agitated again, started circling and whining around us. We figured out what he was doing and you were able to sit just before it happened."

I lick my dry lips. "Your dog is magic."

"He can sense something we can't," she says. "It makes me wonder if there are other dogs who can do the same thing. Even a dog who could keep you propped on your side, and bark for help, could make a big difference. Maybe we can look into it, after we're back."

I rub my face. "Which is . . . when?"

"We crossed Teso's Ford this morning. Do you remember that?"

I strain my groggy mind—it's like trying to see through shifting sand. "Um . . ."

"I'll start earlier. We caught Fala at Tolukum Palace. Do you remember that?"

"Fala, yeah. I remember that." I blink a few times, trying to put all the pieces in the right places. Something important happened after that . . .

"Do you remember . . . what came next?"

It was something *really* important, something bigger and better than anything that's ever happened to me . . .

Lark leans down and presses her lips to mine, and the memory comes flooding back, as real and thrilling as the moment it first happened. My fingers jump to her neck and thread under her ponytail. Her hair is soft, but the rest of her is not— not her skin, or her lips, or her kiss. She's solid and purposeful. Her hand moves not to trail absently, but to tilt my cheek for something deeper, her callused palm pressing into my skin. And when that's achieved, she slides her hand down, her fingers curling around the base of my neck, and her thumb resting lightly over the apple of my throat. I shiver at the feel of her open lips and resting palm, because I know what those hands can do, and instead they're lying warm and enticing on my skin.

The wagon hits a rut, and we jounce, our foreheads knocking. She grimaces and leans back, combing her fingers over my brow and into my hair. My hand slips from her neck and comes to rest at her belt—I can feel the stiff bandages around her ribs through her shirt.

"That didn't happen last time," she says, adjusting her knees under me. "Want some water? Rinse out some of the sand?"

"You don't taste like sand—not like that first time in the stage."

"No, but you do. And anyway, I had my bandanna over my mouth then—and it *wasn't* a kiss. Here." She gives me her arm and helps me sit up, guiding me back against the crate she's leaning on. I take the canteen gratefully and sip. Our shoulders press comfortably against each other.

I lower the canteen. "How are your ribs?"

"Nearly mended. Haven't been able to ride for too long each day, but in another few days they should be fine."

I crane my head to look out the back of the barrel-top wagon we're riding in. The peaks of two more wagons sway behind us, with a few horses and riders in between. We're in a caravan.

My gaze focuses on one of the riderless horses tethered to another. "That's Jema!"

"Yeah. She was in the Tolukum stables." A smile flickers on her lips as she follows my gaze. "I asked about her the morning after we sent Fala to prison. It was partially to escape that audience with the queen Iano was threatening, but it happened anyway. Do you remember that?"

"Bits and pieces."

"Kobok was arrested."

I brighten. "That's right! And he had that gorgeous black eye. He didn't go quietly, either."

She shifts uncomfortably. "No. But—he went all the same."

More things are falling into place now—how Lark had described the way Kobok had been using the Port Iskon name to mask the number and origin of Alcoran slaves, how he'd started using it fifteen years ago to cover up the abduction of the Lumeni princess, how much he howled when he was being led away under the queen's stoic gaze. And then . . .

"You were officially pardoned, weren't you?" I say.

"You were, too, and—the ambassador and the princess." She adjusts her hat anxiously. She's still wearing the patch leather hat I bought her, though the brim is sliced in two places from the blade of her sword. "We were all pardoned."

I look down at my fingers, where my seal ring sits again. "And outfitted with a guard escort and brought to Pasul, and then hooked on to the caravan of freed workers traveling back across the Ferinno," I say. "It's all back now. There was that lion scare a few nights ago, and that wild thunderstorm, and before that . . . Three Lines."

We had stopped, like all caravans must, at the South Burr just below the trace to Three Lines. Unlike the last time we were there, the Burr was running low and clear, with barely more than a chuckle in its rapids. Fording would have involved little more than getting our knees wet. But we didn't cross. There wasn't time. The caravan driver was wary of that stretch of road, knowing its reputation for being thick with bandits. We didn't tell him the outlaw he was most afraid of was traveling in his caravan. Lark had stood at the bank, looking up the slope to the golden mesa, silent. When the driver said it was time to move on, she turned without a word and headed back to Jema.

Now her fingers fidget absently in her lap. Before I can second-guess myself, I reach out and take them in mine.

"I'm sorry you didn't get to go back in and say good-bye."

She curls her hand around mine. "I said my good-byes already. And . . . it's just a patch of desert."

"It was more than that," I say. "It was your home."

"It was a crappy home," she says, looking away. I go silent. I want to tell her that it's okay—that she doesn't have to tough things out anymore, not for me or anyone else. But even in my head that sounds silly and patronizing, so I just link my fingers closer through hers. I brush my thumb incrementally across the back of her hand.

She sighs.

"It worked though," she says. "For a while."

We sway with the movement of the wagon. I sip from the canteen.

"Are you nervous?" I ask. "About getting to Callais. Seeing Rou and Eloise."

"Obviously," she says. "I think I'm . . . more nervous about meeting the queen, though."

"Alcoro doesn't have a queen," I say.

"The *queen*, you absolute knucklehead, the . . . my mother."

"Oh!"

She snorts, and I flush. She reaches with her free hand and wraps her fingers in my hair, tugging gently. I grin apologetically, and my gaze strays to her lips, which are curved upward in a half smile. She doesn't lean closer, though. She lets go of my hair and settles back against the crates with a sigh.

"You probably don't have to worry about that right away," I say, flattening my bangs. "Depending on how long it took Rou and Eloise to cross the Ferinno, I don't think Queen Mona could get to Callais any sooner than we will. And anyway— she never travels to Alcoro. She's famous for it. Even though we're allies and her brother Colm lives there, she's never set foot there. Ma says it's a burned bridge, all left over from the War of the Prism twenty years ago. My guess is she would travel up through Cyprien and wait for you near the border."

Lark gives an anxious hum in the back of her throat. "I don't like the idea of more waiting. I can't stand the waiting." She sighs again and unconsciously adjusts the hat on her head. "But I guess it will give me time to see how my campmates are getting on. Sedge and Lila both have probably been mourning Rose hard. I hate that I left them with all the little ones."

"I'm sure they know you did everything you could."

She puffs out a breath and looks sideways at me. "What about you? Are you nervous?"

"I'm scared stiff about Eloise," I admit with a familiar lurch. "I sort of forgot in Moquoia how bad off she was when she left. Crossing the Ferinno while fighting rainshed fever, and with Rou gone to pieces like he was . . . I just hope they made it okay."

"What about your family? Your ma? Are you excited to tell her all that you did? To show that you could do it all along?"

I open my mouth and then go blank, just leaving it hanging open. I hadn't thought of things like that.

"If you had asked me a few weeks ago," I say, my brain turning slowly, "I'd have said yes. That if I got through those kinds of scrapes alive, the first thing I'd do is point them out to all the people who didn't think I could do it. But the thing is . . .

even though I survived, I don't really feel . . . like I *succeeded*. Does that make any sense?"

"No," she says.

"Well, just think about when you collapsed in the water scrape." I shift uncomfortably. "I was a mess. And then bumbling through Tellman's Ditch, and the Giantess market—I managed to get out of those just by luck, or because you were there. And then forcing you back into being the Sunshield Bandit, botching the attack . . . getting you captured." I swallow. "It may have all turned out okay, but I can't feel like it was a success. I can't feel like the ends justified the means. And I guess . . . I'm nervous for Mama to hear about it all."

"Veran," she says. "Listen—you have to stop thinking that success always comes with trumpets and banners. Success is almost always messy. You did botch the attack." She does that thing again, winding her fingers in my hair. She never pulls hard enough to hurt. I'm starting to like the pressure that comes with it, the connection she's trying to make between us. "But then you got up and walked to Tolukum, and you . . ."

". . . Put my foot in it again," I say, my cheeks heating. "Fala practically had me wriggling on a hook because I was too dense—"

"Hey," she says, sliding her hand down from my bangs to my mouth, planting her palm over my lips. "Shut up, okay? That hero thing you have . . . it's lying to you. I've seen you do brave, smart, painful things—and it's always been in the times you *weren't* trying to be a hero. You believed in me—you've got to believe in yourself, too."

I go silent, worrying that thought in my mind. It feels dangerous to approach it—after everything that's happened, I feel even less ready to believe in myself than I did when I was just fantasizing about how things could be.

"We made it through, I guess," I say finally. "That's what matters."

She grunts. "Yeah, great. Now the hard part can begin."

I laugh and settle against her, our fingers linked as the wagon creaks and sways, rolling onward toward Callais.

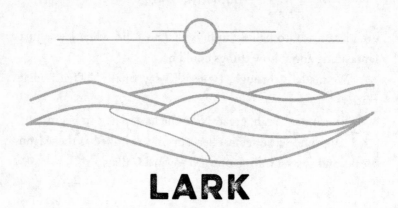

LARK

We splinter off from the caravan after crossing the narrows of the massive canyon of Callais. With the handful of Moquoian guards Iano assigned to us, we ride north along the canyon rim, watching the chasm grow wider and deeper. Soon the river at the bottom is lost to mesas and cliffs within the canyon itself, and then we start seeing hobs, the little clay-and-stone neighborhoods tucked into the overhangs. Before long, the city of Callais rises ahead of us.

I've never traveled into the city itself—the few times I've ventured this far away from Three Lines was to bring Bitty and Arana and the others back to family, and we always said good-bye down at the crossroads. As more buildings sprout up around us, the knot of dread grows in my stomach. It's not helped by the jingling of the guards trailing us—I've never been in a situation where having a guard following me is a good thing, and I can't get used to the feeling now.

Callais is a city of whitewashed adobe, gold stone, and red

tile, and despite the cool of September, the streets and houses radiate sunlight. Sweat trickles down my neck and forearms, leaving grime marks from the long trek out of the desert. To our right, the old royal palace sprawls into the bright blue sky, now home to the Senate in one wing and the university in another. Veran leads the way through the bright streets, heading toward his friends' house, where he's hoping we'll find Eloise, Rou, and my campmates staying with the ex-queen Gemma and my now-uncle Colm. The strangeness and uncertainty of it all is making my hands shake. I don't know what I'll do if my campmates aren't there. I don't know what Veran will do if Rou and Eloise didn't make it, either. We sent a letter ahead a few days ago forecasting our arrival, but there's no way to tell if it's been delivered, or who's on the other end to receive it. Unnerved, I focus on guiding Jema to follow Veran's horse, trying to fight the feeling of being slowly hemmed in by the rising walls.

Veran goes to turn up a street only to find it blocked with wooden barriers. A few city guards lounge on the far side, their weapons idle. Veran reins in his horse while I come even with him.

"Huh," he says. "Main causeway's blocked. Must be a parade today—is it Starfall? What day is it?"

"I don't know." Between the Moquoian calendar and the bubble of the Ferinno Desert, I've lost track of organized time.

He shrugs. "Oh, well. We can use the side streets. This way." He guides his horse away from the barricade and down a series of narrower alleyways, cut with sharp shadows and canopies of hanging laundry. We run into one more barricade, necessitating a dismount and awkward passage through a cramped covered market—our Moquoian guards still in tow—and then we arrive at a tidy row of adobe houses all squashed together and fronted with colorful courtyards. Hedges of brush willow and marigolds swallow wrought-iron gates, and strands of bells tinkle in hand-molded archways.

"There," Veran pants, a note of irritation in his voice. We got fussed at for bringing the horses through the market, but there'd been no alternative. He starts toward a gate standing open in front of a house with a bright turquoise door. Just as we reach the entrance, an almighty shout splits the air. My tired nerves fray.

"Blazes, Sedge, Lila, Sedge, *Sedge*—they're here!"

A figure barrels across the little courtyard and hits me like a crossbow shot. It's Saiph, unhurt, intact, and laughing like a maniac. He throws his arms around me and squeezes. Following him is Andras, his eyes shiny with ointment and his face split into a smile. And past them—

I waver on the spot, my heart dissolving in my chest, unwilling to believe my eyes. Saiph and Andras are the only things holding me up.

"Rose?" I gasp.

An astonished smile spreads across her face. "Lark! Hot damn—I knew you'd make it!"

She's sitting in a wicker chair with big wooden wheels, with her trouser leg knotted neatly at her knee. On a bench beside her are a line of beautiful faces—Lila, Sedge, Hettie . . . *blazes*, Arana is here, beaming. And beside her . . .

Veran sags against the archway, clutching his chest in relief. "Eloise."

Rose wheels forward as I stumble through the gate, leaving the arms of Saiph and Andras. I stop in front of her, hardly daring to breathe, afraid I'll blink and the scene will change, afraid I'll wake up.

"How?" I croak again, my throat full of dust and scratches. "I thought . . . I thought for sure . . ."

"I hung on," she says with a grin. "Thanks to the supplies and the wagon your dandy friend sent. I don't think I'd have made it otherwise."

"But I saw . . ." I begin. "Up in Three Lines, there was a cairn. I saw it, and I thought for sure . . ."

Her face falls, her bright grin replaced by dark clouds.

"It was little Whit," she says softly, reaching out and linking her fingers through mine. "She didn't make it. She died in her sleep two nights after you left."

The rising wave of relief in my chest plunges into a freezing pit. My gaze flies to the others getting up from the bench. "Whit?" I whisper.

Rose nods, her eyes shining. The old, barely-mastered grief over losing Rose that I've carried since Three Lines cracks open again. I squeeze my eyes shut. Little Whit. Her cleft lip, her pale cheeks, her frail body . . . she'd been sick. I'd always known it, I'd watched her slip away bit by bit, and still I'd kept her out in the merciless desert, because I couldn't bring myself to send her to an orphanage or the poor house.

I'd kept her too long.

"You couldn't have saved her," Rose says, knowing exactly what I'm thinking. "Even if you could have gotten her into town, we didn't have the money to pay for the care she needed. She'd have died all the same in a public orphanage. At least this way we were with her. None of us blame you—you shouldn't, either."

A hand touches my arm, and I open my eyes to come face-to-face with Eloise. My breath, already fighting its way through my throat, sticks entirely.

She looks miles better than she did when we last saw her in Pasul—there's a healthy flush in her cheeks and brightness in her eyes. Her hair tumbles loose around her shoulders, the dark golds catching the sun amid the smoky browns.

"I'm sorry about your friend," she says softly.

Oh no—she's crying. Panicking, I realize she's turning into me, her hands sliding past my sleeves—she's hugging me.

Oh no.

Her shoulders hitch under a soft white shawl. "Bless the Light," she whispers into my shoulder. "I'm so relieved you made it."

I flex my hands at my sides, unsure of what to do with them. I cast a panicked look at Veran, who's doing his best to keep sympathy on his face despite clearly wanting to laugh. Hettie—the girl we first called Moll, the girl from the Silverwood Mountains just like Veran, with his jeweled firefly pin still winking on her shirt—is in his arms, clinging to him like a baby opossum.

I clear my throat and pat Eloise once before considering the dirt I'm going to leave on her shawl. I drop my hand back to my side. Rat noses my fingers, and I pull them away so he doesn't make mud out of the road grime on my skin. Still, Eloise doesn't let go, her arms linked around my neck. Her curls smell like honeysuckle.

The others have crowded around now, all dressed in clean clothes in pretty colors, wearing new shoes that fit. I stare at them each in turn, taking in the flushes and roundness in their cheeks. Lila's dark blond hair is shiny and pinned back, and she's wearing a white nurse's smock. Saiph—*Saiph is alive*—is wearing a gray jacket with the emblem of the university on the chest. I stare at Sedge, wondering what's so unnerving about him—his sandy beard has been shaved, and his hair's been trimmed—but then I realize the iron collar around his neck is gone, leaving a discolored band of skin in its place.

And Arana—my gaze lands on my old friend again. She's nowhere close to the stringy, sunburned knife fighter who lived with me in Three Lines. Her bunched muscles and knobby joints have softened, and her various battle scars have faded against smooth, glowing skin.

She grins the same grin, though, and waves at me.

Always knew you had to be some kind of princess, she signs. *All that attitude.*

My knees go watery again, and Eloise stands back, keeping hold of one of my hands. Rose takes the other, smiling at my shock. I don't know what to say. I don't even know if I *could* say anything at all. I feel like a ghost, floating a few feet above my body, watching this all unfold. Rose is alive. Saiph is alive. *Little Whit is not.* Lila and Sedge and Andras and Hettie are here, in one piece. Arana is here. Eloise is here, and she's my sister—we share blood. I look down at our linked fingers, hers delicate and soft, somehow impossibly made of the same stuff as mine. My ears ring.

Somewhere in the distance, a horn blares a fanfare, and filtering over the sounds of the city comes the rattling of heavy wheels, the clop of myriad hooves. Shouts ring out. Our Moquoian guards, gathered outside the gate, suddenly spread into a defensive formation. Beside me, Saiph leaps with excitement.

"Oh, is that them?" he exclaims, racing back to the gate. "It must be them!"

"Must be who?" Veran asks, echoing my own numb thoughts.

Eloise finally looks away from me and out past the gate. "It must be the procession—I'm not surprised. Papa left with Uncle Colm and Aunt Gemma two days ago to meet them in Parnassia."

"Meet who?" Veran asks.

Eloise looks back at him. "Our parents, of course. And probably an honor guard, if I had to guess. Didn't you see the roads closed? They were putting up barricades all yesterday."

"Your parents?"

"*Ours.* Veran, come on. Mother and your parents."

His eyes widen. "*My* parents? They're not—they're not coming here, are they?"

"Of course they are," she says in surprise. "Papa sent a rush letter as soon as we arrived. We got their response a few days ago, saying they'd reach the city today."

I blanch, my insides turning to stone. Where before I felt like I was floating, now it feels like I've slammed back into my body, with every sense on high alert. The ambassador? The queen? They're here—now? *Right* now? I'm not ready—I'm filthy, I'm upside-down. Rose, little Whit . . . I haven't even greeted Arana . . .

Veran gapes at Eloise. "Your mother, too?"

She gives him a look of incredulity. "Our mother *especially,* Veran, honestly. Why would she not?"

He shifts Hettie in his arms. "I thought—with her and Alcoro, you know . . . she never travels here. The war . . . ?" He trails off.

Eloise shakes her head. "Veran." Her fingers still linked through mine, she holds up my hand, as if offering me as evidence. "Veran, you *found my sister.* The entire East is in an uproar."

There's clattering up the road now, and our Moquoian guards have their weapons drawn. Veran sets Hettie down with a pat and hurries out into the road. With the clamor of the oncoming vanguard, he has to shout to be heard, first in Moquoian to our guards, and then in Eastern to the oncoming ones. The front cadre comes even with the courtyard, the horses all tossing their manes and pawing in the cramped space. Behind them rolls the coach, a thing of gleaming wood and gold trim, with a matched six-in-hand. Braces groan. Tack jingles. The driver calls to the guards; a guard shouts back. Rat starts to bark.

It's chaos. The second coach and team stop a little too close to the first, and the cadre in between has to mill around, trying to find a way to establish order in a street meant for little more than donkey carts. Neighbors begin to peer out of windows and doors. A woman driving turkeys around a corner gives a cry of dismay—her flock scatters in panic at the commotion.

Rat is still barking, his tail wagging. I scoop him up and clamp him in my arms, my stomach roiling. Everything in me is screaming for me to get out, to get away—slip over the garden wall and start putting streets between me and this growing mess. The courtyard feels like a trap, with the house behind me and walls and people on all sides. I back slowly away from the gate while Rat wriggles excitedly in my arms.

A piercing, two-fingered whistle shrieks through the air. Some of the clamor dies down.

"Eyes up!" shouts a voice.

On the roof of the second coach, rocking slightly with its movement, is a woman in a green uniform, with copper skin and dark brown hair pulled into a curly knot. She can't be over five feet tall, but she draws in a breath and shouts for the whole canyon to hear.

"I need all cadres to dismount, save one junior officer from each," she bellows. "Mounted officers, take the horses and both coaches and stage them in the plaza. I need an Alcoran captain on that detail." I stare up at her, recognizing the twang in her voice, the shade of her skin, and the thick fringe swinging on her buckskin boots. I'm looking at Veran's mother.

"I need the Lumeni cadre in two files from the road to the house," she continues, pointing, "and the Silvern cadre in a perimeter around the property. I need the Cypri honor guard and each standard bearer in a parade block in the street. Anyone not expressly needed is to stage with the coaches in the plaza. Fall in!"

The crowds of people rush to do her bidding. Boots hit the ground and horses are trotted away. Soldiers in blue uniforms scramble through the gate to form lines on either side. Soldiers in green organize themselves along the walls and around the corners.

"Let's get inside," Eloise says, waving us toward the door. "It'll make things simpler."

I tighten my grip on Rat. I don't want to go inside. Inside is even more of a pen than the courtyard. Rose wheels forward and beckons to Hettie, who's clamping her little palms over her ears at the noise.

"Come on," she says, patting to her lap. "Why don't we all go down to the fountain for a while? We'll come back when things have quieted down."

I lock eyes with her as she pulls Hettie onto her lap.

"Don't leave me," I whisper.

She shakes her head, smiling. "You're fine, Lark. You'll be fine. We're just in the way. We'll see you later. Also . . ." She checks to be sure Eloise has gone in the house, and then she says, "For your information, your sister is a be-damned *delight*. Don't be difficult."

She beckons to the others and they move in a little knot through the gathering soldiers. Soon they've passed through the throngs organizing themselves in the street and are gone.

"Come on," Veran murmurs, pulling my elbow. "Once we get inside, the soldiers can finish forming ranks, and they'll let our parents through."

"Veran . . . ," I begin hoarsely.

"I'm sorry," he says, sliding his arm through mine. "I didn't know it would be like this."

Still clutching Rat, I let him drag me through the turquoise door. My breath seems to only be able to travel to the base of my throat and back up, without actually making it to my lungs. I barely register the room inside—rounded adobe walls, colorful rugs over dark tiles, timber beams and plants in windows. Eloise is shifting chairs and plumping pillows, readying the space for all the people it's about to receive. I circle around the low wicker furniture and gravitate toward the back of the room, putting my back to the wall like I'm about to be jumped. Rat squirms in my arms, whining.

There's a tromp of boots outside, and the door opens. The first to come in are a handful of soldiers, who spread out into the corners of the room. Next is a woman with dark brown hair and a dark purple mark covering the skin of her left arm. Veran greets her as the provost, and when the golden-haired man comes in after her, I realize these two are Gemma and Colm—the woman who was queen, and whose name I borrowed for my horse, and the man whose stage I wrecked all those months ago. Whose money and shoes I stole. Whose face I hit with the handle of my knife.

The man who's my uncle.

Their eyes both sweep the room and land on me, now pressed flat against the back wall. Colm's beard twitches, and I want to believe it's a smile, but it feels more like a grimace. A maid enters behind them, and Gemma breaks her gaze away from me to accompany her through another door, murmuring about refreshments and extra chairs.

Shadows play on the door, and in comes the woman from the top of the coach, and two men—an older one with Veran's crow-black hair, and a younger one about our age.

Veran's mouth pops open. "Vynce?"

The older man locks sights on Veran and sweeps toward him, the hem of his emerald cloak billowing behind him. He closes his arms around him, pelting him with urgent questions. Veran's answers are muffled in his shoulder. His mother, though, doesn't go to him right away. She stands alongside Colm, and does what he does—stares hard at me.

There's thumping on the threshold.

"Please, move—aside, please, *aside*." A pair of approaching servants suddenly splits apart to let another figure through. It's the ambassador, the man from Pasul, the man who, if all this is real and true and not an impossible weeks-long dream, is supposed to be my father.

He looks terrible. He was wild-eyed and crying in Pasul,

but now he looks wrung out and ragged. Both his brown skin and black hair look grayer, and his eyes are bleary. He fixes on me the moment he crosses the threshold, and he freezes, while the two servants wait patiently in the doorway.

He swallows. "Moira."

Oh fire and dust, there's that name again. I should have expected it, but it only adds to the sense of being upside-down and backward, like this moment isn't actually mine. When is someone going to stop and say, *Hang on, are we sure this is really her*? When is someone going to get a closer look and say, *No . . . there must be some mistake*?

He shakes off his paralysis and heads toward me. Eloise starts around the couch, perhaps to intercept him and soften the impact. I press my back against the wall so hard I can feel the uneven surface of the adobe through my shirt and vest.

As they close in, I catch sight of a final shadow in the doorway. Over the shoulders of the oncoming ambassador and princess, a woman appears, tall and slim, in a traveling gown that just brushes the ground. The sunlight from outside lights up the edges of her blond hair, cropped short, and flashes off the pearls in her earrings and cloak pin.

Everyone is looking at me, and everyone is moving and talking. Veran's father murmurs to his mother. His brother Vynce whispers to him. Colm calls after Gemma, asking if he can help. The servants mutter apologies as they sweep through the house, opening windows. And the ambassador is talking to me, and Eloise is talking to him, and I can't hear anything they're saying. Rat twists in my arms, whining—he desperately wants to get down.

I know what I'm supposed to do in this moment. I'm

supposed to move forward and let them all look, let them ask, let them touch me and probably cry. But my feet are glued to the floor, and my back to the wall. Without meaning to, I squeeze my eyes shut.

"Colm."

Her voice isn't loud, not like Veran's mother's, but it cuts through the clutter in the room all the same. I slit my eyes open.

The queen in the doorway doesn't look away from me, but she addresses the blond man—her brother—again.

"Is your study available?"

Colm gives her an affirmative and crosses the room to open the door next to me. The queen glides after him, stopping short of the ambassador and the princess.

"Rou," she says. "Eloise. Give us a moment, if you please."

The ambassador's voice escapes in a rasp. Eloise clasps her fingers together. "Oh, but, Mother . . ."

"Only a moment, Eloise. Not long. We'll open the door when we're ready for you." She lays her slim, pale hand on the ambassador's arm.

The breath seems to go out of him, and he steps back. She presses a soft kiss to his cheek, and then one for Eloise, and then gestures for me to enter the study.

I draw in a breath and glance desperately at Veran. He nods encouragingly.

Still clutching Rat, I unstick myself from the wall and turn into the study.

The queen follows.

The door clicks behind us.

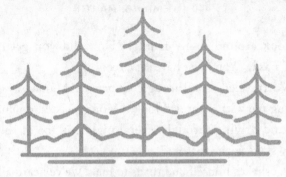

VERAN

There's something like a collective sigh in the room as the door to Colm's study closes.

"Earth and sky," Vynce mutters next to me. "They look *exactly alike,* don't they?"

I give a vaguely affirmative sound. I feel bad. I'd downplayed our arrival in Callais to Lark, because I really didn't think it would be so overwhelming. I knew Rou would be emotional, but I didn't expect Queen Mona and half my family to be here the minute we arrived. And now Lark is shut up in a room with Queen Mona, who's maybe the only other person I can think of who's as terrifying as the Sunshield Bandit.

Rou stands in front of the closed door, rigid, until Eloise takes his elbow and guides him down to the couch. Provost Gemma comes in from the kitchen, carrying a tray. She sets it down on the coffee table, pours Rou a mug, and presses it into his shaking hands.

I look around at my family. "How did you get here so soon?" I ask. "You must have set a record."

"We traveled fast through Cyprien," Mama says. She's watching me with a shrewd look. "Mona insisted on changing teams and driving through several nights. None of the usual lengthy stays with senators."

Papa shakes himself and turns to me. "We've heard all kinds of things, first in Rou's letter and then in yours . . . you didn't really go out into the Ferinno alone, did you? Tell me I misunderstood."

"No," I say. "I did. Twice."

Vynce stares at me, just short of gaping. "And were you really robbed by—" He gestures to the closed door.

"It's . . . more complicated than that," I say wearily.

"Well." Mama's voice is like a branch breaking underfoot. She waves to the chairs. "We've got the time. Sit. Let's get started."

LARK

I stand at the far side of the little room, watching the queen calmly take off her traveling cloak. Even after having come hundreds of miles by boat and coach, she's the most polished person I've ever seen, even compared to the dandified nobility in Tolukum. The door cracks open and a servant slips in with a tray, which she places on a low table in front of a squat adobe fireplace. The queen murmurs her thanks, hands her cloak to the maid, and then we're alone again.

The study is lined with books of all sizes, and maps and notes coat the walls. The breeze from the cracked window creates a quiet ruffle of pages. The queen looks me up and down, from my scuffed, dusty boots to my hat with the splits in the brim. Her eyes are gray—the kind of gray you see in a thunderhead as it towers on the horizon.

Most folk forget that lightning can strike even if you're nowhere near that thunderhead.

"They tell me your name is Lark," she says.

I try to swallow some moisture into my throat. "Yes'm."

"My name is Mona Alastaire," she says. "But I suppose you already knew that?"

"Yes'm."

She nods down at my arms. "Who is this?"

"Rat. My dog."

"Will he come near me, do you think?"

I flick my gaze down to him, where he's piled in my arms with his big, silly ears perked forward.

"Maybe if you sit down," I say.

She moves to one of the chairs by the fireplace and settles onto it. She holds out her hand.

"Here, Rat."

He cocks his head, looking at her empty palm.

"He thinks you're going to give him food," I say.

She plucks a corner of a corn cake off the coffee tray and holds it out to him. "Here, Rat."

He twists in my arms, and reluctantly I let him down. He lopes forward and sniffs her hand. She holds still while he nips the cake from her palm. She pats him on the head, and he plops his rump down next to her, looking expectantly at the coffee tray.

"He's a nice dog," she says.

"He can tell when Veran's about to have a seizure," I say quickly, feeling absurdly like I have to validate my mangy coyote mutt to her. "He gets all worked up, and Veran knows to sit down."

Her perfect eyebrows rise. "Does he now?" She looks at him again, turning her pat into a scratch. "How fascinating—and how helpful. What a smart dog you are."

He closes his eyes lazily. I drift a little closer.

She turns her attention back up to me. Her face is narrow and smooth, with just a few faint age lines around her mouth and between her eyebrows. Freckles dust her cheeks and nose—like mine and Eloise's.

"I'm glad to see your locks are still in," she says. "You always hated your hair loose like Eloise's. After you saw Senator Fontenot's, you declared you wanted them, too."

Her comment makes me realize I still have my hat on my head—surely a rude gesture. I swipe it off quickly, gripping the brim.

"Was it . . . you who got them started, then?" I ask. The question feels bizarre.

"No, I didn't have the skills. I took you to Madame Binoche in Lilou, and she got them started and taught me how to take care of them." Something flickers in her eyes. "I didn't have much opportunity to practice, though. That was the week before the summit in Matariki."

The place where I disappeared.

Without realizing it, I've drifted to the edge of the short couch beside the table. Rat noses the tray. The queen pinches off another piece of cake for him. Slowly, I sink down at the very edge of the couch, with the coffee table between us.

"Do you remember anything from that day?" the queen asks.

"No, ma'am."

"Not a face, or a ship?"

"No."

"Do you remember anything from before?" Her voice, like her face, is unreadable. Not sad, not angry, hardly emotional at all.

"Only . . . small things," I say. "I don't even know if they're really memories . . ."

"Like what?"

"Coffee," I say automatically, though it's a stupid thing to start with. "With cinnamon."

There's the barest twitch at the corner of her lips. "Rou has always taken it that way."

"You don't drink coffee," I say without thinking. I don't know why I recall this, why it came to me just now—that he was the coffee drinker and she the tea.

"No," she says, and we both look down at the coffee tray. The edge of a metal tea strainer peeks out from under the lid of the pot.

She folds her hands in her lap. "What else do you remember?"

"I . . . I think, waterfalls. Water in general. A lot of it."

"That's both Lumen Lake and Cyprien. You had a great deal of water in your early years."

"And . . . some of the names," I say. "They feel familiar. Colm and . . . Gemma."

"Yes?"

"I named my horse Jema," I blurt out. "I don't know why."

She gives another very slight smile. "I'm sure she'll be pleased to hear it."

I start to smile back, just as small as hers, but I quickly pinch my lips. This is going too well, too quickly. Too unreal—I need to slow it down, to pull it back, to let her down gently.

I clear my throat. "Just, um, just so you know—I mean, there are other things, too. Things you should know about me, before you . . . get too attached."

She lifts her eyebrows again, just a little. "Oh?"

"It's just—you know I was an outlaw. Right?"

"I'd heard, yes."

"With a price on my head."

"And a reputation, if I'm not mistaken," she says.

"No. Yes. I mean . . . you're right. And . . ." I look again at her hands, her smooth, fair skin. "I have tattoos. Lots of them."

"Of what?"

"My sword and buckler. A river. A lark. A singing coyote. The sun." I turn my wrists. "These words."

"What do they say?"

"Strength, and perseverance."

She gives a little *hm*, lifting her chin. "Those are good words."

I move on quickly. "Also, I don't believe in the Light."

She gives a short nod. "Neither do I."

That throws me off, so I jump to the important thing. "I've done things that most folk would find . . . objectionable. Downright wrong, in a lot of cases." I make myself raise my chin to match hers. "And I don't regret them."

She holds my gaze. "We have more in common than you might think."

"It's just—you heard about me wrecking Colm's stage?"

"He told me, yes."

"Well, his wasn't the only one. And there were plenty of storehouses I've robbed. Oh, and I worked as a cattle thief for a while."

"What are you expecting, Lark?" she asks finally—coolly, with that same even voice as before. "Do you think something you say will upset me, and I'll storm away and have nothing to do with you? That I'll deny who you are?"

Yes, that is exactly *what I'm expecting.*

I shift at the edge of the couch. "I just want you to know what you're dealing with. I'm not like Eloise."

"You were *never* like Eloise," she says.

Silence hangs between us. Rat sets his head on his paws, one ear cocked back.

Queen Mona lets out a little breath. Some of the crispness slides from her shoulders. She leans forward and plucks a teacup off the tray.

"Has anyone told you anything about the circumstances of your birth?" she asks, filling the cup with steaming tea.

I clench the brim of my hat. "No."

"I got very sick. I'd miscarried twice before you two, and when the healers determined I was carrying twins, no one was very hopeful that we'd all survive. In fact, I had all the documents in place to transition the throne to my youngest brother, Arlen." She sips delicately from the hot cup. "Rou was a ball of nerves. He'd mourned the other two we'd lost, but the prospect of losing anywhere from one to three of us was agonizing for him."

She sets the cup back on its saucer with barely more than a clink. "The details of the labor aren't important—like most mothers, I remember very little of it. Suffice it to say, it lasted hours, and my health was already very poor, but you were both born alive, and I managed to hang on, too. But my most vivid memory from that night is that you cried."

"I was a baby," I say, mystified.

"Yes," she says. "A skinny, red, premature baby who looked

exactly like your sister. Except you cried. She didn't. Great Light, you cried for hours. Eloise was silent as nightfall. I've never heard anything as frightening as that lack of sound. Not a peep out of this tiny, sick infant. The healers, understandably, descended on her in force. They tried everything. Rou and Ellamae helped them. They thumped her feet, they suctioned out her airways, they massaged her body, they pinched and prodded and tried everything to get her to respond. Meanwhile, you lay in my arms, squalling like a stuck piglet. And I remember lying there, barely conscious, and thinking what a picture of health you made—those deep breaths, that red face, the force of your cry. You were strong."

I'm creasing the brim of my hat so hard my knuckles are going numb. I try to relax my grip. Queen Mona swirls her teacup, observing it contemplatively.

"Eloise came around, obviously, but those first few hours of your lives were portentous ones. Because I was so sick, I couldn't produce enough milk for both of you. Eloise would only nurse on me, and only if I held her a certain way, and only if Rou dabbled her with a wet cloth to keep her from falling asleep. You were satisfied with anybody. So you had a wet nurse, while Eloise had me. Later on, Eloise was colicky for months, crying for days and nights on end, while you were content to lie and look at your mobile. So she was coddled and rocked and crooned to by a never-ending parade of family and nurses while you babbled at the little mother-of-pearl fish over your bassinet. Eloise never learned to sleep through the night. You slept like a rock. So her bassinet was pulled right alongside our bed, so I could nurse her without getting up every two hours. Yours was over in the corner, and later in a separate room, so her crying didn't wake you."

She waves a hand. "This continued. For five years it continued. Eloise startled at loud noises. You learned to pull yourself up in your bassinet to see what the loud noises were. Eloise was scared of the water. You tried to crawl into it when you were barely seven months old. Everything made Eloise sick—shellfish, strawberries, goat's milk. You ate anything and everything. You can imagine, then, the discrepancy this led to. The squeaky wheel, as they say."

She takes a long sip from her cup. "It was hard on Rou to figure out how to treat you both. He's one of triplet brothers himself. Eloise is named for one of them, the one he was closest to. But he and his third brother never got along, ever, and he always regretted it. And I think he worried the same would happen to you two. You were so different. So he tried to shower you both with affection—it's a strong point of his. Eloise took to it like a bee to honey. Oh, she loves her father. And you loved him, too, but you also had important things to do. You had missions to accomplish. You would squirm from his grip while Eloise snuggled close to him.

"You came to me instead, Lark. You knew I wouldn't blow raspberries on your belly at any idle moment. You knew I wouldn't plump your cheeks when you tried to talk to me. I had different ways of showing I loved you. To Eloise, I wasn't nearly as much fun as your father. To you, I was stable, predictable. You liked that."

Without warning, that dust from earlier rises back into my throat and up into my nose, stinging my eyes. I realize I've been staring at a divot on the edge of the coffee table for the past several minutes, but I can't make myself tear my gaze away. Everything in my head is muddled again, all swirling and tumbling around like brush in a storm. Another silence stretches out. There's a clink of the teacup on its saucer.

"Do you know how a pearl is made, Lark?"

I don't know why she's asking that question. My gaze slides from the coffee table to her hands holding the saucer—that's as high as I can make myself look. She's wearing two rings, one on each hand. On her left is a large white pearl set in gold filigree. Her wedding band, I suppose. On her right is a mother-of-pearl seal.

"It starts with a wound," she says when I don't respond. "Perhaps a bit of sand gets into the mussel. Maybe it gets nicked. To protect itself, it builds up layer after layer of nacre— mother-of-pearl. In a sense, that's what happened to Rou and Eloise after you disappeared. It broke your father, Lark, what happened to you. He feels things deeply. That third brother, the one he never got along with—when he died, Rou mourned him as if they had been best friends. It's his nature. And he loved you far, far more intimately than he ever loved Lyle."

She sees me staring fixedly at her hands, and she tilts her wedding ring so I can see it better. "So to protect himself, he made a pearl. Eloise is the pearl of his heart and always will be. He nurtured her through her whole life, he cloaked her with love. Oh, he let her live, too, enough that she's more than capable to stand alone, and well at that—she'll be a good queen someday. But she is his, and he is hers—that's how it's always been."

Silence falls again. She finishes her tea and sets the saucer back down on the coffee table. She folds her hands in her lap again.

"Lark," she says. "May I tell you something I've never told anyone else?"

No, no, no, no you may not. I think of all the times I've been caught in sand devils, holding my breath in the stinging whirl-winds, and I could swear I'm caught in one again.

"Not my husband, not Eloise, not my brothers or my clos-est friends," she continues as I persist in staring at her lovely fingernails. "Because it's a guilty thought, Lark. A thought no mother should ever have, and one I hate myself for."

My eyes drop again, to the floor between my feet.

"But can you imagine, that day in Matariki—if it had been her instead of you? Delicate, sensitive Eloise, who despite the responsibilities of a single heir still finds a way to be generous and kind to everyone, without fail. Sweet Eloise, gentle Eloise. What would have happened to her? What would have happened to Rou?

"That day and the ones that followed were the worst of my life, Lark, and I've had my share of very, very bad days," she says. "I've had a hole inside me ever since that nothing will fill—not my second daughter, not my husband. I won't say it was all worth it in the end, because it wasn't. I would take the per-son who took you from us and kill them myself without—as you said—regretting it for one moment. But I sit here and look at you, Lark, and I see who you've become, and I see victory. You are strong. You are mighty. You've fought, and you've won. And I don't care if you hate me for what happened to you—you certainly have the right—as long as you see what I'm seeing. I'm stunned and overwhelmed and relieved beyond belief, but I'm also vindicated. Because all this time, I knew that no mat-ter where you were, no matter what had happened to you, you would beat it. And you have."

I drop my hat. I don't mean to—but my hands aren't work-

ing right anymore. Nothing is. My throat is closed up and choking, my nose is streaming, and my eyes—damn my eyes to the
sun and back. I wipe my nose on my sleeve.

"You can cry," she says quietly.

"I hate crying."

"As do I," she says. "But sometimes we must."

I squeeze my eyes shut and duck my head, tightening my
fists. The tears fall before I can stop them, landing in two fat
drops on my fallen hat. Once they've started, they don't stop. I
jam one of my fists into the bridge of my nose, my breath hitching uncontrollably deep in my chest. There's a rustle of fabric,
and the cushion sinks next to me. Her soft fingers close around
my other fist. She leans until her forehead comes to rest against
my temple, and then she kisses me right where she kissed the
other two. I hear her own uneven breaths, and I know she's crying, too.

It lasts several minutes, the crying. We sit pressed together
on the little couch, her forehead against mine, my tears seeping through my clenched fingers. To my surprise, I find, as the
crying continues, that I feel better and better. I hadn't expected
that, the little release with each thick breath, the way it feels like
I'm pulling something ugly and raw out of my chest. All that
dust. Slowly my fists loosen, and after a while she can circle her
fingers around mine, her thumb brushing the back of my hand,
right over my sun tattoo.

When my tears have slowed to just bleary breaths, and hers
are quiet, too, she kisses my forehead again. Slowly, I look
up and meet her eyes. From this close, I can see the small shifts
and shadows of emotion in her face that from far away only
looked like stone—not the broken-open grief of the ambassador.

Something just as real, but less frightening in its intensity. Something quieter. Something warm, something comforting.

Something that, deep down in the farthest depths, I remember.

I wonder if I should say something, and not just stare, but any words that surface seem alien and awkward. She doesn't seem to expect words, though, content simply to hold my gaze, her thumb tracing my cheek. I blink, and two more tears slip out. She reaches into her pocket and pulls out a handkerchief, cloudy white and embroidered with little plants.

I wave at it, trying to dash my cheeks with the back of my hand. "I'm . . . so dirty, I'll ruin it . . ."

"Embroidery is a nervous habit of mine," she says seriously. "All my friends and family possess an overabundance of personalized handkerchiefs." To prove her point, she reaches into her other pocket and pulls out another one, identical to the first.

Gingerly I take the one she offered. On closer inspection, I realize the little plants woven in thread are cattails—the symbol of Lumen Lake, and my saving grace. I blot my face with a corner. Sure enough, I leave grimy streaks on the fabric.

"I need a wash," I mutter.

"I do, as well," she agrees. "But right now, I think it's only kind to let your father and sister in. Rou is likely beating his head against a wall. Remember what I told you, and try to see things from his perspective. He wears his heart on his sleeve, and the fact that he hasn't burst in here and sobbed over you in his arms means he's showing greater restraint than I'd have expected from him. Be gentle with him."

I take a breath and nod. "All right."

She glances at the door. "Before he comes in, though, just a few more things." She turns back to me. "I'd be remiss if I didn't mention, Lark—you're older than Eloise. You're my firstborn, which technically makes you the first in line to the throne of Lumen Lake."

A bubble of panic swells in my chest, right in the place my tears had cleaned out. Quickly, she holds up a hand. "I only want you to be aware. No decision has to be made right now. I have already rewritten the laws of my succession more than once, and I have no issue with doing it again. Eloise has been raised her whole life to be a queen and could take the crown tomorrow, if the circumstance arose. But I wanted you to be aware that it is officially *your* birthright."

"I don't want it," I say hurriedly.

"That's fine," she replies. "And I want you to understand, too, that you have no obligation to leave Alcoro, if you don't want to. Obviously, we all desperately want to have you with us, but that is your decision to make. If you prefer your life here, you don't have to come to either Cyprien or Lumen Lake. I don't want you to feel pressured otherwise."

"I didn't think you liked Alcoro," I say, and then bite my tongue.

"It's not a bad place," she says mildly, looking around Colm's study. "What little I've seen of it so far. It's time I let go of some things in the past, and my own stubbornness. What I like, though, is not relevant right now. Your preference is more important. If you choose to stay, this will be just the first of many visits."

I fidget with the handkerchief. "Is there . . . I mean, I suppose there's a place for me at Lumen Lake? I mean a—a room, or somewhere?"

She nods, without any hint of amusement at what I'm sure is a silly question. "Oh yes. There has always been a place for you at Lumen Lake."

"I think I'd like to come back, at least . . . to see what it's like," I say. "Then maybe I can decide?"

"That's a good idea."

"I'm not really sure what I'll do there," I admit. "I don't know what I'd be good at."

"If you'll permit me to be honest with you, Lark, I don't give a single pin whether you're good at anything or not," she says, with a hint of wryness. "While I expect there's plenty you can do, you could lie on the shore and throw rocks at ducks all day, and I will still personally exile anyone who says anything against it."

A choked laugh slips from my lips. On the floor, Rat thumps his tail a few times. The queen brushes her fingers over the last tear tracks on my cheeks, and then she rises from the couch.

As she turns for the door, though, something else suddenly springs to mind. My hand shoots out and touches her sleeve. "Um."

She turns. "Yes?"

"What . . . what should I call you?"

"What do you feel comfortable calling me?"

I think a moment, fiddling with the handkerchief. "Mona?" I finally say.

"Mona is fine."

"And . . . ?" I gesture helplessly to the door.

"That may be harder. Eloise calls him Papa. I know he would be an extremely happy man to hear you say the same, but he can wait."

I nod and sit back. She squeezes my shoulder and then turns for the door again. I take the moment to scratch Rat behind both ears, pressing my forehead to his. He huffs another sigh, confused. The door opens and Mona murmurs to the group in the room beyond. I blow a breath out through my teeth and stand.

Eloise comes in first, followed by Rou. He moves slowly, wearily, without the same intensity as before. I've let him down twice already, first by running from him in Pasul, and just now by recoiling out in the parlor. Mona closes the door behind them.

"Thank you for giving us some time," she says. "Rou, please call Lark by her name, not Moira."

He makes a sound deep in his throat, not taking his eyes off me. I swallow and rub my damp palms over my trousers.

"I, um . . . ," I begin. "I'm sorry for running, for leaving you in Pasul. I . . . didn't know what to think. I panicked. I'm sorry I made you upset."

I realize I don't know how to initiate a hug. I hold out my hand, as if waiting for a handshake. His gaze falls on it, and he moves forward and takes it in both of his. But still, he holds back, keeping empty space between us.

"You, um—you can hug me," I say awkwardly. "I'm really dirty, though, just so you—"

He pulls himself forward with his grip on my hand and wraps his arms around me, pressing his face into my hair. One arm clings tight along my back. He lifts his other hand to cradle the back of my head, like someone might do to a child.

Yes, just like that—like a parent holds a child.

"Oh, my precious girl," he whispers. "Oh, my precious, precious baby."

I'd have thought I was all out of tears, but my nose goes

stuffy again, muddling that scent of coffee and cinnamon. Behind him, Eloise presses her palms to her cheeks, her eyes glistening. Mona turns to her and gathers her in her arms, stroking her hair. They haven't seen each other, I realize. This is the first time in months that they're seeing each other, after her long, dangerous trek to and from Moquoia.

"I'm so sorry," Rou says, his cheek resting against mine. His voice is strung with emotion. "For what you went through, for what you had to endure—I'm so sorry."

"It's all right," I say thickly. "I got through it okay."

His grip tightens. "Oh, my girl. I know you did." He heaves a breath. "More than anything, I'm sorry for giving up our hope—for leaving you to think we didn't love you. Do you know how much we love you—how much we've always loved you?"

I let myself sag a little closer, my fingertips pressing the back of his embroidered vest.

"Yeah," I say. "I think I'm starting to."

VERAN

It's another half an hour before Lark comes out of the study with Queen Mona, Rou, and Eloise. By now my voice is hoarse from telling the others the story of our trip, and I'm glad attention can finally shift away from me. Colm is the first to rise when the others come in. He approaches Lark, who looks bleary-eyed but not nearly as anxious as she did when we first arrived. She starts to apologize to him for wrecking his coach, but he doesn't let her finish. He wraps his big arms around her, nearly lifting her off the ground. I grin and lean back against the couch as the others get up and head toward her.

Vynce stays behind with me. He combs through his coppery hair.

"This is wild," he says. "I can't believe you did all that."

"A lot of it was dumb luck," I say, watching Mama introduce herself to Lark, first with a handshake and then with a kiss to her forehead. Lark has to bend down to accept it.

"That stuff in the water scrape, though, and in the canyons . . . I mean, damn, even on all our training runs, when Ma likes to set stuff on fire and all that, we still know there's water somewhere. We still know there's someone to bail us out."

I squirm on the couch. Lark is talking to Mama and Papa now, and her hand keeps flicking in my direction. Over the murmuring of the others, I can't hear what she's saying, but they're listening closely, and it's making me nervous.

"It's like any other landscape," I say absently. "There's power in it, and you have to respect it. It's just a different kind of power from home. I wouldn't have made it without Lark."

He snorts. "Always quoting right from the handbooks. I swear, you know more by heart than my entire rank."

"Mm." I tear my gaze away from Mama. "I notice *you're* not in uniform. You've decided to travel as a civilian now?"

He takes a jam pastry from the coffee tray. "Now and forever—I turned in my badge."

"You *what*?"

"Yeah, a few months ago. I guess you'd left already." He takes a bite and says through it, "Not my thing."

"Not your . . ."

He wipes his mouth. "Well, it was always kind of a guilt thing, working toward Woodwalker. We all thought it would break Ma's heart if none of us took up scouting, and everybody else had one reason or another not to. Viya's always been eyes-deep in politics—it's her first time as regent when both Mama and Papa are gone, we'll see if the mountains are still standing when we get back—and dear old Fighting Ida was always headed to the Armed Guard. And then of course you, and Susi hates to do anything that might tweak a knee and keep her from dancing. You know she's taking lead for the Festival of Emergence this year? Anyway." He shrugs, polishing off the pastry. "I always felt like it was sort of me or nobody. But I never really wanted Woodwalker. I've always enjoyed my music lessons more. I kept showing up late to training because I was playing with the canopy ensemble . . . you should see the drum Hiley's got, it's got three kinds of jingles . . ."

The rest of his words wash over me without registering. Instead, that one phrase cycles in my head over and over, like a moth around a flame.

And then of course you.

And then of course you.

You, who never had a reason to not be a scout. You, who just *were*—you, who just *are*, inherently, by nature of being you, unfit for it.

I stare into the space between us and the group around Lark while Vynce rattles on about fiddle strings and whistles. The thought of him so casually picking up and then tossing away the thing I've wanted my whole life boils in my stomach. Just because he didn't want it. Just because he didn't feel like it.

Lark is still talking to my parents, but now the group is drifting back toward the couches. Beside me, Vynce is still going.

". . . so after I missed the next ridge run, Ma sat me down and told me that I shouldn't be training if I wasn't going to commit to it, and that if there was something else I'd rather be doing, I should do that instead . . ."

"We're one seat short," I say abruptly, shooting to my feet. Before he can respond, and before the others can fully turn their attention away from Lark, I scoop up my coffee and sidle out of the cluster of furniture. On the pretense of heading toward Professor Colm's study for a chair, I slip instead to the staircase leading up to the second floor.

I pad as quietly as I can, leaving the murmur of their voices behind. Clutching my coffee, I head down the hall between the bedrooms—through the door to the spare room I see the floor littered with blankets and pillows, where Lark's campmates have been sleeping. I reach the smaller staircase at the end and climb up it to the door to the roof.

Like most homes in the canyon hobs, the roof of the house is another living space, with a corner filled with garden plants, and another occupied by a hutch of nesting grouse. I go to the corner nearest the canyon and set my coffee down on the adobe wall. I lean forward on my hands, my gaze on the space between my thumbs. The sun is sinking toward the far rim, bathing everything in a rich golden light and throwing purple shadows. In the street below, a line of my parents' guards stand quietly around the house, drawing stares from passersby.

I drag in a breath, my fingers tightening on the wall. I have to remind myself that I'm not angry at Vynce. There's no one *to* be angry at, because it's nobody's fault. It's just my stupid life, always bringing me right back to this reality. Lark was right, all those weeks ago, way back when she and I were traveling toward Utzibor.

Life can't be changed, she'd said. *We're just meant to react to it.*

I'd disagreed with her then, but I'm not sure I do now. Frankly, she's the one who probably thinks differently now. Her life *has* changed. Her reality is completely new. But even with everything that's happened, everything we've been through . . . my reality is still the same. It'll always be the same.

The hatch to the roof creaks. I turn to see Mama appear from below. She climbs through and beats some of the dust off her uniform trousers.

"I saw you sneak off," she says. "What'd your brother say to get you all hot and bothered?"

"Nothing," I lie. "I just wanted to give everybody some space with Lark."

"You might want to reconsider." She joins me at the wall and leans on her elbows. "She'll probably want a familiar face close by these next few days."

"I'll go back down soon," I say. "But you'll see—if anyone can take care of themselves, it's Lark. She doesn't really need me."

"Sounds like you both needed each other on more than one occasion." She looks sideways at me. "Navigating the water scrape with no gear, huh?"

"And flirting intimately with dehydration, yeah," I say, not meeting her eyes. "Not to mention seizing a couple of times and making Lark deal with it."

"Did you expect anything different?" she asks.

"No," I say automatically, before realizing that yes, I absolutely had been expecting something different. I'd expected to make it to Utzibor and back without my body giving out.

She hooks a finger under her silver shoulder cord where it's gotten twisted. "Seems to me taking on the Ferinno—more than once—is pretty significant even for someone who doesn't have to listen quite as closely to their body."

"If I'd been by myself I'd probably have died of exposure," I say flatly.

"I didn't say taking on the Ferinno *by yourself*. What's that got to do with anything?"

I stop short of pointing out the two-night solo trip every trainee has to go through before becoming a scout, but I can't stop my gaze from flicking sideways, landing briefly on the silver florets tacked to her collar, the first mark of rank any scout earns. Hers are tarnished with age, standing out against the more brilliant silver of her badge and the circlet over her brow. Badges and pins may come and go, but scouts don't replace their florets unless one gets lost or broken beyond repair.

I let what I hope is a decent amount of silence lapse before I can change the topic.

"Vynce said he'd quit the Guard," I say casually.

She puffs a strand of hair out of her face. "It was about damn time, too. He was setting a bad example. I've been telling him for years he didn't have to keep it up, but like all my darling children, he doesn't listen to me. He kept thinking he was going to break my heart if he quit."

"Didn't he?"

"Earth and sky, no. I kept telling him I'd rather he commit to something he really loved, but instead he drove me to insanity and made himself miserable in the process."

"You don't have any of us as scouts," I point out.

"Your lives are yours, not mine," she says. "I've always tried to push you all to make your own decisions."

I nod, lifting my coffee cup. "Except me."

"Why except you?"

I wave a hand to appear flippant. "Like the time you wouldn't let me join the Wood Guard."

"When you were ten?" she asks.

"Yeah." I take a hasty sip from my cup.

"When you were ten you were having three or four seizures a week. You remember that time as well as I do—the cushions around your chair, the flock of folk who traveled with you all over the palace, the ban on riding and wading and standing at the top of a staircase. Those years, we were all trying to figure out how best to keep you safe and let you live your life." She sighs. "I never thought you weren't capable, just inconvenienced for a while."

I force myself to stare out at the canyon—which hurts, because the sun is beaming directly across the rim. I drop my gaze to avoid the glare. "Then why didn't you let me start later, when I started having fewer seizures?"

She looks at me, and from the corner of my eye I can see her eyebrows lift. "Because by that point you were getting ready to go to university. You'd been writing to Colm for a year without telling me. I thought you'd moved on, settled on something else. And after you left for Alcoro, you were here in Callais more than you were home."

I hadn't told anyone about writing to Colm because I was so afraid he'd say *No, you'd better stay at home*. I was so afraid he'd say *I don't think we can accommodate you*. I was so afraid he'd say *It's too risky, Veran*. I was so afraid he'd say all the things that I'd internalized after realizing the Wood Guard was out of my reach. If I didn't tell anyone, nobody would have to know when I was turned down.

But he'd said yes, and then to my surprise, my parents had said yes. And I grabbed on to that *yes* like it was the last slip of air in a bottomless pool.

I shrug as nonchalantly as I can. "I liked the university, and studying Moquoian. I'm good at it. But I still wanted to be a scout."

"Want, or wanted?"

"What?"

"Do you still want to be a scout?" she asks.

I lift my cup. "Kind of late now," I remark over the rim.

"Why?"

"Ma, most kids start at age ten."

"And we've established why you didn't," she says, turning to face me fully. She leans sideways on the wall and puts her fist on her hip. "That didn't stop you from building fires on your balcony, or memorizing all the handbooks. You used to steal them from your brother's room—I'd find them under your pillow."

He never noticed, because he barely read them.

"Memorizing facts is a lot different from actually training," I say bitterly. "Case in point—you know how I said we stopped the *ashoki*'s coach outside Giantess and tried to talk to her? We didn't just stop it. We mounted a full-scale attack. It was my idea. I was up top, coordinating everybody with the scout birdcalls. And guess what? I screwed up. I screwed up so bad that Lark got captured and hurt and nearly executed, and Tamsin fell hundreds of feet and nearly died, and we all got separated. I had all the knowledge right here in my head, but I panicked, and it all fell apart. Bet Lark didn't tell you *that*."

"She did," she says, with that sharp tone that means I've been disrespectful. "She said you made some mistakes, but afterward you beat a path to Tolukum Palace and tricked the bigot behind everything into outing herself."

I take a breath, gripping the wall. The sinking sun is flooding the hob now, plunging the far side of the canyon into dark blues and purples.

Mama sighs and shakes her head. "Veran, I admit I didn't do as much as I could have when you were younger to make a place for you in the Guard. But part of that, I think, was that you heard the *not now* as *not ever*."

"*Not now* and *not ever* are the same for me, Ma," I say. "Life . . . can't be changed. I just have to react to it."

"That's crap, Veran," she says flatly. "If life can't be changed, why did you work so hard to undo the Moquoian labor system?"

"*My* life can't be changed, then," I say bitterly.

She snorts. "Not with that attitude. Can you wish away the bows? No, and that's not insignificant. But you never seemed to see it as a lock and key before. What's different now?"

I'm silent, flooded suddenly with the vision of Lark on the ground beside the carriage, of Tamsin disappearing, of Fala hurting so many people.

I take a painful breath, lift my cup, and then set it unsteadily back down again. "I just . . . I made so many mistakes, Ma, *so many*. Mistakes that cost other people . . ."

"Earth and sky, Veran, who hasn't? When I was your age . . ."

"You were a Woodwalker," I say quickly. "Don't try that on me—when you were eighteen, you'd been a Woodwalker for two years, the youngest in decades—"

"And I made *piles* of mistakes," she says, quirking an eyebrow.

"You stood up for the other Woodwalkers, you challenged everything that was happening in the Silverwood . . ."

"You're not listening, Veran." She raises her hands and face entreatingly toward the sky. "Mercy, that I should be blessed with five children who never listen to their mother! Yes, at eighteen, I was a Woodwalker, and a good one, and I knew it—and I let myself believe I owned the place. Shouting at a king may seem brave or legendary a few decades down the line, but it was stupid, and it ruined my life for five years. It would have been longer if I hadn't gotten lucky a few times. It was a bad choice, Veran. And yes, it eventually led to the Allied East, but it just as easily could have not. I was a hundred times more likely to die nameless in some Paroan port. Don't conflate mistakes with failure. Folk don't tell legends about people who made no mistakes. Folk tell legends about the people who overcame them.

"And what's more—look at me, Veran." I glance at her and then slide my gaze down to her florets again, just so I don't have to meet her eyes. "What's more—you making mistakes *isn't* about the bows. You might not be able to change the bows, but you *can* work past your mistakes. They're bruises, not scars. Are you going to let them control you instead?"

My chest squeezes, and I look back out at the sky. It's an honest sunset now, with a few slips of clouds glowing pink and orange near the horizon.

Mama isn't looking at the sunset—she's still looking at me, with her fist on her hip again.

"How long were you out in the Ferinno?" she asks.

"A couple days. A week, I guess, after finding Lark, and then a few more days in the water scrape."

"Did you really revive Lark from dehydration? She didn't make that up?"

"I mean, I was a mess—"

"Yes or no?"

"Yeah, I guess."

"And you tracked her to her camp?"

"Which time?"

She gives me an appraising look. "You did it more than once?"

I try to wave away her scrutiny. "It was just lucky—the first time I used a powder that made her leave a trail, and the second time the ground was all soft . . ."

"That's not *luck*, Veran, that's *skill*, and knowing what you have. Final question—did you rescue a sick person from a burning building and carry her through the desert to civilization?"

"Tamsin? It . . . it wasn't like that, Lark was there, too . . ."

"Good," she cuts me off. "That's not just knowing *what* you have, but *who* you have. Remote camping." She ticks off on her fingers. "Tracking. Wayfinding. Medical emergencies. Knowing your gear. Knowing your team. Knowing yourself. Learning from your mistakes. I think that just about covers it."

She steps back and points at the ground. "Kneel."

My face heats. "Why?"

"Because you're supposed to kneel. Everybody else has to—you're not special."

"Mama . . ." I fidget like a little kid, flattening my tangled hair, rubbing the back of my grimy neck, straightening my beat-up tunic. I know what she's trying to do. I think of all the dozens of ceremonies I've spied on, watching trainees fresh from their nights in the forest get down on their knees in front of her while she swears them in. I think of all the pomp and symbols of the event—the bugle fanfare, the silver florets in a carved box, the presentation of the green shoulder cord, the other scouts watching, the row of Woodwalkers up front, the trainee taking off their smooth boots and putting on their first pair with fringe, the retelling by one of the older scouts of their two nights in the wilds of the forest.

I realize I just went through that last bit, and it wasn't lit with a blaze of glory. It was awkward.

"I didn't do any of it by myself," I protest one last time. "And I don't want to get a spot in the Guard out of pity, just for folk to have to babysit me the whole time."

To my surprise, Ma's face hardens. "Out of *pity*? Do you think I'd place *anyone* in the Guard out of pity? I have a scout who's blind, and one who can't move his legs, and three who think and interact differently from their peers. I expect them to do their jobs, and do them well. Do you think I instated them out of *pity*?"

"No, that's not what I . . ."

"I instate people because their skills meet the needs of the job and their team," she says, her voice iron. "You do the whole organization a disservice by assuming otherwise. You've got to overcome this fixation on doing things by yourself. *Nobody* in the Guard does anything by themselves. Everyone has a cadre. Everyone has peers to rely on. Even the trainees doing their solo nights have people to help them if they get into trouble. *I* always have someone to get me out of trouble. You are so good at knowing *what* you have, but so stubborn when it comes to knowing *who* you have. You're not alone, Veran. You're not a rock in the sea. If you're not willing to rely on anybody else, who can you demand to rely on you?"

She takes a breath, her gaze still locked on me, and when she continues, her voice is a bit gentler, but still firm. "It's your decision to make, Veran, but keep this last thing in mind: if even half the things Lark told us are true, then you've been field-tested more than every single one of my Woodwalkers."

I swallow, my racing thoughts landing on Lark. Lark, who once accused me of living my life all or nothing. *There's got to be something in between.*

Something. Not all, not nothing, but something.

Maybe in chasing after the *all* I missed the *something*.

At long last, I lift my gaze from Mama's collar to her eyes. She must be able to see the resolution in my face, because she nods and points to the ground.

"Kneel," she says.

I kneel.

Mama reaches up to her collar and unpins one of her florets.

"What name do you take?" she asks.

Normally achieving rank would be an opportunity to take a new epithet. But that process deserves thought, and I find myself thinking of the uncomfortable, ant-riddled patch of briar that nettled me to my feet and down the road to Tolukum.

"Veran Greenbrier."

"Do you pledge yourself to the care and keeping of the Silverwood Mountains, the defense of its resources, the preservation of its monarchy, the well-being of its folk, and the upholding of its alliances?" she asks, then, going off-script, adds, "Or whatever country you happen to be in at the time?"

Hot damn, I wouldn't have thought those words would make me emotional. But the number of times I've stood off to one side, listening to her say them to someone else . . .

I swallow, vainly trying to keep my eyes from burning. "I do."

"Address."

"I do, Woodwalker Heartwood."

"Do you dedicate yourself to the Royal Guard, to the Wood Guard, to the deference to your superiors and the support of your fellow guard?"

"I do, Woodwalker."

"What pledge do you make?"

"My might is in my diligence," I recite, my mouth dry. I spent an entire childhood gazing at the words carved over the Guard wing. "My honor is in my loyalty. My strength is in my integrity."

"To which we're all held." This last phrase is normally a shout, ringing around the courtyard and then echoed back by everyone present. But now she says it simply, straightforwardly. No response from a boisterous crowd. The echo instead settles deep in my chest, feeling as big as the canyon yawning up to the sky in front of us.

Mama takes my fraying, sweat-stained collar and pushes the first floret pin through the fabric, tacking the wing down. She repeats it with the other side and stands back. Her collar has two little discolored marks where they've been pinned since she first got them.

"Veran Greenbrier, I bind you to your pledge and pronounce you a member of the Wood Guard of the Silverwood Mountains." She holds out her hand with her seal ring facing out, the carved firefly flashing in the sunset. I lean forward and kiss it.

She jerks her thumb upward. I get to my feet, looking down at the space between our boots, trying to tamp down the stinging in my eyes. Behind her, the sun has finally slipped below the canyon rim, bringing rich new pinks and blues to the arching sky.

"Veran," she says. She sets one finger against my chest. "You are worth so much more than you think. To me, to your pa, to your brother and sisters, to the people around you, and to the good of this beautiful, hurting world we live in. But your worth isn't dictated by how much you accomplish, and nobody loves you because they feel sorry for you. We love you because you're exactly who you are." She prods my chest, gently. "Don't forget it."

I drag my thumb under my eyes and sniff. I nod.

She leans back. "You know you've saddled yourself with another layer of superior rank? Mother, queen, *and* Woodwalker. It's binding now. Sworn and witnessed."

"That's a stretch, Mama," I say hoarsely, grateful for her familiar banter. "Who's my witness? The hens?"

In reply, she reaches up and plants her palm on the top of my head. Slowly, she turns me around, away from the sunset, back to the other side of the roof, where the door to downstairs is still propped open.

Standing on the staircase, her elbows hooked over the hatch and a grin on her face, is Lark.

TAMSIN

"It should be to your specifications," the engineer says, fiddling with a wooden peg. "Single-pull screw, type cast in lead." He points to the big wooden plate on the press—reminiscent of Soe's oil presses, but just different enough to clearly serve another purpose. The plate isn't round, like Soe's, but rectangular.

"Should hold a sheet of parchment or paper big enough to fold a two-sided pamphlet," he continues. "Twenty-six lines per page." He gestures to his assistant, who daubs the metal type in the well with tacky ink. The engineer swings the wooden plate so it faces upward, fixes a sheet of rag paper in place, turns it back over, and hauls down to clamp it to the type. With a sticky kiss, the paper releases, and he pulls it out. I take it from him, my stomach swooping at the lines and lines of crisp, uniform text—currently just the alphabet, over and over, but the alphabet has never looked so beautiful.

I nod in satisfaction, hand him back the paper, and sign to him. A few paces away, Soe—wrapped in a shawl but no longer stiff with bandages—clears her throat. "Tamsin says it's exactly as she specified. Thank you. When can more be made?"

"I have two more in assembly—I wanted your approval before beginning any more." The engineer has already worked with me on multiple occasions and is courteous enough to look at me while he gives his response, something other people don't always think about—they're more likely to look at Soe. The engineer squints an eye in thought. "With the schematics in place, I can have the six you ordered operational in two months' time."

I smile. *Kuludresi*, the last month of the year and the *si* of sharing wealth. The symbolism pleases my poet's heart.

"Excellent. Thank you and your team for your hard work," Soe says.

He gives a short bow. "It is an ingenious device, my lady. I look forward to seeing how people take to it."

I as well, I think as the engineer and his assistant pack up. As the assistant picks up his bag, I notice a tattooed line inside his forearm. It's become something of a trend—though slave brands were ordered obsolete before Lark and Veran left the country, negating the need for freed people to get the painful release line branded through the rings, many workers have been choosing to set tattoos through them, just like Lark's inked longsword. Some are just simple lines, others are words or symbols. The assistant's looks like it may have needles on the end, like a branch of evergreen.

"Hey," I say to him, and he looks at me. Soe recognizes my request for privacy and lowers her voice so the engineer out in the hall can't hear. *Is this post of your choice, or were you grandfathered in?*

While there have been all the tumultuous ups and downs

we expected in transitioning the labor force, one thing we should have foreseen but didn't was managers who threatened or extorted their workers into staying in their roles for as little pay—or in as much debt—as they could contrive. Iano's new Labor Bureau has been auditing as many employers as they can, but it will be months, probably, before that practice is stamped out.

"Oh no, lady," he says, and his eyes spark with excitement. "I was in the Vittenta factories. I applied to the carpentry guild as soon as I got to Tolukum, and Bo hired me without any training at all. He's putting me on the lathe next week."

I let out a breath, relieved at the boy's genuine enthusiasm, and that I don't have to cancel my contract. *Good. You've done fine work—I wish you good fortune.*

"My thanks, lady." He dips a bow again and hurries after the engineer.

I run my hand over the smooth wood of the press, appreciating its strong redwood timber and sturdy screw. This has been built to last—built to work. I let my fingers drift to the giant trays on the worktable, their compartments piled with dark metal type, meticulously organized.

Soe shifts in her chair, rewrapping her shawl. The injuries she sustained in Fala's attack have left her with deep-set aches in her right shoulder, chest, and side where the knife landed, but there's been no infection, and miraculously no organs were punctured. Still, it will be a long time before she regains full mobility again, and her slowness and unconscious wincing reminds me daily that Fala's swift and private execution may have been too kind an end for her.

"It's a long way from my old wine press," Soe says amusedly. "I think you should enshrine my old one, for posterity."

It certainly deserves a place of honor, I agree, and then pause, my fingers resting again on the trays of letters. The thought that's been nagging me the past week surfaces again, born from the time spent at Soe's bedside. In the moments between transforming the labor laws, and sessions with the engineer, and preparing for Iano's upcoming coronation, I hired a tutor—a deaf woman who has patiently corrected some of my signs and trained me with a host of new ones. Slowly I've come to discover an entirely new world. When Lark first showed me the subtle differences between certain signs, I realized there was poetry in this language. My time with my tutor has taken me even further. I can use rhythm, I can use slang, I can show concepts that just can't be captured in spoken words. I can *rhyme,* and not just with the same tired words I've been stuck with until now—*rain, pain, again*. I can use similar handshapes to rhyme *rain* with *wind* and *snow* and *night*, which frankly appeals to my penchant for symbolism more than forcing two unrelated words to couple. My well of creativity that had run so dry out in the Ferinno is once more overflowing—I have three crammed notebooks to prove it.

Soe asked me to conduct the lessons with my tutor at her bedside, to alleviate her boredom and talk to me more easily. It's where I've done most of my composing, as well, both visually and on the page, and she's already declared that in sign language I've finally found my ultimate form of expression—that fusion of lyrics, rhythm, and theatrics I was always destined for.

It's not everything, though, and I can't decide how to ask her what I need to ask. Now I turn to her.

I have a question, I say.

She raises her eyebrows. "Okay."

You can say no, I continue quickly. *And I'll pay you, as a real job—at least, until you're well enough to go back to Giantess . . .*

"Tamsin Moropai, are you couching your words?" she laughs. "Get to the point."

I smile apologetically. *Would you consider staying with me and acting officially as my interpreter? Iano can read my signs, but none of the others in court can. I can't keep relying on my slate during conversations when he's not there.*

She smiles. "I'd be happy to."

I don't want you to feel like you're giving up your voice, I say. *Like you're only to parrot mine. And I don't want to make you leave Giantess.*

"I do love my cabin," she says. "But you're doing big things here, Tamsin. You're changing the balance of power. I'd like to be part of that."

We can go back to your cabin, I say. *I write better there. We can keep a place here in Tolukum, but after the presses are installed in the scribing offices, we can go back to Giantess.*

She smiles. "Sounds perfect." She rises stiffly from her chair, takes a few steps toward me, and wraps her arms around me. I hug her back.

Rain cannot soak dry ground. If the ground's not willing to receive it, it runs off and forms a flood.

Turns out, that's exactly what the world needs now and then.

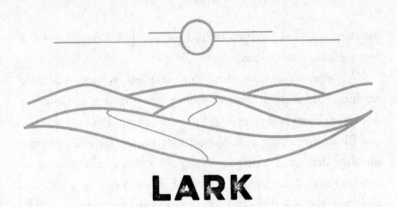

LARK

Andras's house is in the city of Lilou, which I've learned is the capital of Cyprien. I stand with him on the threshold to his cherry-red door. Behind us are Rou and Eloise, and behind them, a few guards trying to be inconspicuous. To keep things from being too overwhelming, everyone else is staying with the coaches and remaining guards a block away. On a whim, as we passed through the market to get here, Eloise bought a box of raspberry pastries and a bouquet of yellow and green flowers that drapes over her whole arm.

Andras reaches up and knocks on his door. A few seconds of silence pass, and then the knob rattles. A tall man in wire spectacles appears. Andras shrieks his delight and throws himself forward. The man catches him, momentarily stunned into silence. And then his knees give way and he cries out, a deep-chested, anguished sound, pulling his boy close, alternately holding him out to look at him and then crushing him against his chest, cupping the back of his head just like Rou did to me a few weeks ago in Callais.

A woman flies into the room, startled by her husband's wailing. And then all three of them are wrapped in a pile in the doorway. Everybody's crying—they're crying, I'm crying, Rou and Eloise are crying. Rou comes along next to me and squeezes my shoulder, and Eloise goes to my other side and lays her head against mine. After the first round of shock come the questions, and then the hugging, and then the thanking, then more crying and then laughing—wild, anguished laughing—and then the invitations to come and stay and eat. We politely decline, and Eloise presses the bouquet and the sweets into Andras's parents' hands.

Andras gives me one final hug. It's the latest in a long string of good-byes I've made since leaving Alcoro—Rose, Lila, Sedge, and Saiph are all staying in Callais, and I still had to find space to grieve for Whit. Rose has started testing false legs that fit to a saddle, with plans to join the surveyors mapping new sections for the Ferinno Road in the spring. Sedge wouldn't budge from her side or his new job, and Lila, despite her old convictions about Lumen Lake, elected to stay with them as well and continue at the children's hospital. They moved into a little cob town home with Arana. Saiph moved to quarters at the university. Between bidding them good-bye, and then Colm and Gemma—which was harder than I expected—I have done more hugging and more damned crying than I can ever remember before.

We've all repeated over and over to each other that it's only good-bye until the spring, when we'll come back this way to meet Tamsin and Iano in Callais. Still, it's left me feeling like bits of me keep flaking off, to be left behind. It's a quiet walk back to the coaches. Partway through the market, an arm slides through mine, and Eloise draws close alongside me. We make an odd couple—she in a pale purple dress with lace at the sleeves and neck, with her curls pinned to one side of her face so they spill down her shoulder, and me in Alcoran boots and trousers, with a new vest and my hair wound high on the back of my head.

The strangest detail between us is probably the least noticeable. In her ears, in place of her fine droplet earrings, are two dingy tin studs. In mine are two small white pearls. We traded a week ago, the last day we spent in Alcoro, and the day we both turned twenty.

I close my elbow more tightly around hers.

Behind us, Rou blows his nose with force.

Back at the coach, Veran is sitting on the running board, scratching Rat's ears. He's been patched up pretty well, in a fresh tunic the same sage color as his eyes and boots with fringe flaring down the seams. Even Rat has a new look, after several baths and my red bandanna tied around his neck, which was mostly so the neighbors in Callais wouldn't try to drive him off for scrounging in their trash barrels.

Veran stands up as we approach, and I catch a flash from the two little silver pins tacking down his collar—he hasn't taken them off since that day his mother gave them to him.

"How did it go?" he asks. "Is Andras all right?"

"Perfect," I say, bending to greet Rat. "He's back home, and he knows how to get in touch."

Rou makes another pass at his face with his handkerchief—Mona didn't lie, it's embroidered—and tucks it back in his pocket. He rests his palm on my shoulder. "You've done a world of good for so many people, Lark."

I let out a short breath. "Not everybody."

"Maybe not," he says, squeezing my shoulder. "But if you only focus on the people you couldn't save, you'll never stop beating up yourself." He gives me a little shake. "You laid a foundation, one we're going to build on. I know it's hard to feel like you're all right when others aren't. But we're going to get there, and we don't forget the people we lose. And that little boy and his family? You saved them, Lark."

I curl my fingers into Rat's fur, my head down. "Thanks, Pa."

He kisses my forehead and then opens the coach door. There's a murmur from inside—a quiet one, which probably means Hettie is asleep in Queen Ellamae's lap. Rou steps up to join the others.

Eloise reaches for my collar and untangles one of my buttons from the cord holding the shard of rock from Three Lines. "You know he's talking about himself, right?"

"Definitely talking about himself," Veran agrees.

I half-smile to them. Eloise smooths her skirts and steps up into the coach after Rou. Veran, though, leans against the varnished wood paneling beside the door, watching me.

"Are you okay?" he asks.

"Yeah." I let out my breath. "I'll miss Andras—I'll miss them all, even though I know it's only for a few months. And . . ." I glance at the open door and then come around to his other side. I set my back against the carriage and lower my voice. "I don't know, I just feel like . . . this is all the good I've ever done, rescuing kids, bringing them back to family. Once Hettie's back home . . . I don't know what I'm going to do with myself."

"You'll find something," he assures me. "Something that fits."

I look sideways at him. "Like you, huh?"

"Well . . ." He shoves his hands in his pockets and shrugs. "We don't know if it fits yet. But Mama said her quartermaster is fixing to retire. Master of gear, you know, the one who oversees all the stuff the scouts use, and who keeps the remote caches in working order."

"Start with what you have," I say with a grin.

"Something like that. And if that Winderan fellow Papa wrote to has dogs that can be trained to buffer me . . ." He looks down and scratches Rat's head again, making his big ears flop.

"You might be all set," I agree.

"We'll see." I can hear the smothered smile underneath his measured words.

"Honestly, you tramping around the wilderness and nit-picking about gear, with a big dopey dog following you—it's only what you did all through the Ferinno, anyway."

He rolls his eyes, his grin breaking through. "Thanks." He turns to face me, leaning on his shoulder. "You'll find something, too."

"Maybe. Or maybe I'll sneak up and steal things from your caches."

"Outlaw." He glances over my shoulder, where the guards are all standing with their backs to us, waiting for us to get in the coach. Then he lifts his fingers and traces the line of my vest down to the first button. He slides the lapel of my shirt sideways, baring the skin just above my heart, where it's still pink and tender from the Alcoran tattooist's needle.

His gaze moves over the three wavy parallel lines in crisp black ink. "How's it feel?"

"A lot better than Rose's old butcher knife." I crane my head to look down at the ancient symbol that led Rose and me into Three Lines, the symbol for water, the symbol for life in the desert. Rose came with me and got a matching one in exactly the same place.

My gaze wanders from the little scar bisecting his eyebrow, to the burn mark taking a divot out of his hairline from the fire at Utzibor, to the fresh scar on his cheek from broken glass. Before he can look up from my tattoo, I tilt forward and press my lips to his. His breath hitches, his fingers tightening on my lapel.

"Lark," he murmurs without actually pulling away. "There are people watching."

I plant my palm on the back of his head, sliding my fingers through his glossy hair. Between the topsy-turvy days in Alcoro—full of long conversations over meals with family, along with meetings at the capitol to plan our return in the spring—and then the trip in the coach with the others, it seems like months since Veran and I were last truly alone together. When he and I first set out into the desert to find Tamsin, I'd rather have been with anyone but him. Now I think longingly of that lonely, wide-open wilderness. It may be a terrible place to keep a camp of kids . . . but there's no denying it's private.

He winds his hand behind my neck and pulls me forward, so his back is against the coach. I lean against him, my thumbs on his cheeks. Down at our feet, Rat leans against our knees, panting.

There's a rustle at the coach door. I slit my eyes open.

"You know there are windows in this thing, right?" Eloise asks, her head poking out.

Veran starts and breaks away, dropping his hands to his waist. I grin and give a leisurely stretch before pushing myself away from him. He quickly smooths his tunic front, his face blazing red.

"Come on," Eloise says, beckoning. "So our parents don't have to keep pretending to ignore you."

I gesture for Veran to go ahead of me. He picks himself off the side of the coach and shakes his head.

"I swear," he mumbles, passing me for the door. But when I brush his fingers, they close around mine, quick and tight.

Inside, the coach is dim after the sunny market. Veran's parents sit on the rear-facing seat. Hettie is asleep in Queen Ellamae's lap, her little legs swallowed by the queen's fringed boots, and the queen's bare feet crossed at the ankle. She quirks an eyebrow at Veran as he slides into the seat next to her, but she doesn't say anything. I coax Rat inside and then sit next to Eloise on the forward bench with our parents.

That's still such a dizzying thought. Our parents.

My parents.

The guards shut the door. Orders are given, and we lurch forward. It's only a short ride, now, to the port, where we'll get on a boat, and then sail north.

The adults pick up the threads of a conversation they seemed to have been having before. Veran's father, King Valien, has a tiny lap desk open on his knees and is making notes with a pressed charcoal stick. They're discussing what they're calling *longitudinal illicit suppression*, which, from my time listening to the Senate in Callais, I now know means stopping a black market of human labor from springing up again in the wilds of the desert. I lean back, sliding my palms between my knees. I still feel out of my depth during these conversations, with all kinds of unspoken etiquette and a hundred different ways to put a diplomatic spin on something. I'd stayed mostly silent during the Senate discussions about hosting the Moquoians and planning the funding for the Ferinno Road.

"The road can be patrolled, but slavers will find other routes to move wagons," Queen Ellamae says, and King Valien scribbles with his charcoal stick. "We'll never be able to monitor the whole desert."

"A key factor is going to be eliminating their havens," Mona says. "Cutting out the places they can resupply and water their stock."

"You might find that difficult," Veran says, glancing at me meaningfully. "People out in the Ferinno already turn in runaway slaves to Pasul and collect bounties. The desert towns would be prime places for slave runners to pick up escapees. If you're trying to eliminate havens, you're going to need to outlaw collecting a bounty first. Maybe set a prison sentence for anyone who's found to have turned in runaways . . ."

"Don't do *that*," I blurt out. "Punish people for collecting bounties? That's a terrible idea."

Everyone in the coach looks at me. Veran stops midword, his lips parted. King Valien pauses with his charcoal stick in the air. The coach jostles off a bump. Queen Ellamae cups Hettie's head so it doesn't hit the door.

I flush, wishing I hadn't said anything. But this—*this*—is what always set my stomach boiling about nobility. They're good at finding problems, but they don't know how to *fix* things.

At the end of the bench, Mona leans forward, her face turned to me. I look down at my knees, feeling her gaze out of the corner of my eye.

"Why is that a terrible idea, Lark?" she asks, her voice cool.

I take a breath, glancing up at Veran. "Sorry. I shouldn't have said that. But all you'd be doing is making desperate families even more desperate. All those towns started hurting when Alcoro shut down the mines and opened the university. You want people to stop taking advantage of a twenty-key bounty, you have to fix it to where twenty keys isn't the difference between going hungry or not. Open up survey teams in the towns, offer folk positions on the road crews, train new stagecoach drivers—something, anything, to get some real, long-lasting income in those towns, or nothing's going to change. Fix the reason for the problem—don't just put a patch on it."

I expect a response similar to the handful of measured, false-smile arguments I heard before leaving Callais, where a bad idea was insulted in the mildest possible terms and redirected. But that's not what happens. Rou props his boot over his knee and leans back against the seat with a full-fledged grin, teeth and all. Eloise gives a satisfied little hum. Queen Ellamae checks to be sure Hettie's still asleep, and then plants her palm on her chest.

"Blessed Light," she says. "Somebody finally gets it."

"Valien," Mona says. "If you please, make a note of Lark's suggestions. Lark, my dear, once you've had some time to get settled at the lake, and when you feel ready, I would very much like you to meet my council. I think you'll have comments they should hear."

I'm struck by how she says *my dear*—not as a throwaway phrase, but as something she actually means. I look down the seat to her. Her face has changed very little from a moment ago, but all the same something strange and deep stirs inside me, some little pocket of memory. Somehow, instinctively, intuitively, whether through the subtle change in her lips, or the shift in her eyes, or some invisible signal I understood as a child, I can *feel* her warmth. It feels familiar, comfortable—feels not like friend or sister or rest or full belly . . . it feels like *mother*.

I look at Veran, wondering if he's pissed that I cut him down, but he's grinning, too.

"Told you," he says.

My cheeks blaze. "Told me what?" Any number of things spring to mind, smug sureties he's now justified in—his comment that I'd find something to do at Lumen Lake, or his long-ago convictions that these people would surely love me, or simply his stubborn insistence that I belong with them at all. It doesn't gall me that he's right, only that he's pointing it out in company.

But he shakes his head. "Not you." He gestures at the rest of the carriage. "Them. Told them you were smart."

"*Inconceivably brilliant* were the exact terms you used, I think," Eloise says, and now it's his turn to flush.

"I'm not," I say. "I just . . . I've been there. That's all."

"It's not all," Mona says. "But, should you want it to, it's what's going to make the difference."

She reaches across Rou and lays her hand in Eloise's lap, palm open. I slide my hand out from between my knees and set it in hers. Her fingers curl over mine. Without hesitation, Rou closes both hands over ours, and Eloise sets hers on top. It's a simple gesture, almost alien in its familiarity, but I don't pull away. I lean my head against the seat and close my eyes, wrapped deep in that sensation, as we continue toward the harbor.

EPILOGUE

Kuludresi 15

Dear Veran,

First and foremost, I'm writing to tell you that
the palace received your gift the day before Iano's
coronation, and I'll have you know it very nearly
overshadowed the ceremony itself. A hundred strings
of Silvern mirror and Lumeni mother-of-pearl! I
doubt a gift this fine has been seen since the palace
was built. You should see how they look hanging
in the atriums—even under cloudy skies, they sway
and flash, and at sunrise and sunset the reflections
are nothing short of glorious. The court is absolutely
preening under them—mirrored buttons and brooches
have instantly become a trend. Kimela's already
written a song titled "Silver and Pearl," and though
her symbolism is rather ham-fisted, she's captured
the fervor of the palace to a T. I've included the lyrics

for your amusement (take a look at my new title-font stamps, while you're at it).

I've done what you requested with the shipment letter, working with the staff to track the number of dead birds they collect. And while we'll have to wait for the spring migration to be completely sure, and summer to test the impact on mosquitoes, I think you'll be thrilled to know that your gift is working. In the month before the mirrors arrived, the staff averaged a collection of two hundred and fifty birds a week. Since the mirrors have been installed, this month has shown a mere forty-five birds collected—for the whole month!—and these are mainly around the terraces where the mirrors aren't hanging. Iano is putting the finishing touches on the new Committee of Natural Resources, which will discuss how to bring that number to zero. Their first report is included (look at the colored ink!). In short, Veran, you've very nearly done it. In a single stroke you've solved our bird mortality crisis, and won over the court. I believe we can expect far fewer obstacles during the Alcoran summit than we've previously had the pleasure of dealing with.

Finally, you'll notice that I've included two additional documents. One is a citizen publication that has sprung up in the past few months—the public have been bringing their compositions to the print shops (we have five now, two in Tolukum and three in the crossroads towns) to be combined into pamphlets. Already it's clear we'll soon have to divide these into literary, news, and instructional publications, we have that many submissions. Make sure Lark sees the newest serial installment of the wildly popular—and suspiciously named—"Adventures of the Sunlight Bandit."

The last is my own composition, a book of poetry and two political essays. Soe is standing over my shoulder and thus insisting I tell you that it has sold twelve dozen copies so far, and the printers are rushing to fill continuing demand. I admit, I am pleased to see my work still resonating with people—now throughout the country, rather than just within Tolukum Palace—but I'm even more pleased to be in such printed company, alongside other writers who now have the opportunity to agree or disagree or simply expound on something else.

I am so, so glad to hear about your new Winderan puppy, and I adore her name. I can't wait to meet her. Soe and Iano both send their regards. We look forward to seeing you again at the end of *Akasansi*.

Hoping you, and all our friends, are well—

Sincerely,
Tamsin Moropai

FEBRUARY 10

Hail to Mighty Lark of the Sands and Waters, Wielder of Righteous Flame,

I hope that salutation was more to your liking than the last one—you know "greetings to . . ." is just how people begin letters, right?

I wanted to pass along this letter from Tamsin. Look at the printing in her book! Look at the public pamphlet! Look at what she says about the mirrors! Lark!!!!!!!!!!! I yelled so loud Mouse tried to climb on top of me to hold me still. I can't think of anything I've done that I'm more proud of.

Another thing happened that I thought you might like to know—two days ago I was out on the ridge, resupplying one of the caches, when Mouse started barking at me. You know how she is—she doesn't bark much unless we're training her. Even though she hadn't warned me of a seizure yet, I figured it was a good idea to keep to her training and sit down. And Lark—I seized. I did. She felt it coming, just like Rat did. When I came around, she was lying against me, and a woodcutter was there—he'd heard her barking and come to investigate. He read the instructions stamped on my leather cuff and helped me get back to the palace.

You can imagine the reactions from my family—Papa paid the woodcutter his weight in keys, and Viyamae actually cried. I think Vynce did, too, though he pretended he wasn't. Idamae brushed Mouse from head to tail, and dramatic Susimae ordered a feast in Mouse's honor and spent the rest of the afternoon tying laurel garlands to hang around her neck—she ended up looking like a big shaggy bear that got stuck in a brushpile. And Mama disappeared for a while and came back with a silver badge that she pinned to

Mouse's collar. So we're official now—Quartermaster Veran Greenbrier and Mouse, Wood Guard.

As for me, I'm feeling better, and I don't mean just physically. It's weird. I don't know how to explain it, but while I was lying in bed yesterday—I couldn't get up, Mouse was on my legs and she has to be close to a hundred pounds now, I swear—I realized I tend to think of my life in segments, like chapters in between seizures. And it's always been hard to think too far into the future, because I know there's another one coming at some point. (Maybe that's the problem with the forethought you like to boss me about.) But after yesterday . . . I didn't feel that way. I found myself thinking about my supply schedule, and which caches I need to get to next and which ones I'll get to next month, and what I'll need to wrap up before we leave for Callais after that. I know my body hasn't changed, but it feels like . . . my grip on it has. With Mouse, I don't have to choose between being all alone, and being someone's responsibility. I don't have to rush through each day, trying to wring out everything I can—I can sit back and take my time, because I can trust that I have that time. She can give me some of that time.

Anyway, I thought you'd appreciate that. You're coming up at the end of the month, right? I want to show you the chestnut groves we didn't get to last time. And, I miss you. Don't look at me like that. I know it's only been ten days since I visited the lake, but I do. I think about you every day, every hour. There

are so many things I want to share with you, or hear
what you think. I want to know what you've been
up to today, what made you smile or frown. It's been
good being back home, but I'm looking forward to our
summer in Alcoro, because we'll be together again,
just like old times. No, not like old times, because
now I've got a dog and you've got . . . a country, I
guess. Two countries. And a last name, and killer new
earrings.

New times. Just like new times.

Give Rat a scratch for me, and say hi to Eloise.

Sincerely,
Veran

MARCH 24

Dear Rose,
Thanks for the letters from Lila, and Irena. I'm glad
everyone is doing well, and that your new leg doesn't
hurt like the old one. Eloise is good and says Thank
You for asking, and she wants to know if you have
thought any more about coming back with us to spend
the autum here. I know you are working on the road
with the surveyers but please think about it—I have
three rooms here and you can have one for as long as
you want, I even have a Bath tub.

We leave in one week for Cyprien, where we'll stay
for a few weeks (Pa wants to show me Lilou and the
other Provinces). And then we'll travel over the ~~Stelera~~

~~Stellerrange~~ Stellarange mountains (I still can not spell
worth a dam). So we will be in Alcoro probably at the
end of May. Both Mother and Papa are coming. Eloise
is staying behind to act as Regent with Uncle Arlen
helping her—that's why she hopes you will come visit.
No preshure but do not break her heart or I will have
to go to War against Alcoro, I think that's how I am
to settle argumments now. No I am joking but we do
want you to come visit, you have to see my Bath tub.
Oh! And my boat. Did I tell you I have a boat now?
It's a small one, and I am learning to sail it. I got to
name it, so I named it the Little Whit. If you come to
the lake I will give you a ride and hopefuly we will not
drown, that would be annoying.

   To answer your questions from your last letter,
yes, actualy, I am enjoying being in the council room.
I did not think I would, but I have made some things
happen here in Lumen Lake that I think are good.
There are so many things you would see right away,
Rose, that sometimes the people in the palace don't
see. So many problems where they are not looking at
what's causing the problems. They'll put people in jail
for poaching pearl beds but don't think to wonder why
people are poaching them. I have been sailing my boat
to some of the outer islands, which are not as rich as
the ones close to the palace, and talking to familys. At
first I think some of them were afraid of me but then
I shouted at a governor at midwinter, I didn't mean
to but she was being stupid, saying stuff about poor

Islanders being criminals, and I kind of shouted a lot. It was at a big party, too, with those little foods that are extra-tiny to be fancy, and I just got mad. I thought Mother might get upset that I made a scene, or that Eloise would be embarased, but they both came and stood with me, and Papa, too, and Uncle Arlen and his family, and I felt kind of bad but I think the governor felt worse. Anyway she's still the governor but now the Islanders talk to me and Mother is having the counsil completely revise their Inter-island trade plans to strengthen the local economys there.

Veran's good. The Winderan retriever pup they got—well, she's not a pup anymore, she's huge—actualy warned him of a seizure last month, and another a few weeks ago. I told you he named her Mouse, right? After the first dog who looked after him. I won't lie, I got a little choked up when he told me but tried to pretend I was only coughing, I still hate crying.

Veran will be here tomorrow with his ma to get ready to travel to Alcoro. I'm glad because I am really terrible at writing letters (as you can tell) and just miss being with him. I miss being with you, too, and can not wait to see you and everyone else. I am starting to love the lake—there is so much sky and so much water, and the waterfalls! But I do need a breath of the Ferinno. I need some time under the sun—I think it must be a different sun out in the desert than here at the lake, under the mists and clouds. That would have seemed crazy to me a year ago, but what can I say. If water is in my blood I think sun must be in my bones, and my heart, and my head. I feel strong in those ways, in those places, like I can finally take what I think and what I feel and actualy do something with them. I feel full, and free.

Anyway, I will see you soon.

All my Love,
Lark Alastaire

ACKNOWLEDGMENTS

I'm so grateful to my agent, Valerie Noble, for her never-failing enthusiasm for this series, and to my editor, David Pomerico, for his expert revision and appreciation for the emotional heart of this story. A huge thank you also goes to my publicist, Holly Rice, and to Mireya Chiriboga, Imani Gary, Paula Szafranski, Victoria Mathews, and the entire team at Harper Voyager—you make so much magic happen. Thanks, too, to Chelsea Stephens, Lauren Ezzo, and Matthew Frow, for voicing Lark, Tamsin, and Veran with such life in the audiobooks.

I had a slew of help with details in this book. I'm immensely grateful to Sarah Watkins, who helped develop Tamsin's learning of sign language, and once again to my agent, Valerie, for her guidance on writing Veran's epilepsy. Thanks, also, to Sarah Remy, who gave me feedback about some horse questions I had, and Serra Swift, who helped me brainstorm appropriate poisons for Veran to panic over.

A big acknowledgment goes to my high school chemistry teacher, Mrs. Nancy LeMaster, who I'm sure many millennial grads of D. W. Daniel can hear singing, "Always *start* with what you're *given!*" This became the baseline for Veran's mantra, ghosted to him by his mother—start with what you have. While balancing chemical equations still gives me anxiety, there are few other bits of advice from high school that have stuck with me so firmly or imparted such wisdom.

Thank you to my parents for their constant support, and to all my family for their enthusiasm. Thank you to Caitlin for being my sister and confidante and partner-in-crime.

And, of course, thank you to my husband, Will. What a journey we've been on. To my girls, Lucy and Amelia—thank you for your inspiration, your energy, your creativity, your resiliency, and your curiosity. I love you.

And finally, thanks, also, to you—the readers and the writers, the artists and the cosplayers, the storytellers and the adventurers. You are the heartbeat of the world of books.

ABOUT THE AUTHOR

An avid hiker and explorer, Emily B. Martin is a park ranger
during the summer and an author/ illustrator the rest of the
year. Her experiences as a ranger have helped inform the characters and worlds of the Outlaw Road duology and the Creatures of Light trilogy. When not patrolling national parks such
as Yellowstone and the Great Smoky Mountains, or the Boy
Scouts' Philmont Scout Ranch, she lives in South Carolina with
her husband, Will, and two daughters, Lucy and Amelia.

EXPERIENCE THE WORLDS OF EMILY B. MARTIN

SUNSHIELD
Outlaw Road, Book 1

A lawless wilderness. A polished court. Individual fates, each on a quest to expose a system of corruption.

Separated by seas of trees and sand, the outlaw, a diplomat, and a prisoner are more connected than anyone realizes. Their personal fates might just tip the balance of power in the Eastern World—if that very power doesn't destroy them first.

WOODWALKER
Creatures of Light, Book 1

Exiled from the Silverwood and the people she loves, Mae has few illusions about ever returning to her home. But when she comes across three out-of-place strangers in her wanderings, she finds herself contemplating the unthinkable: risking death to help a deposed queen regain her throne.

ASHES TO FIRE
Creatures of Light, Book 2

An adult fantasy tale that will surely resonate with young adult readers, *Ashes to Fire* is the story of a queen's desperate journey to secure peace, and the even greater journey to discover herself. *Ashes to Fire* is the captivating and adventurous follow-up to *Woodwalker*—once more with cover art by the author!

CREATURES OF LIGHT
Creatures of Light, Book 3

Queens, countries, and cultures collided in *Woodwalker* and *Ashes to Fire*, the first two books in Emily B. Martin's Creatures of Light series. From Mae's guidance to retake Lumen Lake to Mona's eye-opening adventure in Cyprien, we now see things from Gemma's perspective—a queen in disgrace...and a symbol of the oppressive power of Alcoro.

📖 HarperCollins*Publishers*